HELL DIVERS VIII

KING OF THE WASTES

BOOKS BY *NEW YORK TIMES* BESTSELLING AUTHOR
NICHOLAS SANSBURY SMITH

HELL DIVERS VIII

KING OF THE WASTES

NICHOLAS SANSBURY SMITH

BLACK STONE PUBLISHING

Printed in the United States of America

First paperback edition: 2021
ISBN 978-1-6650-8851-0
Fiction / Science Fiction / Apocalyptic & Post-Apocalyptic

Version 1

CIP data for this book is available from
the Library of Congress

Blackstone Publishing
31 Mistletoe Rd.
Ashland, OR 97520
www.BlackstonePublishing.com

For the Hell Divers readers, you all keep
this series going with your encouragement,
support, reviews, and enthusiasm.
Thank you for diving so humanity survives!

"Either I will find a way
or I will make one."

—Carthaginian General Hannibal Barca

RECAP SINCE
HELL DIVERS VII: WARRIORS . . .

A year has passed since the Hell Divers defeated the machines at Mount Kilimanjaro. The five hundred liberated prisoners, former sky people from the ITC *Requiem*, ITC *Victory*, and ITC *Malenkov*, have all settled in their new home back at the Vanguard Islands, joining the Cazadores, sky people, and survivors from Rio de Janeiro and other far-flung bunkers around the world.

Legendary Hell Diver Xavier "X" Rodriguez remains on the throne of the Vanguard Islands, having defeated Horn and the skinwalkers in Aruba. After killing Horn and destroying the machines, King Xavier thought the immediate danger to his people was over, but a different threat is discovered in a log on Horn's former warship *Raven's Claw*. The scribe reveals a secret and lays bare the truth about the fate of the Vanguard Islands—a fate that both former King el Pulpo and his son Horn foresaw.

The Hell Divers have been grounded since Mount

Kilimanjaro, but they haven't been sitting idle. New divers have joined the ranks, and they deploy with the Vanguard military on raids in Aruba and other locations.

Michael Everhart is now the chief engineer of the Vanguard Islands, working night and day to maintain the oil rigs and keep them secure against the storms. Rodger Mintel serves as a deputy chief engineer and oversees the growing Vanguard naval fleet.

Life in the sky is but a memory for some, but life on the surface has become more dangerous than ever. Extreme weather and failed crops have raised the specter of famine, forcing Vanguard naval ships to deploy to the wastes in search of supplies. But each time, they are obliged to travel longer distances in dangerous red zones, and each time, they come back with fewer supplies—and fewer soldiers. Soon, X will conclude that the way to survive isn't by sustaining what they have. They must expand into other areas, once again taking to the wastes to survive.

PROLOGUE

A fiery sunset spread across the invisible boundary separating the Vanguard Islands from the poisoned world. Somehow, despite all odds, this place still existed. The rigs had survived World War III and its deadly aftermath, the reign of el Pulpo, the war between the Cazadores and the sky people, a plot from the skinwalkers to take the throne, and a devastating attack by the machines.

King Xavier Rodriguez felt a kinship with these oil rigs. Old, weathered, and lucky as hell to be upright. Standing outside the command center of *Raven's Claw* with Miles by his side, he gazed out at the oil rigs in the pale moonlight.

Five days had passed since X slew Horn, el Pulpo's son. In that time, the aircraft carrier had also arrived with the defector units and drones, only to be repelled when the Hell Divers shut down their base at Mount Kilimanjaro.

Still no word from Commander Everhart or

anyone else on that mission, but in his heart, X knew that Tin would return.

Together, they would rebuild.

Torches burned on the horizon, illuminating the work already being done on the trading post rig, which the drones had all but destroyed. On scaffolds, crews of Cazadores and sky people worked by torchlight into the night.

X walked down the platform to Magnolia and Ton, both of them looking at the trading post rig. Victor was too injured to make this journey, but X knew that the former slave would be here if he could.

The warship passed the platform bearing the *Hive*, renamed *Vanguard*. The airship was still secured to the rig but was being prepared to make the journey across the ocean, to find the divers and bring them home.

X would be on that flight, but first, the islands must be safe. That meant tracking down the ITC *Ranger* aircraft supercarrier, which had delivered the machines to the islands.

After the defectors went offline, the carrier had drifted away, into the storms beyond the barrier of the Vanguard Islands.

Raven's Claw was hunting the ship.

The hatch opened behind X. Heavy boots pounded on the platform. A group of warriors, led by the Cazador general Forge, stepped into the command center, on the superstructure known to naval personnel as the "island." The tall, stone-faced general pounded his chest armor in salute to X.

Behind Forge stood the freshly promoted militia lieutenant Wynn, who had helped defeat the machines during their attack on the islands. Beside him was the Barracuda warrior Sergeant Willis, now leader of the elite squad that had helped in the victory against Horn on Aruba. His valor in battle had earned him a new name: "Asesino," or *Slayer*.

By his side was Bromista, a man known for his joking off the battlefield and the accuracy of his crossbow on it. The bald Cazador was the only other surviving Barracuda from the war against the skinwalkers.

Behind the two veterans stood nine more of the most illustrious Cazador soldiers left in the army, including Sergeant Jorge "Gran Jefe" Mata. Gran Jefe was not only the biggest Cazador left, he had also been a member of el Pulpo's personal guard.

On the deck below, fifty more veteran Cazador warriors stood alongside twenty-five militia soldiers.

The bow of *Raven's Claw* cleaved the waves with its whale-skull figurehead, approaching the storms beyond the invisible line. X stood in silence, thinking of the Hell Divers in Tanzania.

They wouldn't all be coming home.

Darkness enveloped the ship as it broke through the wall. Lightning arced across the sky, and thunder echoed in the clouds.

Miles moved up beside X, nudging his leg.

"It'll be okay, boy," X said.

His loyal companion lowered his head in the

gusting wind that blasted the warship. Rain sheeted down on the soldiers on the deck.

Two teams manned the .50-caliber machine guns with the last belts of ammunition. They wouldn't do anything against the aircraft carrier. The restored Mark 45 turret mounts with barrels that fired 127 mm shells could take out any defectors that may be operational.

If it came to that, the torpedoes the skinwalkers had loaded into *Raven's Claw* would knock a good-size hole in the carrier and send her to the bottom.

X hoped not, but he was always prepared for a fight. The wind grew more intense, and he raised his prosthetic arm to Magnolia.

"Take Miles inside," he said.

The thoughts pinballing through his mind ceased when he saw the supercarrier's outline.

The nuclear-powered floating fortress loomed out of the darkness, drifting aimlessly in the storm, or so it seemed.

X unslung his assault rifle, already loaded with armor-piercing bullets, and chambered the first round.

The gray wall of metal grew larger in the distance.

"Okay, you inanimate bastards," he growled under his breath.

"Get ready!" Lieutenant Wynn shouted.

General Forge barked orders in Spanish, and the deck came alive. The MK 45 mounts rotated, aiming their barrels and preparing to fire their 127 mm shells toward the massive dark silhouette.

X went inside the command center.

Captain Two Skulls stood at the helm with his back to X, the death's-head tattoo on the back of his shaved scalp staring out from black eye sockets.

X joined him at the viewports. "Talk to me, Cap," he said. "Tell me this ship is dead in the water."

"Ah, King Xavier." Captain Two Skulls looked over a screen. "Our scans show the nuclear engines are running, but we don't know their available power at this point."

X stared at the distant silhouette, considering the orders he was about to give. He didn't want to risk more lives, but they had no choice. "Keep *Raven's Claw* here," he replied. "We'll take in the boats to board it. You sink that bastard if I give the order, even if I'm still on it. Got it?"

"Pues, sí, my capitán."

Magnolia looked at X, clearly wanting to say something.

"Let's go," X said.

He jerked his chin, and Miles got up to follow him, Magnolia, and Ton down through the interior ladders to the deck. The small boats were already being lowered onto rough chop below.

"Over here, King Xavier," said Slayer.

X joined the Barracuda warrior. Five fellow Cazadores stood with him, armed with the last of the armor-piercing rounds.

"Let's move out!" X shouted.

The fifty-five warriors on the deck started down

the rope ladders to the boats. X bent down in front of Miles.

"I'm sorry, boy, but you got to stay here," he said.

X kissed the dog on his wet head and started climbing down after the Barracuda squad, trying his best to ignore the indignant barking from his loyal companion.

Magnolia and Ton followed him down the rope ladder to the boat.

They unlatched, and Slayer fired up the motor. The bow thumped over the waves, heading toward the monster ship a mile away. X secured his helmet and bumped on his night-vision goggles, seeing the ship's outline in the green hue.

The ship had eight acres of flight deck that once supported dozens of advanced aircraft—all rendered useless in World War III, when EMP weapons knocked them from the sky.

All X could see was the control-and-command island standing six stories tall.

Five other boats fanned out, and the wind drowned out the last of Miles's barking. X focused on the supercarrier, putting aside all his worries about the Hell Divers, the Vanguard Islands, and those they had lost.

As the tiny boat sped over the waves, the ITC *Ranger* seemed to grow even bigger. X felt like a sardine confronting a whale.

X checked his rifle and faced the team. "Stay on me," he said. "You see anything off, you report it."

Slayer repeated the command in Spanish, and the warriors nodded.

"You sure you don't want to just sink the bitch?" Magnolia asked.

X had considered doing just that, but they were low on ammo, and it would take a lot to scuttle the floating city. Boarding the vessel was worth the risk if it meant gaining desperately needed supplies.

"Yeah, I'm sure," he said after a pause. "Now, do your thing, but be careful."

"You got it."

Magnolia reached over her back and hit her booster. The balloon popped out, filling with helium and whisking her up off the deck. At two thousand feet, she pulled the capewells, cutting away from the helium bag and falling back toward the ship. Seconds later, she had deployed her reserve parachute and was steering over toward the towering deck of the supercarrier.

"She's a crazy one," Slayer said.

"You have no idea," X muttered.

He lost sight of Magnolia, then saw her parachute a moment later as she sailed over the deck and touched down.

Five minutes later, she threw a cable down.

"Good to go," she said over the private comm channel.

X secured a cable rider and clicked the button. It plucked him off the boat and ran him toward the ship like laundry on a clothesline.

Magnolia met him at the top and motioned for him to follow. The other teams quickly joined them, bringing their rifles up and walking a few steps before stopping short.

When X saw what had them spooked, he held up a fist and crouched.

The metal carcasses of defectors littered the deck where they had fallen, in neat ranks like soldiers waiting to march. X could almost picture the deck full of them, their laser rifles still gripped in their hard, cold fingers.

It was a gold mine of weapons.

Once, X might have smiled, but no longer. Smiling could lead to the slightest relaxation of one's vigilance in the wastes, which could shorten your life.

"On me," X growled.

He flashed hand signals to the five teams. They spread out, weapons trained on the titanium-alloy machines that had caused the end of the world and, very nearly, the extinction of humanity along with it. They had hunted the humans down like dogs.

Not dogs, X thought. *More like rats, cockroaches. Like goddamn vermin.*

Gran Jefe led the way with a .50-caliber chain gun that he carried at his hip, sweeping the barrels over the deck. Bromista and Slayer were on the big Cazador's flanks with their assault rifles shouldered.

The wind blasted against their armor, and the heavy rain cut visibility to a few feet as they made their way through the scrapyard.

X bumped on the command channel. "Captain, bring up the engineers with their escorts," he said. "I want every laser rifle detached and secured for transport."

General Forge looked over. He was leading his team toward the superstructure. He gave a nod of his spiked helmet, and X nodded back.

Lieutenant Wynn and the militia teams headed belowdecks to the engine room, and X went with Ton, Magnolia, and the Barracudas to search for any vehicles in the cargo holds.

One team remained topside to secure the deck while the engineers and techs were brought up to the salvage operation.

"Captain, got a lock on?" X asked.

"Locked and loaded, King Xavier," replied Two Skulls.

"Good. We're headed belowdecks, over."

X tried the handle on the nearest hatch. It clicked open, and he nodded at Magnolia, the fastest and lightest of the group. X pushed the hatch open for her.

Their helmet lights clicked on, and X shut off his NVGs as they started down into the bowels of the ship, searching for the cavernous cargo hold that had once held most of the aircraft.

They didn't have anyone who could fly one, anyway, but holy Siren shit did he hope there was equipment that still worked!

He followed the Barracudas to an open hatch three decks down. Gran Jefe was the first inside, with the other Barracudas slipping into the darkness after him.

X and Magnolia followed, raking their lights across a sprawling room as wide as it was long. There were no aircraft—only dozens of shipping containers with ITC logos.

Ton seemed to hesitate at the sight of the long steel boxes, and X knew why. It was in a container like these that Katrina had found Ton and Victor along with their countrymen. She saved them from being eaten by el Pulpo's cannibalistic warriors.

X motioned for Ton to stand sentry. The rest of the team followed X through the maze of containers, the tactical beams on their rifles flashing across the sides.

X stepped up and aimed his rifle while Magnolia pulled the bar up over the double doors. She opened the one on the right, and X shined his light inside.

"Holy shit," he said.

"What?" Magnolia stepped up beside him. "Oh, damn, those are pretty!"

Parked bumper to bumper were three armored vehicles with turrets and reinforced viewports.

"These will come in handy if they work," Magnolia said.

A voice called out behind them, and X turned.

"King Xavier, better check this out," said Slayer.

X ran over to another container. Stepping inside, he felt a chill of excitement. Three-by-two-foot crates, stacked six high, were already open.

"Of all my years raiding, I've never found nothin' like this," Slayer said.

X raised a hand for silence. He examined each crate of weapons and conventional ammunition in a wide range of calibers. There were also vacuum-sealed packages of fatigues, hats, and helmets.

Reaching inside, he pulled out a hat with an eagle, a globe, and an anchor. The motto on the bill read "*Semper Fidelis.*"

X didn't know what it meant, but he recognized the old-world logo of the anchor and globe as belonging to the Marine Corps.

"I believe this is what they used to call 'hitting the jackpot,'" Magnolia said.

"Check this out," Slayer said.

He took them to a third container.

X had hoped it held a helicopter, even though he knew it would be crazy difficult learning to fly it. But a tank was even better! Two cannon barrels protruded from the turret, and armor covered the tracks, which looked brand-new.

"Guess I gotta learn to drive this," X said with a grin.

As he moved around the radiation-proof godsend, he was having trouble keeping his self-imposed injunction against smiling in the wastes. This baby would make one hell of a safari vehicle against the mutant beasts out there.

And the loot kept coming.

They found two armored scout vehicles that

appeared to be for nuclear/biological/chemical missions, three more APCs, four transport trucks, and crates containing six drones that looked like Cricket.

Magnolia said, "I'm sure Tin can put those to use if . . ."

"He's alive," X said. "I'm sure of it."

She nodded.

General Forge's voice hissed in his earpiece.

"King Xavier, do you copy?"

"Copy," X replied.

"The engineering teams confirm that four nuclear-powered engines are operational, but the life-support systems have all been cut."

"What about weapons systems?"

"Disabled," Forge said. "What's left of them."

"Good."

"Should we try and bring the power back on?"

X thought on it but feared that doing so could activate weapons systems that might target his people.

"No, pull your teams out for now," X said.

"Copy that, King Xavier," Forge replied.

The treasure hunt lasted another half hour, with many more exciting finds in the containers. He was feeling great about their journey when a new message over the comms made his heart sink.

"We've lost contact with Lieutenant Wynn," Forge said.

"That's Wynn," Magnolia said.

X brought up his minimap. The team's objective was to search the lower decks.

"We'll check it out," Forge said.

"I'm on my way," X said.

"King Xavier, perhaps you should—" Slayer started to say.

"Not a chance."

X had known the militiamen and women with Lieutenant Wynn most of his life. He owed it to their families to find them.

If it wasn't already too late . . .

X took a ladder deeper into the supercarrier. He tried to reach Wynn on the comms, but only static answered.

The grin was long gone now. Maybe coming here was a mistake. Maybe . . .

A scratching noise stopped X in midstride. He held up his prosthetic arm, and the group behind him halted.

X strained to hear what sounded like nails being pulled from very hard wood. The long, deep screeches seemed to be coming from the other side of the bulkhead.

He put his helmet against it, feeling a slight vibration. Magnolia stepped up beside him, and he gave her a nod.

They started toward the closed hatch that Wynn's team had taken to the lowest deck of the ship.

Slayer and the Barracudas formed a line, hand on the next warrior's shoulder plate, ready to move. The scratching suddenly ceased.

With a dip of his helmet, X gave the order to enter the room.

The hatch swung open to an elevated platform stretching around the sides of a vast chamber. Soldiers followed X out, sweeping their beams over the piles of bones below. Mounds and mounds of bones, all of them human.

X started down the platform, his boots clicking on the metal as he searched for Wynn and his team. Magnolia pointed her beam at some barred-off cells across the chamber.

X crossed over to a pile of corpses still dressed in tattered clothes over leathery, mummified skin. Wispy hair hung off dried, eyeless skulls.

The scratching came again, this time accompanied by a pounding noise.

X turned toward the sound. It seemed to come from two hatches across the chamber.

He hurried past the dead and motioned for Magnolia and Ton. Slayer joined them as they scanned the interior of what appeared to be prison cells.

More bodies were inside.

Magnolia waved frantically to X. He hurried over and stared.

Inside, a corpse lay slumped against a wall, still in gear. A Hell Diver.

"One of ours?" she whispered.

X pushed the gate, making a low metallic screech.

As if in answer to the noise, the scratching from earlier intensified, followed by more pounding.

It was closer—on the other side of the bulkhead.

X left the remains of the unidentified Hell Diver and backed out of the cell.

Slayer motioned for them outside an open hatch that led to a dark passageway.

"I think it's coming from in there," he said.

Bromista was mumbling something in Spanish.

X led the way, keeping his rifle and beam on the darkness ahead. The noise grew louder and was joined by a muffled, almost human-sounding voice.

The pounding started again, softly at first, then like someone using a rifle butt.

X opened the hatch, and a body slumped out into the passageway, wearing militia armor.

"Wynn," Magnolia said. "What happened?"

X moved past her into a pitch-black chamber. His beam cut through the darkness, hitting cryo pods secured to an egg-shaped central device.

"What the hell . . ." X muttered.

Slayer entered with Bromista right behind.

"Wynn, where's the rest of your team?" Magnolia whispered.

"Tunn . . ." he stuttered.

"Get him out of here and call in reinforcements," X said. "Everyone else, on me."

Ton, Slayer, Magnolia, and the Barracudas followed X into the chamber, their light beams spearing the darkness. The cryo pods were all open, the lids popped.

Bromista and Slayer fanned out with the other warriors. Gran Jefe lumbered into the center of the room, his heavy footsteps as loud as a Bone Beast.

An electronic wail answered, reverberating from one of the passages.

X aimed his rifle at the arched opening he thought it came from, but it was impossible to tell. He stepped forward, halting suddenly at a new noise, this one human. The scream escalated into an animal cry of agony. The crunching and tearing that followed told X all he needed to know.

There wasn't a defector inside these passageways—there were beasts.

He looked back at the cryo chambers, realization setting in.

Slayer signaled for the Barracudas to spread out toward the walkways. There were ten on each wall—plenty of places to hide.

Another scream issued from the bowels of the ship, ending in the sounds of ripping flesh.

"Stay here," X said to Magnolia.

"But . . ."

"Do it."

Magnolia nodded, and X pushed into the first passageway with Ton, who slung his rifle and drew his cutlass from its canvas sheath.

Trails of blood snaked down the deck, stopping at the mutilated body of a militia soldier.

X froze as his light found the predator.

An eyeless leathery face rose up, blood dripping off its wide grin of a mouth. The Siren sniffed the air as X hit it with his light.

This wasn't a normal Siren. A metal chest rig was

secured around its midsection. It turned on all fours, exposing a spinal column of gray metal that connected to a port in the back of its skull.

Before X could fire off a shot, it leaped to the ceiling and scurried away.

"We got some sort of modified Sirens—"

Another scream cut him off, echoing through the passages. There was no telling how far these went, or how many of these cyborg Sirens were down here.

Gunfire rang out, the reports amplified by the enclosed passageways. Voices called out in Spanish, and the clank of metal came in the respite.

In seconds, more gunfire erupted and edged weapons clanged, as the Barracudas engaged hostiles in the other spaces.

"Back up," X said. "Everyone out. Now."

Hearing a yelp right behind him, X whirled with his rifle, the light hitting Ton as leathery hands yanked the sentry upward.

X let his rifle hang from the sling as he reached up to grab Ton's leg. Ton squirmed, grunting.

Looking up, X saw that Ton's assailant wasn't a Siren. It had a deformed human face with a metal cap. Saliva drooled from a crooked mouth as bulging eyes stared down at X.

Ton pulled a knife from his belt and thrust it up under the cyborg human's chin. Blood ran down onto X, but still the creature held Ton fast.

X pulled harder until he finally freed Ton, bringing the beast down with them.

Bringing up his rifle, X aimed at the half-naked cyborg scuttling away. He fired a shot at the back of the metal head. In the narrow chamber, it sounded like a lightning strike.

The bullet went low, missing the skull but hitting the spiked metal column that connected to the head. Blood spurted out, and the creature jerked spastically.

Ton pushed himself up, his eyes wide in the glow of the lights. He finished off the cyborg with a cutlass thrust to the center of its hairy composite chest.

Magnolia rushed inside and turned to squeeze off a burst of covering fire.

"Come on!" she said.

They retreated to the main chamber. General Forge entered with a squad of heavily armored Cazadores, including one with a flamethrower.

"What the hell are those things?" Magnolia huffed.

"Experiments," X said. "The machines must have modified Sirens, humans, and God knows what else."

"So the virus didn't work on them?"

"Apparently not," X said.

The Cazador teams set up a perimeter outside the passageway entrances and awaited orders as the Barracudas joined them.

Slayer, Bromista, and Gran Jefe were covered in blood and gore, though it didn't appear to be their own.

"General, I want you to burn these creatures out," X said. "Tell your men to watch carefully for any survivors from Team Jupiter."

X doubted there were any at this point. He felt the despair that always flooded him after he gave orders that got people killed. The supplies and weapons hardly seemed worth it now. They certainly wouldn't to the families.

"And the ship?" Forge asked. "Do we scuttle it?"

X looked to Magnolia, unsure.

"Your call, but this ship is cursed, King Xavier," she said.

Another team arrived with flamethrowers. X didn't want to lose anyone else, but this floating city was vital to the future of the islands.

"We clear the corridors and locate any survivors," X said. "Then we move it to a new location until the day comes we need it."

General Forge nodded, and Slayer pounded his chest armor. The Barracudas brought up their weapons, and X raised his rifle, knowing that the day might be closer than anyone thought.

ONE

A year after returning to the Vanguard Islands and helping stop the machines, Ada Winslow was serving as a Hell Diver, though not by choice.

King Xavier had conscripted her into service. She wasn't thrilled to be back in the wastes, but she was still trying to atone for her crime after the peace with the Cazadores—a peace that she almost broke with her actions at sea.

During her exile for that heinous crime, she had seen the real world—a place of wastelands and monsters. From human-size leeches and birds with beaks that could snap a man in half, to trees with vines that could crush *and eat* a human.

But never in her journey had she seen anything quite like Aruba.

She sat in the bow of an inflatable boat racing toward the shoreline.

The lush tropical terrain was now a desolate,

hostile landscape, home to poisonous flora and fauna. None of the plants or animals out here seemed to be strict herbivores. They would eat *whatever* they could. Much as the skinwalkers had when they lived here, Ada thought.

It was still hard to believe that this island was the site of the Outrider Colony. Most humans wouldn't have lasted a week here. But the skinwalkers weren't normal humans.

A year after King Xavier and General Forge had wiped the skinwalkers out, the Vanguard Army and Hell Divers kept coming back to the outpost for supplies and to siphon off the stabilized fuel stored in tanks there.

Today, Ada and her animal companion, Jo-Jo, were on a mission with two teams to explore the ruins of a former gold-mining operation, now centuries old.

The warship *Ocean Bull* and the former research vessel ITC *Octopus* were anchored on the horizon. General Forge had discovered both ships on a mission to the Port of Colón at the northern end of the Panama Canal.

While another team of Vanguard forces went about extracting the last of the oil from the Outrider reserves into the tanker *Blood Trawler*, Ada and Jo-Jo were on a small team tasked with searching the last known location the skinwalkers had used—discovered on a map they had left behind at the main outpost facility.

Ten miles away from the main outpost, they

beached their boats. The group of Hell Divers that included Ada, Commander Magnolia Katib, Edgar Cervantes, Arlo Wand, and the new chief engineer of the Vanguard Islands, Michael Everhart, all jumped out into the surf.

The divers had been grounded for the past few months due to the risks of sending the airship *Vanguard* into the sky, and Michael, who no longer served as a diver, was here as the structural engineer.

Pedro Gonçalvez, the leader of the Rio de Janeiro survivors, was here providing tech support in case they found any computers or other technology in the tunnels. He carried a pack with secured electronic tablets over his suit and a tactical bow.

They weren't alone on this trek. A second boat pulled up alongside, and a Barracuda squad hopped out. Their leader, Sergeant Slayer, flashed hand signals to his team.

The soldiers moved up the beach with spears, flame throwers, and a .50-caliber machine gun that Gran Jefe had propped up on his shoulder plate.

Bromista, the jokester, was all business today, sweeping the terrain with his crossbow.

They were expert monster hunters, though none were as effective as Jo-Jo. Over the past year, Ada had trained the monkey to sniff out danger, and in that time, she had watched the animal grow from 100 pounds to almost 150. Tusklike canine teeth protruded below her lips, and her hands bore claws as long as Ada's fingers, but she was still a gentle giant.

The monkey moved quickly and nimbly on all fours.

Her black nostrils sniffed the air—no hostile scents so far. Ada knew because the animal's black hair lay flat against her muscular body.

As they made their way up the beach, warm rain sluiced off them, turning the dirt and sand to thin soup in minutes.

Jo-Jo stopped ahead, a dozen paces from a ledge of rocks exposed by the receding tide. It took Ada all of a second to see that these weren't just rocks.

Dark, purplish bivalve shells the size of oil drums protruded from the outcropping, their exterior ribs giving away their identity.

Ada had seen such mutant mollusks on her journey into the wastes and knew that they were still alive despite being out of the water. She also knew what the closed asymmetrical shells contained.

"Everyone stay clear of those," she said.

The team gave the shells a wide berth by moving up the slope and around the ledge, but Arlo trod a little too close to one on the path up the ridge.

Cracking down the center, the huge shell opened to expose a rim of teeth and a gooey interior that was the flesh of the mussel. Out slopped the remains of its last catch: a giant leech of the kind that had attacked Ada and Jo-Jo during her sojourn into the wastes.

"Shit!" Arlo cried.

Magnolia pulled him away as the monstrous thing writhed, somehow still alive. Goo peeled away from the flesh as it wriggled toward them.

Drawing one of her sickles, Magnolia cut the monster in half, then wiped the goo off before sheathing the blade.

"Let's go," she said.

Arlo stumbled away from the beast, which gave one last hiss before going limp.

The team kept going until they reached the top of the ridge overlooking a flat, rocky area that stretched away from the beach. A few trees poked out of the dirt, and clumps of bushes with hook-shaped thorns marked the path forward.

The rain came down harder, peppering their suits as they marched onward.

"Hold up," Michael said. He held up his wrist computer behind the group. "This is acid rain, so make sure you're buttoned up really good."

"I'm secure," Arlo said.

Edgar gave thumbs-up.

Ada checked her life-support systems and confirmed that her suit was functioning properly.

"Damn it," Magnolia said.

Michael jogged over to her. "What's wrong?"

"Damn filter," she said. "I just checked it before we left. If it was bad, my sensors would be going off."

"Maybe they aren't working, either," Michael said. He checked her wrist computer with Pedro.

Ada had watched the two men become good friends since Michael helped rescue Pedro and his people from a bunker in Rio de Janeiro. In that time, Pedro had also learned to speak English, although it wasn't perfect.

"Your sensors are offline," Michael said.

"No good," Pedro added. "If you get a tear in suit, you won't know."

Michael looked back toward the shore. "Head back to the boat, Mags."

"No way, I'll be fine," Magnolia said.

"I'm giving you my professional opinion. Take it or leave it."

"It's probably more dangerous to head back alone," Edgar said. "If you do, I'll head with you, Mags."

Magnolia seemed to think on it, then shook her head. "We proceed with the mission. It shouldn't take long."

Ada motioned to Jo-Jo, and the monkey barreled ahead, through the downpour. Visibility was getting worse by the second.

"Stay close," Ada said.

The animal didn't understand, but she also knew better than to run too far ahead.

Ada kept her rifle at the ready as she searched the green field of her night-vision goggles. Not long after, she finally spotted something in a brilliant flash of lightning.

The glow illuminated a fortress of stone in the distance. Most of the walls had tumbled, but this was clearly man-made.

This was their target.

"Eyes on the mine," Ada said over the team comm.

"Copy that, we see it," replied Slayer.

The two squads came together at the ruins of an

ancient gold mine. Above the surrounding terrain rose four distinct structures, all of them built of local stone. Red and blue mold caked the cracks and recesses of the walls with a toxic patina.

Michael pulled out a handheld device. It was all that remained of Cricket 2.0, his old droid, salvaged from the mission to Tanzania.

"Life scan is negative," he said. "Look for entrances to the mines."

The squads fanned out through the ruins to search.

"What's that?" Arlo asked. He pointed to a mound of dirt with a box-shaped metal hull sticking out at right angles.

"An old-world bus," Edgar said. "Probably some tourists, stranded here during the war."

Ada tried to picture people sitting behind the broken windows, but as usual, she found it too hard to fathom what the world was once like.

Two more vehicles sat partially covered by dirt in the center of the mining site. Barrels and crates were stacked outside one of them—evidence of relatively recent activity.

"The skinwalkers were definitely here," she said.

It didn't take long to find the two entry points to the tunnels, both covered with tarps, at the western and eastern edges of the ruins.

Slayer motioned for the group to split up. Gran Jefe led the Barracudas to the left while the Hell Divers went right.

Holding Cricket in his hand, Michael did another scan outside the cave entrance. It came back negative.

"We'll go first and see if it's safe," Ada said.

"That's why I'm here," Michael said. "Pedro, we'll let you know if we find any tech."

Pedro nodded.

"Edgar, go with them," Magnolia said.

Ada pulled back the plastic tarp from the mouth of a stone tunnel to let Jo-Jo and Michael inside. The monkey went down on all fours, staying just in front of him and sniffing the air, as Ada and Michael turned on their flashlights.

The beams flitted over rock walls, pieces of which had fallen away, scattering chunks of rubble on the path. Edgar joined them in the narrow passage, using the tactical light attached to the barrel of his rifle.

"Looks sturdy," he said.

"Yeah, but be careful not to touch anything," Michael said.

Bottles and sundry other debris littered the ground: the head of a hammer, a rusted oil canister, a decaying rubber sandal. The path sloped downward, and Michael went deeper into the mine with Cricket, scanning for contacts or potential weak spots in the ancient timbers.

Drawings marked the ceilings and walls. Ada couldn't make most of them out, but she did stop to look at one of a man with the head of a bull.

"What the hell is that?" she whispered.

"A Minotaur," Edgar said.

"A *what*?"

"Ancient monster from Greek mythology. I read about it when I was a kid. Horn must have worshipped it, considering his helmet and name and shit."

Jo-Jo looked back at them, snorting.

"Let's keep moving," Ada said.

Keeping low, the two divers pushed deeper into the passage. The skinwalkers had added steel posts and shoring in parts where the tunnels had crumbled.

Michael scanned them all, then moved on into the darkness.

"Layla isn't going to be happy to hear you came down here," Ada said as she and Edgar caught up.

"No, I don't suppose she would, but she understands what this job entails, and it's safer than diving."

He looked over his shoulder. "Some days, that is."

After descending for a few minutes, they finally reached another tarp, which was pulled back already, revealing a wide chamber ahead.

"Careful," Michael said. "Watch for booby traps."

He did another scan with Cricket, then cautiously walked inside the room.

Tarps and plastic sheets seemed to be strategically placed to keep the space sealed off from toxins and perhaps radioactive dust, although Ada wasn't picking up much on her Geiger counter.

Jo-Jo went next. Her hair still lay flat—not sensing any creatures.

Edgar and Ada raked their lights across the open space strewn with open supply crates and upended barrels.

"Looks clear," Michael said, lowering Cricket and his rifle. All three divers switched to their more powerful helmet lights. Combined, they had enough candlepower to see the entire chamber.

Ada crossed over to the western wall, where more plastic sheets hung. Jo-Jo was there, sniffing.

"What you got?" Ada said.

Taking a step closer, she realized that the sheets weren't plastic, but sections of tanned human skin.

"Oh God," Ada whispered.

Edgar hurried over to their position. "Damn, these bastards were brutal."

Stepping back from the macabre display, Ada saw something tucked in the corner. She walked over to a big metal chair positioned in front of a square hole where a large stone had been pulled from the wall. Bones and candles had been arranged as a shrine inside the opening.

But it was the chair that held Ada's gaze.

"Must have been Horn's throne," she said.

Edgar lifted a hardcover book out of a small chest under the chair. "What's this—some sort of torture guide?"

To Ada's surprise, the pages were filled with sketches and logs, all the words in Spanish.

Edgar tossed it aside. "Let's keep searching for something we can *use*."

"Hold on," Ada said. She picked the book up. "This could be useful."

"Oh damn, this is what I'm talking about," Edgar said. He propped up the lid of a large chest and pulled out a sword with a gold trident carved onto the hilt.

Ada took a look inside, finding thin, dull black armor that looked different from what the Cazadores wore. There was also a helmet with a beaklike snout.

"Wow," Edgar said, holding the blade up under the light. "I've never seen one like this before. Definitely not Cazador."

"Maybe they found it on a raid," Ada said.

They continued the search, uncovering a few crates of tools and some long-expired medicines, but that was it besides the logs and the sword.

"You find anything?" Ada asked Michael.

He held up the metal case of an electronic tablet. "It's not working, but I might be able to fix it with Pedro."

"Good," Ada said. "It could have some intel on it."

They packed the goods and headed topside.

By the time they got to the surface, the rain was still pouring and the wind was picking up. The Barracudas team was still not back.

Edgar, Arlo, and Pedro huddled under a rock shelf with Magnolia.

"Find anything?" she asked.

"Not really, just a broken tablet," Michael replied.

"Storm's getting worse," Edgar said. "Let's check on Slayer."

The Hell Divers went to the other entrance, where Gran Jefe stood cradling his .50-caliber chain gun. He pointed the muzzle at Jo-Jo as she approached.

"Hey!" Ada shouted. "That's my—"

"*Bestia*," Gran Jefe said. He took a glove off the barrel and gestured for the animal to get back.

Ada whistled for Jo-Jo, who retreated behind her.

"Don't you ever point a weapon at her again," Ada snarled.

"Shut up," Gran Jefe said. He mumbled something else that was obscured by the noise of his breathing apparatus, but it sounded a lot like "*puta*."

Magnolia moved in front of her. "Calm down," she said.

Then she walked up to Gran Jefe. "Where's Slayer?"

Gran Jefe pointed to the tunnel.

"Yeah, I know," Magnolia started to say. "But . . ." She shook her head and walked back to the Hell Divers.

"Slayer, this is Commander Katib," she said over the team comms. "Do you copy?"

"Copy, Commander," Slayer's voice crackled. "We've located a second tunnel and are about to open it."

"Copy that. You need any help?"

"Negative, we've got this."

Magnolia motioned for the divers to get away from Gran Jefe. Ada stared at the big Cazador for a while. He stared back at her through the almond-shaped visor slots in his helmet.

Behind him, flashlight beams streaked out of the tunnel, and Slayer and his crew emerged a few minutes later with a few crates. Nothing that looked to be of much value.

"You guys find anything?" Slayer asked.

"Not really," Edgar said.

"We're still searching the other chamber. I'm heading back down. With any luck—"

A black-winged creature shot out of the passageway behind Gran Jefe. Slayer ducked as it flapped overhead.

"What the hell is that?" Arlo shouted.

No one replied, and for a moment, the only sound was the rain pattering on their armor. Gran Jefe turned to the open tarp, pulling it back. Ada heard something else then—a whooshing sound.

"Everyone, get down!" she yelled.

The big soldier dived to the side as a wave of bats exploded from the entrance. Sleek and muscular, with fangs like fillet knives, they flew out in droves. These were not your average bat.

Ada hit the ground, wishing she could burrow. Pedro crouched next to her, an arrow notched in his tactical bow. He loosed the arrow and got a shriek in answer.

Another quarrel streaked into the air from Bromista's crossbow. Its explosive head detonated on impact, raining down hunks of meat and burning hair.

A flamethrower erupted behind Ada, eliciting high-pitched wails of agony as the flaming stream found more of the flying monsters.

Flapping in vain, winged balls of fire dropped screeching to the ground.

Slayer and one of his warriors used their spears to finish them off while the other soldier kept on spraying the air with liquid fire. Gran Jefe stomped on the flaming monsters and kicked one up into the air. "*¡Anda, pendejo! ¡Vuela!* Go on! Fly, asshole!"

"*Abaixa* . . . Stay down," Pedro said to Ada.

He scrambled over to a bat the size of a chicken and plucked his arrow from its head. The jaw released what looked like a human hand.

"Get back, all of you!" Slayer shouted.

Ada pushed herself up, joining the Hell Divers and Jo-Jo, but they didn't retreat. They raised their laser rifles and fired at the cloud of bats circling the area.

The beasts rained from the sky, landing in heaps on the ground.

In a few minutes, it was over, and the last bats fled into the darkness.

"Everyone okay?" Slayer asked.

Ada checked for injuries, but her team and the Barracudas seemed okay.

"Go check on the others inside the passageway," Slayer said to Gran Jefe.

The hulking warrior nodded and ducked inside.

Slayer turned toward the ocean. "Command, this is Barracuda One, do you copy?"

The Hell Divers gathered together with the remaining Barracudas, their weapons still angled at the sky. Michael held up Cricket, but the scans came back negative. The only animal life registering was human.

A few minutes later, Gran Jefe returned alone, carrying two extra rifles.

"Where's Lan and Hugo?" Slayer asked.

Gran Jefe shook his head and replied in Spanish. Ada didn't need a translator to know that the hand she had seen earlier belonged to one of the warriors.

The Barracuda sergeant looked down and muttered a few words that she couldn't hear. Then he walked away with Bromista and Gran Jefe.

"What about your men?" Magnolia asked. "You don't want to recover them?"

"There's nothing to recover," Slayer said. "Come on. We need to get back to the boats. The captain said a storm is coming."

Hauling the crates of supplies, the teams hurried back to the inflatable launches on the beach. They took them back to the *Octopus*.

As soon as Ada was on board, she pulled the book out from her vest and waved Slayer down. He was changing out of his armor, clearly distraught. She felt bad about pestering him after he lost two men, but she wanted to know what the book said.

"Hey, can you translate this for me?" she asked.

"What is it?"

Slayer opened it, then answered his own question. "Shit! Where'd you get this? It's Horn's log!"

He flipped through the pages slowly, then stopped.

"Holy . . ."

He looked up from the book and met her gaze.

"I need to show this to General Forge," he said. "Thanks, Winslow."

She watched the sergeant trot off with the book.

"I guess we did good today, Jo-Jo," Ada said.

The monkey followed her back to their quarters with an ocean view. Ada sat on her bunk and looked out at the tanker *Blood Trawler*, sailing away from the Outrider Colony port. The ship contained the last of the oil, meaning this would be their last visit to this evil place.

She ruffled the thick hair on Jo-Jo's head.

"Time to go home, my friend."

TWO

The radio tower on top of the Wind Talker oil rig had the best view in the Vanguard Islands. Michael Everhart was in the crow's nest, two hundred feet above the highest point on the capitol tower.

His long hair fluttered below the baseball cap that threatened to skip out to sea on the next strong gust of wind. The thought drew his gaze to the new wind turbines, mounted on six raised platforms across the rig. One of his personal projects, the turbine array continued to provide additional energy to the islands.

The turbines, all scavenged from the wastes, spun quietly, charging batteries. Once full, the batteries would be assigned to the rigs, to restore power that was formerly fueled by gasoline or propane.

Michael brought the binoculars up. Ahead of them, the research ship ITC *Octopus* pushed out to sea, leaving a long wake.

A month had passed since they escorted the oil tanker *Blood Trawler* from the Outrider Colony. Now the new fleet would soon be heading off on another raiding mission.

He centered the binos on the bow of *Ocean Bull*, mounted with a massive spiked grill. As chief engineer of the islands, Michael had fulfilled King Xavier's order himself. He still didn't know exactly what the king was going to use the spikes for, but if Michael knew X, he had a plan. And it probably didn't involve ramming any other vessels.

Today, Michael wasn't up here to monitor the fleet. He was here to check on the wind turbines and then finish installing a new satellite dish that connected to weather drones.

It was storm season, and according to Cazador records, this year was already one of the worst since humans began living on the oil rigs. In the past, they had believed that the barrier would protect them, and though it did blunt the storms' fury, people suffered.

Michael and his team were doing what they could to prepare for the next one.

Pulling Cricket 2.0 from his pack, he ran a patch cord from the handheld computer to the satellite dish to run a diagnostic.

After defeating the machines at Mount Kilimanjaro a year ago, Michael had trekked back out and salvaged the hard drive. He was still reprogramming it, but Cricket 2.0 already had a variety of functions that included in-depth environmental scans as well as communication with the drones deployed outside the barrier between light and dark.

The drones from the ITC *Ranger* helped them monitor the storms from a distance, giving them more lead time to get the crops covered and buildings battened down and the growing fleet of ships and small craft out of harm's way.

A chirp sounded, and data rolled across Cricket's screen.

Michael bumped on the comm and opened a line to Pedro, who oversaw monitoring the drones and assembling the data.

"Pedro, do you copy?"

"*Sim*, copy, Chief. Satellite is online and we are get uplinks."

"Excellent. I'm on my way."

Michael started down the ladder, pausing to brace himself against a gust of wind.

Halfway down, a voice called up. But this wasn't Pedro; it was Michael's deputy chief engineer, Alfred.

Michael hurried down the last rungs of the radio tower and hopped off to the deck. "What?" he asked.

"You better come see this, Chief," Alfred said.

They ran across the middle platform to a hatch that opened onto the command room. Inside, Pedro was leaning over three monitors. The soothing voice of AI Timothy Pepper resonated through the room, explaining something about "miles per hour," "millibars," and a "storm vortex."

Pedro turned and swung an unruly dreadlock back over his shoulder.

"Chief," he said with a nod.

"What've we got?" Michael went to the monitors.

A 3-D image of Timothy rose above the holopod. He had altered his projected image and shaved his tidy beard, exposing dimples no one knew he had. His salt-and-pepper hair had grown out into tightly curled strands.

"Greetings, Chief," he said. "I was briefing Pedro about the data we just received from a drone two hundred miles to the east."

Michael leaned down over the monitor depicting a swirling mass.

"The storm front currently has up to sixty-five-mile-per-hour winds with heavy rain," Timothy said. "We need to monitor it longer to see if it is growing stronger or weakening. For now, it appears the trajectory will miss the Vanguard Islands by fifty miles."

"If it changes course, we could have a problem," Alfred said.

"I will keep eye on it," Pedro said.

"Let me know if it changes even a little bit," Michael said.

"*Entendido*, Chief."

"There is some good news," Timothy said with a smile. "Engineering crew four just finished the solar panel installation at the trading post rig."

"Finally," Michael said.

"Want to go check it out?" Alfred asked.

Michael nodded.

The two men hurried down the decks, passing a score of technicians and engineers who now reported to Michael. He knew them all by name, even the Cazadores who didn't speak English. It was a huge change going from hell diving to this, but he enjoyed the job and it allowed him to spend more time with Layla and Bray instead of risking his life in the sky.

He missed the comradeship and sense of saving humanity, but he was still protecting his people, just in a different way.

At the marina, Michael and Alfred untethered his speedboat, an enclosed armored warcraft that had once belonged to el Pulpo. Piloting it used to bring up dark memories, but Michael had slowly buried that past. Happily, so had the Cazadores.

There was still anger and grief from those who had lost loved ones in the fighting, but defeating the machines and the skinwalkers had helped most of them bury the hatchet. As X often said, the future of humanity would depend on everyone standing together.

Michael fired up the two 400-horsepower engines. Grabbing the throttle, he eased the boat into reverse and backed away into the teal-green water.

"Did you ever think we would make it to somewhere like this?" Alfred asked.

"I dreamed of it as a kid but never thought I would see it in my lifetime."

"Me neither, Chief. Me neither."

Michael smiled at his friend and deputy. They had worked together for a year, but Alfred's time as a technician and engineer went back far beyond that.

Years ago, he had replaced Ty, the former Hell Diver technician who had served Team Raptor with honor. And like Ty, Alfred served with competence, creativity, and a work ethic that never let up.

Both Michael and Alfred were tech geeks, but they had bonded over more than that after Bray was born. Alfred was also a dad with a two-year-old son, and he had been a font of timely advice that helped get Michael through the long sleep-deprived nights.

Alfred also helped at work, especially during the first month, often taking on more of the load so Michael could give Layla a break at home.

It was time to give Alfred a little something back.

"After this, why don't you call it a day," Michael said.

"What about you?"

"I'll finish up work and then head home."

"You sure, Chief? I'm happy to—"

"Real sure."

After docking the boat, Michael and Alfred went into a new single-story warehouse building with windows in the walls and solar panels on the corrugated metal roof.

"What do you think, Chief Everhart?"

A man with green sunglasses propped up on his bald head walked toward them. He wore a tool belt with half a dozen different hammers and hatchets dangling from its loops. He massaged his thick white goatee.

"Looks good," Michael replied.

He walked over to Steve Schwarzer, one of the leading technicians at the islands. Also the top blade-smith, Steve had designed and made weapons for the past fifty years, starting when he was only twenty, after an injury as a Cazador soldier had left him blind in one eye and with two broken legs.

Though twice Michael's age, the man seemed to respect Michael. They had something in common other than their engineering backgrounds. Like Michael, Steve wasn't a Cazador but rather a former prisoner, stolen out of a bunker as a child and raised in the Cazador society.

"The panels are installed and hooked up," Steve said.

Alfred walked up to the entrance to examine the work. But Michael wasn't looking at the solar panels. He was looking at the sign mounted over the door.

The Hive.

It was the same steel sign that once hung in the airship.

"I cleaned her up and installed it since you guys decided to name the school after the ship," Steve said. "Thought it was a nice touch."

"It is," Michael said. "Very nice."

"Good. Say, I've got another project I need to get to for King Xavier, but let me know if you need anything else today, Chief."

Michael nodded and watched the bladesmith hurry off. He could only imagine what type of project X had cooking with Steve.

"I'll finish up here," Michael said. "Go home to Tammy and Leonard."

"Thanks, Chief."

Michael opened the doors and walked into the school. There were twenty classrooms for the 610 kids, and Layla was teaching in one of them. Michael headed straight for her door.

It was ajar, and he stopped outside, out of view. Folding his robotic arm with the real one, he listened to the friendly, engaging voice of his wife.

"During the early days of what would become the United States, horses were domesticated animals often used to haul goods or as transportation," she said. "In those days, over nine hundred different native tribes lived all across North America."

Michael listened to the story he had heard as a kid, about how the colonizers of the country uprooted the people who were already there, killing many of them and placing survivors on reservations.

That same social evil could have happened here at the Vanguard Islands if not for X's determination to make everyone equal. Someone like Captain Leon Jordan wouldn't have done things quite the same way. He would have exiled the Cazadores or killed them outright after defeating them and taking the throne.

And that is how humanity was almost wiped out, Michael thought. *By men like Leon Jordan and el Pulpo.*

Stepping up to the door, Michael studied the kids inside the room. They ranged in age from seven to ten. He knew them all by name, though only a few of them personally.

Alton was there, the boy from Tanzania who Michael had discovered when diving into the machines' camp. He would never forget the kid's filthy, haggard face and wild eyes. Now those eyes were bright and focused on a picture of a horse that Layla showed the class.

It was interesting to think about what each of these kids would become as they got older. Engineers, some of them. And doctors, sailors, electricians, soldiers . . .

Their future wasn't guaranteed, but they all had the opportunity to become something at the Vanguard Islands. A chance to grow up in peace, without having to worry about their next meal or the fateful lightning strike that would send their airship crashing to the surface. And they didn't have to steel themselves against the possibility of their parent dying on a raid in the wastes.

Layla saw Michael and smiled. "Looks like we have a visitor," she said.

The class all turned as Michael stepped inside the room.

"Don't let me interrupt," he said. "Just came by to say hi."

"Is this your husband?" asked a girl.

"Yes, this is Michael, a former Hell Diver and now our chief engineer," Layla said.

"He saved us," Alton said. "I'll never forget that day."

"Neither will I," Michael said.

He moved down the aisle of desks, looking at the animal drawings each kid had made. Some of them were just stick figures, but he could tell they were horses.

"You ever seen one in the wastes?" asked a young boy.

"Me?" Michael asked. "No, horses are extinct, I'm afraid."

"What about mutated horses?" Alton asked.

"Not sure there are any of those, either," Michael said.

"Of course there aren't," Layla said.

"Right."

A knock came from the back of the room.

Alfred stood in the doorway. "Can I see you a minute, Chief?"

Michael nodded and turned back to Layla.

"I'll see you and Bray at dinner," he said.

Layla held his gaze, clearly concerned. Michael joined Alfred outside the building. Pedro was there. That was all he needed to see to know what this was about.

"The storm?" Michael asked.

Pedro handed him an electronic tablet displaying images of the storm pattern.

"The first drone's storm trajectory was *errada* . . . wrong," he said. "We will be going to get hit."

"How long do we have?" Michael asked.

"*Aproximadamente* two days, maybe less."

Alfred sighed. "So much for some time off. How do you want to handle this?"

"Scramble everyone—all hands—and meet me at HQ."

"What about the alarms?"

Michael thought about it for a moment.

"Don't sound them yet," he said. "I need to talk to King Xavier first. He'll know what to do."

* * * * *

Lightning arced across the horizon, its long-delayed rumble almost too distant to hear.

It was the music of the season, a season of storms—and a foreshadowing of what was to come.

X sat in his study, reading over the log, now translated, that Ada had discovered on Aruba a month ago. Under the table sat a wooden crate that contained black armor, a helmet, and a beautiful sword inlaid with a golden trident, also found on that raid.

Only General Forge and Sergeant Slayer knew what the logs said, and until X could figure out a plan, he was keeping it a secret.

OUR JOURNEY TO FIND THE CORAL CASTLE FAILED, AND NOW WE MUST RETURN TO INFORM MY FATHER. HE MUST ACCEPT THAT THE METAL ISLANDS ARE DOOMED UNLESS HE SACRIFICES THE WEAK FOR THE SURVIVAL OF THE STRONG. BUT I FEAR THAT MY FATHER, LIKE MANY OF MY COMRADES, WON'T FORFEIT THE LIVES OF HIS FAMILY FOR THE

BENEFIT OF THE METAL ISLANDS. IF HE
FAILS TO ACT, I WILL.

X turned to the second entry.

TODAY MY FEAR WAS REALIZED. HALF MY
CREW TURNED ON ME IN LIGHT OF MY PLAN.
I NOW CLOTHE MYSELF IN THE HIDES OF
THESE MEN. THE METAL ISLANDS ARE
DOOMED UNLESS WE REDUCE OUR NUMBERS,
AND SOON I WILL DELIVER THAT MESSAGE TO
MY FATHER. HE MUST TAKE THE ACTION TO
SAVE OUR PEOPLE, OR HIS REIGN HAS COME
TO AN END . . .

The log revealed why el Pulpo and his bastard
son had gone to war: over a mythical underwater city
called the Coral Castle. X still didn't know where they
had come up with this idea, but he was going to meet
with Imulah soon to find out.

Coral Castle or no Coral Castle, el Pulpo and his
son had fought for the same reason that humans had
always fought: land—in this case, the only habitable
real estate with sunshine anywhere on the planet.

It was a tough bite to chew, but now X understood what had motivated el Pulpo and his Cazadores
on their raiding missions.

They didn't trap Sirens and human survivors for
conquest—they did it to survive.

Seeing the steady decline of resources at the Metal

Islands during his reign, el Pulpo was forced to travel farther and farther for supplies and food to prevent starvation and the total collapse of the islands.

Even after destroying the machines and killing the Cazador warlords el Pulpo and Horn, the Vanguard Islands were not living up to their name—especially now, with the rigs damaged and supplies dwindling.

Time was again running out, and X knew he needed to make a decision before it was too late—a decision that would once again send men and women into the wastes to die. It was time to finally tell Michael and his other confidants the truth.

A rap came on his door. X took off his reading glasses and stood as Victor entered.

"Sir, the bladesmith has finished his work and is in the garden," he said.

"Excellent," X said.

Miles followed X out of the room as Ton and Victor led the way to the rooftop of the capitol tower. The two former slaves, freed by the sky people, each carried a spear and a slung rifle. They seemed relaxed, but their eyes never stopped moving.

At the orange trees, a man knelt in front of the wooden statue that Rodger had made a year ago. The spot marked the grave containing the remains of the Hell Diver they had found aboard the ITC *Ranger*.

X cleared his throat, and Steve Schwarzer, the master weaponsmith, stood up. The old craftsman took the green sunglasses off the top of his head, which gleamed like a melon in the thin moonlight.

He tucked the shades into his shirt and held up the restored armor X had commissioned.

"Banged it out the best I could, sir," Steve said.

X picked up the chest rig, ran his fingers around the empty cavity where a battery had once powered the suit. Most of the rust was buffed out, and the armor shone almost like new.

"Excellent work," X said. "I'll put this to good use and let this diver rest in peace here."

They still didn't know the diver's name—only that he had served on *Ares,* which meant Commander Rick Weaver would likely have known him.

But like this man, Weaver was long since dead, his memory lost like the souls of billions.

X never worried about people forgetting his name. It meant nothing to him. But he knew that the concept of legacy had once driven men mad in the Old World. Leaders who would do anything to solidify their place in history, even if it meant going to war.

"I can fix that, too, if you want," Steve said, glancing at X's prosthetic arm. "Could make something similar to the spear blade you wore."

"That blade served its purpose," X said, referring to General Rhino's spear, now back where it should be, at his statue.

"Let me know if you change your mind. I'd have great fun making something for you that could come in handy for all kinds of situations."

"I might just take you up on that. Thanks."

Steve bent down to pat Miles. The dog wagged his tail and licked his callused hand.

X had many ways to judge a man's character, and one of them was whether Miles liked them.

"Thanks again," X said.

"Anytime, sir."

X took the armor and left the grave with his dog and his guards. They crossed the domed rooftop of the capitol tower to the eastern edge, where a machine gun was nestled between walls of sandbags. In the distance, he could see *Vanguard*, formerly known as the *Hive*. The beetle-shaped airship rested on the platform, unmoored and ready to fly.

To the east, two trawlers bobbed in the water, hauling up nets in the moonlight to keep the market filled with fresh catch. But it wasn't enough. After the last crop was damaged in the machines' attack, they were playing catch-up, and the next harvest was still two weeks out.

X was doing everything he could to keep the last bastion of humanity alive and working even harder to keep the peace. One thing was certain: he wouldn't be able to keep it if they ran out of food, water, or fuel—the three resources without which peace was unattainable.

Ton and Victor followed X across the tower and into a stairwell.

At the top landing, Miles started carefully down the stairs, as if he couldn't see them well. Each step showed his age. The dog's vision was going, and his hind legs were starting to deteriorate.

Seeing his decline hurt worse than hitting the ground crosswind on a dive.

When Miles went, X would likely not be far behind.

X continued to the library and opened the doors to the long two-tiered chamber. Candles burned in sconces set between the bookshelves on the first level.

On the second floor, a candle flame illuminated the bearded face of Imulah. The lead scribe was right where he had promised to be, sitting at the table with the maps and books.

"Everything you asked for, King Xavier," Imulah said. "But I'm afraid we don't have much information on the Coral Castle—only a single entry about the man who first spoke of such a place."

X put the armor down, took a seat, and carefully opened the logbook.

"One hundred and two years ago, a Cazador raiding party saw a lighthouse in Colón, Panama. When they went there, they found a man wearing the armor and helmet Ada discovered in Aruba," Imulah explained. "He was killed and eaten by that party, but not before he told them about the Coral Castle."

"Did he say where it was?"

"In the Pacific. Under the water. He claimed to have traveled through the canal in a small boat and was looking for survivors to bring them back to this haven."

"Sounds mad, but then again, I found this place, and I was a bit loco, as you say," X said. Still, he didn't think much of the story and quickly went on to the next book—logs of the Cazador warships that had raided Florida and the Caribbean and Atlantic shores of South America for over two centuries.

The hours passed, and X finally put the book down.

"Imulah, do you know why el Pulpo and his descendants focused only on these places?" he asked. "Why did they never try to go through the canal and reach the western shores of South America?"

"They did. Let me search for it." Imulah unraveled a scroll, then another. Then he opened a book and pointed to a passage. "Here . . . The warship *Anaconda* traveled to the Panama Canal forty years ago, during the reign of King Mayac. A second, much smaller vessel, called the *Sea Sprite*, was deployed with them."

He handed the scroll over. From what X could tell, King Mayac had deployed the warship with fifty sailors and a raiding team of thirty marines—quite a number for a vessel that never returned.

"Were they looking for the Coral Castle?" X asked.

"Perhaps, but I think they were just trying to get through the canal."

"No scouts were sent out to look for them?"

"Yes, a vessel was deployed to search. I believe they found the *Anaconda*, adrift in the ocean not far from the Port of Colón in Panama, but the *Sea Sprite* was never recovered."

Imulah put his finger on a line in Spanish and read it aloud, translating on the fly.

"When we found the *Anaconda*, it drifted like a dead fish—no direction," he said. "A boarding party was put together and climbed onto the *Anaconda* to search for the crew. At first, due to the missing lifeboats, it was believed they had abandoned ship during the storm. But then we found the damage to the port side."

Imulah glanced up, stroking his beard.

"And?"

"They found signs of a *kaiju*."

"What the hell's a *kaiju*?"

"It was an old-world term for 'monster.'"

X sat back in his chair.

"General Forge was just in Panama a year ago, where he salvaged the *Octopus* and *Ocean Bull* from the port," X said. "I wonder if he knew about this."

"Maybe, but why does that matter?"

"Do we know if Horn and his skinwalkers went through the canal?" he asked.

"No, I'm afraid not," Imulah replied.

X listened to the rain tap on the shutters and windowpanes. Candles flickered across the quiet room as he pictured what might have happened to the crews of the *Anaconda* and the *Sea Sprite*.

Imulah sighed. "King Xavier, with respect, I know you well enough to understand what you're doing."

"Oh? And what's that?"

"You believe this place is doomed, as el Pulpo did, and you are looking for more places to raid."

X narrowed his eyes. "You knew he thought that?"

"I suspected it."

"And you didn't tell me?"

"I figured you would make your own way as king."

"Do you believe this place is doomed?"

Before Imulah could answer, a knock came on the door. X stood, Miles rising with him.

Michael opened the door and stepped inside.

"King Xavier, you summoned me," he said.

"So formal," X said with a grin. "Yes, please come in. We need to talk."

Michael crossed over to the table, holding a computer in his robotic hand. "I have something I need to talk to you about, too."

X narrowed his eyes and gestured for Michael to take a seat, but Michael remained standing.

"This must be bad," X said.

"I'm afraid so."

X decided to stay on his feet, too.

Michael held out Cricket, and a hologram of Timothy emerged before them.

"Ah, King Xavier, good to see you," he said with a smile.

"Give me the shit news, Pepper," X said.

"The drones have detected a powerful storm heading our way," the AI replied. "The wind is already hurricane strength, and it's getting stronger."

X cursed under his breath.

Time wasn't running out. It was already gone.

Two weeks before harvest, they were about to be hit with the worst storm yet.

He knew then that he could no longer sit around and try to mitigate problems. There was no fixing some of the issues here.

It was time to be aggressive and head back into the wastes.

"How long do we have?" X asked.

"Two days, maybe a bit less," Timothy said. "Pedro is monitoring the data with me and has taken a more conservative approach, thinking it will be here faster."

X shook his head. "Just what we need," he said. "Sound the alarms when I tell you to get everyone prepared and buckled down to ride this one out."

Michael nodded and went to leave, then hesitated. "Wait. What were you going to tell me?"

"Something I should have told you a month ago," X replied.

He handed Michael Horn's logs, translated from the Spanish. Michael read them and looked up with dread in his eyes.

"I'm going to activate the Hell Divers and recruit new ones," X said. "It's time to face our future without fear. I'm sending a team into the wastes to look for more places to raid. We can't hide out here any longer."

"Where exactly are we heading?" Timothy asked.

X pulled over the maps and pointed at the Panama Canal.

"Never thought I would say this, but el Pulpo was right," he said. "Unless we head back to the wastes to search for new supply chains, the Vanguard Islands have an expiration date."

X picked up the new armor and whistled for Miles to follow.

"Where are you going?" Imulah asked.

"To recruit some new allies," X said over his shoulder.

THREE

Kade Long squinted and pulled down the brim of his tattered cowboy hat. Although he had been here a year, he still wasn't used to the bright sunshine at the Vanguard Islands. There were a lot of things he and his fellow sky people weren't used to.

Food, for one. *Good* food, anyway.

The 505 survivors formerly imprisoned at Mount Kilimanjaro weren't used to eating much at all. Most of them had been malnourished and sick when the Hell Divers showed up and rescued them from the machines.

Five of Kade's comrades had died shortly after, unable to hold on long enough to see this wondrous place.

He gazed out from the balcony of his small shack on the second-highest deck of oil rig 15. All the Kilimanjaro survivors lived on this rig, cramped together in dwellings just like his. No one minded the tight quarters.

Laughter came from the balcony above him, where his neighbors were joking around.

Sounds he never used to hear—very different kinds of noises from those he had heard in the machines' prison. Gone were the constant coughing and sobs of starving, sick people.

Here was laughter, deep and joyous.

He enjoyed hearing those happy noises, but he also enjoyed the sounds of the ocean: the keening cries of the seabirds, the rumble of fishing boats heading out early in the morning.

All these sounds were new, just like the views. The clear blue-green water, the colorful shoals of fish, and the bright colors of the Cazadores' clothing and jewelry made him feel like a blind person seeing for the first time.

He closed his eyes.

This was paradise, but the thought often brought on survivor's guilt, as it did now. Feelings of regret and loss bubbled up, along with the horrible question that ate at his broken heart.

Why was he alive when his family was dead?

He thought of his wife, Mikah, and their boys, Sean, Jack, and Rich—all of them gone. Killed by the machines all those years ago when Captain Rolo had chased the signal to Mount Kilimanjaro and fallen for the trap.

Anger festered in his guts, though not at the captain. Kade had long since forgiven Rolo. In fact, Kade had been on the crew that decided it was worth the risk to chase that very signal.

Maybe surviving after his family had perished was only what he deserved—a punishment that would never end.

He went back inside. Besides the little square table and a plastic chair, the two-hundred-square-foot dwelling also boasted a custom-made bed and armchair. Resting against the armchair was his only other belonging besides his clothes and hat and six-shooter: his guitar.

Normally, he would sit down and pick a few tunes every day, but today he didn't feel much like playing.

He left the shack and headed to the top of the rig. The supper bell sounded from a lookout platform off one of the sundecks, drawing hundreds of hungry mouths.

The scent of fish stew and fresh-baked bread led them all to the center of the deck, where tables and chairs were already occupied by the early birds.

Kade knew every person here. They all had suffered together, seen each other at their worst. He walked past Janice, who had been friends with his wife. She bit off a hunk of bread and nodded at him as he walked by.

In his mind's eye, Kade recalled a night five or six years after they were imprisoned at the machines' camp. He was in a cell with Janice and three others, two of whom had since died. Starving, sick, and thirsty, Janice had come to Kade, offering her body in exchange for his water ration.

He had gently declined her offer but gave her the rest of his water.

Kade was filled with memories of moments that had brought out the worst in the captives. Times when people had fought and even killed over food and water.

Doing whatever they could to survive.

He fell into line behind Thomas, who had lost an arm in an accident running a laser-cutting machine at the camp. The severed limb hadn't gone to waste, though—several other workers had cooked it that night and eaten it.

"G'day, Kade," Thomas said.

"How you doing, mate?" Kade dipped his cowboy hat, speaking with whatever remained of the accent that had taken to the sky with their ancestors during the war. "I'm still full as a butcher's dog from last night's feast," Thomas said while patting his belly. "Sometimes, I can't believe this is all real."

"Aye, almost like someone pulled the wool over your eyes, yeah?"

Thomas chuckled.

As the queue shuffled forward, another memory surfaced, of the lines he once stood in for the thin soup that the machines served in the camp. A droid unit that looked like a wastebasket had served them all from vats that contained a mystery soup. Some days, it was just broth; other days, it had small chunks of meat or herbage.

Kade used to think the rare scraps of meat came from rats, until the day he learned the truth.

People would often push and fight their way into

the line, anxious to get the first ladlefuls, thinking these would have the most meat. In the early days, Kade didn't care about his position in line. He had lost his will to live, and with it, all his instinct to survive.

He let his rations go to people like Tia, the daughter of a fellow Hell Diver who had died years before their airship reached Africa.

Kade didn't see the teenager here today, but he did see another kid, this one born in captivity.

Eight-year-old Alton was sitting at a table with his mum, Kaitlyn, shoveling fish stew into his mouth. Long, shaggy brown hair hung over his eyes.

Unlike most of the other sky people, Kade was blessed—or, in his mind, perhaps cursed—with the natural athletic ability and killer instinct that kept him alive.

He had lived in that camp for over ten years, until the day the angels stepped from the sky.

Finally, a joyful memory emerged: the moment Michael Everhart and Arlo Wand had landed at the building where Kade was held prisoner.

He breathed deeply, exhaling the memories as he took a bowl from a stack. When he got to the front of the soup line, he held it out. Molly, a widow with long brown hair and a pretty smile, spooned a hearty portion into his bowl.

Kade thanked her politely and took his bowl, and was headed back to eat in his room when a youthful voice called out.

"Hey, Cowboy Kade, will you tell us some stories today?" little Alton asked.

Sorry, Kaitlyn mouthed.

Kade hesitated. Not because he wanted to eat by himself, but Alton reminded him of his sons. He had a hard time with painful memories of his family whenever he was around kids.

"What kind of story you want to hear?" Kade asked.

Alton gestured to the hat as Kade kicked out a chair and sat down.

"For starters, where'd ya get *that*? I know that's why they call you 'Cowboy Kade,' but . . ."

"I'm no cowboy," Kade said.

Alton pulled out a book from his backpack and opened it in front of Kade. "*These* are cowboys," he said. "They got the same hat you got on, and they rode these things called horses."

Kade looked at the picture of a man astride one of the old-world beasts. The rough-looking guy wore a leather hat and chaps, and held a lasso in one hand and a pistol in the other.

"He sure looks like you," Alton said. "Even got your gun."

Kade had forgotten he was wearing his six-shooter on his hip.

"The Monster Hunter."

He turned toward the cocky female voice and found Tia. She wore a tan tank top and the turquoise necklace she never took off—the last thing her dad ever gave her. Or, rather, that Kade had given her for her dad, who died on the very day he found it.

Tia ran a hand over her buzzed head. The Maori tattoos inked into her scalp recalled her distant ancestors. Those first Polynesians had a fierce warrior culture.

"Where've you been?" Kade asked. "I haven't seen you."

"Trying to find work." Tia shrugged. "Not much to be had if you only know how to shovel dirt and sit in cages."

"There's got to be something."

"Aye, but maybe you should teach me how to use *that*." Her green eyes flitted down to his pistol.

The barrel was rusty from sitting in the dirt during all the years of Kade's captivity, but he had recovered it after the Hell Divers freed him and his people.

Now it stayed in the holster, ready for the day he might need it again.

"Teach me how to shoot," Tia said.

"Yeah, me, too!" Alton said.

Kade snorted and then chuckled while shaking his head.

"What's so funny?" Tia asked.

He sighed. "That's not the kind of life your dad wanted for you."

"Well, he's dead along with pretty much everyone else, and I want to do something with my life now that we got this second chance."

Kade turned back to Kaitlyn and Alton. "Excuse me for a—"

"No need," Tia said. "I was just heading out."

"To go where?"

She hurried off without answering. Kade considered getting up and trying to talk to her, but he knew Tia all too well, and chasing after her would make things worse. Long ago, her father, a Hell Diver on Kade's team, had asked Kade to help look after Tia if anything happened to him.

Kade had agreed, but after her father's death, Tia grew more and more distant and rarely listened to anyone. Now, with freedom all around her, she listened even less.

He sighed again and turned back to the table.

"She's a hurt soul," Kaitlyn said.

"What's that mean, Mum?" Alton asked.

"It means you have a broken heart."

The truth was, Tia thought Kade a bit of a bastard, when he was only trying to help.

Alton pointed at the book again. "Were cowboys kind of like Hell Divers?" he asked. "You really look like this guy."

Kade studied the picture of the cowboy and saw the resemblance. They both had thick mustaches, a strong jawline, and a brown leather hat.

"No, I don't think so," Kade finally said. "It's just a coincidence."

"So how'd you get that hat if you're not a cowboy?" Alton asked.

Kade set the spoon back down as another memory engulfed him, this one a nightmare.

"I found it in a building a long time ago," he said. "Place called a museum. Same place I got my revolver."

Alton reached out for the hat, but Kaitlyn chided him.

"That's not yours to touch," she said.

"It's okay," Kade said. He handed it to Alton. "Go ahead, try it on."

"Really?" The boy's eyes widened.

"Aye, long as you give it back."

"Crikey!" Alton put it on and tipped it up.

"Heya there, mate, I'm a cowboy," Alton said in a deep voice.

Kade gave a rare grin. "Sweet as, pal. You look just like one."

"Okay, give it back now, Alton," Kaitlyn said. She took the hat and handed it back to Kade with a shaky hand.

He noticed then that her skin was paler than normal.

"Thanks," she said.

Kade would have asked her if she was feeling okay, but not in front of her son. He knew that frail, pale look. It was how everyone had looked back at the camps. But this wasn't from starvation and exhaustion. This was the sickness, or what many in the camps referred to as the "reaper."

"Alton, do me a favor," Kade said.

Alton nodded enthusiastically. "What do I get to do?"

"Go and get my guitar, okay? It's leaning against the big stuffed chair at my shack."

"Heck yes!" Alton jumped up and sprinted away from the table.

"And don't run with it!" Kade shouted after him.

As soon as the kid was gone, he leaned forward.

"How long?" he asked.

Kaitlyn knew exactly what he was referring to. "About a month now," she said. "Doctor says it's back again, and not much he can do."

"I'm sorry," Kade said.

"I have a few good months left, maybe more." She drew in a deep breath. "I got to spend a year with him here, but I just don't know what he's going to do without me."

She met his gaze, eyes burning into his.

"I know this is a lot to ask," she said, "but, Kade, you're a good man. One of the best. Promise me you will look after him some. I don't mean you got to take him in, but just make sure he finds his way."

This wasn't the first time someone had asked Kade to look after their child.

He reached out and put his hand over Kaitlyn's. Something he would have done decades ago whenever his wife was worried.

He patted her bony hand. "I will," he said. "You have my word."

Kade quickly pulled his hand back. He hadn't touched a woman for as long as he could remember.

Alton returned a few minutes later, reverently carrying the guitar.

"Will you play us a cowboy song?" he asked.

"I don't think I know any cowboy songs," Kade said.

"Sure you do," came another voice.

Kade turned around to see Captain Rolo with the former chief engineer, Carl Lex, also known as "the Charmer" for his toothy smile and a certain knack for getting his hands on whatever he needed over the years, both on the ship and in the machines' camp.

From what Kade had seen, Charmer was doing the same thing on this rig, running a full-fledged scavenging and bartering operation. Dressed in a new beige tunic with a silver-lined collar, he seemed to be using his skills also to purchase the best for himself. He even had a new suede eye patch to cover the socket gouged out by one of the defector machines.

With the two men were an entourage of officers from the other two airships that, like the *Victory*, had followed the signal to Mount Kilimanjaro in hope of finding a place like this.

Captain Linda Fina, from the ITC *Requiem*, and Lieutenant Olga Novak and Ensign Dmitri Vasilev, from the ITC *Malenkov*, took seats at a table. Their bowls were topped to the rim with chunky fish soup.

Some things never changed.

Kade had understood the need to keep rank and

discipline in the camps, but these people had never gone a day without eating or drinking more than their share.

"So, you going to play us a tune?" Captain Rolo asked.

Kade hadn't planned on performing. Hell, he hadn't put on a show since the night before the ITC *Victory* went down.

"Please?" Alton said, putting his hands together.

The voice reminded Kade of his son, who had begged him to play that night. Mikah smiled her beautiful smile, and Kade gave in, playing for a crowd of clapping and dancing passengers who were their neighbors, friends, and family.

"How about 'Tumbling Tumbleweeds'?" Rolo said. "Sons of the Pioneers. Mikah used to like that, right?"

Kade looked around, all eyes on him. He realized he really didn't have a way out without looking like a bastard.

"For you, Mikah," he whispered, picturing his wife.

Taking a deep breath, he put a foot up on a bench and brought up the guitar. It was a Cazador instrument, crafted here at the islands.

Plucking the guitar strings with his fingertips, he broke into song.

> *"See them tumbling down,*
> *Pledging their love to the ground!*
> *Lonely but free, I'll be found,*
> *Drifting along, with the tumbling*
> *tumbleweeds."*

Playing and singing reminded him of the best days of his life, when he was with his family and his Hell Diver comrades back on the *Victory*. There was never enough to eat, and they never knew if tomorrow would be the day the airship finally crashed, but he would trade anything for another day with his family.

He would give up the light for the darkness just to see his wife and kids again.

He opened his eyes, but the crowd was no longer looking at Kade. He lowered his guitar and turned to see a one-armed man with a bulging backpack slung over one shoulder. An unruly black beard with gray streaks covered half his craggy face.

At his side stood a wolflike dog with bright blue eyes that were currently fixed on Kade.

"King Xavier," Captain Rolo said.

He stood up with the rest of the officers.

Kade almost didn't recognize the king. He stiffened and lowered his guitar.

"Hey, don't let me interrupt," X said, gesturing to Kade. "That was getting really good."

Kade tipped his hat.

"What brings you to our humble abode, Your Majesty?" asked Rolo.

Kade started to sit, then hesitated at what the king said next.

"I'm here to talk to Kade."

Kade turned slowly, meeting Rolo's eyes first, then the king's.

"Finish your food, then meet me on the top deck," X said.

"I'm all done," Kade said. He handed his guitar to Alton. "Watch this for me, please."

The kid took the guitar as if he were being handed the Holy Grail.

Kade pushed his half-eaten bowl of soup over to Kaitlyn.

"Ta," she replied.

"Yeah, thanks, Cowboy Kade," Alton said.

"Cheers." Kade walked through the crowd, ignoring stares—and some glares—from comrades as he followed X to the top deck. Troughs and platforms covered in dirt supported plots of pole beans, corn, and vegetables, most of them nearly ripe, that swayed and dipped in the wind.

X walked down a path to the edge of the rooftop and looked out over a darkening horizon. A storm brewed, firing silent bomb bursts through the clouds.

"You and I are a lot alike, Kade," X said. "You just don't know it. We've survived when others have died, and I bet you wonder why that is. I sure as shit did."

"Aye, sir," Kade replied.

X turned. "And I bet you feel guilt."

"Every damn day."

X nodded at the horizon. "There's a storm coming, and I need people," he said. "People I can trust. People with experience."

"I could use work."

"Not sure this is the type of work you want," X

said, grunting as he unslung his backpack. He unzipped it and pulled out a shiny chest rig and armor plates.

"I need Hell Divers, and I'm told you made a fine one in your day. You don't have to decide now, but I need to know by tomorrow."

X eyed the hat and said, "Someday, you'll have to tell me how you came by that. Never seen one of them before on the surface."

"It was my son's," Kade said.

X looked at it for another hard second before patting Kade on the arm. "The armor will be on the *Vanguard* waiting for you if you want it."

"Aye, gratitude, Your Majesty," Kade said.

"We sure could use your help, but no pressure. I understand if you want to just . . ." He looked around them. "Enjoy this place, but it's going to take good men and women to protect what we've got."

The king walked away, leaving Kade to contemplate his offer. The warm wind beat against his tunic, ruffling his hair.

He wasn't sure how long he stood there, drifting in the past, thinking about the future, and feeling his heart kick in his chest.

Kade Long was still alive, while everyone he ever loved was dead.

Voices snapped him from his trance. Not the joyous laughter from earlier. These voices were close, and he turned as his people flooded out onto the rooftop, looking at something in the east.

He followed eyes and pointing fingers toward the only remaining airship in the world: the *Vanguard*.

It rose into the sky, sirens blaring.

For those around him, this was a warning about the incoming storm. But to Kade, it was a call to arms—a chance to protect this place, to make sure the families that had survived could continue to live in peace.

To live a life he had been robbed of.

As Kade turned to go, he noticed another life that had been robbed. On a boat racing across the water, Tia sat with a group of five sky people. Behind the wheel was a Cazador soldier, and on the bow another, holding a spear.

"Shit," he whispered when he realized what she was doing.

There was work that anyone could get on the islands: soldiering.

He thought they had escaped death and war, but it seemed, no matter where humanity lived, soldiers would always be in demand.

Just like Hell Divers.

FOUR

A bright green flash, a shade brighter than Magnolia's hair, streaked across the horizon. Something to do with the earth's magnetic field and the incoming storms—a precise synchronicity that made this moment of rare and fleeting beauty.

Magnolia stepped away from the portholes in *Vanguard*'s launch bay. The big empty space looked pretty much the same as the day she first stepped into it over a decade ago, back when she was just a petty thief with an attitude.

In the center of the room, technicians prepped the recently restored launch tubes for the training dive. Hundreds of divers had come and gone over the years. All that remained besides memories were the stickers on their lockers and the banners of the diving teams.

Reporting here, she had thought her life was over, but it was really the start of a journey that would lead her people to a new home and save her from a life of misery.

Magnolia walked past the veteran divers of Team Raptor at their lockers. Her best friend, Sofia Walters, was braiding her hair. She looked good for having given birth just six months ago to Rhino's son.

"It's just training," Sofia said, glancing over at Magnolia. "I'll be fine."

"I know, but it's never safe," Magnolia replied.

Sofia sighed. "We can't let Arlo have all the fun, can we?"

"Fun?" Arlo said. "Not what I call this. I call it my contribution to humanity."

"Like the time you landed in a Siren pit?" Edgar asked. The militia soldier turned Hell Diver had survived fifty-nine jumps and the war with the machines. Unlike happy-go-lucky Arlo, Edgar was a no-nonsense, get-it-done kind of diver, always following orders and putting the team first.

"We got out of there just fine, didn't we?" Arlo said.

"Some of us did," Edgar replied.

Magnolia remembered the death of Alexander Corey, who had sacrificed his life so the team could escape in Rio, not long after Arlo almost ended up as Siren shit.

Edgar shook his head in resignation.

A low grunting came from across the room. Ada Winslow was feeding her companion animal, Jo-Jo. Ada was here not by choice but by conscription, as Magnolia had once been.

For Ada, this was a second punishment for her terrible crime against the Cazadores. But she had accepted it with grace and had already proved that she had what it took to be a Hell Diver.

At first, Magnolia didn't like the idea of Ada diving with the beast, but they had trained over the Vanguard Islands for months and had mastered the tandem dive.

"Sorry, she's hungry," Ada said.

Magnolia watched the young woman feeding the animal, who had grown a foot since they returned from the wastes a year ago. Sharp white canines protruded like tusks below her dark lips. The liquid black eyes were riveted on the pile of dried fish Ada had placed on the deck.

The twenty rookie divers stood by watching, some of them with revulsion, others with friendly curiosity. And then there was Jorge "Gran Jefe" Mata, who looked as if he wanted a bite of the fish.

Half a head taller than anyone else in the room, the Cazador was brawny as well—easily one of the strongest men in the Vanguard Islands. He had fought for el Pulpo, and last week he had transferred from the Barracudas in answer to the call for Hell Diver recruits. Sergeant Slayer had personally blessed the move.

The irony wasn't lost on Magnolia, but she was willing to put the past behind them.

They all were survivors here. Fifteen new Cazador divers, along with two from Rio de Janeiro, and three of the sky people from Kilimanjaro.

Like her, these men and women had endured

hardships unthinkable to most people. And with grit, vigilance, and a bit of luck, they were here now, ready to dive so humanity might survive.

"Okay, listen up," Magnolia said, "especially you greenhorns. Today we're jumping from twenty thousand feet, free-falling through storm clouds."

The launch-bay doors opened behind the rookies, and Magnolia looked up at whoever had just interrupted her briefing.

A tall, muscular man came in, wearing a burned leather cowboy hat. He took it off, revealing a weathered face with kind brown eyes. "Commander Magnolia Katib?" he asked.

"Yes, and who are you?"

"Kade Long," he said. "King Xavier asked me—"

"Oh, that's right . . . But you're *late*."

"Aye, sorry, Commander, I—"

She cut him off again. "I heard you were a damn fine diver on the airship *Victory*."

"That was a long time ago."

"Well, I don't know how things were done on the *Victory*, but around here, we respect the clock."

"Yes, ma'am. Won't happen again."

Magnolia jerked her chin at the lockers. "Choose one. Then we'll find you some armor and gear."

"I got the armor covered," Kade said, shucking off his backpack.

"Who's that?" Edgar asked.

"Cowboy Kade," Arlo said. "Heard he once rode a horse against a pack of mutant wolves."

Edgar laughed. "No such thing as a horse any-more—not in the wild, anyway."

"No? So you've explored the entire world?"

"Guys, cut the shit," Magnolia said. "As I said, we'll be jumping from twenty thousand feet into what is so far a mild storm, to simulate what it's like in the wastes. But very soon, the best of you will be heading to the wastes on a classified mission."

Kade looked at Magnolia. Unlike most of these divers, he had no fear in his eyes. She saw something else, too—a sense of sorrow.

Magnolia had heard a few stories about him, mostly from Michael, who had discovered the survivors at the machines' camp. Kade had helped them fight back, and with his background, she hoped he would be a valuable asset.

"Our DZs are the weather deck of the *Octopus* and of the *Ocean Bull*," Magnolia said.

"Those rust buckets are going to be slick," Arlo said.

"*Es el punto*," Gran Jefe said. "The point."

"Plan accordingly," Magnolia said.

The divers finished suiting up and fastening their armor before moving on to check their gear. Magnolia made sure Kade had a chute that was already checked and prepped.

Thirty minutes later, Captain Rolo's voice crackled over the PA system. "The ship is in position."

Magnolia stepped in front of the veterans and said, "All right, who's going first?"

"I will," said a voice from behind her.

Magnolia turned, surprised to see that it was Kade.

She couldn't help but smirk. "Not questioning your commitment, but how long has it been since you dived, Kade?"

"Ten years, give or take."

"So maybe you should sort of *ease* into this."

"And all due respect to you, Commander, but diving isn't something you forget." He shrugged the chute harness over his back and stepped forward. "King Xavier asked me to dive, and from what I understand, we don't have much time before this airship leaves."

"You're right." Magnolia brushed a strand of green hair from her face. "Go ahead and be the first, then. I'll come down with you."

Judging by his hesitation, Kade didn't seem to appreciate that she wanted to go with him. But this wasn't a suggestion. He was here on King Xavier's wishes, not hers, and she didn't like diving into the wastes with someone until she trusted that they could get the job done. A training run with him would be a way to start building that trust.

"The rest of you, pair up with the other greenhorns and follow, one by one with your new recruit, in the following order: Edgar, Ada and Jo-Jo, Sofia, and finally Arlo."

The veteran divers moved to buddy up with the rookies.

"I really got to go with this guy?" Arlo asked, side-eyeing Gran Jefe. "No offense, amigo, but you are . . . how do you say—oh, right, *el gordo*."

None of the Cazadores laughed, especially Gran Jefe.

Magnolia whistled before the soldier could smack the grin off Arlo's face.

"God damn it, Arlo," she hissed.

"Sorry," Arlo said.

Gran Jefe glared at him and then turned to Magnolia.

She cinched her helmet and stepped up to the row of launch tubes.

"Pick a tube," she said to Kade.

She climbed down into the one she always used, and her boots hit the glass bottom. The storm clouds were too thick to see through, but by looking at her HUD, she could tell they were at twenty thousand feet, directly over the Wind Talker rig.

Three minutes later, after all final checks, the glass slid open and dumped Magnolia and Kade into the darkness.

As soon as she was out of the tube, the wind sent her banking hard into a pocket of turbulence. She fought into stable position, holding out her arms and legs at right angles while searching the sky for Kade.

To her surprise, he was already in stable position and, according to his position on her HUD, almost directly over the drop zone.

Magnolia started to reposition her body in that

direction, cutting through the clouds. Lightning flashed to the east, but the static wasn't powerful enough to mess with their electronics.

She watched the altimeter tick down. At seventeen thousand feet, she was closing in on Kade. It seemed he was right about not forgetting how to dive. He looked like a seasoned Hell Diver.

She moved closer, giving a thumbs-up, which he returned.

At fifteen thousand feet, they hit a patch of turbulence that would have knocked a rookie diver out of form. But Magnolia and Kade were soon through it.

They hit another pocket at twelve thousand feet, and this time Magnolia broke from her dive and angled into a suicide dive, tucking her arms and straightening into an arrow.

Kade was doing the same.

When they hit eight thousand feet, she slowly worked back into a stable fall. Kade was already in it, arms and legs out.

"Nice job, cowboy," Magnolia said over the comms. She bumped on the team channel. "Edgar, you're up."

"Copy that, launching now."

Another five thousand feet zipped by before Magnolia hit the rain. The droplets pecked at her armor, but the neoprene suit kept her dry.

She studied the floor of clouds below them, searching for the DZ.

At four thousand feet, she blew through the

clouds and finally got her view of the oil rig and the marina. The *Octopus* and *Ocean Bull* were docked on opposite sides of the rig, each ship lashed to two of the four massive cylindrical concrete columns that anchored the rig to the seabed. Huge rubber tires, scavenged from big trucks and earthmovers on foraging runs, cushioned the contact between ship and rig.

The decks and command centers were blacked out to simulate an actual dive in the wastes.

But there was a third ship down there with its island lit up, which told her exactly which one it was.

Raven's Claw.

X was probably down there, watching.

"Deploying chute," Kade said over the comm.

Searching the sky, she found the blue glow of his battery pack, illuminating the canopy over his head.

Magnolia pulled her chute a moment later. She watched Kade steering toward the deck of the *Octopus* as she pulled her pilot chute and let it go. She felt the opening shock, but it wasn't until she started spinning that she realized something was wrong.

Heart racing, she looked up at her canopy. The lines had twisted around themselves four or five times.

"Oh, shit!" she yelled.

She still had her reserve chute, but at two thousand feet, she had some time to kick out of the line twist.

"Mags, what's wrong?" Edgar asked.

"Lines . . . twisted," she replied.

"You know what to do. Just keep calm and kick your way around. You got time. Now, throw that leg!"

This is what the training is for . . .

Pulling the risers apart, she kicked in the opposite direction, but the lines twisted again, and again.

"Shit, shit, *shit*," she said.

Magnolia tried again, straining to kick and pull on the risers, but she kept spinning.

Her stomach felt queasy, and soon the centrifugal force could make her lose consciousness.

No. This isn't how you die!

At one thousand feet, she was running out of time. And with Edgar a minute above her and Kade many seconds below, she was on her own.

"Commander, can you cut away and deploy your reserve?" Kade asked.

"I'm . . ."

The spin made it hard to drag her hands up to the capewells and release the main chute.

"Just keep breathing," Kade said calmly over the channel. "Push the risers together and run your hand up the lines, twisting as you go."

After pressing the risers into her left hand, Magnolia ran her hand up the skein of lines and twisted out the bottom coil. Twisted again, and the spin slowed as another coil unwrapped. She checked her altimeter: four hundred feet. But it wasn't the lack of altitude that made her heart skip a beat.

She was too far away to land on the *Octopus*, and heading right for the ocean.

But she wasn't alone. Kade was following her.

The line still had three wraps, and for every one she twisted out, she lost another fifty feet.

The ocean came screaming up at her. She had to slow her descent more, or it wouldn't be much better than cratering into the ship. The impact would break bones and knock her unconscious, drowning her before any boat could reach her.

"You got this, Commander," Kade said. "I'm with you; just stay calm."

Working fast, Magnolia finished untwisting the lines, allowing the chute to inflate fully above her, with maybe a hundred feet to spare. Six feet from the surface, she pulled both toggles and flared, stopping her forward motion.

It felt like hitting concrete. The collision knocked the wind out of her as she slammed into the ocean. The weight of her armor pulled her down, but she hit the helium boosters on her arms and took a breath of reserve air.

After sinking for another few seconds, she stopped and started to rise.

She broke the surface and quickly got enwrapped in her lines and chute. A wave broke over her, pushing her deeper into the tangle.

"Hold on, Commander," said a voice out of nowhere.

A hand grabbed her, then another. She was pulled up into a red inflatable rescue craft. Kade was here, too. It seemed that he had pinpoint landed right *in* the boat. He had already shucked the harness and had his helmet off.

"You okay, Commander?" he asked, leaning down.

She took off her helmet and stared into the kind eyes of a man who simply exuded calm.

"Yeah," she said, sitting up. "Saving my ass on your first dive—I'd say that's a good start, Cowboy Kade."

"Aye, it was the one thing I used to be good at," he said, "until I couldn't save the ones who needed it most."

* * * * *

Raven's Claw pulled up alongside the massive rig that the Cazadores had turned into a dry dock. The great doors were open, exposing scaffolding and cranes that could hoist even the largest fishing boats. Soon, either the *Octopus* or the *Ocean Bull* would be docked inside to protect it from the storm.

X watched as the other divers landed one by one on the *Octopus*. The veterans guided the rookies through their flares and landings without any trouble—a relief after seeing his best diver splash down in the ocean.

Even the big Cazador soldier Gran Jefe, who had volunteered to dive, made it safely onto the deck—with Arlo, no less.

As *Raven's Claw* drew even with the rig, X piloted the ship's motor launch the quarter-mile to the docks. He walked over to wait as a rescue boat pulled up.

Kade and Magnolia climbed out onto the deck, their armor dripping.

X couldn't believe it. Kade had stuck the landing in a moving inflatable boat, then pulled Magnolia out of the water—after not diving for a decade.

Kade was right. It wasn't something you forgot.

Seeing him, both divers straightened.

"King Xavier," Magnolia said.

"Had me worried there for a moment, Mags," X said. "Good thing you had Cowboy Kade with you."

"Good thing," she replied.

"Well done, Kade," X said.

Kade just nodded.

"Finish up the training and get to the capitol tower for a meeting, Commander Katib." X looked to Kade. "You, too. I want you there."

"Aye, Your Majesty."

X walked down the dock to the open entry doors to the rig. Inside, teams of technicians and engineers were still pulling small boats out of the water. It was a remarkable system the Cazadores had built over the years to keep their precious vessels safe during storms.

Michael wasn't far, working late into the night with Alfred, Pedro, and Rodger in the offices on a third dock. X opened the door and stepped inside, yelling over the racket of compressors, cutoff wheels, and pneumatic riveters.

Pedro sat staring at a monitor, his dreadlocks dangling over the back of the chair like short, fat snakes. Rodger was next to him, glasses propped high on his nose.

"How's that storm looking?" X yelled over the noise.

Michael looked up from a metal table covered in blueprints and logs.

"It's getting stronger," he said. "It's a level-one hurricane but about to build to a level two."

"What's that mean? What kind of winds are we talking about?"

Michael looked to Alfred, who held up Cricket.

"Sir, the drones are picking up winds around one hundred miles per hour," Alfred said.

"How long until it reaches us?" X asked.

"Five hours before the edge hits, maybe a bit more," Michael said.

"How are we doing on getting everything locked up?"

"Most of the small vessels are secure, but we still have the *Octopus*, *Ocean Bull*, and *Raven's Claw* in the water. Same with *Blood Trawler*, which is currently offloading into our reserve tanks on rig nine . . ."

"Bring it up to about the halfway mark; then bring *Blood Trawler* here and fill up the *Octopus* and the *Ocean Bull*," X said. "I don't want to put all our precious fuel in one place."

"Good idea," Michael said. "Rodger, can you handle that?"

"Well, yeah, I'm on it, Chief."

X looked at the time: almost 10:00 p.m.

"At midnight, meet me at the capitol tower, in my study," X said to Michael.

"I'll be there."

X returned to *Raven's Claw*, where Ton and Victor had his speedboat ready to launch in the boat bay. They motored out in the rough water and beelined it back to the capitol tower in the raging storm.

Miles was waiting for X in their quarters. X grabbed his satchel, whistled to the dog, and headed straight for the same study where el Pulpo once determined the fate of his people. The irony wasn't lost on X, who was now doing the same thing.

Imulah waited at the long table. "I have the maps you requested, King Xavier," he said.

"Thank you." X pulled a book out of his satchel and began to go over the documents.

A little before midnight, the door cracked open. Ton and Victor stepped aside to let General Forge inside. The tall, muscular man was fifty, fifty-five at most, although the weathered features and the many scars made him look older.

A line traced the right side of his face, the top of his right ear was gone, and what teeth he had left were sharpened. Still, he was a handsome man in a rugged sort of way, with a certain presence about him.

X stood to greet him.

"King Xavier," the general said. "I'm glad to attend this gathering."

X gestured toward a wooden chair. Forge had tried his best to learn English over the past year, and X had tried his best to learn Spanish. It was remarkable how much both of them had picked up in that short time.

"Gracias, General."

A few minutes later, the other attendees filtered in, soaked and huffing. Michael and Magnolia, his most trusted confidants. Joining them was Kade Long. He took off his cowboy hat and nodded politely.

Next came Pedro, carrying a tablet and a crossbow that he handed off to Ton and Victor. They didn't search the next two participants, Captain Rolo and his XO, Eevi Corey, the former militia investigator and Hell Diver.

"Thank you all for coming," X said. "Please, have a seat. We don't have a lot of time."

As soon as everyone had taken their chairs, he said, "This storm is just the beginning of the threats we face. Before the brunt of it hits, I'm deploying the airship *Vanguard.*"

"We're going to the poles to turn on the weather tech?" Magnolia said. "About damn time!"

X shook his head and glared at Magnolia.

"Sorry," she said.

He rotated a map of South America and Mexico so all the attendees could see.

"I'm scouting out a place to add an outpost, with the goal of starting a new supply chain to keep the islands safe," X said, pulling a pencil from behind his ear.

"A year ago, after the defeat of the machines, I promised we would feed everyone and keep the peace." He let out an uncharacteristic sigh. "But no matter what we do here, the Vanguard Islands have an expiration date unless we expand."

"What the hell does that mean?" Magnolia said. "There's always been storms here."

"This one is . . . how do you say . . ." Pedro extended his arms. "*Un monstruo.*"

"The difference between now and the past is raiding," Imulah said. "The Cazadores brought back a steady stream of supplies from the eastern shore of South America, but those supplies have been exhausted, and the once-great Cazador navy is down to a few ships."

"We may survive this storm, and we may have enough food to last the year after this harvest, but what about next year?" X asked. "What happens then?"

He pensively scratched his beard. It was time to share the secret he had harbored for the past month.

"El Pulpo knew this place wouldn't last forever," X said. He pulled out the logs that Ada had found.

"The former king sent his son Horn to look for a place called the Coral Castle, but when that mission failed, Horn turned on his father. He believed the only way to save his people would be to murder and eat half of them."

"Wait, what the hell is the Coral Castle?" Magnolia asked.

"A fantasy, based on a man a Cazador raiding party found in Colón, Panama," X said. "They ate the guy before he could say much more."

"So we know nothing about this place? Because if el Pulpo thought it existed, maybe . . ."

"We only know that it is a place of coral, somewhere in the Pacific Ocean."

Michael looked to Pedro. "Have you ever heard of the Coral Castle?"

He shook his head, dreadlocks bouncing.

X didn't want to dismiss the possibility of a secret haven—after all, his people had survived in the sky, but there was no evidence to support the story—only the sword and armor of a very unlucky man.

To hunt for it seemed a fool's errand. But it had given him an idea about the canal. He pondered what he was about to ask, but his gut told him it had to be done. They had the weapons and vehicles from the ITC *Ranger* to fight within the wastes. It was the *people* he was afraid of risking.

Sending young people out potentially to their deaths when he had to remain behind weighed heavily on his heart. It was what he had learned to hate most about being king, but it had to be done.

"We must head back to the wastes and start raiding the western shoreline of South America," X said. He put a finger on the map. "To do that, we will set up an outpost somewhere along one of the greatest engineering feats of human history: the Panama Canal."

The others hovered closer to the map.

"We're sure it's clear?" Magnolia asked.

Imulah spoke. "In 2031, they punched a deeper,

wider channel, getting rid of the locks at Miraflores—he pointed on the map—and here, at Gatun Lake. So theoretically, yes, it should be wide enough for our vessels. Whether it's clear in terms of hostiles, I'd err on the side of caution and say it is unlikely."

"Which is why I'm deploying the *Vanguard* to Panama as soon as it's ready to fly," X said. "To figure out what *is* down there. Magnolia, I want you to dive in with Team Raptor and recon the area. Find us the best place to set up an outpost."

Kade stared anxiously at X.

"Kade, you're on backup just in case we need you," X said. He turned to Rolo next.

"Captain, you and Lieutenant Corey will lead this mission and leave as soon as we finish here."

"Aye-aye, sir," Rolo said.

X looked over the maps again. "What happens next will go to the council," he said. "But if we find the Panama Canal is clear, then I'll deploy our navy and engineering teams to establish an outpost."

General Forge nodded. "I will work with Chief Engineer Everhart to prepare our fleet."

"So that's why you wanted the mounted rams? Just in case you need to push something through the canal?" Michael asked.

"Yes. But this is just the beginning of my plans," X said. He used a pencil to draw a line over the map from Panama down to Colombia and Ecuador, stopping to circle the known ITC bunker locations.

"I want to set up outposts and keep a steady

supply coming to the islands from these locations,"
X said. "That's how we stay alive until the day we're
strong enough to go to the poles and power up those
weather modification devices."

He put the pencil down.

"I'm with you," Michael said.

"It shall be done," Forge said.

"We dive so humanity survives, X—er, King
Xavier," Magnolia said.

X gave an authoritative nod and followed them
out of the room. They each had their own duties to
keep this place safe, and X had his. Tonight, it was to
make damn sure the *Vanguard* got away before the
storm hit.

FIVE

It was almost two in the morning when Michael secured the last of the heavy-duty canvas tarps on the top of the agriculture rig. A loud humming filled his ears. He wiped the rain from his goggles and looked to the sky as the *Vanguard*'s thrusters fired. The blue torches burned in the darkness.

"Good luck, my friends," he said.

The airship blasted over the rig.

"There she goes," Alfred said.

"Hope she has better luck than the last crew that went to Panama," Steve said.

"What's that mean?" Alfred asked.

"I was just a boy, but I remember it well. About two years after a Cazador crew found my people and brought them here as slaves. That same crew went to Panama and never came back."

"Does X know about this?" Alfred asked.

"Yes," Michael said.

"Good. I figured as much," Steve said. He pulled

out a hammer and drove a nail into a metal sheet covering a trough.

The crew fanned out across the acres of crops to make final preparations. By now, tarps covered most of the plants that weren't ready for harvest, but if the winds got worse, they would blow away like ash in a firestorm.

Even the metal panels Steve was installing over some of the troughs wouldn't work if the storm grew worse than they expected.

"I think that's the last of them," he called out.

"Okay, good work," Michael said. "Let's get down to the livestock."

Rodger's voice crackled into his earpiece.

"Chief, we just finished securing the port," he said. "All boats are lifted out of the water and buttoned up the best we can get them. Still working on draining *Blood Trawler*, but the *Octopus* and *Ocean Bull* are full now."

"Copy that," Michael replied.

Lightning flashed nearby, and the thunder crack made him flinch. He had thought working as a chief engineer would be less dangerous than Hell Diving, but right now it was a lot like diving, only without the armor and protective gear.

"Shit, I felt that one," Steve said.

"With all those tools, you're a walking conductor," Alfred said, laughing.

Steve looked down to his tool belt, filled with all sorts of hammers and multitools. "I've been wearing this for thirty-five years, no problem!"

"Famous last words!" someone said.

The crew laughed as they headed down to the livestock corrals.

Michael took a ladder down three levels, where hogs squealed and chickens squawked, sensing the impending storm. The farmers tended the animals on the lower levels, trying to calm them down. Each was precious for the milk, eggs, or meat that it contributed to the fragile ecosystem.

"I'll finish up here, amigos," Steve said. "Why don't you two get to the marina and make sure everything's secure."

"Thanks," Michael said. He rushed back to his boat with Alfred and lowered it into the roiling water.

Nights like this reminded Michael how fragile things were at the islands. He got into the boat and pulled away from the rig, the distant cries fading in the wind.

Gripping the wheel in his bionic hand, he headed for the Wind Talker rig. He had promised Layla he would be back home before the worst of the storm hit.

The radio crackled as he navigated the sloppy seas. Reports of damage to the rig that housed half the Cazador population. Another report of damage to the trading-post rig. Then a message from Pedro that made his gut clench.

"*Incendio en el tanque,*" he said.

"*What?*" Michael said in a stunned tone. But he knew he hadn't misheard.

"Fire on the tanker. *Bomberos*—fire teams—on the way. I go there now."

"Be careful, Pedro, we're on our way!"

He steered away from the cargo rig to the Wind Talker rig, their last oil production source and the site of the wind turbines.

If *Blood Trawler* exploded, it could take the entire rig down.

The implications gave Michael a chill. It wasn't just the loss of life and the lost fuel that scared him, but the poisoning of the water they relied on for much of their food supply.

The speedboat powered over the waves, and within a half mile, Michael could see the glow of the fire.

"Alfred, get us a sitrep."

"They think it was lightning," Alfred said over the radio, "but I don't know. It sounds like the crew is abandoning ship."

"What! They have to get it away from the rig!"

"I know," Alfred said as Michael tacked into the waves.

A few minutes later, Michael spotted the red lights of other vessels flashing in the storm. He glanced at the fuel gauge. It was almost on empty—yet another reminder of how precious fuel was at the Vanguard Islands.

"Tin, are you there?" his wife's voice said on a private channel.

He shook his head. Layla was never going to stop calling him by his childhood nickname. "Copy," he said.

"What's going on?"

"Lightning hit *Blood Trawler*."

"What?"

"We'll put it out," Michael said, going for his most reassuring voice. "Don't worry. Tell Bray I love him and I'll be home soon."

"Michael, please be careful."

He heard the edge of concern in her voice. "I will."

He slowed the boat as he came upon the western side of the oil rig, where four levels rose above the main platform that supported the drilling module. The two-hundred-foot-tall rig was a dirty brown color after centuries of exposure to the elements.

Not a single fleck of paint was left on the hull, and soon there wouldn't *be* a hull if they didn't put out the fire on *Blood Trawler*, which was still docked on the eastern side.

Flames raged on the bow, belching dark smoke into the storm. The rain wasn't doing much, if anything, to quell the flames that vented from the bow.

Michael docked his boat in the enclosed marina, where a crew was waiting. Two Cazador workers tethered the craft while he and Alfred jumped off.

A few minutes later, Steve pulled in with his crew.

A toothless Cazador covered in grease hopped down off a ladder onto the dock in front of them. He coughed as he ran over to them.

"Chief," he gasped, "*el tanque no se mueve.* Stuck!"

"*Repite, por favor,*" Michael said, hoping he had misheard.

"No move it!"

"We have to get someone to move it!"

"No move it!"

Steve spoke in Spanish to the frantic Cazador, then turned to Michael.

"He says the engines are offline and that is why the crew abandoned it," Steve said. "Most of the crew, that is, but a few stayed behind and are in the engine compartment, including Rodger and Pedro."

"No, no," Michael said. "We have to help."

He turned to go back to his boat, but Alfred grabbed him by the arm. "Only way to get on the ship—or the safest way—is from the deck of the rig. I'll get someone on that crane."

"You guys serious?" Steve asked.

"You know what will happen if this rig blows?" Michael asked. "We have to get *Blood Trawler* as far away from the islands as possible."

"The fishing grounds." Steve looked out over the ocean, apparently realizing what Michael had already grasped.

"I'm coming with," Steve said. "I'm an old man. You're young and have families."

"No, stay here," said Michael. "I need you to make sure the rig is protected."

"But . . ."

"I put Rodger on this task. It's on me."

Steve nodded. "Gotcha, boss. Just come back, okay?"

"I will."

Alfred and Michael started up an enclosed ladder

to the first level. Michael's boot slipped on the third rung, but his robotic fingers held him fast.

They both coughed from the smoke already making its way inside the rig. At the top of the ladder, he stood on a landing, breathing through his sleeve.

Alarms rang throughout the passage on the first level, and panicked voices called out in English and Spanish.

Michael ran toward the retreating workers. A stairwell took him to the command center on the top deck, with a direct view down to *Blood Trawler*. A group of rig workers stood looking at it through the viewport.

"What in hell are you all doing watching!" Steve shouted. He yelled something in Spanish, and the team all took off to their various stations.

Michael stopped briefly to stare at the inferno blazing below. The tanker, still half full, sat fairly low, hardly moving as the big waves slapped against it, dousing flames that returned the moment the water receded.

The waves were pushing the ship closer to the rig. It wouldn't be long before the bow collided with one of its supporting columns.

Turning from the window, Michael and Alfred rushed out of the room to the emergency supply room. Heavy fire jackets and helmets hung neatly on hooks, and air tanks lined the shelves below.

"Chief, I got a bad feeling about this," Alfred said.

"We can't lose this rig or the ship," Michael

replied. "We lose this ship, and we lose our energy lifeblood. And then there's the fish it will kill off."

"You never told me this job might get me killed," he joked. But Michael caught the little tremor in his voice.

"We'll be okay," Michael said. "Just keep your eyes open and stay close."

They finished getting into their fire gear and hurried back outside to the deck. Steve was there waving up at the operator in the cab.

Smoke swirled across the western side, and the rising wind beat against Michael and Alfred as they crossed the deck to the crane. It lowered a box in front of them.

Michael climbed inside the box.

"You sure you want to do this?" he yelled at Alfred.

"Are *you* sure?" Alfred shouted back.

As Michael reached up to signal the crane operator, he considered his promise to Layla. It wasn't just the two of them now. Their year-old child was at home.

But Michael couldn't just sit by and do nothing if Rodger was still alive and there was still hope of saving the tanker.

He motioned to the crane operator, making circles with his upward-pointing finger, and the box lifted off the deck.

It began to rotate in the gusts.

The wind slammed the jib, rocking the box like

an empty can on a string. But the jib swung slowly left as it lowered them toward *Blood Trawler*'s stern, away from the smoke roaring out of the bow section.

"Good luck!" Steve shouted.

Mountainous waves bashed against the tanker's hull, threatening to drive it into the rig. Indeed, the water seemed to be the only thing keeping the fire from spreading even faster, but if the tanker hit one of the rig's legs, it would burst like a bomb, setting off an inferno that could end the Vanguard Islands.

As the box lowered, Michael prepared to jump.

"Get ready!" he yelled.

Alfred pulled off his helmet and vomited over the side into the rain, nearly falling out when a strong gust shook the box. Reaching out, Michael hauled him back inside.

"Oh, shit," Alfred moaned.

Gripping the sides, Michael looked over the edge.

Cracking sounded over the wind—a noise that sent a chill up his back. A glance over his shoulder confirmed it.

The jib buckled at its attachment point to the boom, and the box started to drop the last ten feet to the oil tanker's deck.

"Hold on and bend your knees!" Michael shouted.

They had only an instant to brace themselves before they hit. Michael bit his lip and tasted blood.

He rolled out of the box and slid to a stop near the tanker's command tower. Alfred helped him to his feet.

"You good, Chief?"

"Yeah . . . I think so."

They headed toward the hatch in the command tower that would lead them to the engine room.

As soon as they were inside, Michael felt the heat. He pulled out Cricket and did a scan of the hull.

The first reading came back at 110 degrees, and they weren't even close to the fire yet.

Sweat trickled down Michael's forehead as he worked his way through the dark passages, guided by his helmet lamp.

The scorching heat reminded him of working in the guts of the *Hive* when he first became an engineer, before his diving days.

Hearing a loud rumbling, Michael halted.

"Those are the engines," he said. "Rodger must have gotten them back online. Go topside and get on the wheel. I'll find him."

Alfred turned back the way they had come while Michael kept pushing ahead.

"And look for Pedro on your way up!" Michael shouted.

He moved cautiously, flitting Cricket back and forth and up and down for scans. The engine room wasn't far, but the heat was getting worse with every step down the ladder. It was almost 130 degrees here.

He turned around a landing and discovered a body of a worker, his skin pink and eyes bulging.

A touch to the neck confirmed death, probably from smoke inhalation.

Michael continued down the stairs, his muscles tense. If the vessel exploded, he reminded himself, he wouldn't feel a thing. He thought of Layla and Bray and considered turning back.

You came this far. You can't abandon Rodger and Pedro.

A few minutes later, he was at the engine room. The hatch was closed, but the handle wasn't hot to the touch. He spun it open and stepped into the engine room.

A body was hunched against the main engine. The peg leg sticking out of the jumpsuit confirmed his fears.

"Rodger!" Michael cried.

He ran over and put a finger to his friend's neck. There was a pulse, and his chest was moving gently up and down.

Michael shook him.

"Rodger, you need to get up," he said. "We have to get out of here."

Rodger blinked and slowly looked up, sweat and tears rolling down his face.

"We got it back on," Rodger said. "Pedro . . . where . . ."

Rodger slumped over.

"Rodger," Michael said.

He moaned but didn't respond. Michael got up to look for Pedro, but the man wasn't here. He returned to Rodger and scooped him up in both arms, cradling his body.

"Hold on, buddy," he said. "I'm going to get you out of here."

* * * * *

X grunted as he put on his Hell Diver jumpsuit in the enclosed marina under the capitol tower. The insulating layers would help protect him from lightning, but it wasn't going to do much against the fire on *Blood Trawler* when he boarded.

And he was boarding that ship as soon as he got close enough.

Michael and Rodger were on board, and Pedro was missing. No one was going to stop X from saving them if they were still alive.

"They are steering the boat away from the oil rig," Imulah said. "You really should let the engineering team deal with this, King Xavier."

"And you really should stop telling me what to do," X snapped back.

"He's right, we can handle this," said Steve over the radio. "The ship is already moving away from the rig."

The engineer and weaponsmith was supervising the crew at the oil rig where *Blood Trawler* had been refueling other ships.

"I'm on my way," X said.

"Okay, sir," Steve replied.

Metallic cranking sounds rose to compete with the shouts of crews lowering vessels into the choppy sea. Two other boats would be joining X on the water.

He finished putting on the protective suit and stepped over to his boat, the *One-Armed Bandit*. Ton and Victor were already aboard, preparing the armored yacht that Michael had helped restore as a gift to X.

"We're coming to help, King Xavier," Victor said in his thick African accent.

"You don't know how to swim," X said.

"Then don't drive bad." Victor smiled and Ton laughed, which, due to his missing tongue, sounded almost like choking.

"Be careful, King Xavier," shouted Steve. "I'll be right with you."

X strapped goggles over his eyes and lugged a bag of equipment over to the boat, which was hoisted out of the water by a convertible electric/manual lift. Miles tried to board, but X motioned the dog back.

"Stay with Imulah," X said forcefully.

The dog sat on his haunches, whining.

"But, King Xavier, I really think you should . . ." Imulah began to say.

X glared at the scribe, who put his hands up, before crouching down to Miles. "Come here, my friend."

The dog growled at Imulah, and this time X couldn't help but chuckle.

A familiar and frantic female voice ended it.

"X, wait!"

He turned to see Layla running down the dry dock with something clutched in her arms.

Not something—someone.

"Just what I need," X grumbled.

Layla stopped in front of the boat, a crying Bray in her arms. The yearling wailed like a Siren.

"Tell me what's going on," she said. "Michael told me lightning hit *Blood Trawler*."

X couldn't lie to Layla.

"It did, but—"

"I'm coming with you."

She handed Bray off to Imulah, who acted as if the baby were a live bomb.

"Take him," Layla said.

"But, Mrs. Everhart . . ." Imulah protested.

"It's a dog and a child," X said. "Deal with it."

He reached out and helped Layla onto the boat.

X led her into the command center of the yacht. Two chairs faced the dashboard, and behind them were two couches. Ton and Victor stood, but Layla took a seat next to X.

"Let's go," she said.

"I'm working on it," X said. He pushed the button to lower the boat into the water. Waves slapped the hull as it met the violent sea.

He guided the boat past the rows of other lifted boats. There hung the *Sea Wolf*, rarely used now.

The marina doors opened to a hellish sight of lightning, rain, and big waves that dashed themselves against the viewports.

"Go," Layla said.

She put her hand over his and pushed the throttle down.

The boat motored out, its two 400-horsepower engines growling as if they couldn't wait to cut loose and roar.

"Easy," X said. "I want to get there, too, but we do this safely."

Layla took her hand off his. The radio crackled with static as they entered the storm.

X gave her a side glance, spotted the tears welling in her eyes.

"It's going to be okay," he said. "Michael's going to be fine."

That was how he always dealt with things: reassuring himself even when he wasn't sure the words were true.

It was how he had gotten through decades of diving and losing people close to him.

But he wasn't losing anyone else today.

He flicked on the high beams, which speared through the heavy rain.

He steered the boat over the growing waves, riding them up, then down, in a way that made Ton and Victor finally sit down.

The rain pounded the viewport, and waves rushed over the bow.

Even with the beams, X couldn't see much in front of him.

"Steve, do you copy?" he said.

Static broke from the dashboard transceiver.

"Buckets of Siren shit!" X growled. "Layla, see if you can get us a working frequency."

She fiddled with the radio, but the storm was interfering with everything. All X could hear were the muffled voices of the different crews.

He steered around the oil rig that served as the trading post, keeping his distance. From the raised command center, he could see the rig's bottom deck. Pieces of metal sheeting had come loose and were flapping in the wind, threatening to peel away and slice someone's head off.

A tarp flew away like a cape, vanishing into the night.

X swallowed hard, the implications poisoning his gut with worry. If this turned into a full-strength hurricane, they could lose an entire crop and hundreds of lives.

He wasn't the praying type, but he hoped the vortex would pass through quickly.

"I've got something," Layla said.

She turned up the radio, filling the cabin with the chatter between Deputy Chief Engineer Alfred and a Cazador officer aboard the flagship fireboat.

"I think I can make it . . ." Alfred said.

Layla picked up the transmitter.

"Alfred, this is Layla on the *One-Armed Bandit*. Do you copy?"

"Copy . . . Layla . . ."

His voice was faint, but she definitely heard them.

"Where's Michael?" she said.

"He's with Rodger, but he's okay."

X heard that loud and clear and smiled at Layla. She seemed relieved.

"You have to get off that ship!" she said after a pause.

"We will as soon as we get to the following coordinates."

"Plug those in," X said.

Layla tapped them into the dashboard as he rattled them off. When she finished, X looked at the digital map.

"They're making a run for the edge of the Vanguard Islands," Layla said.

"Yeah," X said. "That sounds exactly like what Michael would do. Get as far away from the rigs as possible to keep the oil from polluting the waters."

Layla stared at X with wide eyes.

"It'll be okay," he said.

But now he really wasn't sure he believed his words.

"Hold on," he grumbled.

Pushing the throttle down, he braced himself for the rough waves ahead. The storm was getting stronger, but he had no time to waste.

For the next half hour, the *One-Armed Bandit* skipped over the waves, chasing *Blood Trawler*. By the time they were approaching the border of the islands, the radio was useless—just static from the almost constant lightning.

But X didn't need to hear updates from Alfred to

see the location of *Blood Trawler*. Away in the darkness, a flame rode the waves like a bobbing candle.

"There she is," X said. "Keep trying the radio."

"It's not working," Layla said.

Other boats had joined the effort—all emergency vessels that didn't have the yacht's speed.

Layla got out of her chair to stand, and X did the same thing, holding the wheel tight in his hands. He steered past the other boats, coming up on the stern of *Blood Trawler*.

"What are we going to do?" Layla asked.

X didn't have an answer.

The ship was heading out to keep it from poisoning their fishing waters, and perhaps Michael, Alfred, and Rodger were also trying to save the precious cargo of oil.

Steering to starboard, X pushed the throttle down as far as he could. Waves slammed the hull, and a monstrous wall of water rose, threatening to sink them.

He turned into it, riding up it the best he could, but water still broke over the decks and slammed into the viewport.

As it cleared, he saw the fires venting out of *Raven's Claw*'s bow. They didn't seem as bad now. Maybe the rain would put them out.

"See if you can spot any fire in the tower," X said. "Binos are on the ledge."

Layla snatched them up and twisted the center wheel to zoom in when the center of the deck burst upward. A second blast blew up in front of the command center.

"NO!" Layla shouted.

X turned the wheel, steering them away as *Blood Trawler* exploded in a brilliant, thunderous blast. Shrapnel whizzed through the air, peppering the yacht and shattering two of the viewports.

Ducking, X reached out to Layla, who let out a scream unlike any X had heard in his life. He realized a moment later that he, too, was screaming out a deep roar of pain.

Layla turned and moved past X, pulling out of his reach as she grabbed the hatch.

"Stop!" X shouted.

Ton and Victor grabbed her before she could get outside. They held her as she screamed in anguish at the sight of the burning ship.

All X could do was stare as the sea opened its mouth and swallowed it whole.

SIX

The airship *Vanguard* hovered directly over the Panama Canal, having beelined it there at maximum speed to escape the storm.

Standing side by side in the launch bay were the members of Team Raptor. Arlo, Edgar, Ada, and her companion, Jo-Jo, all faced Magnolia. Even the monkey appeared anxious. Kade and Sofia were there, too, with the most promising rookie of the twenty volunteer divers: Gran Jefe. He wore part of his Cazador armor, along with a chest rig and battery unit that the technicians had managed to piece together at the last minute.

Only four from Team Raptor would be diving, with the others staying behind just in case they needed backup.

Everyone stared at Magnolia, waiting for a briefing.

But this wasn't about her words.

In her hands, she held a tablet with a message

from King Xavier, prerecorded for this very moment. She held it up and turned it on.

"A message from the king," she said.

"The nature of this mission is simple: to survive, we must expand. And once again I must call on the heroes of the sky," X said in his gruff voice. "I wish I could be there with you, but I have placed my faith in you all and Commander Magnolia Katib. She helped us find the Vanguard Islands, and I have no doubt she will help find the perfect location for the first of our new outposts."

The king paused, perhaps for effect, or maybe to consider his next words. Magnolia had listened to the message several times, and her bet was on the latter.

"This mission has the potential to help secure our future and provide a lifeline to our families and friends," X continued. "We can't fail in providing this lifeline. Without it, we are doomed. Good luck, divers."

Magnolia handed the tablet back to a technician and clapped her hands together.

"All right, Ada, Arlo, Edgar, you're up," she said. "We dive in ten."

"Wait," Sofia said. "What about me?"

"You're sitting this one out," Magnolia said. "I'm sorry, but we need Jo-Jo on the ground with Ada and—"

"That's not why, Mags, and you know it."

Sofia stormed off, clearly miffed, not that Magnolia blamed her best friend. Truth was, she didn't want Sofia going because of the risk.

Kade stepped over to Magnolia.

"You sure you don't want me to come?" he asked.

She reached up and cinched his parachute harness down tighter. "Look, I know you can dive, but there's more to it than the actual dive. My team is used to working together, and adding a new member could . . ."

"Aye," Kade said. "I'm here if you need me."

The technicians and other divers cleared the room, leaving Team Raptor alone at their launch tubes. Magnolia looked at her people as they made their final preparations and cross-check.

Edgar and Arlo were diving heavy, with extra shotgun shells, magazines, and flares stuffed into their vests. Their blasters and pistols were secured in their holsters, and laser rifles were strapped tight over their battery units.

It was a new way of diving, without supply crates, and that was for a simple reason: they were likely dropping into a hot zone with mutant beasts. They wanted to be armed to the teeth from the moment they touched down.

Ada stood in front of Jo-Jo, giving her a hand of bananas. The big primate had already eaten a bag of apples and oranges. And if Magnolia wasn't mistaken, her friend was still growing.

Jo-Jo grunted and reached up, brushing Ada gently on her face.

Magnolia saw the same bond of love between X and Miles.

A warning light flashed in the bay, and the technicians checking the last tubes left the launch bay.

Flashbacks from Magnolia's first days surfaced in her mind as she climbed into her tube and secured her helmet.

As she checked her life-support systems, the open comm channel crackled in her helmet.

"We're directly over the canal," said Captain Rolo. "Our sensors detect a yellow zone on the surface, and some lightning on the drop in. Be careful, Team Raptor."

"Always, Captain," Magnolia replied. She bumped the comm channel to Team Raptor for a sound-off.

"All systems clear," Edgar said in his usual all-business voice.

"Ready, boss lady," Arlo said.

"We're . . . good," Ada said. "Although I think Jo-Jo needs to take a crap."

"I thought I smelled something!" Arlo said with a laugh.

Magnolia shook her head and checked her heads-up display. She saw all three beacons, plus a fourth for Jo-Jo.

Blue light swirled in the launch tubes, and Magnolia looked down through the ballistic glass beneath her boots. Lightning bloomed in the floor of clouds miles below.

The countdown ticked from one minute, and Magnolia bit down on her mouthguard, thinking of Rodger. She hoped he was safe and warm during the storm, but she had a feeling he was working.

She hadn't even gotten to say goodbye. They saw each other more back when they were Hell Divers.

The final seconds ticked down on her HUD, distracting her from her thoughts.

"Cleared for launch, Team Raptor," said Captain Rolo. "Good luck."

Blue light swirled in Magnolia's tube.

"We dive so humanity survives, baby!" Arlo shouted. "Whoo-*ee*!"

The glass floor opened, and Magnolia slipped into the darkness, plummeting toward the thick mattress of clouds. She flipped before maneuvering into stable position, with arms and legs out and bent. The three other divers fanned away from one another.

Lighting forked under their flight path and fizzled away.

"Hold position," Magnolia said over the comms.

Her HUD snowed, then solidified.

She checked each diver. They had covered their glowing blue battery units for stealth, but she easily saw their IR tags, which showed their names in red.

Ada and Jo-Jo were in stable free fall and closing on Edgar. He tracked away, easing into the dive like one might an old lost shirt.

At fifteen thousand feet, a shelf of clouds lit up with multiple flashes. The hair on her neck prickled from an arc that sizzled unnervingly close.

"Screw it," she whispered.

Tucking her arms against her side and straightening her knees, she pulled into a suicide dive, plummeting like a dart and gaining velocity.

The comms crapped out, but she knew that the other divers were doing the same thing.

Magnolia mentally calculated her time to the surface. Her last observed reading was 110 miles per hour at twelve thousand feet altitude; now she was falling nearly twice as fast.

She peered into the clouds, trying to get her first glimpse of the ruined surface.

There were only a few logs in the Cazador archives about journeys to the Panama Canal. The Cazador ships *Anaconda* and *Sea Sprite* had tried to find a way through, and neither ever returned. But a Cazador rescue party had discovered the *Anaconda* drifting off the coast of Colón, with no sign of the crew and only a log entry that the *Sea Sprite* had continued into the canal.

Rumor had it the skinwalkers had also tried to make it through but failed. Something was definitely out there—something terrible.

She counted the seconds, flinching at a lightning flash that came uncomfortably close.

Glancing up, she spotted Arlo and Edgar's IR tags. Ada and Jo-Jo were off course but moving back toward the DZ.

At six thousand feet, the carpet of clouds began to thin. The storm weakened over the next two thousand feet, and Magnolia bumped the comms back on as her HUD activated.

She gasped to find that she was already at three thousand feet.

Rolling out of her suicide dive, she hooked her

thumbs in the sleeve loops of her suit to deploy the braking wings Rodger had designed for her. He had told her he got the idea from an archival video of some small old-world rodents called flying squirrels.

At two thousand feet, she had reduced her speed to under a hundred miles per hour, just in time for a first glimpse of the Panama Canal's southern extremity, Balboa.

In the green hue of her night-vision optics, her eyes traced down a small section that was the only thing she recognized from this vantage. She had to check her minimap to tell which side of the canal was their DZ.

Arlo's and Edgar's IR tags slowed suddenly in Magnolia's HUD as both divers pulled their pilot chutes. Ada did the same with Jo-Jo.

A moment later, Magnolia pulled her pilot chute. It caught air, the parachute exploded from its pouch, and the lines didn't twist. She grabbed her toggles and steered toward the others as they sailed toward Cocoli, once an expensive enclave a few miles north of the port of Balboa. Along with Panama City to the east, Balboa had been devastated by a nuclear blast, and the resulting tsunamis had flattened most of what remained.

The crater was on the eastern side of the city—its bustling commercial epicenter now a vast bowl surfaced with dark glass where the extreme heat of the blast had melted the underlying sand. It was hard to imagine this place bristling with skyscrapers.

Magnolia toggled over to the DZ that they had selected for its proximity to the entrance channel of the fifty-mile-long canal. Five hundred feet down, and she was low enough to make out the rusted masts and upended prows and superstructures protruding above the surface.

But not all the ships had sunk. A single container ship stood in the canal. Flying over it, Magnolia thought the deck didn't seem as damaged or weathered as the others.

This one had come here *after* the war.

She considered changing course, but it was a bit late now that Edgar was already leading the way toward the DZ—a command center that once served to guide those ships through the canal.

Edgar was the first one on the ground, stepping out of the sky and shouldering his laser rifle.

Magnolia flared and gently touched down. Ada made it down without crashing onto Jo-Jo, but Arlo was a little less graceful. He landed crosswind and face-planted in the dirt, sliding to a stop entangled in his lines a few yards away. Fine dust poofed up around him.

"Some things never change," Magnolia said. She secured her gear, listening for Sirens, but the shrill electronic voices were mercifully absent.

All she heard was the breeze and Arlo's muted cursing. She went over to help him while Edgar and Ada both stood watch with their laser rifles at the ready.

"You good?" Magnolia asked.

"Yeah," Arlo said.

She helped him to his feet, then checked her Geiger counter. The reading was still in the yellow zone.

"Pack up fast," she said. "We need to move."

With their gear secure, Magnolia flashed hand signals, moving everyone toward a lookout tower over the canal. The concrete structure was still standing, but the two adjacent buildings were completely destroyed, their blue roofs caved in and the white brick walls now reduced to piles of rubble.

Jo-Jo sniffed the ground as they trekked toward the tower. Ada had taught her to search for other creatures, and for that, Magnolia was grateful. On their last mission with the Vanguard navy, Jo-Jo had sniffed out a Siren nest before anyone even suspected them in the area.

Magnolia followed the beast through a door hanging on one hinge. Only a few overturned tables and chairs remained inside the room. She cleared it with her rifle and moved to the stairwell, stepping over vines that snaked across the dusty floor.

"Edgar, on me. Arlo, you and Ada stay here with Jo-Jo."

She and Edgar took the stairs to the second level, cleared it, and moved to the third.

Stopping before a blown-out window, Magnolia pulled out her binos to scan the canal.

"I saw a ship on the drop," she said. "I wonder if it's the *Sea Sprite*."

Edgar stepped up next to her, cradling his weapon. "Where?"

"About a mile from us. I can't see it from here."

She moved the binos slowly back and forth, switching to infrared.

"Negative on life scans," she said. "Come on."

They went back down to the first level.

"See anything?" Arlo asked.

"No, but I want to check out a vessel I saw on the way in," Magnolia said. "Come on."

They moved back out into the industrial zone, marveling at the destruction surrounding them. All that remained of huge skyscrapers was the concrete foundation and a few steel girders.

"Looks like a tsunami rolled through here after the initial blast over in Panama City," Edgar said dryly. "Bet it was an entire dead zone."

"Yeah," said Ada. "Nothing could have survived here after the war."

"I'm not worried about humans," Magnolia said. She halted halfway out into the field as a tremor shook the ground under her boots.

Jo-Jo froze.

"You feel that?" Magnolia asked.

"Earthquake?" Edgar wondered.

"I don't think so," Magnolia said. "It feels like something's right under us."

* * * * *

X steered the *One-Armed Bandit* through the storms, navigating the towering waves the best he could with a broken heart.

An hour had passed since *Blood Trawler* exploded before his eyes. And for that hour, he had searched the water for Michael, Rodger, Alfred, and any crew who had made it off. So far, there was no sign of any survivors, and the storm continued to worsen, along with the odds of finding anyone alive.

Steering the boat up the next wave, he felt the hope drain from his tired old bones.

"Have they picked up an SOS?" Layla asked.

X knew she had to know the answer. If they didn't get to a lifeboat, there would be no beacon, and so far, he had no indication that anyone had even made it off the ship at all.

"No, but that doesn't mean they aren't out there somewhere," X replied after a pause. "The storm could be interfering with a beacon."

He didn't know if that was true, but the storm was definitely interfering with the radio. The dashboard transceiver crackled with a message from Lieutenant Wynn.

"King Xavier, the storm is picking up," he said. "Timothy highly encourages you to return to the capitol tower. You can start the search back up after the storm."

Layla, still standing at the viewports, shook her head.

"We can't turn back," she said. "They could still be out here."

"I know, but that storm is . . ."

X had a choice to make: give up on Tin, or use precious resources to search for him even though he was probably dead.

"A little longer," X said. He picked up the handset. "Tell Pepper to focus on updates about the storm, not dispensing advice. Got it?"

"Copy," Wynn replied.

Water splashed against the starboard side and slapped the glass. Layla stumbled but kept steady at the viewport.

"At least take a seat, okay?" X said.

He wasn't the only one not listening to advice.

"Layla, please," he said.

Finally, she took a seat while X kept the boat pointed into the waves. He scanned the water for a lifeboat or life jacket but saw nothing in the bright glow of the beams. So he turned the vessel with the waves, heading back for another pass over the area they had already searched.

Two other boats came into view, riding up and down waves that dwarfed them. They weren't much bigger than his, and they seemed to be struggling.

He lost sight of the flashing red lights a moment later.

For the next hour, X stared at the water, searching. The pain inside him mimicked the pain of the cancer that once metastasized through his body.

But he knew the difference between the pain of loss and the real thing.

Layla broke the silence in a voice just above a whisper.

"I thought he would be safe," she said. She glanced over at X. "I thought, when Michael gave up diving for us, that he would get to grow old, to see Bray grow up."

"He will," X said.

Layla shook her head, sobbing, unable to hold herself together.

"Layla, come on," X said. "Michael is out there, and we're going to find him and Rodger."

She wiped the tears away and took a deep breath.

"Then we don't give up," she said. "We don't turn back."

X exchanged a look with Ton and Victor. Both seemed to understand what she was saying. They gave him a nod of support, but they would have done that no matter what the situation.

Their loyalty was like Miles's: unwavering.

X's eyes flitted over the waves, back and forth, searching. Of *course* they would have bailed if the boat was going to blow . . . unless they didn't know it was going to blow.

He checked the radar for the other vessels to make sure they weren't too close, when he noticed one of the dots had gone offline.

"Shit," he muttered.

"What?" Layla asked.

"I think we lost a rescue craft."

He turned the wheel slightly and jerked his chin.

"I need you on the radio," X said. "See if you can reach the *Falcon*."

Layla unbuckled and went over.

"This is the *One-Armed Bandit* calling the *Falcon*, do you copy?" Layla said.

White noise crackled from the comms.

She repeated the message as X piloted them toward the *Falcon*'s last known location.

On the third pass, he knew that the vessel was gone—another victim of the storm. He didn't need to check the manifest to know that meant at least four dead sailors and another lost boat.

The *One-Armed Bandit* arrived at their last known a few minutes later.

"Ton, Victor, get ready," X said.

Both men were standing at the back hatch, life vests on. Again it occurred to X that they couldn't swim.

"I see something!" Layla shouted.

"Victor, take the wheel," X said.

X joined her at the viewport.

The beams from their boat illuminated three Cazador sailors wearing orange life jackets, bobbing in the water. Then X noticed a fourth, with no vest, treading water as it rode up and down the mountainous seas.

These Cazadores had lived on the sea since birth and could all swim, but that didn't matter in storm waves.

"Get us close to them!" X yelled.

He rushed out of the command center and onto the deck with Victor. They went straight for the port rail, where rescue lines lay coiled with life buoys tied to the ends.

Ton flung a buoy into the sea. X threw another.

Rain hit them horizontally so hard, it felt like

blown sand. X thought of storms like this as living beings—live enraged beasts bent on vengeance.

Ton began hauling the line back, with two frail Cazador men clinging to the life ring. The next wave lifted men and boat alike, and reaching over the edge, he grabbed one of them by his life jacket and dragged him over the gunwale.

The second Cazador man, wearing only tattered cutoff dungarees, grabbed the rail, and X helped him aboard while looking for the last two, who had drifted farther out.

Seeing nothing, he turned to the command center behind him and waved to Victor through the viewports. "Come about!" he shouted. "Hurry!"

Timing his move between swells, Victor brought the boat around. Even with his skills, navigation in such heavy seas was harrowing. A wave broke over the gunwale, hitting Ton and the two sailors they had just rescued with a wall of water that knocked them to the deck.

X landed hard on his backside and winced.

Pushing himself up, he launched into a stream of profanity that lasted several seconds, then went back to the railing with Ton while the two sailors headed for the safety of the cabin.

X searched the water for the other two, but the man without a life jacket was gone, swallowed by the sea.

The spotlights finally captured the other sailor.

Ton picked up a rope and flung the life ring at

the orange dot bobbing on the waves. X picked up the other rope. He was going to get only one shot at saving the man.

In the bright glow of the lights, he saw that it wasn't a man but a boy of thirteen or fourteen years. Hardly old enough to join as a deckhand in the navy, and not nearly old enough for the military.

X wound up, then threw the buoy—precisely as the boat yawed violently, knocking him into the railing and over the side.

Where he stopped short. His boot had caught in a coil of rescue rope, which his weight drew taut, to leave him staring down at the raging sea.

He flailed about for something to hold on to, but the yacht's tapering hull left him dangling free, nowhere near anything. All he could see was the newly painted words "*One-Armed Bandit*" on the hull and the churning water below.

The boat yawed, and he closed his eyes and held his breath just before being submerged up to his waist. Water went up his nostrils.

Powerless to help himself, X could only pray that the loop of rope biting into his calf would hold him.

The boat righted itself, and he opened his eyes. Spitting and coughing, eyes stinging, he again watched the water rise up to meet him. Then hands were on him, grabbing his life jacket and hauling him back over the gunwale.

He collapsed to the deck to find Ton and Layla hovering over him.

"You okay?" she shouted.

Nodding, he got up with her help.

"Come on!" Layla shouted.

He hesitated at the railing, looking back over the water where he had last seen the kid. The life ring was out there, but no sign of the boy.

X searched for another moment before following Layla and Ton back into the command center. The two rescued sailors were inside, panting and coughing.

"I'll take over," X said.

He took the wheel from Victor and turned the boat to look for the two lost sailors. The lights danced over the water.

But the young sailor and the other man were gone, lost forever to the sea.

X blinked his burning eyes. His heart ached as he spoke.

"We have to call off the search," he announced. "We can't let anyone else die."

"I know, Tin wouldn't want that." Layla stepped up beside X, a hand on his shoulder. "But *we* can stay and search, right?"

X closed his eyes for a second, picturing Michael as a child with his foil hat on in the medical bay after a storm had injured dozens of passengers. He was an empathetic, kind boy, always looking out for others.

And now X had to abandon him. He couldn't make Bray an orphan by risking Layla's life, too.

"Tin would want you to go back, too," X said. "I'm so sorry, Layla."

She bowed her head and nodded, her face hidden behind the cascade of hair.

"King Xavier," Victor said. "King Xavier, I see something."

X stared out through the rain sluicing down the viewports. Layla joined him there, both of them searching the turbulent waters in the glow of the beams.

One of the sailors rose to his feet, shivering, saying something about a "*bote salvavidas.*"

"Do you understand what's he saying?" X asked Layla.

"I think he's talking about a lifeboat they saw when they were taking on water, before they went under."

X held back a grin.

Layla perked up, too, her eyes frantically searching the water.

"There!" she shouted.

X followed her pointing finger to a wave on the horizon, with a patch of orange rising up the side. As they watched, the orange splotch resolved itself into a boat hull.

"Everyone, hold on," X said. He gripped the dashboard and braced himself as a wall of water crashed against the bow and washed over the deck.

The yacht's beams hit the lifeboat. They were closing in. X checked Layla's life jacket, knowing she would never stay inside the command center.

"Victor, take over," X said.

X left the cabin with Layla and Ton.

Victor piloted the boat expertly through the waves, bringing them right up to the bobbing craft. A hatch on the top popped open, and a figure wearing a life jacket emerged, waving its arms. Grabbing a boat hook, X reached over the railing and snagged the lifeboat's grab line.

Water dripped from wet dreadlocks. It was Pedro, the computer technician from Rio de Janeiro.

Ton threw him a ring and Pedro caught it. He helped another man out, then a third, but X didn't see Michael, Rodger, or Alfred among them.

One by one, the three men clambered aboard the *One-Armed Bandit*. X stared at the lifeboat hatch, his heart thumping with anticipation as each new face emerged.

When the final man had climbed out, Layla shouted, "Where's Michael!"

Pedro shook his head and yelled back, "Not with us!"

X finally tore his eyes away from the lifeboat and helped the rescued men into the command center. Victor closed the hatch behind them, sealing out the howling wind.

"Did you see Michael, Rodger, or Alfred on *Blood Trawler* before it exploded?" X asked.

Pedro nodded. "Yes."

"Did they make it off the ship?"

"I don't know," Pedro said. "I seen them before the boat blew up, heading to weather deck, but nothing after."

Layla looked destroyed. But then she turned to him and said, "There's hope. See, X? We found this lifeboat. Tin and the others could have made it off in another."

X wanted to nod and feel the same sense of hope, but his gut told him this was a miracle and that there wouldn't be a second.

SEVEN

Michael lugged Rodger away from *Blood Trawler*'s engine room.

"Come on," he grunted.

Rodger was alive, but the smoke was getting to him. He leaned on Michael as they moved through the dark passage.

"Alfred, how you doin' up there?" Michael said into his headset.

"Steering us away from the rig, Chief," Alfred replied. "This ship's a beast. What's your status?"

"I've got Rodger. We're on our way to you."

"Copy that."

Rodger slumped against Michael, nearly collapsing them both to the deck. With an assist from his robotic prosthetic, Michael kept him on his feet.

"You have to stay alert," he said. "Do you understand?"

Rodger nodded. "I'm sorry, I . . ." He coughed violently.

Michael reached down and pulled Rodger up by one arm. But this time, Rodger kept coughing so hard, his shaggy brown hair fell over his goggles.

"I've got you," Michael said.

Bending over, he hoisted Rodger over his shoulders. Then he trekked back toward the ladder as fast as he could, with Rodger still coughing and retching on his back.

"Hang on, buddy. I'm going to get you out of here."

Near the stairwell, the heat increased. He could feel it even with his suit on. Sweat stung his eyes.

Entering through the open hatch, Michael started up the stairs, hauling Rodger up, taking the landings one by one.

"Almost there," Michael said. "Hang on!"

At the top passage, he set Rodger down to open the hatch. A wave of heat rolled out, singeing the hair on Michael's bare flesh. He leaned down to Rodger, but this time Rodger shook him off.

"I can make it," he said.

Rodger staggered a few feet and collapsed, breaking into another coughing fit.

Again Michael picked him up and lumbered down the passage. At the exit hatch, Rodger was still coughing, and Michael knew that his friend was going to have major respiratory damage if they didn't get him somewhere safe now.

Summoning his last reserves of strength, Michael managed to run all the way to the hatch and out onto the deck. The smoke followed them into the rain.

Michael gently set his burden down. Rodger lay gasping for air, blinking at the sky.

Flames still poured from the bow as that compartment of oil burned off. Rain sheeted down, slowing the inferno's spread. But the ship could blow at any point if any of the lower decks should be compromised.

"You okay?" he asked Rodger.

Rodger was sprawled on his back, coughing at the sky.

"I . . . think so," he said.

"Stay here. I'll be right back."

After waiting a moment to monitor Rodger, Michael started across the deck. He looked around him for any oil rig to give him an idea of where they were. Lightning speared the horizon, but he saw no silhouettes of rigs in the burst of light.

The farther away they could get from the islands, the better.

A wave crest broke over the railings, sloshing across the deck. Alfred kept the ship heading into the storm.

Michael opened a hatch and flew up a ladder to the command room. Alfred was at the wheel, looking out through the viewports.

"Where are we?" Michael said as he made his way over.

"We're about ten miles west of the boundary," Alfred replied.

Stepping up to the controls, Michael looked down at a map. They weren't far enough away from the Vanguard Islands yet.

"Can we put this thing on autopilot?" he asked.

"Yeah, but there's no telling if the storm will push it off course. We have to keep going, Chief."

Michael gave a reluctant nod.

"Is Rodger gonna be okay?" Alfred asked.

"He took in a lot of smoke, and he has some burns."

"Get a lifeboat ready and get Rodger inside," Alfred said. "I'll stay up here for now."

Michael left the command tower but stopped when he saw movement at the front of the tanker, past the raging fire.

"You see that?" he asked.

Alfred followed his gaze and then grabbed a pair of binoculars.

"I think that's Pedro," he said. "He's with two other sailors."

"Did you try them on the comms?"

"Yeah. I don't think Pedro has a headset or radio."

"They look like they're trying to lower a lifeboat."

"Okay, keep an eye on them," Michael said. "I'm heading back down."

He was relieved that Pedro and a few other sailors had survived, but they weren't clear yet. He pounded down the ladder.

Feeling the seconds tick off was like watching the fuse on a stick of dynamite burn down shorter and shorter. And each second that passed took him farther away from Layla and Bray.

When Michael reached Rodger, he was on all fours, coughing.

"Can you walk?" Michael called out.

Rodger pushed himself up.

"Yeah, I'm good . . ." He paused while another spate of coughing racked him.

Michael half-lifted and half-dragged him over to the railing on the starboard side, where an orange enclosed lifeboat hung over the side on its davits, just above the lower deck.

The next wave crashed into the hull, splashing the deck above and soaking Michael and Rodger.

A violent tremor suddenly shook the ship, making the lifeboat swing and knocking both men down. Michael grabbed a post and pulled himself up as flames shot from a vent amidships.

"We have to get the lifeboat ready to launch!" Michael shouted.

"Okay!" Rodger yelled back.

They moved over to start the first preparations by removing pins and disconnecting the electrical charge cable.

"Alfred, how far out are we?" Michael yelled into his headset.

"Almost twenty miles now, Chief."

He would have liked to be much farther, but it

was time to bail. The second fuel compartment was about to blow, and when it did, the ship would sink.

"Alfred, put us on autopilot and get down here," Michael ordered.

"On my way."

Michael helped Rodger into the orange lifeboat, dragging him and then lugging him through the hatch. He locked Rodger into a seat and fastened a belt around him.

Rodger was pale and his lips were blue.

"You're going to be okay, buddy," Michael said.

"Mags is going to kill me *twice*," Rodger mumbled. He pushed his goggles up in his hair and fiddled with his glasses. "She's going to think I'm a gimp."

"She'll be glad you're alive." Michael managed a smile. "I'll be back in a sec. Sit tight."

Leaving the boat, he looked at the bow and then the water, scanning for Pedro and the others, but there were only waves.

"It's done!" Alfred shouted. "Let's bail!"

"Did you see Pedro?"

"Yes, they launched a few minutes ago."

Michael trotted with Alfred across the deck to the lifeboat.

Another vicious quake shook the ship, knocking them to the deck. Alfred slid toward the rail. He had his hands out, trying to brace himself, but he hit a post headfirst. The crack was audible even over the howling wind.

"Alfred!" Michael yelled.

He slid over and bent down, afraid to move him.

Groggy, but conscious, Alfred reached up to the wound.

"Let me help you," Michael said. He put his robotic arm under Alfred's armpit and helped him to his feet.

"Can you walk?"

"Yeah," Alfred said.

They started down the rail to the section directly over where the lifeboat hung in its davits. Alfred staggered in his grip, unsteady, like a child taking its first steps.

"Almost there," Michael said. "You can make it."

A deep roar ripped through the hull. Alfred grunted as Michael hauled him over the deck.

"Hold on to the rail," Michael said. "I'll help you over in a second."

Michael straddled the rail, one foot in the lifeboat, and reached back to Alfred.

Alfred took his hand and swung a leg over the rail. They were both directly over the lifeboat now. Rodger was coughing in the open hatch and trying to raise a hand.

Michael jumped down onto the top of the orange craft and motioned for Alfred to do the same.

A blast rocked the ship as Alfred jumped. He hit the bow of the lifeboat but slid backward. Michael scrambled across the overhead and reached down, grabbing him by the wrist.

"I got you!" Michael shouted.

"Shit!" Alfred screamed.

He looked down at the waves slapping up toward his boots.

"Rodger, I need a hand!" Michael yelled.

A few seconds later, he felt Rodger grabbing his legs with both hands.

"Pull him up!" Rodger shouted.

Flames erupted out of the hull at the stern of the ship. The heat rolled over them. Michael closed his eyes and felt the burn on his cheeks.

Their time was up. It was escape now or go up in flames.

With a grunt, Michael started pulling Alfred back onto the overhead of the lifeboat. He had him almost all the way to the top when the boat lurched.

The nose dropped to a forty-five-degree angle.

"One of the cables snapped!" Rodger cried.

He held on to Michael's feet, and Michael kept his grip on Alfred's wrist and forearm, but Alfred slid back over the gunwale, his feet dangling over the violent water. The flames on the decks above grew more intense. Michael squinted and coughed as smoke drifted over them.

"I can't hold on much longer!" Rodger shouted.

"Don't let me go!" Alfred screamed.

There was terror in his voice—the same tone Michael had heard many times when a man knew he was about to die.

But Michael wasn't going to let his friend die.

He pulled Alfred back up, their eyes locking.

"I got you, mate!" Michael yelled.

There was a loud pop, and the right side of the lifeboat dropped.

Alfred slipped from Michael's grasp, plummeting the twenty feet to the water and vanishing into the boil.

"NO!" Michael shouted.

The lifeboat fell a moment later as the last cable broke free.

They hit the water with a jarring splash, and Rodger pulled Michael inside. Michael blinked and wiped the water away as he searched the waves.

"Alfred!" he yelled. "Alfred!"

A wave slapped him in the face. Blinking the salt-water from his eyes, he popped back up, staring out into the ocean as the lifeboat bobbed up and down.

Water sloshed about their ankles.

An explosion above made Michael duck on instinct. He pulled the hatch down as the fireball rolled over them.

Rodger picked himself up off the sloshing deck, dragged himself up into the pilot's seat, and seconds later was going full throttle away from the blazing tanker. Michael stood under the hatch, trembling in anguish.

"I had him," he said. "I *had* him."

Michael opened the hatch and stood up with his top half out of the boat, gazing at the floating conflagration behind them. As he stood there gaping, a billowing mushroom of fire rose above the raging sea. He gazed in wonder for several seconds. Then a force greater than anything he had ever known hit the lifeboat, and the world stopped.

* * * * *

More tremors rippled across the earth. They came and went as Team Raptor advanced along the canal's edge. Magnolia swept the shadows with her laser rifle barrel while scanning the phosphor-green terrain through her night-vision goggles.

The rumbling faded, but she didn't let herself relax. This wasn't lightning strikes—the noise was resonating from somewhere *below* them.

The radiation levels reflected the power of the storm. Magnolia's Geiger counter put the ionizing radiation levels at the top of the yellow zone. They wouldn't survive for long out here without their protective gear.

She hunkered down to scan the industrial area west of them. Nothing stirred across the dark terrain. A few steel girders and beams poked up out of the ground ahead. Across the canal, a line of containers had blown over like dominoes.

She motioned for the team to keep moving along the rolling terrain flanking the canal. There wasn't much cover—only scattered boulders and rusted-out old-world vehicles.

In the distance, another concrete lookout tower had survived, but the top was blown off, leaving the viewing area a jumble of twisted metal.

The lack of cover did have one advantage, though: the divers could see if anything was hunting them. They moved in combat intervals toward the ship she had seen on the dive.

Another vibration rumbled.

"What is that sound?" Arlo asked.

"Quiet," Edgar said.

He was on rear guard with Arlo. Magnolia was right behind Ada, who had taken point with Jo-Jo. The beast sniffed the ground, stopping every few minutes to peer into the darkness.

Magnolia spotted a fire in the city—lightning, no doubt. She hoped the heat would draw whatever beasts they had heard back at the DZ.

Two hours after landing, Team Raptor was closing in on the ship. She could see the stern now, its Chinese characters still visible on the hull.

As they got closer, she noticed signs of the postapocalypse-style retrofits familiar to her from other Cazador vessels: mounted harpoon guns and railings festooned with razor wire. Whoever abandoned this ship had gone to great lengths to keep others off.

All the way around the vessel, rows of metal spikes protruded from the hull.

Magnolia raised her fist, then waved everyone behind a wall bordering the canal. She brought her binos up and saw more evidence of recent life. And a battle.

The hull had long, deep gouges in the metal.

Magnolia crouched back down. They all knew

that something had killed the crews on the *Anaconda* and the *Sea Sprite*, neither of which ever returned from their mission through the canal.

The long marks on the hull gave Magnolia a bad feeling, but then, that was what they were here to do: discover monsters.

"Edgar, with me," she said. "Arlo, stay here with Ada and Jo-Jo."

Nods all around.

Magnolia hopped over the wall and started toward the ship. The long hull rested against the left side of the canal. Oddly, a platform had been extended down from the deck to the ground. It was as if someone had just stopped here, put down a ramp, then fought a battle.

She saw no evidence of the fight having occurred as much as a decade ago.

She motioned for Edgar to follow her over to the chains hanging off the stern. Eight feet of dark water separated them from the ship.

"Gotta run and jump," she said.

"Yup, I'll go first," Edgar said.

He took a few steps back, then ran and leaped into the air. His boots hit the hull with a loud thud as he grabbed one of the dangling chains. With his boots only inches from the water, he twisted the slack once around his leg for a brake.

Then, pulling himself up, he let the slack run down and around his leg. After climbing up ten feet or so, he let the coil around his leg tighten and gave his forearms a few seconds rest before starting up again.

Magnolia leaped and grabbed the chain to Edgar's left and started up the side at once, wanting to put distance between herself and the inky water below.

Halfway up, the chains next to Magnolia and Edgar started to jingle.

"What the . . . ?" Magnolia noticed a ripple through the water, then a second and a third, each seemingly created by a distant rumble.

Above her, Edgar twisted back toward the industrial zone, where the other divers had sheltered behind a hill. Magnolia couldn't see them—only their beacons on her HUD.

"Keep climbing," she said.

As they neared the top of the hull, the jingling of chains became a loud clanking, and the ripples were now wavelets.

Looking over her shoulder, Magnolia saw the source of the quakes.

Across the rolling terrain, beyond the hills rimming the canal, geysers of dirt burst into the air. She bumped off her NVGs to see unaided, using the glow of lightning.

Out of those holes, creatures clambered out. Magnolia squinted to get a better look at the one closest. Pointy yellow legs emerged from the shell of what looked like a dog-size sea turtle. But the resemblance to a turtle was only superficial. Rather, it seemed to be a hybrid of several species, including a crab and an iguana.

Across the terrain, great curved turtle beaks

chopped like guillotines while releasing little clicks and shrieks. Spiked green tails slithered behind the beasts as they skittered over the ground on six legs and two pincer-wielding arms.

Ada and Arlo took off running through the mine-field, with Jo-Jo leading the way. All around them, the ground swarmed like a kicked anthill.

Ada fired a bolt at the pincers snapping behind her. The laser seared a hole into the beak and face, eliciting a gruesome screech.

The head vanished inside the shell as Ada punched simmering holes through the armor. Green fluid trickled out.

"Run!" Magnolia shouted.

Arlo fired as he backpedaled, only to trip and fall. Ada paused to help him up.

Magnolia watched in horror for a second, then went back to hauling herself up the hull. At the top, she rolled over the barbed wire, snagging a strand. She hit the deck and got up, using her knife to cut through the tangled wire.

"Edgar," she said.

A quick scan of the deck showed he wasn't there.

"Edgar?" she said into the comms. "Where'd you go?"

No answer.

Heart thrumming, Magnolia brought her rifle scope up for a close-up visual of the beasts chasing her comrades.

Spiky red hair surrounded the wicked beaks

on their armored faces, and those long, pointy legs scuttled so fast, she had trouble sighting up a target.

Her burst went high. The next hit one of the creatures in the head, blowing out green juice. It bucked and slashed at the air with its sharp legs.

Another dirt geyser erupted in the direction Jo-Jo, Arlo, and Ada were running. Arlo had his back turned to fire and didn't see.

By the time Ada warned him, one of the creatures skittered toward him, slicing the air. He turned just in time to bring up his rifle and parry a pincer, but the other claw snapped around his arm.

A scream of pain rang out over the comms.

Ada fired a laser bolt into the head, and the beast finally let go and fell back, legs kicking the air. A second turtle clattered toward Ada, but a snarling Jo-Jo grabbed both pincer arms.

"Get Arlo out of here!" Magnolia shouted over the comm. "Get a tourniquet on that arm and take him back up to the ship!"

She had to give the team a window to escape. Ada crouched next to Arlo. She had applied a tourniquet and was taping a sterile dressing over the wound.

Jo-Jo finished off the hybrid creature by ripping off both clawed arms and then beating the head to a pulp with her powerful fists.

Ada's mascot packed a hell of a punch.

"I'm cold," Arlo said over the comms.

"Stay with us!" Magnolia shouted. "Edgar, where the hell are you!"

She dare not turn to look for him, so she just kept choosing shots, picking off the turtle creatures surrounding the divers. Jo-Jo got in front of Ada and Arlo, raising her fists and letting out a roar that Magnolia could hear from the ship.

She zoomed in on Arlo. He slumped against Ada as she finished wrapping his wound.

"Get him out of here!" Magnolia shouted.

Ada helped Arlo to his feet and punched his booster. The canister fired, filling the helium balloon and yanking him skyward.

"Ada, run!" Magnolia yelled.

Jo-Jo howled and swung at the beasts as they closed in.

Magnolia aimed and fired, aimed and fired, trying to give them a chance to escape. Ada and Jo-Jo took off running up a hill bordering the canal.

As they crested it, a massive bulge of dirt pushed up, revealing pincers as long as a man. They pushed up, supporting a white shell with red markings that was the size of a small airship.

"Oh my God," Magnolia murmured. She gazed in wonder at what had to be the mother of this turtle brood—a beast far bigger than any animal she had ever seen.

Ada stared up at the monster.

"Ada, get in the air!" Magnolia shouted over the comm.

Turning, Ada grabbed at Jo-Jo. The animal fought in her grip, but Ada managed to get a safety strap around her and fashion it into a crude harness. She reached over her shoulder and hit the booster, firing two balloons.

Magnolia held her breath as the hellish thing broke through the ground and swung its massive head upward. Sighting the diver and her companion, it let out a roar that filled the night.

She had raised her rifle to fire when she saw something drop. Not something . . . some*one*.

The monkey fell almost twenty feet to the ground.

The monstrous turtle snapped at the air below her feet while the babies swarmed around their mother. Ada toggled away from them, toward Jo-Jo, then cut away from the booster.

"Ada!" Magnolia shrieked over the comm.

She fell, feet together, and executed a textbook parachute landing fall. Rolling up to her feet, Ada kept running after Jo-Jo, who was loping along on all fours.

Magnolia crouched at the rail, heart pounding. The roar of the gigantic shelled beast surged across the canal, and she looked over the railing once more at the nightmare brood swarming the low hills.

Magnolia pulled herself away, keeping low to search for Edgar. His beacon wasn't far, but he still wasn't answering on the comm.

"*Edgar!*" she hissed.

The turtle clambered across the ground.

She kept working her way toward the bow, between containers and past barrels secured with a chain.

"Edgar, do you copy?"

Still nothing.

Magnolia knew it now: something had happened to him. Perhaps there were baby turtles on this ship, too, or maybe a Siren.

She followed the beacon on her minimap and stopped at a container. Darting around the side, she found her missing comrade, hanging upside down from a chain thrown over a beam. His arms hung lank, hands touching the deck.

Magnolia didn't see any blood.

She got low and searched the deck for contacts, but nothing moved in the green field of her NVGs or an infrared scan.

As she reached him, she heard a click.

Magnolia turned just as a net whipped up around her, slamming her against a container. The lines tightened around her, pinning her against the rusted metal wall.

Squirming, she tried to unsheathe the crescent blade at her back, when a figure moved out onto the deck, wearing an old-style sniper's ghillie suit.

But instead of a helmet, a birdlike face with a long beak stared at her with shiny black eyes.

Magnolia bumped off her NVGs—lightning would give her a more accurate look.

Green and black feathers spiked off the ghillie suit and rippled in the wind around the bird face. It raised a humanoid arm, and a hand that gripped a hammer with a head on one side and a spike on the other.

Magnolia fought to free herself. "No," she said. "No, please, stop!"

The turtle in the distance stared at them with black eyes the size of truck tires.

The bird creature turned the weapon from the spike side to the hammer, raising the other hand as if to silence her, but Magnolia kept squirming against the net.

The clicking and screeching grew louder as the mother turtle skittered across the dirt and up the hill for a better look.

Magnolia's eyes flitted from the beast to the bizarre plumed creature ahead of her.

"No!" she said, raising her voice.

Before Magnolia could move, the beast smacked her in the helmet with the hammer.

EIGHT

"I just got a report of a fishing trawler taking on water," said Wynn. "The rest of the fleet is getting beat up pretty bad."

"Son of a bitch," X said as the lieutenant delivered his report.

Wynn kept focused on the radio dashboard in the command center at the top of the capitol tower. They had put shutters over the reinforced glass, but X could still see out through a narrow gap.

He stared at the lightning that flickered on the horizon, picturing Tin, Rodger, and Alfred. There was still no sign of them. Four hours had passed since he watched *Blood Trawler* explode with them on board.

Two hours had passed since he was forced to discontinue the search. It was simply too dangerous, especially since Pedro, who was in the command center now, never saw Michael or the others get into a lifeboat. The last he saw them, they were in the command center, steering the ship away from the islands.

But Pedro did have an idea how to find them. Using one of the weather drones, the computer engineer was searching for their beacon, which was traceable only within a certain range.

X stepped up behind him.

"Any luck yet?" he asked.

Pedro pulled off his headset. "Not yet, sir."

A tear ran down X's face, but he didn't wipe it away. He didn't care who saw him cry. Besides Ton, Victor, and Miles, only General Forge, Lieutenant Wynn, and Imulah were here, monitoring the situation with Pedro, and they were all too busy to notice an errant tear.

The clink and clatter of hand tools announced someone new, and X turned as Steve walked into the room. He heaved a deep breath and unbuttoned his jacket, which was soaked.

"Our engineering crews are overwhelmed," he said.

"That's why we need you here," X said. "With Michael, Rodger, and Alfred MIA, you need to take charge."

"King Xavier, I'm more of a hands-on . . ."

X's look silenced him. "I need a leader, and you're all I've got right now."

"You got it, sir," Steve said. And taking a seat, he grabbed a radio.

Wynn looked up from his monitor.

"Another report coming in about a lightning strike at rig fifteen," he said. "We've already got a crew putting out spot fires."

X paced back and forth behind the group of men trying to keep things together. The islands were holding on by a thread. So was X.

General Forge spoke in Spanish to his soldiers, who were moving people to safety from compromised sections of other rigs.

As the first major edge of the storm barreled into the Vanguard Islands, X began to see their weaknesses. The problem wasn't lack of preparation—Michael had done everything he could to secure the rigs. The problem was that each rig was on its own, with no easy way to send additional help if the teams on those rigs had trouble.

X had thought they were ready for the storm, that they had everything battened down, and that people would be safe. But now he saw the truth that el Pulpo had seen firsthand: humanity couldn't live here forever.

It was only by a series of miracles that they had survived this long.

Another tear escaped. He blotted it with his shoulder.

The divers would be at the Panama Canal by now, probably even on the ground. They were fighting, and X would, too.

Reports continued to flood into the command channel.

"Rig fifteen has taken some structural damage to the civilian quarters on decks four and five," Wynn announced. "Rescue teams are relocating the residents to the center of the rig."

X stopped pacing. Standing here while his closest friends and family were out fighting for their lives and while the islands were being torn apart was worse than being stuck in a Siren pit.

He slammed the glass with his fist, drawing the attention of everyone in the command center. Miles whined, got up, and trotted over to X.

A child sobbed, and X turned to see Layla in the open doorway, holding a wailing Bray.

X loved the kid, but that was the last thing he needed right now.

"Damn it," he grumbled.

He went to Layla and forced his features into what he hoped was a kind expression.

"I'm sorry," he said. "I didn't know you were there."

She didn't respond or ask if there was an update on her husband. Instead, she leaned down to whisper to Bray.

"Your dad is going to be okay," she said quietly. "It's okay, don't you worry, my love."

X returned to the viewports as something whipped past in the wind.

"The hell was that?" he asked.

"Tree branch," Steve said. "We're going to lose a lot of them."

X swallowed hard. He could only imagine what the rooftop and gardens were going through.

"The wind is now one hundred and five miles per hour," Pedro said. "According to drones, worst of storm is about to be hitting us."

"General, can *Raven's Claw*, *Octopus*, or *Ocean Bull* survive in these winds?" X asked.

"Maybe," replied the general, "if they don't run out of fuel and if you have someone who knows how to turn into the waves."

"I know, but we're getting hammered out there," X said.

"Captain Two Skulls has experience sailing in storms like this, and is currently aboard *Raven's Claw*," Imulah said. "But we have to keep in mind that as of four hours ago, we lost over half our oil reserves."

"I'm well aware," X said. "I'm also aware our fishing trawlers are getting beat to shit, and considering what's happening to our crops, we can't afford to lose any of them."

"I'm sorry, King Xavier, but my job is to—"

"To give me guidance, not tell me what to do."

Imulah nodded.

X instantly regretted being a dick. But standing here doing nothing while everyone else was risking their lives made him crazy.

He felt like a coward. He felt helpless.

But he wasn't hopeless. There was something he could still do here at the capitol tower, which was by far the most secure of all the rigs.

"Contact all the rescue crews here and have them meet inside the marina," X said to Steve.

The engineer nodded.

"General, deploy *Raven's Claw*," X said.

"Deploy it where, sir?" asked General Forge.

"Here," X said. "We're going to board it with all the help we can get, and then go where we are needed. Send the most at-risk fishing trawlers to take their place at the hangar. Get them hoisted above the wave action. We gotta save the fishing fleet."

He turned away from the windows and went to the hatch.

"Where are you going?" Imulah asked.

"For some fresh fucking air," X said.

He left the command center after motioning for Miles to sit. The dog whined but stayed behind, sitting on his haunches.

X took the three stairs to the top of the roof. The wind on the other side of the hatch howled like a thousand Cazador warriors screaming from the Sky Arena.

He took off his hat and his shirt and laid them on the landing. Then he went to the top landing and opened the hatch.

The wind tugged at him. Except for the blown debris battering his body, it felt like diving through a pocket of turbulence. He forced the hatch shut and staggered out onto the rooftop.

The trees whipped and swayed violently back

and forth, held in place by posts and guylines. Every fruit tree was already bare, the limbs picked clean, ripe or not.

Staring at the storm clouds as the rain and wind beat against him, X raised both fists—one metal, the other flesh and bone.

"Fuck you!" he shrieked.

He wasn't even sure who he was cursing. He didn't believe in a deity, but there was something out there, some sort of energy that bonded him with other organisms and with the universe. Whatever it was, it continued to punish humanity.

He often wondered if humanity deserved this. Maybe they should just throw in the towel and roll over and die. But X was the perfect example of the human spirit, relentless and unwavering.

A gust slammed him to the ground. He pushed himself back up and wiped his muddy hands on his chest and down his front. Rain pelted his scarred hide, each wind-driven drop a needle.

The pain helped him focus and remember the most important thing. He couldn't fight back, but he could still help those who needed it.

X fought the wind back to the hatch, stopping to unlatch his prosthetic arm. It came loose and sailed away in the wind.

Putting his head down against the howling gusts, he tried to hurry back to the hatch. It occurred to him that more than just the wind was howling.

X opened the hatch and yelled at a madly barking

Miles to get back. The dog moved out and grabbed him by his pant leg, pulling.

"Miles!" X shouted.

Ton and Victor were there, too, staring wide-eyed.

"King Xavier, what are you doing!" Victor said. "That wind is throwing things—big things."

Ton made a clicking sound, probably trying to tell X he was an idiot.

Miles tugged on his pant leg, and X moved back into the passage before the fabric ripped. Victor shut the hatch, sealing out the wind.

Soaked, cold, chest heaving, X started back down the stairs without saying a word. The moment in the storm had given him the adrenaline to focus.

When they got back to the command center, Layla and Bray were gone. Pedro, Steve, General Forge, and Lieutenant Wynn stared at the mud and the red welts on X's hand and face, but they didn't say anything, either.

X wiped his face clean and threw his shirt back on. He put his hat on a table.

"Steve, I'm going to take you up on your offer," X said. "When this is over, build me something I can use."

"You got it, King," Steve said with a grin.

Wynn stood in front of the viewport.

"Here she comes," he said.

X stepped up. Through the glass, he could see lights on the horizon. *Raven's Claw* plowed through the waves, with Captain Two Skulls at the helm.

"Okay, Wynn, you have the command center," X said. "General Forge, Steve, meet me in the marina in ten minutes."

X threw on a life jacket and took a radio. Then he left with his guards and his dog and hurried down the stairs to the residential wing. Sky people hung out in the hallway, trying to talk over the noise of the storm.

He found Layla and Bray in their quarters. Rhino Jr. was here, too, in a crib, with the Cazador nanny Sofia had hired to look after the child.

"I'm heading out there," X said. "Once things let up, I'll start the search back up for Michael and the others, but in the meantime, please look after Miles."

Layla bent down in front of the dog with Bray in her arms.

"It's going to be okay," X said. "I promise."

He left with Ton and Victor and didn't stop until he got to the enclosed port below. Before he even opened the hatch, he heard voices.

Opening it, he saw the source.

A hundred men and women, in bright clothing and wearing life jackets, were crowded inside the marina. Water sloshed over the docks and splashed the boats that hung from their lifts as the people awaited orders.

X walked toward them, and the group parted to let him through. He scrutinized each face, seeing sky people, Cazadores, and survivors from around the world.

They all had gathered together for one thing: to help each other.

Both Steve and General Forge were among them, ready to hear their mission.

A radio crackled on X's vest, and he pulled it out.

"King Xavier, *Raven's Claw* is docking now," Wynn said. "There's been a major incident at the rig with the people from Kilimanjaro."

"What kind of incident?"

"We got a message about a platform collapsing and trapping some of the people sheltering there."

There was a pause.

"Sir," Wynn stammered over the radio, "the platform has trapped fifty people, and their shelter is filling with water."

"We're on our way," X said. He turned to the rescuers and then waved them onward. "Follow me!"

He opened the hatch, running out into the gusting wind and needles of rain. *Raven's Claw* was docked outside, cushioned from the rig's massive columns with five-hundred-pound earthmover tires, scavenged for just that purpose. An open hangar, with ramps extended, allowed the teams to board.

By the time X got to the CIC, everyone was on board and the warship was carving through the storm waves. At the helm, gleaming under the overhead lights, the death's-head tattoo leered back at him from the bald pate of Captain Two Skulls.

The ancient Cazador sailor gripped the wheel with cracked and weathered hands, staring through the reinforced glass as they plowed into the storm.

"*¿Adónde vamos?*" he asked. "Where we go?"

General Forge responded in Spanish, but X understood exactly what he said.

To save the sky people.

* * * * *

"Magnolia, Edgar, do you copy? Over," Ada whispered.

Terror wrapped around her like a straitjacket as static crackled over the channel. Crouched behind a thornbush, she watched the turtle from hell clamber up onto the canal wall in the distance, while hundreds of its brood combed the area for Ada and the other divers.

She checked the beacons on her HUD. Arlo had made it back to the *Vanguard*, but Edgar and Magnolia were somewhere on the ship in the canal, not far from each other. She zoomed in with her binos.

The monster clambered over the pitted concrete wall and perched there, rotating its head in search of prey. It seemed to know that the humans were there.

"Magnolia, Edgar, answer me with a hiss if you can hear me," Ada whispered. "Anything to let me know you're okay."

Static.

Ada kept her rifle aimed at the deck. Maybe there was interference from the ship's hull, or maybe they were . . . She stopped herself. No need to dwell on the maybes.

And she had to find Jo-Jo. During the attack, her companion animal had taken off into the jungle—not a huge surprise. The monkey had lived in a habitat much like this before Ada found her on that beach.

Stashing the binos, she turned and headed deeper into the mutant jungle.

The tracking beacon she had implanted beneath Jo-Jo's skin showed that she wasn't far. She scanned the canopy above her for the animal, who would spend most of her time in the trees, given the choice.

Seeing nothing, Ada walked on under purple banana leaves.

An ant the size of a guinea pig crawled over her boot and around the base of a tree. She kicked it away with a crunch. The creature made a clicking noise with its mandibles and darted into a hollow rotting log. As if on cue, the log came alive with huge, angry ants.

Moments after kicking the creature, she was racing through the jungle, being pursued by dozens of its irate brethren.

Clicking and low whistles followed her as she ran harder, leaping over roots and sidestepping the thorny bushes that could kill her with a scratch.

Everything out here could kill you if you weren't careful. She didn't even want to think about what those clacking mandibles would do if they caught up with her. And to be *stung* . . .

But the insects were merely a distraction. What mattered more was the strong reading from Jo-Jo's beacon.

The creatures finally stopped their pursuit just as

she came upon a clearing. The trees around the edge were shriveled in what appeared to be a dead zone.

She switched off her NVGs and turned on her helmet light for a closer look. The beam went straight down into darkness. It explained why nothing grew in the clearing—there was no ground for anything to grow on.

A hole had opened in the earth, and everything around it was dead—not a single tree, bush, or vine left alive.

"Jo-Jo," Ada whispered.

She stepped up to where the monkey should be according to the tracking beacon.

It occurred to Ada then: the monkey had gone below.

What would drive you underground? Or did something take you?

Ada looked over her shoulder to check for the huge ants, but they were all gone now, apparently spooked by the dead zone.

Heart thumping, she stepped up to the edge of the crater and peered over the other side. The pit wasn't too deep, maybe twenty feet.

Ada slipped back into the trees for cover, trying to figure out a game plan.

"Edgar, Magnolia, do you copy?" she whispered into her headset.

White noise filled her helmet.

She cursed and closed her eyes.

You're good. Jo-Jo is fine. You guys will get through this.

But Ada wasn't sure she believed her own little pep talk. Tendrils of dread wormed through her insides as she recalled the horror and loneliness of her exile into the wastes.

You're stronger than you were then, and Jo-Jo needs you.

One thing was certain: Ada wasn't going to leave her friend.

She uncoiled a rope from her gear and tied it around a tree. Clipping it through her rappel device, she crouched over the hole and scanned it a second time with her light.

Seeing the route was clear, she shut off the beams and started down. Seconds later, her boots hit the bottom. She brought up her rifle and turned her helmet back on.

Three different passages led out of the crater. She set off down the likeliest one according to her HUD, but underground it was hard to tell.

Her helmet beam swept over curved, ribbed walls that looked like the gut lining of some monstrous beast. The passage opened into a cavernous dirt chamber.

Ada halted in midstride, eyes flitting over carcasses of various animals. Some were nothing more than bones and fur. Others were fresher kills.

Her eyes locked on a black, furry mound.

"Jo-Jo," she whimpered.

Ada ran to the body. Crouching down, she put her gloved hand on the cold, bloated flesh of a dead monkey.

"No," she sobbed.

A whimper answered, and she raised her laser rifle at two big, shiny, black saucer eyes.

"Jo-Jo . . ." Ada whispered.

Lowering the rifle, she ran over to the corner of the chamber to find her friend hiding in a rocky alcove, shivering in fear.

"It's okay," Ada said. She stroked the animal on the head and reached out to embrace her. Six months ago, Ada could practically cradle the monkey. Now the monkey could cradle her.

"You're okay," she said. "We're okay."

Ada looked over at the monkey body that she had mistaken for Jo-Jo. The question was, what had killed it along with everything else down here?

"Come on, we have to go," Ada whispered

She pulled on Jo-Jo, but Jo-Jo pulled back.

Frustrated, Ada said, "Jo-Jo, move, *now*."

A shriek answered her raised voice, and she turned back in the direction from which she had entered the chamber. Her helmet beam flitted over the carcasses. That was when she saw the Sirens. Two of the hairless, eyeless creatures lay sprawled, their pale, leathery skin drawn tight over their limbs.

Now Ada knew why Jo-Jo was so frightened.

She had blundered or been pulled into the lair of a beast so terrible, it could kill and feed on Sirens.

The shrieking resonated for a few seconds before fading back to silence.

Ada took Jo-Jo gently by the hand.

"Follow me," she whispered.

The monkey stood up, hesitantly at first, and started after her through the darkness, stepping around animal remains and crunching over dried insect shells. An ant the size of Miles lay with its back broken open and the meaty insides removed.

She chose a different tunnel from the one she had come in. It twisted and snaked under the mutated jungle, taking her deeper and deeper below the surface.

Stopping to check her minimap, she realized they were heading toward the canal—in the same area where the turtle-crab things had attacked.

She also checked her HUD for the other beacons.

Edgar and Magnolia were still online, and their heartbeats were escalated from fear or exertion.

She wanted desperately to try contacting them again, but it was too risky.

Keeping her rifle up, she moved down the passage with Jo-Jo right behind her, until a scratching sound stopped her short.

Ada turned, but the noise didn't seem to come from behind them.

She crouched to listen, still unable to pinpoint it.

A thump followed, shaking dirt from the ribbed ceiling. The noise grew louder, but it was seeing the two beacons on her HUD wink off that made Ada flinch.

"Oh, no," she groaned.

Both Edgar and Magnolia were . . .

Ada stared in horror at her HUD. No, her eyes weren't playing tricks. Both divers were dead.

Filled with dread, she listened. There was no time

to contemplate the fate of her friends. A fiery orange glow came from the passage behind her.

Another thump shook the floor beneath them, and again dirt sifted down from the ceiling as she sprang up to move with Jo-Jo. She flitted her light back and forth over the rocky footing, trying to spot anything that would trip her.

The light grew brighter behind her, forming an orange halo in the tunnel.

Then she heard it. A whipping sound, like a strong wind combined with a crackling or hissing. Almost as if something was burning.

When the passageway widened, she risked a glance over her shoulder, unable to quite comprehend what appeared to be a humanoid figure that was on fire.

Ada aimed her weapon at a waxy-looking skull with flaming eye sockets and a ruff of horns around the neck. Blackened skin sagged over thick, well-defined humanlike muscles. It staggered along on two feet, almost shuffling.

Jo-Jo pulled on Ada, but she held her aim. There was no hiding from this abomination.

Moving her finger to the trigger, she sighted up the flaming eyes and pulled the trigger. The laser cracked into the head, sheering off a burning piece of skull.

Tight lips moved around the mouth, but the noise that came out wasn't a shriek of pain or agony. It was a scream of anger.

Jo-Jo pulled harder on Ada, and this time she didn't resist.

NINE

"You're going to be okay," Sofia called out.

Kade hung back with her and Gran Jefe while two medics worked on Arlo on the launch-bay deck.

He was breathing but in bad shape, judging by the sheer volume of blood on his armor and suit. He had lost a lot in the air. The medics had removed his armor and were inspecting the terrible gash and open fracture in his arm.

Sofia bent down. "Come on, Arlo," she said quietly. "Pull through. I know you can."

Kade looked on, wishing he could do something to help. Sofia and Arlo had dived on the mission that saved his people from the machine camp at Mount Kilimanjaro. Sofia was a kind, strong woman who had recently given birth to the child of a man Kade had never met but had heard many stories about—the famous General Rhino.

While he was still learning about their past, the fact that Sofia was still diving after giving birth six months ago showed her dedication to the society they were rebuilding.

It was the same reason Kade had dived when he was a father. Not just for the extra rations it put on the table for his wife and their sons, but because it kept the ITC *Victory* in the air—right up until the day they were blown out of the sky.

The launch-bay doors hissed open, and Captain Rolo stormed inside. His white uniform perfectly matched his thinning hair and beard. He had changed dramatically since that fateful day. Once a proud, strong man with a commanding physique, he now walked with a slight limp and slumped shoulders.

"What the hell happened down there?" Rolo growled.

His booming, angry voice was one thing that hadn't changed over the years.

"We're not sure yet, sir," Kade said. "Arlo's unconscious."

"He's the only diver who made it back?"

"Aye."

Rolo shook his head. "I feared this would happen, but Magnolia insisted on—"

"I think he's coming to," said Sofia.

She slapped Arlo on the cheeks.

"*Despiértate, amigo,* come on," she said. "Wake up."

Arlo fluttered his eyelids and looked around as if trying to focus. He let out a grunt and tried to sit up, wincing in pain.

"Take it easy," said one of the medics.

"What happened?" Arlo muttered. "How'd I get back here?"

"We were hoping you could tell us," Sofia said.

He blinked and looked at her as if he was trying to remember something.

"Where's . . ." He looked around him in the launch bay. "Where's the rest of my team?"

"You're it," Kade said. "The only one that came back."

"Arlo," Sofia said softly. She put a hand on his chest. He looked down at her hand, then at the bandage the medics were wrapping around his arm.

He groaned in pain.

Kade hunched down in front of Arlo, wanting to see the wound up close. The gash had a nasty orange color around the openings and already looked infected.

"Can you continue this convo in the medical bay?" asked the lead medic. "He needs stitches and antibiotics, pronto."

"Hold on," Rolo said, holding up a hand. "Do you remember anything?" he asked. "Anything that could tell us what happened to the other divers."

Arlo closed his eyelids, his lips quivering. "I remember landing at the canal and feeling this tremor through my boots . . . There were some kind of turtle things," he continued. "They came out of the ground and attacked us."

"What happened to the other divers?"

Arlo slowly wagged his head, his long locks

swinging out with each shake. "I . . . I can't remember. I'm sorry . . ."

"It's okay," Sofia said. "We'll find them."

She looked to Captain Rolo.

"We're ready to deploy," she said. "Just give us the word, Captain."

Rolo appeared to consider it as the medics carried Arlo away on a stretcher. When he had left the launch bay, Rolo shook his head.

"We can't risk it," he said. "We have no idea if the other divers are already dead. If they are, I don't want to risk the rest of you."

"But what if they're alive?" Kade asked.

"Buckley's chance of that," Rolo said.

"What's that mean?" Sofia asked.

"It means chances are slim and none."

"Then you don't know Magnolia." Sofia sounded confident.

"I know that a lot of hard-to-kill divers never came back from missions in yellow zones, let alone red zones," Rolo said. He eyed Kade. "And he knows it, too."

"Aye," Kade said. He had many memories of dives where the strongest and fastest of his teammates never made it back up to the airship. He was one of the lucky ones, and not because he was the best.

Sofia walked over to her launch tube. "We're not leaving them down there, Captain."

"Yeah, we didn't come to sit on our asses," Gran Jefe said.

The man with a massive head and impossibly wide shoulders lumbered over in his custom armor. He pulled a hatchet from his duty belt. Tapping the hammer face against his palm, he said, "The *tortuga* Arlo spoke of. Tastes good. *Muy sabroso*, like dolphin."

"You're sick," Sofia said.

Rolo glared at Gran Jefe as if he were psychotic.

"The answer is no," the captain said. "You're all staying put, and we will wait to see if anyone else comes back. Got it?"

When Sofia didn't respond, Rolo walked over to her.

"Do you understand?" he asked firmly.

"Yes, sir," she snapped back.

Rolo held her gaze. "Good."

On the way out of the room, he stopped at the weapons crate. He pulled a silver chain out from his collar and took it off. A key hung off the chain. Bending down, he used it to lock the crate.

"Seriously?" Sofia said.

"Don't make me send the militia in here."

The captain went to Kade next.

"Keep an eye on these wank . . ." Rolo looked over Kade's shoulder. "This bunch of drongos. They seem to have a death wish."

"They're just worried about their comrades, sir," Kade said.

"This is what happens in red zones. They should know this."

Rolo left the room, leaving Kade alone with Sofia and Gran Jefe. They were both staring at him.

"He's an asshole," Sofia said. "No offense, Kade."

"We call them bastards," he replied.

"So, you gonna try and stop us?" Sofia asked as soon as the doors closed. "Because I'm not going to leave my friends down there."

Kade scratched at the perpetual five-o'clock shadow on his square jaw. "Captain Rolo trusts me and always has. If I help you, I break a trust built over decades."

"I get that, but there are divers on the surface that need our help," Sofia said.

"If they are alive," Kade said.

He walked over to the weapons crate.

"What are you doing?" Sofia asked.

"Lock the doors," Kade said. "And let's get on with it, then."

Sofia took off, and Gran Jefe grinned, showing off his sharpened teeth.

"You bad man, Cowboy Kade," he said. "*Muy malo.*"

Kade bent down to the crate and unlocked it with his own key, which Captain Rolo had given him when he boarded.

Inside were the laser rifles from the ITC *Ranger*, as well as assault rifles, grenades, and other explosives.

Gran Jefe reached down and grabbed an assault rifle with a grenade launcher attachment. He then pulled out a bandolier of grenades.

"We need these," he grunted.

Sofia came running back from the doors. By the

time she got to the crate and pulled a weapon, the pounding started.

"Hey!" shouted one of the guards. "Open up!"

Kade put on his helmet and finished securing his gear.

"You ready?" Sofia asked.

"I'm not here to fuck spiders," he said.

"*¿Qué?*" Gran Jefe said.

"It means let's get on with it," Kade said. "Old saying my dad used."

The PA system crackled through the space.

"Kade, what the hell are you doing?"

It was Captain Rolo, and there was anger and shock in his voice, reminiscent of the day the machines lured them to Tanzania.

"We're searching for Team Raptor," Kade replied over his headset.

"You're not going anywhere," Rolo said. "I've locked the launch tubes."

Sofia had already moved past them and was standing in front of the wide hatch that they often used to bring in supplies—something the captain had clearly forgotten about.

Suited up, with their weapons loaded, the three divers lined up at the hatch.

"Ready?" Kade asked.

"I'm not here to fuck spiders, either," Sofia said.

Gran Jefe pumped his hips and laughed.

Sofia hit the launch-door button, prompting a siren and red lights throughout the room.

"Fair go, Kade," Captain Rolo said. "I'm warning you."

In his mind, Kade was being reasonable. For his entire career as a diver and then at the machine camp, he had followed the captain's rules and orders. It had kept them alive, but it had also gotten several of their comrades killed.

He blocked out those memories, keeping them in the past where they belonged.

"We dive, *para que la humanidad sobreviva*," Gran Jefe said in broken English.

He was the first up to the edge. It was his first dive into the wastes, but the Cazador warrior didn't hesitate. He walked right out, falling into the darkness.

Sofia leaped into the storm next.

"Sorry, Captain," Kade said. "But we can't sit around idly like we did back at the camp. We have a second chance, and it's time to extend that to the people that saved us."

Arching his back, he jumped into the darkness.

Kade thought back to the dive that Captain Rolo had sent him and his comrade Johnny on when they arrived at the source of the beacon at Mount Kilimanjaro. It was a day of hope—a day that all the passengers on the ITC *Victory* had waited their entire lives for—a day that they could set down.

But that day was not to be.

Kade owed it to the divers who had made the journey across the sea to save what remained of his people. He was diving for *them* now. He was diving so humanity would survive.

He speared through the darkness, hands to his sides, his body an arrow of muscle and grit. The laser rifle strapped to his chest clanked against the armor covering his dead heart—a heart that, on that fateful day, had lost everything he held dear.

Kade wasn't afraid of dying. His purpose was no longer as a father or a husband. It was as a steward of humanity.

At twelve thousand feet, the storm knocked out his HUD. He closed his eyes, rocketing earthward without a worry on his mind. Thunder boomed around him. He counted down the seconds.

A full minute later, at around four thousand feet, he opened his eyes again. His HUD was back online, and he instantly identified the positions of Sofia and Gran Jefe. Still in free fall east of him, they were about to pull their chutes.

Kade opened up out of the suicide dive and scanned their DZ with his night-vision optics. He made out the green-hued canal and the ship masts and bows and superstructures sticking out of the water.

He wasn't sure what to expect on the ground, but with only one diver making it back up to the airship, he had to fear the worst.

Reaching down to his right thigh, he pulled his pilot chute.

The canopy burst out, suspension lines pulling

taut. He toggled toward the DZ that Team Raptor had chosen. As the ground rose to meet his boots, he searched for their beacons.

Only one came online. Ada and her companion animal.

Kade swallowed hard. He had liked Magnolia, and Edgar, too. Maybe they were just out of range.

Although Kade knew how unlikely that was.

He sailed over the mounds bordering the canal. A rather fresh-looking crater had pushed up out of one of them. Double-checking his map, he confirmed what he feared. Ada and Jo-Jo were underground.

Toggling away from the riven holes in the earth, he flared and stepped out of the sky onto the mound about a mile to the north. At once, he began stuffing his chute.

By the time he finished, Sofia and Gran Jefe were on the ground. Kade ran over to hold security with his laser rifle.

Somewhere in the distance, an unholy roar rose from the ground. Kade zoomed his scope in on the closest bulge of dirt.

"What the hell was *that*?" Sofia said.

Gran Jefe took a grenade from his bandolier and loaded it into his launcher.

"*El diablo blanco,*" he said.

Kade turned to Sofia as Gran Jefe started down the mound. "What'd he say?" Kade asked.

Sofia paused, then said, "The white devil."

* * * * *

"You have to get this damn boat running," Michael whispered.

He couldn't believe it. They had escaped *Blood Trawler* two hours ago, narrowly surviving the blast that slammed into their lifeboat, only to be lost at sea before the rescue boats could find them.

Worse, after racing away at twenty-five knots from the burning tanker, the lifeboat had stopped dead in the water. No engine meant no dashboard. And without a dashboard, he had no idea whether there was a working beacon on the boat. The radio was down, too, and every time he tried to connect Cricket 2.0, the signal failed.

The droid was still connected to one of the weather drones, but every time Michael tried to send a transmission, he got an error message.

What he *could* do was see the data the drone was collecting. As of five minutes ago, the winds were at 105 miles per hour with heavy rainfall.

"The islands are getting battered," Michael whispered.

He could picture residential shacks being blown apart across the rigs. But those they could rebuild with scrap from the wastes. It was the crops they couldn't replace.

Leaning down, he held Cricket up, spreading its glow into the mechanical compartment containing the two-stroke engine. Twisted wires and cobwebs filled the space under the deck.

Michael still wasn't any closer to figuring out what was wrong with it, and Rodger wasn't much help. He had taken in a lot of smoke and had burns on his arms and cheeks. He sat in one of the bucket seats, dabbing ointment onto the burns, groaning and mumbling something about his ass hurting.

Michael continued working, fishing carefully through the wires and pulling cobwebs away from components, checking for an open circuit.

After a few minutes, Rodger said something coherent. "How's it coming, Tin?"

"It might be the ignition coil, but I'm not sure. The Cazadores did their maintenance, but everything down here is old as hell."

"I'll help. Just give me a few more minutes."

"I can handle this, Rodge. You rest."

Michael tried to focus on fixing it, but the image of Alfred falling into the ocean was seared into his mind. He kept seeing Alfred struggling to keep his head above the surface and then drowning.

He still didn't know if Pedro had made it off the ship, either.

Often on dives, Michael had imagined dying in the wastes, being marooned out in the darkness and left to the creatures. But a cold, watery grave seemed somehow even worse.

He closed his eyes, trying to block out the images of Alfred drifting down through the depths, his bones being picked clean by all sorts of creatures.

I'm sorry, buddy. Michael thought. I'm so sorry . . .

The deputy chief had given his life to get the ship safely away from the islands. To protect his family and to keep their fishing grounds safe. Now Tammy and two-year-old Leonard would never see him again.

"I shouldn't have let him come," Michael said. "I should have—"

"It wasn't your fault," Rodger said.

"I couldn't save him."

"We can't save everyone. It's the reality of this world."

Rodger got up from his seat and sloshed through the inch of standing water in the boat. He went down on one knee and peered into the engine compartment.

"What a piece of shit," he said.

"Tell me about it," Michael replied.

The archaic two-stroke engine had likely swallowed some debris, preventing proper carburetion.

"Let me take a look," Rodger said. "In the meantime, see if you can figure out where we're at." He paused abruptly and pulled his head out of the engine compartment. "Have you tried patching Cricket to that interface?"

Michael brightened. "Damn, I never thought about that . . ."

He sat in front of the dark control panel.

"Come on Cricket, help me out, buddy."

The droid chirped as he inserted the patch cords into the interface. The main screen flickered on, spreading a cool blue through the dark compartment.

"Brilliant, Rodge!"

Michael tapped the touch screen to bring up their location. The digital map showed they continued to be pushed farther away from the Vanguard Islands. They were now twenty-five miles from the western boundary and completely at the storm's mercy.

Michael knew there wasn't much mercy to be had in the wastes.

He tried the radio, but static from the storm obliterated any signal.

One thing was certain: if the beacon was working, someone would come looking for them. He tapped through the control panel, trying to locate it.

It wasn't a matter of whether X would mount a rescue; it was a matter of whether they could survive long enough for a rescue team to find their beacon and chase it down.

"I don't see the EPIRB," Michael said. "This boat has to have one, right?"

"I didn't want to tell you earlier."

"Tell me what?"

Rodger glanced up, pushing his glasses up on his nose.

"Emergency position-indicating radio beacons are dedicated to transmitting distress signals, and if ours works, it will have turned on when we launched the boat. However, without satellites, the only way they can find us is from the weather drones. And right now they're probably too far away to detect us."

"One is close enough I can see the data," Michael said.

He tapped Cricket, pulling up the data. The screen flickered, indicating the signal was already weakening.

Michael swallowed hard at the realization. The drone was already starting to move out of range.

"We need to turn this tub around," he said.

Michael looked out the viewport above the dashboard. Walls of waves rose and subsided under almost constant lightning.

At this point, he must put his faith in the people who would be searching for them, beacon or no beacon.

Rodger coughed and then backed out of the engine compartment. The deep rattle in his chest was hard to ignore.

"You okay?" Michael asked.

Rodger wiped snot from his nose and sat back in the bucket seat.

"I'm having a hard time breathing."

"You need to rest. Let me handle the engine."

After settling Rodger in his seat, Michael bent down to get back to work on the engine compartment when he noticed the scent of gasoline.

"What the hell?" he whispered. He went back to the control panel and tabbed through the dashboard to look at the gauges.

"Fucking shit," Michael growled.

"What now?" Rodger asked.

"We're low on gas."

"This day just keeps getting rosier!"

Michael cursed a blue streak that X would have approved of.

Even if they could get the engine running, they didn't have enough fuel to get back to the islands. And without a transmitting beacon, finding them would be like finding a dropped snowflake before it melted.

They would never see home again. Never see their loved ones.

As Michael shook his head in despair, something slammed into the boat, knocking him to the deck.

"What was that!" Rodger cried.

"I don't—" Before Michael could finish his thought, something hit them again, knocking him against the hull.

"Strap in," he said.

Michael climbed into his seat and secured his belt.

Rodger said, "Man, I never pictured my life ending like this. But, Tin, if we die, I'm proud to be by your side."

Michael took his hand.

"Thanks for coming back for me," Rodger said.

"Handle your present with confidence. Face your future without fear, brother." Michael smiled.

"I try, but it seems like everything's always trying to kill me."

"I can relate to that."

The two men stared out the portholes, waiting for whatever had slammed into them to do it again. Michael didn't even want to imagine what was out there.

"Maybe it was just a wave," Michael said.

They were silent for a few moments.

"I just hope Mags is okay," Rodger said after the pause. "I wish I could still dive. I would do anything to be with her, but this damn foot of mine . . ."

He shook his head.

"You ever miss diving, Tin?"

"Only every day."

"Maybe if we survive this, we'll dive again someday, together, just like old times."

"My diving days are over. I made a promise to Layla to keep safe."

Rodger didn't answer, but Michael knew what he was probably thinking.

There wasn't anything safe about his job now.

They would be lucky to survive this, and even luckier if the islands survived the storm now pummeling them.

Once again the gravity of the situation hit Michael like a heavy weight.

The divers were heading on a dangerous mission, he was drifting aimlessly in sixty-foot seas without a working engine, and the Vanguard Islands were being hammered mercilessly by what would soon be a hurricane.

It was astonishing that humanity had survived this long.

TEN

The stench of rot made Magnolia gag. She had woken in a dark, damp space, with a pounding headache.

Another breath picked up the scent of something so awful, she didn't recognize it.

But how could she smell . . .

Panic gripped her at the realization that she wasn't wearing a helmet.

She tried to move, only to find that she was paralyzed.

No, you aren't, she thought.

Moving her fingers and toes, she confirmed that. But she felt something cold binding her—a material that felt like metal.

She squirmed, swaying slightly.

It was then she noticed that the pressure in her head wasn't from a headache.

She was hanging upside down, without her armor and helmet.

Her first instinct was to scream for help, but the

memories came rushing back of the bird-faced creature that had hit her on the deck. The same creature
that captured Edgar.

She stared into the darkness, searching for her
comrade, but it was simply too black to penetrate.

"Edgar," she whispered. "Can you hear me?"

No response.

Magnolia replayed the events in her mind. First
the turtles, then the massive mother, and finally the
beaked beast that had ambushed her on the deck.

Was it some sort of highly intelligent Siren?

She tried to move again, but all she could really
do was sway her body. The chains or whatever held
her feet were wrapped around her chest and arms as
well, making it difficult to do anything but squirm.

After a few minutes of trying, she stopped to rest.

Magnolia breathed in the same putrid scent of
rotting flesh and raw sewage.

Her stomach felt queasy. It was probably from the
scent, but it could also be from a low dose of radiation
poisoning. Without her suit, she was at risk.

Grunting, she swung her body back and forth,
the chain whining and the overhead creaking.

A banging thud answered the noise.

She stopped struggling at once, her body slowing
until she was hanging still.

The sound grew louder. Footsteps. Right above her.

A scratching sound sent a chill down her spine,
to her toes.

This was it. Something was coming to eat her.

She cursed herself for being so stupid. There was a reason the crew of *Sea Sprite* had never returned and no other Cazador crew had tried to get through. The canal was a death trap.

As the steps moved closer, she did what she often did when she was scared. She thought of Rodger.

This time, regret burrowed into her heart—regret that she had never fully given herself to him even though she loved him and he loved her. Regret that they would never have a chance to get married or have a family.

It always seemed as though moments of fear made her regret not doing those things before, but then, after that fear passed, she would go right back to putting them off.

She had given everything to her life as a Hell Diver—far more than she had ever given Rodger.

She blinked away a welling tear. *Don't do that*, she thought. *You don't get to do that!*

If Magnolia had learned one thing in the wastes, it was that you always had a chance to survive, however bad the situation. But you had to be positive, you had to be smart, and you had to *fight*.

She gritted her teeth as the footsteps tapped closer, until they were right outside the room where she hung.

Metal creaked, and the hatch clicked open, allowing a spear of light inside the space. She saw a sign on the hatch in a language she didn't recognize, but she could make out the symbols.

She was above the ship's sewage ejectors.

The hatch creaked open a few inches more, allowing in more light—not electric light, but some sort of flame, like a candle or torch.

Magnolia remained still but kept her eyes open. And what she saw in the glow made holding still very difficult.

Directly in front of her was an open hatch down to a primary receptacle for sewage.

Footsteps entered the room, and something sharp poked her in the side hard enough to make her yelp.

The beast answered with a hiss.

She squirmed hard, swaying back and forth.

"I'll kill you!" she screamed. "I'LL KILL YOU!"

Shouting was all she could think to do, hoping that whatever creature was behind her would back off and leave her alone until she could break loose and escape.

The hissing response continued, and the light danced around the room as the thing holding the torch moved. She bucked and struggled like a being possessed, swinging and squirming, screaming as loud as she could.

Something sharp stabbed her arm. She screamed in pain, only to hear a demonic roar in the distance.

That shut her up, and the torchlight flitted out of the room.

Magnolia felt the warmth of blood running down her arm as the awful screeching continued in the distance.

There was no mistaking that sound—or the tremors that came with it.

A quake rumbled through the overhead, rattling the chains that secured her feet.

She hung there waiting for the creature that had captured her to come and finish her off, but whatever the thing was, it just hovered in the doorway, listening to the chitinous abomination outside what she assumed was the ship in the canal, where she was being held captive.

Suddenly, the light moved again, and Magnolia stared at a long beak and feathered head. The creature leaned down until she was face-to-face with it.

She recoiled as it brought up a clawed finger to the tip of the yellow beak, as if telling her to keep quiet.

Magnolia flinched as it reached up to its head and removed, not the head of a mutant bird, but a wildly decorated helmet, revealing the youthful Asian features of a man.

"You're *human*," Magnolia whispered.

The young man, who couldn't be any older than sixteen, put the gloved finger back to his lips. "*Shh-h-h!*" he said.

She managed a nod as she tried to piece together what was happening. The hissing was actually this kid trying to shush her, but the helmet had muffled the sound.

She stared at him, wondering whether he had been a passenger on this ship.

If so, where was everyone?

The glow of the torch provided part of the answer.

In the rust-stained container below, she saw the source of the stench. Skeletal remains filled the tank. Broken orange and yellow shells were discarded with fish skeletons as well as what looked like human bones. The sewage ejectors had been turned into an offal bin.

Magnolia looked back up to the youth, wondering. Had he killed the other passengers? He looked innocent at first glance—the freckles, the eyes incapable of murder. But if he had survived out here, he had to be *very* capable of killing.

She also knew that he was probably hungry and now had a chance to eat something other than the local mutant wildlife.

"Please, let me go," she said. "I can help you."

The kid tilted his head, long brown hair falling over the right side. He brushed it back with a gloved hand.

"I can help you," she repeated.

He didn't seem to understand English.

"I come from the sky . . ." She jerked her head toward the overhead. "We have an airship. We can take you to a place where the sun shines, and . . ."

The young man's eyes widened as a long, ethereal shriek sounded outside the ship.

He stood and put his helmet back on.

"No, wait," she said. "Please!"

He pulled a machete from a sheath on his belt and held it up.

"NO!" Magnolia screamed.

She closed her eyes. But instead of a blade hacking into her flesh, she felt his hand push her body to the side.

A clicking sounded above her, and the chain holding her dropped her to the deck. She lay there stunned as the hatch clicked shut.

Slowly, she worked her way up into a sitting position and clamped her palm around the wounded arm. The cut wasn't deep, but blood was flowing freely. She wondered whether he was trying to hurt her, or just keep her quiet.

Looking back, it seemed like the latter.

Although he could still come back and barbecue her.

She sat there for a moment, trying to get her bearings by mentally recalling what she had seen in the space with the torch. Then she started crawling over toward the hatch.

She found the handle. It was locked.

Magnolia rested her back against the cold hull, trying to keep calm. She was alive for now, but she wasn't going to be after a few weeks of radiation poisoning.

But maybe the radiation didn't penetrate this far, she thought.

The kid had taken his helmet off, and he had lived out here for years.

She decided not to worry about radiation, since she couldn't do anything about it anyway. Instead, she focused on escaping.

Standing, she ran her hand along the hull until

she got to the other side of the room, where she tried to search for her armor.

After a few minutes searching by touch, she had discovered nothing.

The quakes continued, but the sounds from the monster seemed to be getting farther away.

Magnolia froze at a new chirping sound.

She felt her way back to the hatch and put her ear to the metal. Footsteps echoed on the other side.

An orange glow spread under the hatch, and she stepped back with her fists up. The handle twisted but then clicked back into locked position. The young man on the other side of the hatch turned, the glow moving away now.

He suddenly darted away, footsteps pounding the deck.

Magnolia lowered her fists and stepped back up to the door. For several more minutes, small tremors vibrated through the hull of the ship.

A long, deep whistle sounded, almost like a whale calling out. The sound was different from the earlier shrieks and clicks that the chitinous abomination had made. This cry seemed . . . lonely.

The alien noise echoed and faded away, leaving only silence.

She backed away from the hatch and rested her back against the hull. The darkness enveloped her, prompting a wave of panic.

Snap out of it, Mags. You don't have time for this.

Pushing herself up, she pressed her fingers to the

overhead, feeling for a way out. Maybe there was a passage or some ductwork . . .

But she wasn't finding it.

The only other opening in the room was the tank full of human and animal remains.

She felt the despair returning and raised her wrist to cover her mouth.

A voice suddenly called out in a language she didn't recognize.

Magnolia returned to the hatch.

Thumps, grunts, and another shout in the foreign tongue echoed somewhere outside the room.

It all stopped a minute later, quiet once again filling the dark void.

A light slipped under the door—not a torch, but an actual electric beam.

She stepped back as the handle clicked and the metal screeched open.

Magnolia squinted in the bright glow.

"You okay?"

With an involuntary cry of relief, she practically charged Edgar, embracing him in a hug.

"Easy," he said, wincing.

She looked past him to a body sprawled in the passage. The teenager in the ghillie suit and bird helmet lay in a fetal position, bleeding but alive.

Edgar went to stab him, but Magnolia stopped him by pulling on his arm.

"Don't!" she hissed.

"What? Why?"

"I don't think he was going to kill us. I think he was just scared and—"

"Pretty sure he was going to eat us." Edgar gestured to the exit. "Come on, then, we got to find our armor and get out of here."

They walked over to the young man, who was moaning in pain. Edgar had taken his weapons and tied his hands.

Magnolia flicked on her flashlight and followed Edgar through the bowels of the ship.

A few minutes later, they followed the glow of a lit candle into the former captain's quarters, where they discovered their armor.

Hardcover books lined the shelves. The small bed was neatly made with thick blankets, and the desk was laden with maps. A second desk was covered with bullet casings and knives, all apparently custom-made.

"You think it's just the kid here?" Magnolia asked.

"I don't know, so stay alert," Edgar said. He found his armor stacked neatly in the corner of the quarters.

As Magnolia dressed, she couldn't help but think the young man was more of an asset than a threat.

A quick search of the room turned up her laser rifle, which the kid had stowed in a locker. Edgar grabbed his, too, and they hurried out to a ladder. The top hatch was sealed by what looked like a weld.

"Someone went to great lengths to keep people in this ship," Edgar said.

"Or to keep monsters out," Magnolia said.

She hesitated as Edgar started down the passage, looking for an alternative route off the ship.

"What are you waiting for?" he asked.

She turned back the way they had come.

"We can't leave him here," she said.

"Yes, yes we can. He could have killed us, and he still might try."

"But he didn't."

"We don't know anything about him, Commander."

"No, we don't, just like we don't know anything about this place." Magnolia gestured for Edgar to follow her, but he stood his ground.

"Don't you see, Edgar?" she said. "We came here for recon. And no one knows this place better than that kid."

* * * * *

X tried to keep his mind off Michael, Rodger, and Alfred and stay focused on saving those he could right now.

He had boarded *Raven's Claw* with a crew of soldiers, rescuers, and volunteers. They were closing in on a rig housing the five hundred-plus survivors from Tanzania after it sent a distress transmission.

From where he stood on the island of the warship, X could see most of the rig. The ship's spotlights raked across the decks, giving them a view of the damage.

The platforms at the very top, occupied by fields of vegetables and cisterns of fresh water, were intact except for one, which had fallen, the legs buckling and the platform smashing through the deck.

Rain cascaded through the opening, flooding compartments below. The center of the rig had turned out to be a trap for some of the people sheltering there.

As *Raven's Claw* drew closer, a sheet of corrugated metal streaked through the air.

Seeing the shacks and homes stripped away so easily filled X with dread. These people had been through much, living in camps for years and doing manual drudgery for the machines. Starving, sick, and suffering under extreme conditions.

This place was supposed to be their refuge, but now they were being punished again, by something X couldn't fight: Mother Nature.

As with the machines, there was no reasoning with the storm. There was only mitigating the damage and saving as many lives as possible.

"Keep us as steady as you can," X said to Captain Two Skulls. "It's as close as we dare go in these waves."

The captain nodded, and X rushed down into the lower decks, holding on to railings as the ship pitched and yawed. On the third deck below, eighty-five people waited. Most of them were rescue workers, assigned to the capitol tower but no longer needed there now that it was secure.

Firefighters, medics, technicians, soldiers, and volunteers stood ready. They all wore helmets, goggles, life jackets, and bright vests. A group of engineers huddled around Steve, who was supervising the distribution of tools ranging from axes to riveters and welding rigs.

A hundred soldiers and sailors had also gathered. General Forge had taken command, splitting them up into rescue groups to help locate the trapped people on the rig.

The Barracudas were here, too, with Sergeant Slayer and his second in command, Bromista.

"Anyone got a schematic of this rig?" X asked.

Sergeant Slayer held up a blueprint that was already marked with the damaged interior shelters. A glance confirmed they were all near the top level, right below the platform that had collapsed.

"This compartment was damaged as well," Slayer said, pointing.

"Split up the crews," X said. "General Forge will take one group, and I'll head to the main chamber.

"Slayer, you're with me," X said to the Barracuda warrior.

"It's an honor, sir," Slayer replied.

"You, too, Steve."

Steve zipped up his fire jacket and picked up a fire axe.

"We're secure," said the captain over the radio.

"Let's go!" X yelled.

His bodyguards, Ton and Victor, both in the fire gear, stepped to his side. Minutes later, they were on an outboard launch, closing the distance to the rig. As they neared the rig's exterior dock, three cables snaked down from the boat derrick above. Slayer and

Steve managed to get them hooked into the thick eyebolts at the prow and stern. The winch engaged, and in no time the boat was hoisted above the reach of the waves. From the derrick platform, they took an enclosed stairwell up a twisting ladder for two hundred feet.

Outside the rig walls, the wind roared like a sea monster.

Steve and Slayer took point at the top landing and opened an interior hatch. The power was off, and the team turned on their tactical lights in the dark passage.

Water trickled from the ceiling onto the deck.

"This way," Slayer said.

They ran toward the center of the rig. Some of the shelters were repurposed storage tanks. Others were offices or dormitories built centuries ago for the workers on these rigs.

Candles burned in the distance, and a single flashlight beam speared through the darkness.

"Help us!" a voice called out.

Slayer ran toward it, and X got his first look at the civilians. There were only ten.

Two were limping; another was holding her hand to a scalp wound. A few were slumped on the deck, unconscious.

"Bring the medics up here," X said.

Slayer called it in over the radio.

"Help's on the way," X said as he passed the people.

Now that they were deep inside the center of the

rig, the wind was hardly audible at all. But he could hear other noises: cries of agony, more calls for help.

The rescue crews fanned out through the rig. The farther in they got, the darker and hotter the passages became. Smells of sewage and body odor drifted on the sultry air.

They passed more civilians in the hallways, standing outside their designated shelters and talking quietly. Some asked if they could help, but Slayer shook them away.

"How much farther?" X asked.

"Not far, King Xavier."

The team advanced two more levels, just below the rooftop. Water poured from gaps in the overhead and ran an inch deep in the passage. Slapping through standing muck that had mixed with sewage, they finally reached the central chamber.

Clanking and banging echoed off the hulls.

"Right up there," Slayer said.

"This is an old holding chamber," Steve said.

X stepped up to the hull and put his ear to it.

"Help!" someone inside yelled.

The voice was faint, but it wasn't alone. Some of them sounded like kids. He could hear what sounded like splashing, too.

"Shit," X said. "How the hell do you get in?"

"Over here!" Steve called out.

They ran to the next passage and found the source of the banging. A group of people were at a hatch, pounding it with hammers and axes.

A man with an eye patch and fancy tunic turned toward them and said, "Thank the gods you're here."

It was Charmer, the former chief engineer for the ITC *Victory* and, from what X had heard, a huge pain in the ass.

"Get back!" X yelled.

Most of the people stepped away, but a skinny bearded man in a life jacket kept hitting the door with an axe. Chest heaving, sweat dripping down his face, he kept doggedly at it.

"My brother's in there!" he shouted.

"Let them through, Tilly," Charmer said.

Bromista grabbed the man when he did not relent, but Tilly wrenched free and hit the door one last time before Bromista finally wrestled him back. The other Barracudas stepped up.

Tilly struggled some more, but Charmer grabbed him. "Don't be a wanker," he said. "They're here to help."

"How many people inside?" X asked.

"Fifteen," Charmer said. "Maybe more."

"How long has it been flooding?"

"I don't know, maybe an hour."

"It's a huge chamber, and if it's been flooding that long . . ." Steve shook his head. "We better be prepared to swim once we crack her open."

"You heard him!" X yelled. "Get back!"

The other civilians moved farther away.

Slayer moved to the front of the hatch and fired up the metal-cutting chainsaw. The tool choked, rumbled, and fell silent.

"Come on, you pile of Siren shit." He pulled the cord over and over, to no avail.

"Give me that," X said to Tilly.

He took the axe, and pointing the blade at the hull a few feet away from the hatch, he said, "We're going to make our own door."

The six Barracuda warriors started hacking away, their axe bits crunching into the thick metal.

"Almost through!" Slayer yelled.

X swung hard, and the blade broke through the panel. Water jetted out in his face. The other warriors fell to, their axes opening up gashes that spurted more water.

Slayer and two of his men worked together to cut a door into the bulkhead. When they had cut a crude outline, Steve stepped up.

"Everyone, get back!" X shouted.

Steve swung the hammer, slamming the metal bulkhead multiple times until it finally gave way. He went down in the wall of water that followed the panel into the corridor.

Slayer and another soldier grabbed Steve and pulled him to safety. The rush of water continued for several seconds, spilling out several of the fifteen people trapped inside.

X could see that some of them were already gone, their bodies limp and lips blue.

"Medics," X yelled. "Get the medics up here!"

A team standing by rushed over to pitch in.

X ducked inside the doorway and shined his light

through the cylindrical metal structure. There were more people inside. At the other end, a boy clung to a woman.

Rushing over to them, X bent down. It was Alton, the kid born in captivity at the machines' labor camp.

"Please, help my mum," Alton said. "She's sick."

Feeling her neck, X confirmed a pulse. She was breathing, too, but each breath was as shallow as her heartbeat.

"She's going to be okay," X said. He motioned for a medic and then looked to Alton. "Be strong, kid. Your mum needs you."

Only then did X see that the kid was shivering and his legs were shaking.

"You treaded water in there, didn't you?" X asked.

"Yes."

"You saved your mum, kid."

Alton smiled and leaned back down to hold his mother as a medic finally got to them.

Charmer ducked through the opening.

"Thank you, King Xavier," he said, blinking his single eye. "It seems your people are the real-life version of angels for us."

"Don't mention it," X grunted. "You'd do the same for us."

The radio on his vest crackled and he left the chamber.

"King Xavier, this rig is *listo*—secure," said Captain Two Skulls. "We gotta get back out there."

X's breath caught. Had they found Michael, Rodger, and Alfred?

"One of our fishing trawlers had some trouble," said Two Skulls.

"Any word on the chief engineer and his crew?"

"Negative, sir."

X heard splashing behind him and spun about. General Forge and his team had arrived and were standing in the ankle-deep rainwater outside the chamber.

Forge put a hand on X's shoulder.

It was the first time he had ever touched X.

"Have faith, my king," said the general. "I have seen many miracles at sea over the years."

"Damn straight," Steve said. "Hell, the Vanguard Islands themselves are a miracle."

ELEVEN

Michael stared through the front viewport at the roiling sea. They would need a miracle to get home. Low on gas, with a dead engine and a beacon that wouldn't save them unless the drones got closer.

And in a hurricane, that wasn't happening.

Cricket 2.0 couldn't even connect to them now.

Michael tapped the screen and got the same "No signal" error message.

The storm continued to batter the lifeboat, pushing it farther and farther away from the islands and the drones.

On the one hand, it was good to be out of the worst of the storm, but on the other, it made getting home almost impossible.

At least, they seemed to have evaded whatever creature slammed into them hours earlier.

"How's it coming?" Michael asked. "Anything I can do?"

"I think I almost got it," Rodger said.

Michael hovered behind him, his stomach queasy with the boat's constant rocking. For the past few hours, they had worked on an engine with a faulty coil and a loose drive belt.

They had fixed the latter, and Rodger had almost finished rewinding the coil, scrupulously counting every turn. He pulled his hand out of the compartment and wiped his glasses on his shirt.

"The moment of truth has come," he said. "Go ahead and prime the engine."

Michael switched places with Rodger, and Rodger took the starter pull.

"Let's go, sweet baby," he said, yanking on it.

The engine rumbled, groaned, and cut out.

"Come on, sweetness . . ." Rodger pulled it a second time.

The engine rumbled again but didn't catch.

"Worthless fornicating pile of pot metal!" Rodger shouted.

"Take it easy, Rodge. You'll break the magneto and then we'll be *really* screwed!"

Michael took the T-grip rubber handle, and Rodger moved out of the way. Then, instead of yanking on the cord, Michael pulled it gently.

The engine turned over, this time with a chugging noise.

"Wow, how'd you do that?" Rodger asked.

"Having a kid teaches you to be patient and gentle."

Michael ducked under the overhead and plopped

down behind the steering wheel. He checked the map and punched in the coordinates of the Vanguard Islands.

"How far are we now?" Rodger asked anxiously.

"Sixty-seven knots to the north."

"And how much gas?"

"Quarter tank, which *might* get us halfway there."

Michael had scarcely belted in when a wave caught them broadside, and the lifeboat slid down it, listing steeply to port before its superlow center of gravity righted them.

Patience, he thought.

The engine had just enough speed to turn into the waves—*most* of the time. Timing his tack between swells, he got the boat turned all the way around toward the islands for the long journey back home.

But it also meant they were heading back into the storm. He held the wheel steady and kept it at half throttle to conserve gas.

"Better buckle in," Michael said. He tried to keep his mind off his family by talking to Rodger as he settled into his seat. "You ever think about having kids with Magnolia?" Michael asked.

"We're getting old."

"Yeah, but you're both healthy."

"I don't think she wants kids."

Rodger frowned, and Michael could tell he had hit a sensitive spot.

"I do, though. I want a normal life with Mags, as normal as we can have, but I don't care about getting married or all that. I just want to be with her."

Turning back to the viewport, Michael said, "I understand. I think she wants that, too."

"I don't think she would ever give up diving, and as long as she's a diver, I don't think she's ever going to settle down."

Rodger coughed, then continued.

"If I do make it back to the islands, I'm going to have a talk with her and let her know how I feel."

"Good, Rodge. And we *will* make it back."

"You think she'd say yes if I did ask her to marry me?"

Michael turned around and met his friend's gaze. "Of course I do."

"She's always kind of been her own person," Rodger said, "and I'm not sure she has ever really, fully committed to the idea of *us*."

"She has in her own way, Rodge, don't worry."

Rodger sighed again. "Thanks, Michael, you're a good friend."

"So are . . ."

Michael narrowed his eyes at something on the horizon that came and went in a flash of lightning.

Rodger huddled behind Michael to look. "What did you see?"

"Thought I saw something," he said. "Must have been my eyes playing tricks."

He stared for another moment and then glanced at the digital map to confirm they were still heading for the islands.

Michael concentrated on the ocean. All that

mattered right now was getting home. Lightning flashed through the swollen storm clouds as the waves rose higher, coming at them in one long, endless set.

Rain hit the hard shell of the lifeboat with a sound like bullets.

He squinted as another flash of lightning illuminated a funnel shape on the horizon, reaching up into the clouds.

"Oh, shit," he said.

"What now?"

"Things are about to get rough."

He checked the fuel. They had already burned through half their supply and were still forty-two miles from the closest oil rig.

The oncoming waves beat them for another hour. Michael could barely see anything through the viewports.

"I feel like Arlo last time he mouthed off to Mags," Rodger said. "She slapped him around good."

Michael chuckled. "What did he do to deserve that?"

"Something about having big dick energy, I don't know."

"That guy is something else."

Another half hour passed, bringing them another five miles closer to the islands. But the closer they got, the stronger the storm grew.

Sweat dripped down Michael's forehead, stinging his eyes and further impairing his vision. They crested a wave—the largest yet, giving a momentary view of the horizon. Was this an optical illusion?

"Brace yourself," Michael said.

"What? Why . . ."

Before Rodger could finish, the boat skidded down the wave and was halfway up the next. This time, there was nothing Michael could do to keep them steady.

"Hold on!" he shouted.

The bow went up, up, until there was no more up.

Michael felt the sensation of being topsy-turvy as they kept tilting backward and splashed into the ocean upside down. The water swallowed them, submerging the entire vessel.

Rodger screamed, but Michael said, "No worries. She'll right herself."

And sure enough, in what seemed like slow motion, the lifeboat popped back up through the water and rolled over, righting itself.

It took him most of a minute to get them pointed back into the waves. Immediately, something slammed into the boat.

"What was that?" Rodger asked.

Something long and gray moved past the viewport. Michael held his gaze on the water, searching the darkness.

"Tin, what was—"

"*Shh!*" Michael hissed.

"What? Why?"

"I saw something."

"What *kind* of something?"

Michael wasn't sure what he had seen, but something had hit the lifeboat. Maybe a huge fish, or perhaps a shark . . .

He checked the map again and the fuel gauge.

"No," he said quietly, staring to confirm what he already knew.

They were heading away from the islands again, farther from their loved ones.

An expanse of gray flesh filled the viewports.

His gut tightened.

They weren't alone after all.

"Tin . . ." Rodger said.

Michael held a breath in his chest as an eye the size of a dinner plate peered inside, right at the two men.

* * * * *

Ada still didn't have any idea what the strange glowing beast was that she had shot in the skull. Part of her wondered if she was going crazy down here.

For the past few hours, she and Jo-Jo had trekked through the tunnels, hiding from the creatures that dwelled in the darkness. Once again, they stopped to listen for shrieks or skittering claws.

Hearing nothing, they continued down the passage, which narrowed into a bottleneck up ahead. Jo-Jo moved on all fours with hair lying flat, indicating that she detected no immediate threats.

Ada needed a real break. Finding a corner with

a view in both directions, she motioned for Jo-Jo to sit and rest. After making sure they were alone, she pulled out her second water bottle and handed it to the monkey, who drank it greedily.

That was okay. Ada had a reserve supply that she could access from the straw in her helmet. As long as they weren't down here for too long, they would be fine.

She took a moment to get her bearings by scrolling through the minimap on her wrist computer. They were four miles from their original landing zone at the canal, and right beneath the outskirts of Panama City.

Even if Edgar or Magnolia had somehow survived and their beacons came back online, she was too far out of range to see it on her HUD—not just because of the distance, but also because she was underground.

Switching to the environmental data on her mini-computer, Ada saw that the radiation readings had climbed. That made sense, considering her proximity to the blast zone.

They must head back toward the canal, even if that meant running into those hellish turtle monsters.

Normally, she wasn't the claustrophobic type. After all, she had grown up on an airship, packed with too many people in too small a space.

This was different, though. Being trapped underground, in a high-rad zone, with a fire monster and carnivorous turtles, was enough to drive fear into the boldest, craziest warriors she had encountered over the years.

Not even Sirens had survived in these tunnels.

This was a nightmare, the hell below the hell that was earth.

Ada had to remind herself, *You've survived worse.*

The solo voyage to Florida, finding Jo-Jo, the journey back. The memories reminded her that she was strong. That she could survive this.

But maybe this was cosmic justice—another punishment for her sin of killing the Cazadores in that container after the war.

The hair on Jo-Jo's back spiked.

Ada shut off her headlamps, leaving them in darkness her night vision couldn't penetrate. She could hear something, though. A clicking. Scratching.

Deep but faint rumbles in the ground. It had to be the chitinous beasts that made these tunnels.

Standing, she flicked on her light and started down the narrowing passage with Jo-Jo. At the next intersection, she went left, toward the canal.

They trekked for the next hour. The noises had long since faded, and the hair on the monkey's back was flat again.

Still, Ada kept her rifle up, sweeping the darkness for hostiles.

Three miles from the landing zone, a faint dot pulsed on her HUD. Then two . . . three.

Beacons. *The other divers!*

Kade, Sofia, and Gran Jefe had come back for her and the others.

Ada turned on the second light and ran harder,

the rifle clacking against her chest armor. They made it another mile before the tunnel widened. A ramp of scree sloped down into a cavernous passage. This was more chamber than tunnel.

She slowed as she entered, raking her light over a ceiling that had to be twenty to thirty feet overhead. It stretched as far as she could see.

Mud sloshed under her boots as she started across the terrain. Rock lay strewn about, but upon closer examination, she noticed they weren't all rocks. Orange shells and pincer claws littered the rock floor.

This place seemed to be some sort of graveyard.

Jo-Jo stuck at Ada's side all the way across until they came to a narrowing part. The entrance was not of dirt, but of stone.

No, that wasn't right, either, she realized. The walls were *concrete*.

Cautiously she stepped up under the broken entrance to what appeared to be an old-world subway. Using her helmet light, she flitted the beams over mangled train tracks and hunks of concrete rubble.

According to her minimap, they led back to the canal.

Jo-Jo followed her into the tunnel, and on they went until they came across an overturned train car. There were three of them: one on its side, one on its back, and the other crushed like a tin can.

Ada ducked inside the first railcar but found nothing besides the filthy plastic seats. In the next, she found a bent pair of eyeglasses and a broken bottle.

She pushed on. The beacons on her HUD were also moving. Kade, Sofia, and Gran Jefe were all on the surface and heading in her direction.

She tried the comms.

"Calling any divers on the surface. This is Hell Diver Ada Winslow. Do you copy? Over."

Static hissed over the channel.

She would have to get closer.

Jo-Jo climbed up onto a platform that ran alongside the tracks. They followed it for another few hundred feet. She almost missed the door in the concrete wall.

Ada held up her hand to Jo-Jo and reached for the handle. A rusted sign hung sideways.

She turned the handle. Locked.

Jo-Jo kept going, and Ada brought her rifle back up as they came across another hole in the tunnel walls.

Through the opening was another set of rails. Ada scanned them with her light but decided to stay on the current route.

After another five minutes of walking, she tried the comms again. Still nothing but static.

All three beacons had stopped. The other divers were probably trying to figure out what had happened to Team Raptor.

Ada thought again of Edgar and Magnolia. Maybe they were still alive. But after all she had seen down here, it was a long shot.

Cold dread sank into her gut.

Jo-Jo let out a whine, every hair on her body spiking at once.

It took Ada a moment to see what had spooked the monkey.

A greenish-yellowish glow pulsated down the passage.

The radioactive beast had returned.

Jo-Jo darted through the black, guiding them with her night vision. Behind her, Ada ran blind, heart thrumming, sweat stinging her eyes.

Fighting was not an option. Only fleeing could save them now.

Ada ran hard until her boot snagged on something and she crashed to the concrete. Rolling off the platform, she landed between the tracks, her armor taking most of the impact.

A long echo clattered down the tunnel.

The noise sustained like a gong.

As if in answer, the tremors returned, rumbling through the ground, sifting dust from above.

Jo-Jo hopped down, frantic. Though Ada couldn't see her, she felt Jo-Jo's breath only inches from her face.

Pain shot up her ankle when she tried to stand.

"No, damn it!" she hissed.

The tremors grew louder and seemed to be coming from the canal, where she was headed.

They were about to be cornered.

And then the light was gone, leaving them in the darkness. Whatever was coming had spooked the glowing creature.

She hobbled over to the concrete platform and climbed up, then started along it, back the way they had come. Maybe they could hide in the trains. If they could get there.

The noises grew louder, tremors rattling the passage.

A shriek roared through like a tornado, bringing with it a wave of hot air that spiked the temperature gauge on her HUD by thirty degrees.

She watched as the source of the noise and heat squeezed through a hole in the tunnel wall. Dirt and rock rolled down from a wicked curved beak. Clawed legs slashed through the wall, dumping rubble and dirt over the tracks. A mammoth yellow and black shell took shape.

Behind the snapping jaws, a dozen bulbous eyes stared.

Ada lowered her rifle. It would be like trying to shoot a mountain. She turned and ran on her injured ankle, crying out in pain. She kept hopping, but the beast was gaining easily.

They would never make it to the train cars.

She searched the tracks for a place to hide, but there was nothing within view of her beams. She considered shutting them off, but she doubted that would save her and Jo-Jo. Anything that lived down here doubtless had night vision as acute as the monkey's, and without her lights, she would fall again.

The tunnel curved ahead, and Ada made it around

before the creature caught up with them. Around the bend, she saw the door that she couldn't get open earlier.

Ada hobbled toward it as fast as she could, motioning for Jo-Jo. Using the shoulder stock of her laser rifle, she bashed the handle, but the lock wouldn't give.

Taking a step back, she fired at the door, blasting it open just as the monster came around the corner. Her light captured crablike figures dropping from the bottom of the carapace.

The merely human-size spawn skittered ahead.

Ada moved into the room with Jo-Jo and closed the door, backing away as the first of the babies slammed into the other side.

Frantic, she searched for a way to barricade the door, but the narrow tunnel was empty, and the rickety thing wasn't going to hold for long.

Turning, Ada started toward another door at the end of the long passage, where it seemed to widen. The door was wider and thicker.

And wide open.

Ada brought her rifle up as they approached. Jo-Jo was first inside, ignoring orders to stay back.

By the time Ada entered, the monkey was already halfway across a sizable chamber. Bunks and tables lay thrown about.

This was some sort of bunker.

Ada hobbled over to the door's keypad and pushed a button. It hissed and began to close, clanking, and grinding.

She aimed her rifle at the beasts already surging forward, their red eyes glowing in her lights.

Pulling the trigger, she unleashed a volley of laser bolts into their shells. Green fluid dribbled out of holes in the ravenous creatures charging on their clawed legs.

The door was taking too long to shut. Ada could tell it wasn't going to happen in time. So she kept firing calculated shots as she had been taught, keeping the weapon snug against her shoulder and blasting pieces of shell across the floor.

The two creatures in the lead went down, blocking the passage for a few short moments before the next batch climbed over their dead brethren.

Ada went down on one knee, firing right until the gap was only inches wide. And she kept the barrel up even as the crossbar dropped into place and locked.

The monsters on the other side shrieked and scratched at the door, but they weren't getting through.

And, of course, the downside: Jo-Jo and she were not getting out.

Ada started poking around for another way out. Supply boxes were scattered throughout the room. Rusted food cans and plastic wrappers littered the floor. From what she could tell by the evidence, no one had been here in decades, maybe longer.

A hall led to quarters furnished with beds and desks. Filthy, tattered clothing and torn bags were draped over the beds. Shirts still hung from clotheslines.

Across the dark space, a mess hall was a similar scene of upended tables and chairs. She found a pantry that had long since been stripped clean.

It appeared that a fight had gone down here against the monsters. Empty shell casings lay scattered on the floor. But there were no bodies or even remains.

When she reentered the chamber, the scratching continued outside. It was joined by another sound: a rumbling that seemed to come from the walls themselves.

Ada walked over to them, listening.

She followed the noise down the wall, back to the passage, and into the quarters. Finally, it came from the mess hall.

She turned her light up. As she watched, cracks appeared across the ceiling.

Oh, no . . .

Ada hopped back, but it was already too late.

The roof came crashing down, burying Ada to her chest. Pincer claws broke through the opening and popped up through the dirt.

The juvenile turtle creatures clambered toward Ada. She squirmed and tried to move, but she was well and truly stuck.

Jo-Jo tried to pull on Ada's armored shoulder plate and her free arm.

"Run!" Ada screamed. "Get out of here!"

The creatures climbed over her, slicing the air with their sharp claws. One of them snapped a pincer claw at Jo-Jo, drawing blood from her side.

With a howl of pain, Jo-Jo smacked the beast in the face, crushing the skull. Grabbing another by the pincer, she twisted it off and stabbed it into the face of a third beast.

Jo-Jo tried to fight them back, but the army of monsters kept crawling and falling out of the ceiling. In seconds, they had Ada overwhelmed. She watched helplessly through her visor as they clambered over her helmet.

The howl of pain and anger from her animal friend grew louder and louder.

"Run!" Ada shouted. "GO!"

A claw smacked on her visor, cracking the glass.

She bumped her comm channel on.

The cobweb spread across her visor, threatening to shatter.

She shouted into her headset. "HELP US!"

TWELVE

"Ada, do you copy?" Kade said.

Only static. He had thought he heard something earlier, but maybe it was nothing. According to the beacon on his HUD, she was alive. And so was Jo-Jo.

"Ada, do you copy?" he repeated.

Getting no response, he climbed down from the tower and joined the team, huddled in the former observation post over the canal. Kade had selected the position for the view and the concrete shell that protected them from the wind and acid rain.

He moved his binos to the window frame and glassed the crater he had sailed over on the dive. Ada was underground, but across the canal there was no sign of Magnolia or Edgar, or the monsters that had taken them.

Their beacons were offline, which meant they were either without their armor or dead.

Kade wasn't fooling himself. Captain Rolo was probably right about Edgar and Magnolia having Buckley's chance of being alive now.

After a final scan, Kade whispered to the other divers, "We head to the crater, scope it out, and if it looks safe, I'll go search for the divers."

"I'll go with you," Sofia said.

Gran Jefe didn't offer his services. He was a soldier but still very much a greenhorn.

"Stay close and keep alert," Kade said.

They moved out of the building and into the storm. The rain turned the fine, loose soil into mud, making progress difficult. It also left behind their tracks.

Kade used docking stations along the rim of the canal for cover, moving from one to the next and scanning each time for contacts. Derelict industrial equipment—wrecked cranes and container lifts, ruined derricks—littered the slopes ahead.

He worked his way down into a field of overturned containers for the added cover, but cleared each with his rifle. Inside, the contents were long since raided or washed away by the tsunamis that obliterated this place.

It took an hour to get near the crater. By that time, the rain had stopped. Kade kept an eye on the radiation level, which rose the closer they got to the opening.

He almost didn't see the smaller hole ahead. Gran Jefe reached out and grabbed his arm, stopping him short.

In front of them were dozens of smaller vertical shafts in the ground, all looking quite fresh.

Kade motioned for the divers to spread out through the maze of holes. It didn't take long to find tracks.

He crouched down to inspect the boot prints, which had to be from Team Raptor. But they weren't the only tracks.

Long claw marks gouged in the dirt had filled with water.

"Over here," Sofia said.

She bent down and poked what Kade at first took for a rock. But as he drew near, he saw that it was the shell of a creature with a leathery tail and hard, sharp legs. It had a turtle face with a beak-shaped muzzle.

"Thing's as ugly as a hat full of arseoles," Kade said.

"Huh?" Sofia asked.

"Means very ugly."

"I've seen worse," Sofia replied. "But I've never seen one of these before."

Kade looked over the terrain, imagining the ambush, the divers fleeing.

If Arlo was the only one to get in the sky, it meant that whatever happened had gone down very fast. Now at least, Kade knew what awaited them.

He gave the signal to advance.

The team pushed on to the rim of scree surrounding the large crater. Kade stepped up to the edge and looked over. Using his NVGs, he studied the tunnel with the strangely ridged walls. The bottom was maybe two hundred feet down, with a bowl-shaped floor.

Ada was down there somewhere.

They saved you. Now you gotta save them.

He pulled out a rope with a figure-eight knot clipped to his belt by a screw-gate carabiner.

Gran Jefe took three aluminum stakes and jammed them deep into the dirt, forming a triangle. Then he looped some webbing to equalize the tension, clipped two biners into the webbing, and clipped the rope.

"Keep that line secure, mate," Kade said.

"*No hay problema, güero*," he boomed.

After clipping in to his rappel device, Kade nodded at Sofia and Gran Jefe.

And down the shaft he went, his boots knocking clumps of dirt from the wall. With each push off, he lowered deeper into the darkness.

Halfway down, a crunching sound came from the wall behind him. Then a skittering of hard limbs. He eased the rifle around on its sling to train it on the wall as he rapped down.

Braking the rappel with one hand, he pointed the weapon into a cave in the wall of the shaft. He thought of shining his light inside but decided it wasn't worth the risk. The night-vision optics allowed him to see enough without it anyway.

Looking down, he spotted more horizontal tunnels in the wall of the shaft. Nothing emerged, but he could hear something moving inside.

Rifle in one hand and rope in the other, he rapped past the holes, with the unsettling sensation of being watched.

Miscalculating his next bounce off the wall, he fed a little too much rope through and swung into a tunnel.

Heart pounding, he half expected creatures to scuttle out and tear his legs off. But nothing came, and within seconds he had pushed off again and was rappeling smoothly down the wall. Passing another tunnel, he angled his rifle inside. When again nothing came for him, he rapped the rest of the way to the floor. He stood there a moment, looking around.

Several other passages led away, including one of reinforced concrete. This wasn't just the home of mutant life forms. He was near a former subway station.

He pushed onward, toward the twisted wreckage of an old train knocked on its side. The metal hull was riven open, and seats lay scattered across the tracks.

From maps of the area, Kade remembered the subway that had run from Panama City, under the canal, to the resorts.

He walked toward it, but the rope brought him up short.

"Kade," Sofia said over the channel. "You down?"

"Aye, but stay put, I'm checking this out."

Reaching down, he unclipped his rappel device, then started across the open area with his laser rifle roving over the darkness. He could hardly see anything with his NVGs—mostly just outlines.

Ada's beacon seemed to be somewhere in the train tunnel not far ahead, with Jo-Jo close.

He entered through an opening carved by a monster. Stepping over hunks of rubble, he started down the tracks, moving heel to toe, heel to toe. Just the way he was trained to do as a young Hell Diver two decades ago.

Light faded with each step. Soon, not even his NVGs would penetrate the dark void. He resisted the urge to turn on his helmet lamp when he heard what sounded like hard little running feet.

Crouching, he listened for the source, but the sound seemed to grow distant, as if its source was moving away.

He kept moving until he got within a few feet of where the beacons should be. There, he turned off the NVGs and activated his helmet light. He raked the beam over the tracks and platform, back and forth.

A sticky trail snaked away from the tracks, toward a crack in the concrete. He shined his light on the gooey ribbed body of a worm easily ten feet long, with an eyeless T-shaped head.

That head swung around toward him, opening a mouth full of needle-sharp teeth.

Kade backed away, but the creature seemed just as afraid of him. It slithered into a hole in the cracked concrete wall.

He turned off his lights and, with rifle up, stepped carefully to the toppled train car. Stepping up to the back door, he stopped and looked at his HUD.

Both beacons were ten feet ahead.

"*Ada*," he whispered. "Ada, you in there?"

Something stirred, followed by a shuffling sound.
Kade halted at the back entrance to the car.

Taking one hand off his rifle, he reached up and
flicked on his helmet light. The beam lit up the back
of the train car, capturing the spiky black hair of a
large creature hunched in the doorway.

A pair of saucer eyes stared at him.

"Holy shit." He took a quick step back as the
monkey hopped out of the car. It reached out to Kade
as if to show him something.

"Where's Ada?" he whispered.

The creature led him into the train car, the beams
guiding them inside the rusted compartment. Upon
entry, Kade stopped and angled his light at gooey
orange lumps covering a body.

He checked out the rest of the train car and found
skeletal remains on the floor and seats. A body hung
from the ceiling by some sort of cartilaginous net.

Kade tried to make sense of it. Was this some sort
of feeding ground?

Whimpering, Jo-Jo went over to the body, which
had to be Ada. He ran his light down the saffron-hued
lumps and found armored legs protruding from the
mass.

"Bugger me," he breathed. "What in the dingo
shit . . ."

Slinging the rifle, he drew his combat knife and
leaned down.

"Ada," he said.

He shined his light over the gelatinous substance

covering her upper body. He touched one of the lumps with his knife. Inside, a tiny black embryo no larger than a tadpole squirmed and wriggled in a sac of fluid.

Kade reared back. "*Shit a brick!*" he whispered.

She was covered in some sort of eggs, and she was alive, just not conscious.

Using his blade, he began gently scraping the lumps away. Several burst open, releasing their contents. He took a moment to examine a slithering yellow body. As soon as the sac encasing it burst, the creature writhed and died with a faint hissing noise.

Jo-Jo grew frantic, waving a clawed hand as if to tell him to stop.

But Kade continued cutting away the lumps, eventually freeing her torso and chest. With each cut, the creature tried to stop him.

"She'll be right," Kade whispered, using slang.

He leaned down and finished removing the eggs around her neck and helmet.

"Ada, wake up," he said.

Upon closer inspection, Kade saw the reason she wasn't answering. The eggs had gotten inside her cracked visor.

Jo-Jo moved closer to him as he twisted her helmet and pulled it off.

As soon as it was off, Ada's eyes met his.

Kade wasn't sure what to do at first. The egg sacs clung to her face, so that only her eyes, nose, and part of her mouth were visible.

"Ada," he whispered.

She blinked rapidly.

"Ada, can you hear me?"

Her blue lips moved slightly, but no words came.

"It's okay, I'm here to help," he said.

Kade painstakingly removed the eggs attached to her face and in her hair. She was breathing rapidly but still wasn't moving, as if her body was paralyzed.

"Blink if you can understand me," Kade said.

She blinked.

"Blink if you can't move anything," he said.

She blinked again.

Kade nodded. "I'm going to put your helmet back on, okay?"

Another blink.

He twisted it back on her head and reached down to pick her up.

"Better yet, Jo-Jo can carry you," Kade said.

The monkey was smart enough to figure out his gestures and picked Ada up. They left the train, treading on the removed sacs, which hissed as the embryos burst.

A staccato clicking sounded in the distance, followed by a rumbling.

Kade jumped out the back of the train and motioned for Jo-Jo to follow him back toward the main chamber.

"Sofia, Gran Jefe, do you copy?" Kade whispered.

"Copy," Sofia replied.

"Get ready, I've found Ada and Jo-Jo," Kade said. "Send down a second rope."

"On it."

Kade reached the chamber a few minutes later, flitting his lights around the vertical shaft for contacts. The rumbling grew louder, shaking the ground under his feet.

Something was coming. Something very big.

He clipped the dangling rope to Ada, who was still draped over Jo-Jo's shoulder.

"Ada's secure," Kade said over the comm.

The rope pulled up, lifting Ada off Jo-Jo's shoulders.

Kade had no idea how he was going to get the monkey out of here, but he wasn't leaving her behind.

Sofia tossed another rope down. Kade grabbed it and had just clipped the biner to his belt when the rocky floor beneath his boots pushed upward.

He didn't even have time to reach over to Jo-Jo as a quake shook the shaft, dislodging chunks of dirt and rocks.

Jo-Jo took off running.

With Sofia and Gran Jefe busy pulling up Ada on a Z pulley, Kade was on his own. He jumped onto the muddy wall and started jumaring up the fixed rope with his ascenders.

As he made his way up the wall, the ground seemed to be rising up toward his boots.

It took him a moment to realize that the "ground" was actually a shell.

"Bloody hell," he stuttered.

He clambered up the wall as a chitinous shell the size of a small airship rose out of the ground.

Looking up, he saw that Ada was almost at the top. But there was something else along the walls around her. Orange shells popped out of the holes he had passed on the way down. Claws reached out, snapping at her.

Kade planted his boots and fired at the closest turtle beasts, forcing them back into the tunnels, as Gran Jefe and Sofia cranked Ada upward to safety.

The shots announced his location to more of the shell abominations climbing out of holes around the shaft.

Below, pincer claws big enough to snap a man in half snaked up toward him.

He felt a sudden slack on the line and fell a body length down the wall before it caught and he was jerked upward, just out of the reach of the nightmarish claws.

Looking up, he saw Gran Jefe, pulling his rope up with no pulleys, using only a pair of jumars. No one else in the Vanguard Islands possessed such strength. Sofia stood at the rim of the tunnel, aiming her laser rifle and picking off the beasts skittering over the walls.

Several lost their footing and fell, to splat against their mother's hard shell. The beast let out a roar so loud that Kade's ears rang.

Above him, Sofia vanished, then returned a moment later with Gran Jefe's rifle.

She aimed it at Kade.

"What are you doing?" he shouted, bringing a hand up to shield his face.

A projectile thumped past him, and something exploded below his boots. He looked down as two more grenades thumped out of the rifle and slammed into the massive shell. Orange and green fluid spattered his boots.

The creature shrieked louder still and sank back to the ground, dragging itself into a dark tunnel.

He tried to calm his breath as Gran Jefe kept working the jumars, hoisting him to the top. Near the top, Kade hooked his heel over the rim and pulled himself over, rolling onto his back in the dirt.

Chest heaving, he lay there, partially in shock.

"Where's Jo-Jo?" Sofia asked.

"Ah, bugger me!" Kade said, shooting up to his feet.

He had forgotten about the monkey.

The three divers looked over the edge at the shaft, its dirt wall alive with the scuttling turtle beasts.

They had awakened a nest, and Jo-Jo was trapped inside it.

* * * * *

Raven's Claw plowed through the violent seas, water splashing over its bow and surging across the weather deck.

X searched the waters from the island, trying

to keep it together. There was still no word about Michael and the others who were missing.

His heart held on to the thread of hope that they were still alive out there, but with these swells, it seemed impossible.

You can't give up, X.

He rubbed his scruffy beard as the warship approached the last known location of the fishing trawler *Mako*. It was four in the morning, and the storm winds were gusting up to sixty-five miles per hour.

Rain slid down the windows, making it almost impossible to see even with the mounted spotlights raking over the water.

"I don't see it," he said.

Captain Two Skulls gripped the wheel's spokes in his weathered hands. "King Xavier, I believe we're too late," he said.

"What the fuck were they doing out here?" X asked. "I thought we ordered all trawlers into the hangar."

"They were summoning the octopus gods," said Steve. "I consider myself a Cazador now, but even I don't believe in the power of the octopus."

"I wish it were true," X said. "We could use a little juju right about now."

"Over here!" yelled a spotter with binoculars.

X ran over to the viewport.

The spotlights flitted across the waves, over floating storm debris: a wooden door, a barrel, a buoy, and what looked like . . .

"Get a rescue team out now!" X bellowed.

An alarm sounded on the warship, and crew members in life jackets fought through the winds to get rescue ropes into the water. Secured by lines of their own, the men and women worked carefully.

X would be down there with them, but this was something he couldn't do with only one arm. He used the downtime to gather his thoughts.

Everything seemed to be coming down around him in a single night. The crops were being damaged and destroyed, they had lost half their oil, and now they had lost another of their precious fishing boats.

The losses made the Hell Divers' mission to Panama all the more important. If they brought back promising recon from the canal, then he would take it to the council and launch *Octopus*, *Ocean Bull*, and *Raven's Claw* on the expansion mission as soon as possible.

He stepped up closer to the window, watching the rescue.

Twenty minutes after arriving, the crews had pulled up only two fishers.

"We got to keep moving," said Captain Two Skulls. "If there were more, we would have found them."

"How many were on that vessel?" X asked.

"She had a crew of thirty, sir," Steve said.

X bowed his head.

Radio reports flooded in on damage to rigs, and a few minutes later, he gave the order to move on from the rescue.

Raven's Claw pushed on through the storm to their next destination: the trading post rig. He could see it easily in the distance because its roof was burning.

"Those must be propane tanks," Steve said. "They'll burn themselves out soon."

X studied the flames through a pair of binoculars. The fires raged despite the pouring rain, and the fire crew assigned to the rig wasn't answering the radio.

He put on his jacket and secured the goggles over his eyes.

"King Xavier, perhaps you should let the rescuers take care of this one," said General Forge.

X looked at him.

"Very well, sir," Forge said.

They boarded the rig a few minutes later, following a team wearing breathers to protect them from the smoke. Slayer and his Barracudas were with them.

Bromista cracked a joke in Spanish on the long slog up the internal stairwell. Something about getting his nuts burned for the second time in his life, prompting a muffled laugh from the squad. X didn't join in the laughter.

Flashlight beams speared through the dark passages. On the sixth deck, Slayer stopped on point. X could smell smoke now.

The men with breathers wore heavy fire jackets and moved ahead of the others.

"Stay back here until we give the all clear," Slayer said.

X remained behind with a group of rescuers, Steve, and General Forge.

Their radios went silent for the first time in hours, leaving them in a strangely peaceful silence.

X's thoughts kept returning to Michael. "I hope you're right about miracles, General," he said.

"Miracles are—"

Before Forge could finish his sentence, a loud boom echoed through the rig. Dust and bits of acoustic insulation drifted down from the overhead, and the shaking kept up for several seconds.

"The hell was that?" X said.

The radio on his vest crackled to life. It was Slayer, with a panicked edge to his voice.

"We need help on level seven! Bring up more breathers and bottled air!"

X spoke to the men behind him. Two took off back the way they had come, returning to *Raven's Claw* for more supplies.

"Come on," X said to the others.

Forge led the way down the passage. Minutes later, their flashlights found Slayer and his team.

The group huddled around several bodies on the deck outside a closed hatch.

X could smell the burned flesh as he approached. These were the firefighters who had called for support. But this was still two levels below the trading post.

"Son of a bitch," Steve said. "This wasn't just propane tanks. A gas line must have ruptured."

"Why weren't they shut off?" X asked.

Steve hesitated as a wail of agony echoed in the passage.

"Steve, why weren't they—"

"Someone must have forgot. I don't know, King Xavier."

Someone fucked up bad, X thought.

But what mattered right now was getting the line shut off and helping the injured.

X shined his flashlight at the firefighters, checking for signs of life. The four here were all dead.

"Medic!"

X sprang to his feet at the distant cry for help. It was Slayer, and he sounded close.

They followed his voice three passages over and found Slayer with his men, leaning down next to six injured workers. Two were still moving, writhing in agony from burns across their flesh. The others were already gone.

"Out of the way! Move, move!" yelled a medic. "*¡Vámonos!*"

A group of three rushed into the passage. X got out of the way to let them pass.

"We're going to get you out of here, Manny," Slayer said, lifting one of the injured firefighters by his gear. Bromista was also bending down over the guy.

"You have to shut off the gas lines," Manny said to them. "If you don't, this rig is . . ."

He gave a deep, racking cough.

"We'll get them shut down, don't worry," Slayer said.

A medic unfolded a stretcher and set it beside Manny as Bromista got out of the way.

"He's right, King Xavier," Steve said. "We don't shut off those lines, and this rig is toast."

X wasn't sure how that was possible, until he thought about where they were—in the center of the rig. The fire wouldn't consume just the inside; it threatened to blow the entire midsection out, which could destroy the integrity of the entire station.

"What the hell are we waiting for?" X asked. He slung an air tank over his shoulder and put the mask over his face.

Steve, Slayer, and General Forge all knew by now not to argue. They had brought their own tanks, and with a team of three others, they pushed onward.

"Take care of my brother," Slayer called out.

Manny raised a defiant fist as the medics lifted him onto a stretcher.

"The gas lines all have their own shutoff valves," Steve said. "Should be this way, but we have to pass through some dangerous areas."

"Lead the way," X said.

Steve opened a hatch ahead. On the other side, more bodies littered the deck. These were burned to charcoal and still simmered audibly.

X took in a deep breath of the compressed air. He knew he was risking his hide now, but it beat sitting back at the command center in the capitol tower, listening to all the pleas for help.

He ran after the others until they got to the mechanical room.

"There," Steve said. "We can shut off the main lines here. There should be shutoff valves in each compartment."

"Let's split up," X said.

The teams separated, Steve and General Forge following X. Smoke choked the passages on the way to the mechanical room, making it almost impossible to see even with the lights.

X found the door and checked the handle with his glove. It was warm to the touch, but that was normal.

He cracked the door and, when no fire billowed out, opened it and stepped inside. So far, the mechanical room was clear of fire. Steve rushed over to a valve, pulled a wrench from his belt, and began twisting it.

"Got it," he huffed.

"Okay, let's keep moving," X said. Back in the passage, his radio crackled.

"All the lines are off," Slayer confirmed. "Now we can start putting out fires."

They left the mechanical room and set off back into the hallway.

As Forge turned the corner, the passage vibrated. A split second later, a deep explosion thumped through the center of the rig.

"What was that?" he cried.

"Must have been a room that filled with gas and somebody made a spark," Steve said.

Screams in the distance told X what had happened. One of the other crews had been in the blast radius.

X ran down the passage, his light bobbing in the thin smoke. They got to the next hatch, opened it, and were hit by a draft of superheated air.

Down the hallway, flames burned and bodies lay sprawled, some still on fire.

X went toward them. A hand yanked him back. When Forge pulled him into the passage, he saw why.

A propane tank hissed, sending flames dancing across the overhead and passage walls. Several armored figures broke through the cloud of smoke. One of them was Bromista, his arm around Slayer, who was limping.

"It's going to blow!" Slayer yelled. "Close the hatch!"

More Barracudas followed, some of them carrying the injured.

When most of them were through, General Forge closed the hatch.

"What are you doing!" X screamed. "We have to save them!"

"No." Forge shook his head. "King Xavier, unless you want to end up like my comrades, we need to go now. This is no longer a rescue mission."

A scream came from the other side of the hatch, and someone pounded on it.

"HELP!" they shouted.

"We have to open it!" X yelled.

General Forge stepped in front of him, his goggles inches away from X.

"We need you, King Xavier," he said gravely. "We need you alive. You open that hatch, and we're dead—all of us. We have to suffocate those flames."

The smoke swirled around them as the Barracudas carried the injured away, but X stood his ground with Steve and the general.

"This is what Rhino would have done, too," Forge said. "He died saving you, and I will, too, if that's what it takes. You want me to go in there, I will, but you get out of here now!"

"I'll help them," Steve said. "Give me your fire jackets."

The general and X both looked at the weaponsmith.

"Do it now!" Steve shouted.

X and Forge shucked off their fire jackets and handed them to Steve, who tied them around himself.

"Now, get back!" he yelled.

Steve turned and waved at them. "GO NOW!"

They turned the corner, losing sight of him, but the screams grew louder when he opened the hatch.

X stopped halfway down the next passage, sweat dripping off his body. He took in a breath from his mask and stared back into the smoke haze.

Shouting, then cries of pain, then footsteps.

A moment later, a figure broke through the smoke. It was Steve, carrying an injured man. X and Forge ran over as the two collapsed on the deck.

Steve pulled off the two extra fire jackets, both badly singed, and handed them back to X and Forge.

"Put them back on," he said. "You might need them yet."

The seventy-year-old got to his feet, grunting, and nodded at X.

"Come on, gentlemen," he said. "We still have fires to put out."

THIRTEEN

The distant explosions had brought a smile to Magnolia's face when she first heard them. Sofia's voice over the comms made that smile wider yet.

The other divers had come to the rescue.

Magnolia and Edgar were on their way to meet them. In tow was the teenager, bound with the same chains he had used on the Hell Divers. The tables had turned. He was now their prisoner, and he was not happy about it.

The chains clanked as they led him away from the canal, toward the field of craters. He kept trying to pull away, but Edgar had a good grip on the chains.

"Stop," he said. "Or I'll knock you out and carry you."

The kid didn't seem to understand a word of it, and he yanked on the chains again.

Edgar yanked back and raised a fist.

This the kid seemed to understand, and the beaked helmet looked down in an attitude of submission.

A crackling sounded over the comms, followed by the smooth voice of a man who had saved her life once already.

"Commander Katib, where the hell are you?" Kade asked.

"We're about ten minutes out," Magnolia said. "If you're attacked, get in the air. Don't wait for us."

"Copy that, but we got . . . is missing . . . and . . . not conscious . . ."

Loud static blotted out the rest.

"Kade," Magnolia said, stopping. "Kade, come again."

This time, she heard the message loud and clear. Jo-Jo was missing, and Ada was unconscious and paralyzed.

"I'll explain when you get here," Kade said.

Magnolia fell into a run, and Edgar pulled on the youngster, who tripped, regained his balance, and ran after them.

The trio worked their way through a maze of containers. A light rain fell, turning the ground into a mixture of mud and grit.

As they advanced, Magnolia checked the radiation numbers. They were about the same as before, maybe a bit higher. The readings reminded her that she likely had been exposed to a dose significant enough to make her sick, or perhaps worse.

She would deal with that when the time came, but right now she had to get Ada to a doctor and find Jo-Jo.

An electronic shriek pierced the darkness as they neared the crater.

The kid jerked hard on the chains, nearly pulling Edgar to the ground.

"Son of a bitch," Edgar said. He yanked back, knocking the kid off his feet and on his back with a thud.

Magnolia bent down and helped him up. She wasn't sure why, but she had empathy for the kid, and hurting him wasn't going to help anything.

She turned to the skyline, where electronic wails resonated through the skeletal buildings. Zooming in with her rifle scope, she glassed the ruins. Leathery, hairless flesh flapped past the sights. She was looking at the frayed wings of a male Siren.

"Shit. We're about to have more problems," she muttered.

The kid spoke rapidly in an unknown language. He probably couldn't see the beasts, but like Magnolia, he knew that electronic-sounding oscillation of their voices and had learned to associate it with terror.

"Move it," Magnolia said.

She stayed next to the kid and ran after Edgar. They were out in the open now, away from the shipping containers, and nearing a flat stretch that they had to cross to get to the other divers.

Magnolia eyed the sky as she ran. The abominations of nature had changed course and were now flapping toward the canal.

"They know we're here," she said.

They ran harder, and now the kid was cooperating, keeping up the pace.

"There they are," Edgar said, pointing toward the other divers. The group huddled about a thousand feet from the rim of a vast crater, behind a shipping container on its side. When Magnolia got there, Kade was crouched by Ada, with Gran Jefe and Sofia holding security.

They both raised their weapons as Magnolia and Edgar approached with their prisoner.

"What in the hell is this thing?" Sofia asked.

"Not a thing," Magnolia said. "It's a young man."

"If you can call him that," Edgar said.

"He lives out here?" Sofia asked.

"We don't know much about him, but we will once we get him to the ship," Magnolia said.

Sofia walked over. "Captain Rolo won't like you bringing back a prisoner."

"*¿Eres Cazador?*" Gran Jefe asked the kid, who didn't respond.

"I'm serious, Mags," Sofia said. "He didn't even want us coming after you guys."

Magnolia cursed under her breath.

The old bastard was going to leave us down here? Fuck him.

She hurried over to Kade and Ada, crouching down.

"What happened to her?" Magnolia asked.

"Those turtle things covered her in eggs and now she can't move, but she can hear us," Kade said. "She blinked at me."

"You're sure?"

"No doubt in my mind."

"And Jo-Jo's missing?"

"She took off during the last attack."

Magnolia looked around the rolling, rub-ble-strewn terrain, but Kade pointed to the crater.

"She's down there," he said.

The electronic wailing of the Sirens grew closer, and Sofia aimed her rifle at the sky.

"Hostiles at three o'clock, just below the clouds," she said.

Magnolia saw a vee of the monsters sailing closer, keeping high in the sky as they scanned the terrain with their radar.

One suddenly let out an otherworldly wail, the pitch rising and falling like an emergency siren. The noise sent a chill through Magnolia.

She put a hand on Ada to comfort her. "You're going to be okay," she said. "Hang on. We're taking you home."

"What's the plan?" Kade asked.

Magnolia hated doing it, but they couldn't search for Jo-Jo. Her beacon was over a mile away, some-where underground.

"It's safer to get Ada into the air than move her," Magnolia said.

"I'll take her," Kade said.

A faint groan came from Ada, and Magnolia leaned down. She was trying to move her lips to say something, but Magnolia couldn't make it out.

"Ja . . ."

Magnolia realized then, Ada didn't want them to leave her animal.

"We'll come back for her," Magnolia said. "We have to get you to the ship, see a doc."

"Jo . . ."

"I'm sorry," Magnolia said. She stood, guilt setting in as she looked at Ada, who was blinking rapidly. She knew how much Ada cared about the animal, but they couldn't risk human lives to save a monkey, not with the Sirens and hybrid turtles out here.

"Edgar, you want me to take the kid?" Magnolia asked.

"I got him," Edgar replied.

Magnolia walked over to them and pointed at the sky.

"We're going up there," she explained. "You're coming with. Okay?"

The beaked helmet didn't move.

She snorted. There was no use explaining anything.

"Edgar, you hold on to him tight," Magnolia said. "Use a locking biner. I don't want to lose him."

Kade and Sofia helped Ada sit up, and with Gran Jefe's help, they got her on her feet. Sofia made a web harness for Ada, securing her to Kade.

Magnolia pointed as their prisoner watched.

"This is what we're going to do with you," she said.

The kid seemed to understand and backed away, shaking his head.

Out of nowhere, Edgar hammered him in the side of the helmet with his fist. The boy crumpled to the ground.

"Edgar!" Magnolia snapped.

"Only fair—he knocked us out first."

Edgar picked the kid up. "Besides, less squirming this way."

"Okay, we're good to go," Kade confirmed.

"Edgar, you and Kade go first," Magnolia said. "The rest of us will cover you."

Reaching over his shoulder, Kade tapped his booster. The helium balloon exploded from the canister and rose into the air.

It whisked him off the ground with Ada limp against him. She was still trying to protest, begging them not to leave Jo-Jo.

"I'm sorry," Magnolia said.

Edgar went next, with their prisoner, who also hung limp in his harness.

Raising her rifle, Magnolia aimed at the vee of Sirens. Ten of the pale abominations flapped toward the crater. She sighted up the lead beast and moved her finger to the trigger.

Their alien calls echoed through the night as they broke formation to scan for prey.

Kade and Edgar had moved into the cloud cover without being detected.

"Gran Jefe, you're next," Magnolia said.

The big man fired his booster. The helium balloon filled, plucking him off the ground, pulling him skyward as Magnolia and Sofia covered his ascent.

"Thanks for diving down to this hellhole," Magnolia said.

"You're my best *amigocha*—what did you think I would do, leave you?"

"Did Captain Rolo really want you to?"

A Siren shriek cut her off, and she ducked instinctively. One by one, the monsters peeled off the formation and dived toward the two women.

Magnolia led the first one in her sights. "Hold your fire until they get close," she said.

The beasts rocketed toward the ground, shrieking as one. As if in answer, the earth beneath them rumbled.

Magnolia glanced down, then pushed Sofia toward the shipping container. They ducked behind the rusted metal box.

"Get ready to run," Magnolia said.

"What? Run?" Sofia asked. "We can take them . . ."

Her words trailed off at the violent shake beneath her feet. The formation of Sirens tried to pull up as the mounded dirt rolled aside and four sets of orange claws pushed up out of the ground.

The creatures flapped away—all but one that didn't pull up fast enough. The massive pincers were quicker, snatching the Siren from the sky.

"NOW!" Magnolia said.

She took off running with Sofia as the yellow-domed monster clambered up onto the surface, shedding great clods of soil and dust.

After running a quarter-mile, Magnolia gave the order to launch into the sky. They hit their boosters and were whisked up off the ground.

Below them, a giant pincer brought the hapless Siren to the gaping beaked jaws. The electronic shrieking grew more frantic, then abruptly ended.

"That's a different one," Sofia said over the comm.

"What do you mean?"

"Gran Jefe did a number on the first one with his grenade launcher. That one down there is not the same beast."

Magnolia stared in amazement as they sailed over the Panama Canal. The sector wasn't just high in radiation, it was home to a variety of mutant monsters.

And somehow, the teenager who had captured her had survived it all.

She looked up at the storm roiling above them. They would get their prisoner back to the ship and, with some linguistic help from Timothy, have a conversation about how he managed to survive so long on the surface. His knowledge and experience would enable them to return and take the canal with the Cazador navy—and, with luck, find Jo-Jo. The monkey was born and grew up in a place like this. She would find a way to survive.

Magnolia ascended to the launch-bay doors of the airship *Vanguard*. They opened up, allowing her and Sofia to maneuver their balloons into the chamber.

The doors closed under their feet, and Magnolia got out of her harness, dropping a foot and a half to the deck. Inside the glass dome, antiseptic antirad mist sprayed the two divers.

The decontamination unit finally opened to a sight of two militia soldiers armed with crossbows, flanking Captain Rolo. He stood there, hands behind his back, looking stern and imperious.

The other divers had already gone, along with their prisoner.

Magnolia stepped out with Sofia.

"Commander Katib, good to see you made it back," Rolo said. "Unfortunately, we're going to have to put you into quarantine for the trip back to the islands."

"To the islands? We're headed back already?" Magnolia asked.

"I'm afraid there's some bad news," he said. "That storm was worse than we feared. We lost *Blood Trawler*, and apparently, Michael Everhart and Rodger Mintel were on board."

* * * * *

X stood at the top of the capitol tower, Miles at his side, gazing out over the Vanguard Islands as the sun rose. It was hard to fathom that the tranquil sea had risen to twenty-foot walls last night. The last storm clouds melted into the invisible barrier, leaving a scene of devastation in their wake.

Every rig had taken damage, and the scribes would soon start collecting data on crop damage.

What X knew so far was worrisome. Fifty-one people were confirmed missing, including Michael, Rodger, and Alfred. Twenty-five were confirmed dead from fires, smoke, and drowning.

The *Mako* had sunk, and so had *Blood Trawler*, but it was still too early to know whether the lost oil would taint their fishing waters.

What X did know for certain was that they were frighteningly low on gas.

Below, a dozen boats of different shapes and sizes waited on the piers. More were being lowered to the water from their lifts in the enclosed port, to help with rescue and rebuilding efforts.

On the horizon, two construction boats were already sailing toward the trading post rig, which was still smoking. The clank of armor preceded the gruff voice of General Forge.

"King Xavier, we have news from Captain Rolo."

X turned slightly but kept gazing out over the sparkling sea.

"The *Vanguard* is on its way back to the islands," Forge said. "I'm told they have a prisoner with them, a human they discovered at the canal."

"A Cazador from the *Sea Sprite*?"

"No, they never found that vessel. This man is from another far-off land."

The news gave X a hint of hope in a time of despair. "And the divers?" he asked.

"Arlo Wand was severely injured, as was Ada Winslow, but they are alive, King Xavier."

X nodded, trying to keep his emotions in check.

He had a soft spot for Ada despite her horrific crime. She had survived her exile, helped save the islands, and served as a Hell Diver to atone. Hearing she was hurt added to X's unhappiness.

"Anything else?" he asked.

"This is all I have heard, my king."

X nodded, and General Forge backed away.

For the next few minutes, X remained in the same position, staring off toward the horizon, wondering if Michael, Rodger, and Alfred could still be alive out there somewhere.

Pedro had diverted all weather drones to searching for them, now that the worst of the storm had passed. But they couldn't afford the fuel for search vessels when they could be anywhere.

X had to be diplomatic while at the same time husbanding their dwindling resources. He couldn't send the entire fleet off to look for three men who were probably already dead.

The thought pained him, but it was reality.

They needed their vessels to help repair the islands, and gas was now more precious than ever before.

He stepped away from the balcony, feeling a deep dread in the marrow of his old bones. Miles sensed his unease and nudged his leg.

"It's okay, boy," X said.

But that was a lie. Everything was falling apart, and it had happened in a single night. This was precisely why they must expand and create outposts.

El Pulpo was right—something X had never thought he would say. And it wasn't just el Pulpo. His predecessors had also expanded with outposts in the Caribbean and along the continental coasts.

X took in a long breath of fresh air, trying to invigorate himself for another long day of agonizing work. This was the burden of being king: overseeing the lives of so many and being responsible for those who died.

He patted his leg, and Miles got up, following him across the roof. They went to the elevator cart, where Ton and Victor waited. They looked exhausted after staying up all night with X in the rescue effort.

He would give anything for a stim pill right now.

A nip of shine would be nice, too, or a jug of wine.

But those days were behind him.

He took the elevator down to the marina, which was a hive of activity as people gathered to clean up and rebuild. He spied Layla's blond pigtails hanging down her back, and as she turned, there was Bray, tucked in a pouch at her chest.

She had two volunteers: Shelly, who had served as head seamstress on the *Hive*, and Katherine, the widow of former captain and Hell Diver Les Mitchells. They were preparing to head out in the *Sea Wolf*.

The cage set down, and X opened the doors and trotted off toward the piers.

Imulah spotted him and walked over, holding up a clipboard. "King Xavier!" he shouted.

Ton and Victor kept close to X as he moved

through the crowds. There were people from all societies here. People from Rio de Janeiro, the Cazadores, sky people, and the survivors from Kilimanjaro. But today X didn't see differences in race or cultural traditions.

He saw citizens of the Vanguard Islands. All of them prepared to help their fellow humans.

X had considered saying some words this morning, but these people didn't need to hear what he had to say. That would come soon enough. They had work to do.

X moved through the crowd, wearing shorts, T-shirt, sandals, and the Marine Corps baseball cap with its eagle, globe, and anchor.

He remembered their motto, "*Semper fidelis*"—always loyal. Last night, he had been forced to break one of their cardinal rules. He had left a man behind.

He walked over to Layla as she supervised the loading of the *Sea Wolf*. Bray was sleeping.

Shelly and Katherine bowed slightly to X, who frowned at their formality.

"I'm going after him," Layla said, stowing the last duffel. "He's alive. I know it."

"Take Ton," X said. "He can help you with the sails."

Bray opened his eyes, squinting into the sunlight to look at X.

"Hey, little guy," X said. He gave the child his fingertip to squeeze.

"What about the Hell Divers?" Layla asked. "Have you heard from them yet?"

"They're on their way back," X said.

"Does Magnolia know?"

"I imagine so."

Layla handed Bray to Katherine as a voice called out. "I'm coming with!"

A girl ran past X and hopped onto the boat. It was Les and Katherine's nine-year-old daughter. She had seen more than her fair share of suffering over the past few years, after losing her older brother in a dive, and then Les on the mission to Tanzania.

"Phyl, I told you to stay here!" Katherine yelled.

"I want to help find Michael," Phyl said.

X nodded at Ton, who hopped aboard the *Sea Wolf.*

"Be careful," X said.

X made it only a few steps down the dock before Imulah stopped him to hand out his infamous clipboard.

"These are the current tallies, King Xavier," he said.

X looked at the figures as he walked toward his boat. The scribes were already radioing in crop information from the other rigs.

"No," he breathed upon reading a single line.

Almost a total loss . . .

X swallowed hard. He had to see this for himself.

"Bring up my boat," he said, handing the clipboard back to Imulah.

The *One-Armed Bandit* was ready to go. A team of Cazadores stood at attention as he boarded.

X went up the ladder to the boat's command

center and fired the engines as Victor cast off the mooring rope. He reversed away from the dock, drawing alongside the *Sea Wolf*. He waved to Layla, who was behind the wheel. Phyl had lost the argument and was on the deck holding Bray and standing next to Shelly, who would look after them.

Ton looked up from inspecting the sails and rigging and waved to X, who nodded back. Then X pushed the throttle down, powering away from the capitol rig toward the main agriculture rig, where he was needed most right now. His heart tugged at him with every beat to join the hunt for the castaways, but he had chosen to accept the burden of leadership, and that meant caring for all his people equally.

The boat skipped and banged across the wave tops, the engines purring with restrained power.

"Sir," came a voice.

It was Victor.

"I'm sorry about your son," he said.

"My son . . ." X blanked for a moment before realizing that his friend and guard was referring to Michael. "Thanks," he said.

The ride to the rig gave X plenty of time to think— enough time for the feeling of dread to sink into despair.

A warm tear ran down his face.

He wiped it away and motioned for Miles to join him.

For the next hour, X toured the damaged plots and orchards with his dog. Tarps flapped in the wind, exposing areas where the dirt had been ripped away.

In other sections, cornstalks were broken or ripped out entirely.

X bent down and picked up a handful of moist dirt. The future of the islands had been in this dirt. Now it was gone.

His radio crackled.

"King Xavier, this is Pedro, do you copy?"

"Copy, go ahead, over."

"One of our drones picked up beacon from a lifeboat."

X stared at the radio. Could it be possible?

"On my way," he said.

X dashed across the ruined field, Miles hot on his heels, and into a stairwell. The dog wagged his tail, barking playfully. When they got to the boat, Victor whipped the mooring line off the cleat and jumped aboard. X roared away from the piers and out across open water, sending Miles sliding across the deck.

"Sorry, boy," X said.

The dog picked himself up and jumped up on the captain's chair as X stood at the wheel.

"Layla, do you copy?" X said into the radio.

"Copy."

"Pedro picked up a beacon. I'll send you the coordinates."

"Is it him?"

"No one knows," X said. "Go ahead and run the engines, though."

"Thank you, X."

"See you in a few minutes."

X buried the throttle the rest of the way as they flew past the trading post rig. The construction ship was already there. A fleet of smaller boats, some of them without engines, were already docked.

On every level, people were hard at work, cleaning up the mess on the rig. They would rebuild, but to survive they would need food.

One thing at a time.

Thirty minutes later, the *One-Armed Bandit* broke through the barrier between light and darkness. Lightning flashed across the black vault of sky, and thunder rattled the cockpit fittings. The water began to slap against the bow as it shot over the waves.

When he arrived at the stated coordinates, a Cazador naval speedboat was there. He raked his overhead beams across the water, but it wasn't until he steered around it that he saw the orange lifeboat.

Victor joined X on the deck. "It is from *Blood Trawler*," he said.

X nodded, staring at the orange hull, praying that Michael, Rodger, and Alfred were inside.

Lights from another boat hit their position, and X brought up his hand to shield his eyes from the glare. The *Sea Wolf* bobbed up and down on approach.

"Michael!" Layla screamed.

She stood on the bow, gripping the rail as Ton, behind the wheel, nudged the boat close.

X felt his gut tighten. Something was wrong. If Michael and the others were on board, why hadn't they popped the hatch?

Layla swung a leg over the railing and looked ready to jump when X called out. "Wait. Let us secure the boat!"

"No way!" she yelled back.

X waved for Victor to get him a little closer.

When the *Bandit* came alongside, X hopped from the gunwale onto the enclosed lifeboat. Sliding on the wet fiberglass, he fell and very nearly went into the drink. Layla was right there and helped him up.

They clambered over to the hatch. The moment of truth . . .

X hadn't felt his heart pound this hard since he lost his arm.

Layla released the latches, and the hatch popped open.

"Tin!" Layla yelled.

She slid down through the hatch, but X already knew there was no one inside.

He fell to his knees, defeated.

"Tin!" Layla cried. "Rodge . . ."

X let her cry for a moment inside the empty lifeboat, then finally went over and reached down.

"Come on, kid," he said. "They aren't here."

She took his hand and let him pull her out.

X wanted to tell her to keep the faith and not lose hope, but at this point, he couldn't bring himself to lie. Their chances of being alive now were all but nonexistent.

He stood on the deck, scanning the waves.

Where are you, Tin?

FOURTEEN

Kade threw on fatigues and hurried out of the brig as soon as the hatch opened. For the past two hours, he had sat in a small cell during quarantine.

Protocol normally called for a simple spray-down upon return to the airship, but this was something else entirely.

Two militia guards led him away from the brig. The other cells looked empty except for the last one. Kade heard the deep snoring and looked inside as he passed.

Gran Jefe lay on a bed, naked, one massive leg dangling off the side, exposing rather more of himself than Kade would have preferred. He suddenly sat up, scratching his balls.

"*Hola*," he growled. "You guys gonna let me out now?"

The guards both laughed, but the image would forever be seared in Kade's mind.

"Good God, mate, cover yourself!" he said.

"*¿Qué?*"

Kade shook his head and kept walking while one of the guards unlocked the cell and handed Gran Jefe a set of fatigues.

When Kade and Gran Jefe got to the launch bay, Magnolia, Edgar, and Sofia were already there. They looked a bit the worse for wear but were alert.

"Any news on the Vanguard Islands yet?" Kade asked.

"Just that the storm was bad and Michael, Alfred, and Rodger are among the missing," Edgar said.

"I'm sorry," Kade said.

Magnolia simply nodded.

"Knowing my friends, they are alive," Edgar said, giving Magnolia a concerned glance.

"Better believe it," Sofia said. "Those three are pretty hard to kill."

Kade went to Magnolia. "I'm sorry, but don't lose faith," he said.

"I'm not." She glanced up. "Thanks for coming for us."

"No worries, mate. I know you'd do the same." He paused, looking over his shoulder for a minute to see if anyone else was in the launch bay. "So, wanna tell me what's up with the quarantine?"

"We'll show you," Magnolia said.

"What about food? I'm starving," Gran Jefe said.

"Go and eat, then," Sofia said.

Gran Jefe grunted but followed them out of the launch bay.

They headed to the medical ward, which was also quarantined off. Inside, Josh Stamos, a doctor from the airship *Victory*, was dressed in a white CBRN suit.

Arlo was on an operating table, with tubes running to ports in his chest and arms. The doctor lifted a pad covering the wound on his right biceps, revealing pink, inflamed flesh.

"Oh, damn," Kade said.

He moved along the glass panel for a better view. Ada was in the same room, unconscious and lying on a table, with an IV tube in her wrist and a ventilator in her mouth.

"They were infested," Magnolia said. "Dr. Stamos says it's some sort of parasitic annelid worm."

Kade had seen people infected on dives years ago, but he had never seen anything like the eggs he discovered all over Ada.

A voice grumbled behind them.

Gran Jefe wedged himself up between Edgar and the bulkhead, both men staring through the viewport.

Doc Stamos applied a new dressing while they watched.

"So do we know anything more about this guy yet?" Edgar asked. He tilted his head toward the other end of the room.

The teenager that Magnolia had captured was sitting on a bed in an enclosed room, looking out at them. Kade had seen that look before on frightened animals: a mixture of anger and fear.

"I just got out of quarantine, too," Magnolia said.

Footfalls sounded behind them.

They all turned and came to attention as Captain Rolo strode down the passage.

"Any news of the islands?" Magnolia asked him.

"No."

Rolo stopped in front of them, looking at Kade first, then Sofia.

"You disobeyed a direct order," said the captain. He raised a gray brow and glanced at their prisoner. "Not to mention you brought back this hostile creature."

"This young man completes our mission," Magnolia said.

"Come again?" Rolo replied. "I thought you said 'completes.'"

"Our mission was to recon the area, was it not, Captain?" she asked.

Rolo eyed her up and down. "I know damn well what the mission is, and three Hell Divers jeopardized it by disobeying a direct order. I understand you all do things differently than we do, but let me remind you who's in charge."

"Sir, all due respect, but that prisoner holds the key to the Panama Canal and the area that King Xavier wants to expand into," Edgar said. "We brought him back to share his knowledge of the area with us."

Rolo gave Edgar a quick glance, then walked over to Kade and Sofia.

"I knew you'd be trouble," he said to her. "But I expected more from you, Kade."

The captain turned and walked away, saying, "I will have the prisoner escorted to the bridge for interrogation in an hour. Magnolia and Kade are the only ones authorized to speak to him."

"Oh, thank you so much, Captain," Magnolia said sarcastically.

She rolled her eyes as Rolo left.

"He means well," Kade said.

"Yeah, so did Captain Jordan," Magnolia said.

"Who?"

"Just imagine if the Almighty were to breathe life into a two-hundred-pound heap of Siren shit, then add arrogance and a truly foul personality. Then you would have the former captain." She let out a sigh and returned to the window as Doctor Stamos walked over.

He pushed an intercom button, and Kade joined Magnolia at the glass.

"How are they doing?" she asked.

"Arlo is stable now, but he has a fever and a case of necrotizing fasciitis."

"What's that?"

"It's the technical term for flesh-eating bacteria, although this seems to be a new strain. It's working faster than any I've studied. I'm going to have to remove more tissue to save his arm."

"And Ada?"

Stamos shook his helmet. "I'm still running tests, but she is in a coma."

Sofia put a hand on Magnolia's shoulder.

"She will pull through," Sofia said. "Hell, she survived the wastes. She will survive this."

"I'll keep you updated," Stamos said.

"How about our friend?" Magnolia asked.

"He's dehydrated and his body fat is about five percent, but other than that, he's just really dirty," said the doctor. "I'm treating him for body lice and some infections."

"Hard to believe he survived down there," Kade said. He couldn't wait to talk to this kid. There was no telling what he had been through or what parts of the world he had seen during his time on that ship.

An hour later, Kade and Magnolia were on their way to the brig, where the militia had transferred the prisoner to a quarantine cell.

When they got there, the soft glow of a hologram emerged. The ship's AI, Timothy Pepper, flashed a kind smile.

"Hello, Commander Katib and Kade Long," he said politely.

"T, I told you to stop being so damn formal," Magnolia said.

"I apologize, but that is how I was programmed."

Kade had never met the old version of the AI, but this new version had been reset to the original operating system, erasing all memories from the time he had spent with the sky people, and the trauma of losing his family and his own life at the Hilltop Bastion.

From what Kade understood, Timothy didn't

remember his former life as a human, which was probably just as well.

"All right, Timothy, let's see if you can get him to talk," Magnolia said.

The AI's hologram stepped up to the cell door.

The young man huddled in the back of the small cell, clearly frightened of the AI's ghostly image.

"Probably the first time he's seen one," Kade whispered.

Timothy started talking in Mandarin to see if he would understand, but the prisoner remained silent. For the next ten minutes, the AI had no luck at all, even when he switched to Cantonese, Hakka, Fukien, and finally other East Asian languages.

Magnolia reached into a satchel over her back and pulled out an apple. She held it up and gestured to the kid.

"You want this?" she asked, holding it out.

The kid stepped forward, then hesitated.

Magnolia pointed at her chest.

"Magnolia," she said. Then she pointed at the kid.

"Yejun," he replied.

"Ah, that isn't Chinese," Timothy said. "He speaks Korean."

"Good," Kade said. "Now we're getting somewhere."

"Ask him how long he was down there," Magnolia said.

She took out a knife and cut off a hunk of apple, which she tossed through the bars. The kid caught it, stuffed it in his mouth, and held out his hand.

"Tell him I'll give him more if he answers our questions," she said.

Timothy explained, and Yejun replied.

"He says he was down there for the past five years of his life," Timothy said.

Magnolia and Kade exchanged a glance.

"Ask him where the rest of his people are," she asked.

Again Timothy spoke in the foreign tongue.

While they waited for the kid's answer, Kade suddenly wondered if they had stolen this young man from a family or friends.

That thought vanished when Timothy turned to Magnolia and said, "He says he is the last of his tribe."

Magnolia held out another piece of apple.

"I'm sorry," she said. "Tell him that."

"He has a question, too," Timothy said. He shook his head. "Wait. No, that isn't right. It's not a question; it's a request."

"What's that?" Magnolia asked.

Timothy turned his head slightly. "Yejun wants to talk to our leader."

* * * * *

"Keep swimming," Michael said.

"I can't," Rodger replied. "I have to stop. My foot is killing me, and my . . ."

Michael kept swimming in the direction of the Vanguard Islands, the life jacket keeping his head above the water. Rodger rolled onto his back, bobbing up and down over the waves. He had taken off his prosthesis and was treading water with one foot and a stump—no easy feat.

Rodger coughed again. A deep, heavy rattle in his lungs.

"You okay?" Michael called out.

"Yeah. Just need to rest a bit." Rodger kept on his back, still coughing.

Michael paddled over to his friend.

They had abandoned the lifeboat when it burned its last drop of fuel. The sea creature that had checked them out earlier must have moved on for easier prey, for they had seen no sign of it, and Cricket had found no large life forms with its last scan. A welcome reading, to be sure, but Michael wasn't about to relax his vigilance. No one even knew what sorts of mutant beasts may have been disturbed by the hurricane.

Kept afloat by his life vest, he tried not to think of what lurked below. He wondered what stroke and kicking style would be least likely to draw the wrong sort of attention, and finally settled on a modified backstroke using a frog kick and arm movements that stayed below the surface, avoiding any splash.

In his mind, he kept picturing a gigantic shark biting him in half or swallowing him whole. Or a giant octopus wrapping him up and dragging him down into the cold black.

He shook away the thoughts and focused on conserving his physical and mental energy. They had two bottles of fresh water—enough to get them through a day at least—but he was already knackered.

He pulled the dry bag containing Cricket from his vest. According to the digital map, they were still thirty-five miles from the Vanguard Islands. They had swum three miles over the past three hours.

He made himself wait to take a drink. Hoping to forget his thirst for a few moments, he did a life scan with Cricket. It came back negative—nothing near the surface but the two of them.

"How much farther?" Rodger asked.

"Not too far," Michael replied, tucking the droid back into the dry bag.

"Don't lie to me, Tin. You're terrible at it."

"Want some water?"

"Yes, but don't change the subject."

Michael handed him a liter bottle. As Rodger drank, Michael told him the truth.

"Damn son of a . . ." Rodger broke into a new spate of coughing and nearly dropped the bottle.

Michael reached out to hold his hand steady. "Careful, man. That's all we got."

Rodger held it up above the water. "Sorry, I just can't stop coughing."

It was obvious now, the smoke had not been kind to his lungs.

Michael looked up at the lightning storm above them, resting his limbs as Rodger drank.

"We're going to make it," Michael said. "I promise you."

"I trust you."

"You ready?"

"Yeah," Rodger said. "Let's do it."

He handed the bottle back, and Michael took a sip.

Rodger rolled onto his chest. He couldn't see well without his glasses, but then, there wasn't much to see.

After securing the water bottle, Michael kicked and started swimming. It was almost impossible to do a front crawl with the bulky life jacket, which made him even slower. And to make things worse, the salty waves continued to sting his eyes. He chided himself for not grabbing his work goggles before the mission.

For the rest of the morning, as the sun climbed the sky, they kept a rhythm of swim, rest, swim, rest, with a long pause for water. Michael kept charge of the bottles so Rodger wouldn't notice how little Michael was drinking. Then, with the sun at its zenith, the wind shifted several degrees. The stroke of luck gave Michael reassurance when he needed it most. Even the current seemed to be cooperating.

Over the next three hours, they made it another five miles.

"Only thirty to go," Michael called out.

"When will we be able to see the sun again?" Rodger asked.

"I think that's about twenty-three more."

"Maybe Magnolia will be back by the time we get there," Rodger said. "Better get moving—she doesn't like to be kept waiting."

He pulled ahead, swimming faster than Michael had seen him go since they abandoned the lifeboat.

"That's the spirit, pal, but pace yourself," Michael said.

They pushed onward, but neither of them kept up the pace, and an hour later they were sucking air, exhausted. And they were almost through an entire bottle of water.

Michael handed it to Rodger. "Drink the rest," he said.

"I'm okay," Rodger replied. He stared up at the sky. "I think it's getting lighter on the horizon.

Michael studied the clouds. Lightning tendriled through the bulges.

"No, I don't—*aagh!*" He screamed as something bumped into his foot.

"What!" Rodger cried.

"Something touched me!" Michael said.

Rodger flailed in the water until Michael grabbed him and pulled him close.

"Hold on to me and don't fucking move," Michael said. "Got it?"

Rodger nodded, eyes wide.

Slowly Michael eased Cricket's dry bag out of his suit, but Rodger tightened his grip.

"Loosen up," Michael whispered. "I need to get Cricket booted up."

"You said don't move . . ."

"I know, but . . ."

Rodger was right; not moving was better.

The next few minutes felt like an eternity, but nothing came up to snatch them or tear them into octopus chum.

"Maybe it was just debris," Michael said.

"Could it be your mind playing tricks?"

"No way."

Scanning the waves, Michael searched for any floating debris that might have bumped him. If something was floating in the water, they could hold on to it.

In a lightning flash, Michael spotted movement—something smooth in the rough water.

Holding on to Rodger, he turned around, making a complete revolution.

"What?" Rodger said in a feathery voice. "Did you see something? I can't see . . ."

"Quiet."

In the next flash of lightning, he saw what had touched his foot.

A fin sliced the surface.

Not just one.

Three fins circled the divers.

Michael's heart sank—not with fear but with despair. He wasn't going to see Layla or Bray again.

"Don't move," he whispered.

"What?" Rodger cried.

Michael tightened his grip with his robotic arm, silencing Rodger.

"Listen very carefully," Michael whispered.

"I'm listening."

"Three sharks are circling us, and if we stick together and don't move, we'll be fine, okay?"

"Three . . . sharks?"

Michael instantly regretted telling Rodger, whose voice had jumped an octave. The slight movement attracted one of the fins. It approached.

Without so much as a stick between them, the two men were helpless.

Closing his eyes, Michael prepared for the end.

"Watch out!" Rodger yelled.

Michael opened his eyes as a gray body leaped over them, rotating on its axis the whole way before splashing into the water. Two more of the big creatures jumped and came crashing down.

"Those aren't sharks!" Rodger shouted. "It's a pod of spinner dolphins!"

Michael let go of Rodger and turned to watch the mammals jumping and cavorting in the dark water.

He reached out a shaking hand, and one swam over, making a moaning and then a whistling sound. Then it gave him a little bump.

"I think it wants to give us a ride," Michael said.

Rodger kicked over to them.

"We're saved!" he announced. "They are going to rescue us!"

Michael grinned ear to ear as he touched the wet dolphin flesh. The creature kept up the whistling until he put a hand on its dorsal fin. Another dolphin nudged up against him on his left.

He grabbed the fin with his other hand.

As soon as he did, the two creatures swam away, pulling him over the water.

"Hold on, Rodger, they're going to take us home!" Michael yelled.

Laughing deliriously, Rodger grabbed two fins.

Michael closed his eyes to protect them from the sting of salt water as the dolphins picked up speed, their broad tails powering them almost effortlessly through the water.

He held on tight and opened his eyes again as lightning forked across the skyline.

In the wake of the glow, Michael noticed scars on the flesh of the dolphin at his left. He instantly recognized this animal from the islands. It was the same one Magnolia had spoken of over a year ago—the same dolphin she and X had helped save from ending up on a Cazador dinner table.

Now it was returning the favor.

But how had it known they were here? Or that they were friends?

The Cazadores were known for eating anything and everything in the sea that they didn't worship. Maybe these magnificent creatures could somehow tell that these two humans were different.

Whatever the case, these dolphins were saving them.

Michael held on the best he could, but eventually, his hand began to cramp. He didn't want to switch to his robotic hand, which would hurt his rescuer.

After an hour of swimming, the animals stopped

to rest, circling, jumping, and making their distinctive spins, glossy in the lightning's glow.

They returned, and the journey continued for another hour until Michael suddenly felt both his mounts dive under the waves. Forced to let go, he kicked back up to the surface, bobbing in his life jacket.

"Where are they going?" Rodger shouted.

Michael swam over to his friend. He grabbed him and held on as the fins vanished into the ocean. For the next few minutes, the two men turned and turned, searching for their friends.

"They left us," Rodger said. "Why would they leave us?"

Michael kept searching the darkness, trying to pick out dorsal fins in the water, but all he was saw were waves.

After a few minutes, it became clear. Their rescuers had gone.

He rolled to his back and booted up Cricket.

"Where are we?" Rodger asked.

"Eighteen miles from the closest rig," Michael said. He put the device back into his pouch and took a drink of water.

"Come back!" Rodger shouted. "Don't leave us!"

"Stop yelling," Michael said.

"COME BACK!"

"Rodger, stop it, man . . ."

He quit speaking when he heard the rumble. It started as a low hum, then rose into a loud whining noise. At first, Michael thought it was a watercraft. He stared out over the water, trying to spot a boat, until a deep humming came from directly overhead.

Glancing up, he saw what had spooked the dolphins.

A beetle-shaped airship lowered from the clouds, spotlights on its bow and stern sweeping over the waters.

"Mags!" Rodger shouted.

Michael let out a long, deep sigh as the ship descended, its turbofans blasting them with wind.

"See?" Michael said. "I told you we'd be going home—I just didn't realize it would be to our *first* home!"

"The *Hive* just keeps on saving us," Rodger said.

FIFTEEN

Magnolia listened to the cable winch whine and strain, pulling Rodger up out of the sea. She had checked it three times and was still nervous.

"Almost there," she whispered.

Sofia, Gran Jefe, and Edgar were waiting in the launch bay, along with two technicians.

If Magnolia didn't know better, she would think Rodger was unconscious by the way he hung limp in the harness. It wasn't until he reached up with one hand that she began to relax.

A hundred feet below, Michael bobbed in the waves, waiting his turn.

"*Permíteme, por favor,*" said Gran Jefe. "Let me!"

Crouching next to Magnolia, the burly Cazador flashed her a pointy-toothed grin as he reached down and pulled the dripping Rodger into the launch bay.

"Rodge!" Magnolia cried.

"Mags," he croaked.

Gran Jefe pulled him up through the open hatch

and set him down—a bit roughly, in Magnolia's opinion—on the launch-bay deck.

As the winch lowered the harness to fetch Michael, Magnolia leaned down and hugged Rodger, squeezing a cough out of him.

"Rodge, I thought . . ."

"Easy," he said.

"I thought I had lost you."

"Yeah, and I thought I was fish food."

She chuckled and pulled back to look him in the eyes.

"You're okay?" she asked.

"Yes. You?"

"We lost Jo-Jo, and Arlo and Ada were both hurt," Magnolia said. "But we found something amazing."

"Yeah?"

Rodger sat up as the winch pulled Michael into the launch bay. Gran Jefe reached out and pulled him over, and Sofia handed him a bottle of water. He sucked down half of it before coming up for air.

"How . . . How'd you find us?" Michael asked.

"It was Pedro," Magnolia said. "He recalibrated the weather drones to look for Cricket's signal. We picked it up on our way back to the islands."

"You haven't been back yet?"

"No," boomed an authoritative voice.

Captain Rolo entered the room, flanked by two militia soldiers.

"Glad to see you two are okay," he said. "You're damn lucky to be alive."

"Thanks for the lift," Rodger said.

"Yeah," Michael said. "Much appreciated, Captain."

"I suppose we're even now," Rolo said.

Magnolia was taken back by the statement. Stopping to pick up the two stranded men was hardly repayment for what Michael had done in Africa, but Magnolia was too happy to have Rodger back to care what the old grump thought or said right now.

"Let's get you guys to sickbay," Magnolia said, taking Rodger by the hand.

He coughed several times on the way to the airship's med ward. Michael, on the other hand, seemed to be in decent enough shape.

Dr. Stamos was working on Arlo again when they arrived. Glancing up, he gestured for Magnolia to open the door.

"I'll meet you both back in the launch bay," she said to Edgar and Gran Jefe.

They took off as Rodger and Michael followed Magnolia into the medical ward.

Stamos stepped away from Arlo, who sat up, wincing.

"Wow, you guys look like a Siren shat you out," Arlo said.

"And you look like you lost a fight in a Cazador brothel," Rodger said.

Magnolia rolled her eyes.

"I quit going," Arlo said with a shrug.

They shared a laugh, but it died away when they

saw Ada. She was still in a quarantined room, intubated and as pale as a Siren.

"Dear God!" Michael said. "What happened to her?"

Magnolia explained the story as Dr. Stamos listened to Rodger's lungs.

"A few days' rest, and you'll be back on your feet," Stamos said.

"And Ada?" Michael asked.

The doctor looked at her for a moment, then said, "Honestly, I'm not sure. I'll know more once we get her back to the islands, where I have better equipment."

Magnolia turned to Michael. "Follow me," she said. "There's something you need to see."

"Wait," Rodger said.

"Doc's not done with you yet," Magnolia said.

"I know. Just want to say something to Michael."

"Yeah?" Michael asked.

"Tin, I owe you my life," Rodger said. "Thank you for coming for me."

"It's us who should thank you, Rodger Dodger. If not for you, the oil from *Blood Trawler* would have poisoned our water."

"Now we have Pedro to thank, for saving both our asses."

Michael nodded. "He's even smarter than I thought."

"We're all lucky to be back together," Magnolia said. She snatched Rodger up in another fierce hug.

"I love you, Rodge," she whispered into his ear.

"I love you, too, Mags."

Magnolia pulled away, and Rodger sat back down on the bed. She left sickbay with Michael and hurried to the brig.

Two militia soldiers let them inside. "Last one on your right," said one.

Michael walked up to the cell where, years ago, Magnolia had spent months for stealing from the *Hive* trading post.

"Who's this?" Michael asked.

"Yejun," Magnolia replied. "We captured . . . actually, *he* captured Edgar and me before Edgar escaped and freed me."

Michael looked through the bars. The kid couldn't be more than fourteen. He was sitting on the bunk, legs up to his chest, eyes pinned on Michael.

A loud pop came from the speakers, making Yejun flinch.

"This is your captain," Rolo said over the PA system. "We will be docking at the Vanguard Islands in fifteen minutes. Prepare for landing."

Magnolia smiled at Yejun and pulled a device from her vest pocket. She pushed a button, and the hologram of Timothy appeared.

"Hey, Pepper, can you translate for me again?" Magnolia asked.

"Certainly, Commander," he replied.

"Yejun," she said, "in a few minutes, we're going to show you something you've heard about all your life but have never seen. You're going to see the sun, and then you're going to meet our leader, King Xavier Rodriguez."

Timothy relayed the words, and Yejun got up off his bunk and walked over.

He spoke to the AI in Korean.

"Well?" she asked.

"I'm not sure I understand what he said," Timothy replied.

Yejun spoke again, and again Timothy looked confused.

"What?" Magnolia asked.

"I *think* he said he wants to go home," Timothy said.

"To Korea?"

"No, I don't think so. I think he wants us to return him to his *ship*."

"Tell him we're taking him somewhere much better," Magnolia said. "He will see very soon."

Timothy interpreted, but Yejun shook his head and banged on the bar, repeating the words over and over.

"Let's leave him alone and let X talk to him," Michael said.

He led the way out of the brig, leaving Yejun banging away on the bars. They went straight to the CIC, where Captain Rolo stood at the helm with his XO, Eevi. She turned, all smiles, but Rolo wore his customary scowl.

"We're two minutes out," he said.

Magnolia went to the viewports as they approached the barrier between light and dark. Rain drizzled down the windows.

They passed over the first rig a few minutes later. Even under gray skies, Magnolia could see the damage from the storm.

It was far worse than she had imagined. Tarps fluttered in the breeze over shacks that had lost their roofs. The wind had left thousands of people exposed to the elements. The water around the rigs was thick with floating debris: clothes, carvings, splintered furniture—long-cherished heirlooms that had been in families for generations.

The relics would be missed, but it was the lost livestock and crops that mattered most. From the looks of it, they needed to find alternative food sources if they were to survive.

The airship passed over a dirt field that, only days earlier, had held a bountiful harvest of corn, beans, and spinach. Now all the crops and half the soil were gone.

Magnolia prayed that the farmers had salvaged some of it, but judging from the damage to the rigs, she doubted that much was spared.

It was all a reminder of why setting up a supply chain was so vitally important. It also reminded her that her time here was limited. While she had hoped to spend a few days with Rodger, she had a feeling she would soon be heading back into the wastes.

The airship passed over the Wind Talker rig,

where only one of the turbines spun. Two were missing blades, and the other had a buckled mast. Shattered solar panels lay scattered on the decks.

"Damn," Magnolia muttered.

The airship continued toward the capitol tower. The structural damage wasn't bad, but the gardens and forest had taken a beating. Broken branches and uprooted bushes littered the area around the Sky Arena.

On a horseshoe-shaped platform jutting from the top of the tower stood a group of people, one of them missing an arm, with a dog beside him.

Magnolia felt a wash of relief. If anyone could save them, it was X.

The moment the airship set down, she left the CIC with Michael and headed down a ramp.

Layla was waiting with Bray in her arms.

"Tin!" she whooped.

As Michael ran down to embrace her and the baby, X looked up at Magnolia. His worried gaze told her that she hadn't seen the worst of it. She walked over.

"Take a few hours with your families and rest," X said. "At dusk, the work to rebuild our home begins."

* * * * *

Relief filled X like a candle flame in a dark room. Michael and Rodger were safe, and the Hell Divers had all made it home.

In the past, the heroes of the sky were the only hope for the human race, and tonight they had once again brought hope. That hope burned bright inside X, but he knew that a single ill-timed gust could blow it right out.

He sat at the desk of a man who had led an army that hunted sky people, enslaved them, and even ate their flesh.

El Pulpo, king of the Metal Islands, was an evil man, whom X never thought he would understand.

Until tonight.

As he sat at the desk where el Pulpo had once sat, he read over a line from the translated log of the former king's bastard son, Horn:

"But I fear that my father, like many of my own comrades, won't forfeit the lives of his family for the benefit of the Metal Islands. And if he fails to act, I will."

Between the lines, Horn had advocated murdering and eating their own. And if X didn't act, it could still happen.

He pushed the log aside to examine the map of the Panama Canal. The Hell Divers had returned with intel describing a radioactive terrain dominated by monsters. But they also brought back video of a canal that would give them access to the western coast of South America, for a new supply chain that could save the Vanguard Islands. It would risk many lives, but if X didn't act, *all* the lives at the islands were at risk.

But there was another option.

He rolled out the two maps that Pedro had provided a year ago. They showed the locations of the two weather modification devices: one in Antarctica, and the other on the north polar ice cap.

It would be a huge risk, traveling halfway across the globe to reprogram the weather-mod devices. But if they could restore the climate, they would have infinite places to plant crops.

X doubted there was time. Even if they could find a way to activate the machines, no one knew how long they would take to work. Years? Decades? Longer?

The option seemed less plausible by the day.

The door to the chamber opened, and Slayer stepped inside. He had bandages on both hands, and a clear gel on his facial burns, but he had insisted on coming back to work.

"We're ready for you, sir," Slayer said.

"How's your brother?" X asked.

"Manny's going to make it, gracias."

"Good. He's strong, like his older brother."

X blew out the candle, returning the room and its secrets to darkness. Using the key on a chain around his neck, X locked the study hatch and followed the Barracuda warrior down the stairs.

They went to the cells below, where X had visited Ada over a year ago. He thought of Rhino. It was here the general had asked X to kill Ada.

"Stay here, Miles," X said.

The dog settled down on his side for another nap.

Slayer hung back as X entered.

Lieutenant Wynn stood guard with Ton and Victor outside the cells. Magnolia was also there, holding a transmitter. Bromista, the Barracudas' second-in-command, hung back in the shadows, holding a crossbow. He gave a subtle nod to Slayer.

In the third cell, the young man of Asian descent sat on the bed, hugging his knees. His straight black hair hung lank to his shoulders. The dark eyes narrowed at X.

X nodded to Magnolia, she pushed the button, and Timothy emerged, spreading his blue glow over the brig.

"Greetings, King Xavier," said Timothy.

"Pepper, I want you to translate," X said.

"Of course, sir."

X stepped up to the cell and looked in at the young man, who appeared to be in his early teens. It was hard to believe he had survived on his own out there.

"Tell him who I am and tell him we want to know everything he knows about the canal," X said. "Or anything he wants to tell us about where he came from."

Timothy spoke to Yejun, who responded quickly.

"He says it's an honor to meet you, and he will do as you wish, if only you promise one thing."

"What's that?" X asked.

Timothy turned slightly to look at X.

"He wants you to take him home, King Xavier . . . to the ship where he was found," Timothy clarified.

"He said the same thing to me," Magnolia said. "He wants to go back to the canal."

"Okay. Tell him I promise I will take him back there, but I want to know why he was there in the first place, and where he came from."

This time, Yejun spoke longer.

"He says his family lived in an underground city in North Korea, built during the war with South Korea centuries ago," Timothy explained. "But when that war ended, the city was forgotten about until World War Three. It was during those days that his ancestors went there for refuge."

X listened, interested. He often wondered if there were cities out there like the one this kid spoke of. More importantly, he wondered if some still existed. It quickly became apparent that many of them might have suffered the same fate as this one.

"Over the years, their underground gardens failed, and disease killed off many of the survivors. When people turned on one another over the existing supplies, his family left with others on a ship, which they took to search for a new home—a place they could be safe. They searched for years, along the African coast, then crossing the Atlantic to the shores of North America, where they discovered an abandoned settlement not far from the ruins of a city he doesn't quite remember."

Timothy looked to Yejun, who seemed to be trying to find the right words.

"*New* something," Timothy said. "Maybe New Orleans?"

The AI kept listening, then added, "Yejun says they found maps there of multiple safe havens in South America and the Pacific Ocean. They were en route there when the ship had engine failure and became stuck at the south end of the Panama Canal. Monsters attacked them."

Yejun stepped closer to the bars, speaking faster.

"He says our people stole him and now he can't finish his mission," Timothy said.

X's first instinct was to mention that the kid started it when he captured two of X's best divers, but he kept it friendly. He wanted to know more about this mission.

"Tell him I'm sorry," X said. "We want to help, and we will let him go as soon as he accepts our offer of friendship."

X wasn't just going to let the kid loose, but he wouldn't keep him in a cell, either. The longer he did, the more unsympathetic he looked to Yejun.

Another flashback entered his mind, this time of his first days as a prisoner in the Metal Islands. It had taken him a lot to trust the Cazadores after that, and some of them he still didn't trust.

X turned to Lieutenant Wynn. "Give me the key," he said.

"But, King Xavier . . . We don't know if he is—"

"Key, Lieutenant."

Wynn fished out the key ring and handed it to X.

"Now go topside and make sure no one's around," X said.

"Sir, with all due—"

"Lieutenant, are you having trouble hearing me today?"

Wynn backed away, hurrying past Ton and Victor.

X inserted the key in the door and unlocked it. Yejun stepped away from the bars and retreated to his bed.

X held up his hand. "It's okay," he said quietly. "Timothy, tell him I'm not going to hurt him."

Timothy translated, but Yejun still cowered in the back of the cell. How had this kid survived so long in the wastes by himself? Then again, how had X?

X reached in his pocket and took out a watch he had found on a dive. He handed it to the kid. "As an offer of friendship."

Hesitantly, the kid reached out and took the watch. He seemed to know what it was and nodded at X.

"Come on," X said. He stepped aside and motioned for Yejun to come out into the hallway.

"You sure?" Magnolia asked. "He's a tricky little shit—did a number on me and Edgar."

"And yet, you're alive, right?"

She shrugged. "Yeah."

"We need to know what he knows, and this is the only way."

"You're the king."

"Wynn, you and Slayer clear the rooftop," X said.

"Okay, sir," the lieutenant replied, and hurried away.

Yejun followed them out of the cell and into the stairwell. They climbed to the top of the tower, where X awaited Wynn's confirmation that the roof was indeed clear.

After getting the all clear, X opened the hatch and motioned for Yejun to follow him. They stepped outside to exactly what X had hoped for: a gorgeous sunset. The horizon was ablaze with hues of blood orange and ripe grapes, the last glint of sun rimming the distant clouds in platinum fire.

Yejun stared in awe at the impossible beauty of it all.

Ton, Victor, Slayer, and Wynn fanned out, setting up a perimeter so he couldn't escape. Bromista also watched, keeping behind the trees with his trusty crossbow.

But Yejun was too busy gawking to present a flight risk. Evidence of destruction was all around, but the beauty overshadowed it. Yejun was spellbound.

Slowly, he went down on one knee and picked up the dirt, letting it filter through his hands. He looked at X and spoke a torrent of words while Timothy translated.

"He said it reminds him of the place his family was looking for."

"Maybe they were looking for the islands," Magnolia said.

"No," Timothy said. "He claims there is a place like this with dirt and green trees, but without the real sun."

Yejun walked over to the railing and pointed at the water.

"What's he saying?" X asked.

"He's saying they were on the way to another underground city," Timothy said. "Or . . . I think he is saying an under*water* city."

X walked closer, recalling the Cazador story about the man in Colón, Panama, who called the Coral Castle an underwater city.

"Where is this city?" X asked.

Timothy asked, and Yejun shook his head.

"He says he doesn't know. He only knows how his parents described what it would be like."

"His *dead* parents," X said, cursing.

Yejun spoke again, and Timothy smiled.

"He says the locations of these places are recorded on the ship he was taken from, and that if you return him, he will help you find it with maps he hid there."

X scrutinized the kid's face for a lie. But why would he lie? And even more importantly, why would he want to leave paradise for hell?

Unless he knew there was a better paradise.

In his gut, X felt the kid was telling the truth.

"This map on your ship," X said. "We're going with you to get it. But, son, I highly recommend you come back with us."

Yejun shook his head when Timothy translated.

"Ask him why he wants to stay there and what his mission is," X said.

Timothy spoke again, listened, then looked at

X. "He thinks his family might still be alive and he needs to help them."

X sighed. He stepped up closer to Yejun. "I spent a decade on the surface, kid. In hell, like you. Your family is gone, and they would want you to move on."

This time when Timothy translated, Yejun grew more agitated.

Timothy seemed unsure again.

"What?" X asked.

"I think he's saying he has seen his family, but they changed," Timothy said. "I'm not quite sure, King Xavier."

"Tell him to take a few minutes, get some air. There's plenty of time for questions later."

Yejun walked away to explore the roof with his following of soldiers and guards. Magnolia stepped up by X to watch.

"Well?" she said.

"Well, the kid is completely nuts—a shame, but not surprising. On the bright side, if these maps are real, we might have more than two options after all. Expand into Panama, go to the weather modification sites, or search for this underwater kingdom that might not be a myth."

"None of those options are good, but I like the last one least," Magnolia replied.

"Lieutenant, find this young lad quarters and give him some good food," X said. "Post a guard outside his door, but don't scare him."

"Yes, sir," Wynn said.

Miles followed X through the gardens with Magnolia. A team of horticulturists had already pruned the trees and watered or replanted what crops had survived the storm. Soon, they would plant new seeds to replace those lost in the wind.

Voices called out as they headed back toward the rooftop. It was Michael and Layla, with Bray in a pack on Michael's chest.

X had spent only a few minutes with Michael when they found him hours ago, and seeing him now brought back the wave of relief.

Jogging over, X hugged Michael, prompting laughter from Bray.

"Careful," Layla said. "He's not yet mended all the way."

"Sorry," X said, pulling back. He hugged Layla next. "I told you we'd find him," he said.

Layla hugged X back. "Thank you," she whispered. "For everything."

They all turned to the water as the ocean swallowed the sun. The water darkened. Soon, it would be time to head back to that darkness.

"At midnight, meet me on *Raven's Claw*," X said. "We have a new mission, and, Michael, I'm going to need you back in the saddle."

"But Michael just came home," Layla said.

"Don't worry, kiddo," X said. "I won't ever let anything happen to Tin."

SIXTEEN

Tammy stood in the open doorway of the small apartment she had shared with Alfred. In the background, Leonard stood in his crib, sobbing and reaching for his mother—and perhaps his father, too, whom he would never touch again.

"I'm so sorry," Michael said. "Your husband was a good . . . a *great* man, and he did what he did for you and everyone else on the islands."

Tammy's eyes were swollen from crying.

"Did he suffer?" she asked.

"Not long, no. The sea took him quickly."

She looked down, then back up.

"I tried to save him, but . . ." Michael's words trailed off, replaced by the image of Alfred, falling . . .

"I know you did all you could." She let out a long, juddering sigh. "He respected you more than anyone else in this world. You were his good friend."

Michael bit down on his quivering lip.

"I'll miss him greatly," he said. "If there is anything Layla and I can do, please let me know."

"Thank you."

Tammy hugged him. He had thought it would bring relief when she didn't blame him. Instead, he just felt guiltier. Especially when he returned to his apartment.

He opened the door to find Layla in front of the window overlooking the ocean. She held Bray in the moonlight.

"How's Tammy?" she asked.

"About as good as can be expected."

Layla shook her head. "My heart breaks for her and Leonard. But, Michael, that could be Bray and me."

"I'm lucky to be alive. I know that," he said. "But I couldn't leave Rodger or let the ship explode."

He slouched down in a tattered chair.

"I'm sorry," Layla said. "I'm sorry. I know Alfred was your friend, and you did everything you could to help him."

"We have to do something for Tammy and Leonard."

"I know. I'll bring them some food first thing tomorrow. It's a start."

She handed Bray down to Michael. He took the child in his arms, looking down into brown eyes that searched his.

Holding his son eased some of the hurt, but as with all the other losses Michael had dealt with in his young life, a piece lingered.

"I love you, little man."

Bray smiled and reached up to grab Michael's long hair.

"Even he wants you to cut that," Layla said.

"Yeah, yeah," Michael said.

Having a baby had changed his life. Nothing was more precious than Bray and Layla. Everything he did now was for them.

"So are you going to tell me where you're going tonight?" Layla asked. "Because X doesn't send you out on a mission into the darkness for no reason— especially after you almost died."

Michael frowned. She was right, but he didn't know where he was going.

"I don't know," he said.

"You don't know," she huffed.

"I swear, I don't."

Bray stirred in his arms, features tightening as they always did before he cried.

Michael rocked the child. "It's okay," he soothed.

Layla put her hand on his arm. "Sorry, I didn't mean to get worked up."

"Don't be," he said, "I understand. But I swear, I don't know where X is taking me tonight."

He looked at his watch, then handed Bray back. It was almost time to leave.

"I'm sure this won't take long," he said. "Try not to worry, my love."

"Easy for you to say."

He kissed her lips, then kissed Bray's head.

"Soon he'll be walking," Layla said.

"An ankle biter, as X likes to say." Michael chuckled.

Layla didn't laugh, her mind clearly still dwelling on the mission.

"We'll be okay," he said. "I promise."

An hour later, Michael was in the command center of the warship *Raven's Claw* with a small group that included General Forge, Sergeant Slayer, Lieutenant Wynn, Steve Schwarzer, Pedro, Rodger, Magnolia, X, Ton, Victor, and, of course, Miles.

They cruised past the damaged rigs. Michael got updates on engineering issues and was anxious to get back to work, but apparently, there was something more important right now taking him away from the rigs.

Rain pattered against the viewports, and lightning speared the horizon as they left the sunshine of the islands and broke through the barrier into darkness. The ship pushed on as lightning split the sky over the bow.

X still hadn't told them where they were going, but Michael guessed what they were looking for long before he saw the long hull of the ITC *Ranger* emerge through a wall of mist in the darkness surrounding a small island.

"You didn't scuttle it," Magnolia said.

X shook his head. "I had it moved here just in case we need it someday." He faced them all. "Today is that day, amigos."

"Where are we?" Michael asked.

"Saba, southeast of the Virgin Islands and in the northern part of the Leeward Islands."

Michael didn't need to look at a map. Those island chains, all near the Vanguard Islands, had been picked over from years of Cazador raids.

As *Raven's Claw* sailed closer, Michael felt a chill at the sight of the supercarrier, tucked away in Cove Bay at Saba Island, where it had weathered the hurricane.

X said to Forge, "General, soon I will suggest to the council to continue the mission to develop an outpost at the Panama Canal. It will get us access to the Pacific and down the western coast of South America. "I want you to start preparing your troops to thin out the mutant beasts that have nested there."

"*Sí*, King Xavier," Forge replied at once.

"We have the weapons, the vehicles, and a nuclear-powered ship to get us there," X said. "The ITC *Ranger* brought the defectors to destroy us. Now they lie rusting on the sea bottom, and their ship will help save us."

"She needs some paint and a new name," Rodger said.

"You're in charge of that, Rodger," X said with a grin.

He turned to Michael, the grin already gone. "Chief Engineer Everhart, I want you to get the supercarrier seaworthy as soon as possible. I also want *Ocean Bull* and *Octopus* ready to go with *Raven's Claw*."

"Understood."

X looked to Steve next. "We need to make sure every Cazador soldier has a blade worthy of a fight in the wastes to back up his rifle." He held up his stump. "And I need something for *this*."

"I think I can come up with something," Steve replied.

"Good, what's important now is that we all come together, to face our future as one."

"People are already coming together like I've never seen," Steve said. "Old enemies are new friends."

"Let's hope it stays that way," X said. He looked at everyone in turn, and then nodded. "Okay, let's get to work."

Michael left the command center with Rodger, stopping in a barrack to put on a radiation suit and helmet. Then he headed to the bow, where Lieutenant Wynn had two squads of militia soldiers and Cazadores. Slayer was there with the Barracudas.

The two squads had trained together for the past year and were assimilating better than Michael had hoped.

He grinned. A shared threat had a way of doing that.

He climbed into a boat with Rodger, Steve, and five technicians and engineers. The boat putted away from *Raven's Claw*, into the mist.

Twenty minutes later, they had a stern view of the mammoth supercarrier. The aft loading elevator was already lowered to the second deck, just above the waterline. The smaller Cazador boats pulled up, unloading soldiers onto the deck.

"Stay close," said Lieutenant Wynn.

Michael followed the team off the boat and onto the deck. They crossed a cargo hold, toward an open hatch. Flashlight beams flicked on.

There was an eerie calm inside—only the tap of boots and a clanking deep in the hull.

Wynn, two militia soldiers, and a pair of Cazador soldiers stayed with them as they advanced, but Michael still felt uneasy.

He kept a hand close to the revolver he carried on his duty belt.

"This place creeps me out," Rodger said.

"It's safe," Lieutenant Wynn said. "We scoured these passages for days after we first boarded—cleared out the remaining cyborgs, disabled the weapons systems."

"What's left?" Steve asked.

"Some turrets, fifty-cal machine guns, but we stripped the ammo," Wynn said. "The main weapons were the defectors and drones."

Michael had heard the clanging and still worried that something lurked deep in the ship. They took a ladder down to the third and fourth decks, stopping on each for life scans, which came back negative.

Finally, they got to the lowest deck, the engine room, deep below the water line. The hatch at the bottom of the landing was closed. Wynn gave Bromista a nod.

Wynn kept his laser rifle shouldered, looking

as anxious as Michael felt. Even Steve, who was no man of war, gripped a six-pound sledgehammer like a battle-axe.

Bromista opened the hatch, and they slipped into the vast engine compartment. It reminded Michael of the *Hive*. But this was many times larger and more advanced than any he had ever seen.

Using Cricket, Michael located the control units for the carrier's nuclear reactors. He sat at one of the operation terminals—a touchscreen with a keyboard. Ducking down, he found the interface, then connected a cord between the panel and Cricket. With a tap of the button, he was in.

"Okay, showtime," Michael said.

The operation screen flickered, and Steve and Rodger hovered behind him, reading the data scrolling up the screen.

"Looks like the main system is online, but the life-support systems are all offline," Michael said. "Air filtration, water-distilling units, mess, barracks—all down."

"I guess the machines didn't need them," Rodger said.

"Can you get them back on?" Lieutenant Wynn asked.

"We're about to find out," Michael said.

He walked the room, holding up Cricket to scan equipment that even he was unfamiliar with. He finally got to a dashboard with banks of monitors and gauges.

"I think this is it," Michael said. He spoke into the comm mike. "King Xavier, we're in the control room, about to try and power up all systems."

"Copy that," X said. "Watch your six."

Using Cricket, Michael activated the systems.

All the monitors in the engineering bay glowed to life, spreading a greenish glow over the men. The Cazador soldiers looked around, uneasy. They were superstitious about this carrier and the "metal gods."

"We're in," Michael said.

A male AI voice replied. "Greetings, user," it said. "My name is Tyron."

"Why is that name familiar?" Rodger asked.

Michael knew it, too, from somewhere.

"Please enter your access code," said the AI.

"Well, shit," Michael said. "We might need Timothy for this part."

"Please enter the access code," Tyron entreated.

Michael pushed the comm link back to his mouth.

"King Xavier, we've got a problem. There's a sentient AI named Tyron that requires an access code to turn on the rest of the power and the life-support systems," he said.

"Don't do anything until I get there," X said.

By the time X arrived, Michael had brought up Timothy's hologram through Cricket. The AI created a second glow in the room.

X walked inside with Ton, Victor, and Sergeant Slayer. He stepped in front of them.

"My name is Xavier Rodriguez, and this is Timothy Pepper," he said. "Who are we communicating with?"

"Tyron," said the AI. "Tyron Red."

Timothy suddenly turned to X and then to Michael, his dark eyes widening. "Shut the power off, Chief Everhart," he said.

"Wait, please don't—" Tyron started to say.

Sensing something amiss, Michael powered down immediately.

The monitors switched off, leaving only the blue glow of Timothy's hologram.

"What the hell," X said.

"Who's Tyron Red?" Michael asked Timothy.

"Yeah, why's that sound familiar?" X asked.

"Tyron Red was the founder of ITC and, depending on how you view history, the man who destroyed humanity," said the AI.

X and Michael exchanged a glance.

"So let me get this straight," X said. "His AI is in control of this ship?"

"Yes, well . . . kind of." Timothy paced a few steps, putting a finger on his clean-shaven jawline. "Clearly, Tyron—however much of him is left—can't do much, if anything."

"Can we purge this asshole from the hard drive or whatever the hell he's living inside?" Steve asked.

"Possibly. Let me check something." Timothy's image flickered several times before solidifying a few seconds later.

"Interesting," he said. "It seems the virus we

uploaded in Tanzania wiped out a shell that makes up this AI." Timothy raised a brow. "I believe he is like me, in a way—more like his original, human self but without memories—though it's hard to be sure."

Michael stepped back from the consoles. "Maybe we should have destroyed the ship after all," he whispered.

"Yeah," Rodger agreed.

"If Tyron were dangerous, he would already have attacked us," Timothy said. "However, there is the possibility that he has been waiting to do so."

X seemed to think on this a while. After a minute of silence, he said, "Bring up *Raven's Claw* and aim everything we have at the supercarrier. We'll try and purge the AI first, but if we fail, we put this supercarrier on the bottom. Forever."

Michael knew that this vessel could determine the life or death of the islands, but he was conflicted.

"I want everyone off this ship now except Timothy and a security team under Lieutenant Wynn," X said. "Pepper, I'm counting on you to purge Tyron."

Timothy drew a deep breath, much as a human would.

"I will do my best, sir," he said. "However, if I fail or sense a threat, do not hesitate to eliminate me as well."

Michael handed Cricket to Wynn.

"You'll need this," he said. "Good luck, Lieutenant."

* * * * *

Ada couldn't see, but she could hear voices. They sounded right there with her, but distant at the same time.

And she heard the noise of monsters. Hard little feet scuttled over her, and the clicking of mandibles filled her ears.

Nothing worked when she tried to move. Not even her lips. She couldn't even make a sound.

But she was breathing. She sucked in the filtered air—the plastic-like scent told her she was still wearing a helmet.

A blue glow flashed overhead, giving a fleeting glimpse of her surroundings—an underground lair with walls of rock and soil. An open roof gave her a view of a vertical shaft carved out of the dirt.

Red vines cascaded down like a frozen waterfall from the surface far above. Lightning flashed, illuminating the shaft and holes carved into the walls, as well as the creatures inside the tunnels. Dozens of red eyes stared down at her in the blue glow.

Ada remembered everything then: the fire creature, the chitinous monsters, the bunker, being captured.

It all came crashing back over her in a wave of panic.

Able to move only her eyes, she flitted them back and forth. She was trapped inside a place similar to the first graveyard, with remains of several species in varying stages of decay.

In the sporadic glow of the lightning, she saw

something different about these remains. To her right, a Siren lay in a fetal position, the hairless flesh shriveled but mostly intact. Only a few gashes marred its muscular torso.

But for the twisted mouth, it might have looked innocent as a baby. But the horrifying wormy lips were stretched into a crooked grin. A rotting tongue hung between the jagged teeth lining its jawless mouth.

She stared for a moment, thinking that she saw the tongue move.

In the next flash of lightning, she saw that the tongue *was* moving. Only this wasn't a tongue.

The thin lips opened, and out climbed a baby crab on black legs. The lips peeled back farther as more claws ripped through the flesh. Two miniature crabs popped out of the ears, and another split open a nostril.

Ada stared in horror as dozens of the shelled creatures broke out of every visible orifice.

They crawled over the skull for a few seconds, tearing off and scarfing down putrid flesh before moving down the body.

Within minutes, they had consumed most of the carcass.

Distant voices called out again. This time, it sounded as if they were calling for *her*. She could swear she heard someone saying, "Ada? Ada, are you there?"

I'm here! I'm here, come help me!

A brilliant flash of lightning turned the chamber

to daylight, and she could see something covering her armor.

The glow faded, and again she lay in darkness.

In the next lightning flash, she saw gooey yellow lumps on her chest, arms, and legs.

No, no, please God no.

She was covered in the eggs, and soon they would hatch, just as they had inside the baby Siren.

Ada willed her body to move, but it no longer answered to her. She was paralyzed, poisoned, or perhaps both.

As she tried to squirm and twist, every nerve in her body ignited with pain so intense that darkness encroached and she lost consciousness.

When she awoke, she could sense her body moving, but she couldn't see anything. The darkness was impenetrable, and there was no lightning to provide sporadic clues about her surroundings.

Perhaps that was a good thing. She remembered the crabs. Watching herself be consumed by the little monsters would be a bad way to go.

Terror gripped her again as she bumped over rocks. She tried to look up at whoever had her in their grip.

Was it a Hell Diver? Some unknown mutant beast?

She didn't hear the voices, but she did hear a familiar sound: the shuffling of paws, and the heavy panting that came from exertion.

Jo-Jo! The monkey had come to her rescue.

Hope flooded Ada. She tried to speak, but she still couldn't form a single word.

The next thing Ada knew, judging by the clank of her armor, she was being lugged into something metallic.

A train car, she realized.

She could hear Jo-Jo panting, squeaking in a low tone, trying to wake her.

I can't move, Jo-Jo!

Ada wanted to scream, to pull the monkey close, but she couldn't do anything. Frustration brought anger and more pain.

The burning sensation passed from her neck to her face. Her body was trying to fight off some toxin or pathogen.

She lay there in the dark, praying that it would pass and she would be able to get up and flee this place with Jo-Jo. To escape back to the surface, where the other Hell Divers were.

It occurred to her then that her HUD was offline. She tried to look at her visor, but all was black.

She wasn't sure how much time passed before she saw the first light.

Was it her comrades?

The orange glow illuminated the train tunnel, and her heart sank. The divers used white beams. This was a *fiery* light.

Jo-Jo whimpered and leaned down, her liquid black eyes reflecting the flickering glow. She grew frantic, trying to pull on Ada.

Ada finally managed to form a word that Jo-Jo knew. "Run," Ada croaked.

But even with the fire approaching, the monkey stayed by her side.

Voices called out—the same ones from before.

"Ada, can you hear me?"

The voice was familiar, stern . . . Could it really be?

A bright white light replaced the orange glow. It dazzled her eyes. She woke again, but she wasn't in the train. She was in a room under a bright overhead light.

She tried to squint against the glare.

"Ada, can you hear me?"

This was a different voice, not familiar at first.

"Yes," she stammered. "Where . . . where am I?"

"You're safe," said the stern voice from earlier.

"King Xavier?"

"Yes, I'm here with you, and you're going to be okay."

Ada sucked in a deep breath of relief as she realized she had awoken from the nightmare of her captivity.

The dreams had seemed *so* real, though.

"Where am I now?" she asked.

"You're at the Vanguard Islands," X said. "You were in a coma but just woke up."

"Ada," said the other male voice, "this is Dr. Stamos."

She blinked, her vision clearing to see a man in a biosuit. He leaned down and held a cold metal instrument against her chest.

X was wearing one, too.

"Why are you in those?" Ada asked.

"Precaution," said Dr. Stamos. "You were infected with an unknown contagion, but the toxicity levels have all dropped, and at this rate, I believe they'll be gone by tomorrow."

"In other words, a full recovery," X said.

Panic struck again when she recalled the Siren's head disgorging the tiny monsters and then being devoured by them.

Ada squirmed in bed, trying to get a look at her body.

"But the crabs, they . . ." she started to say.

"What crabs?" X asked.

She tried to sit up.

"Easy," X said. "You'll have plenty of time to tell us what happened."

"I'm okay. I remember everything. I saw a creature I can't explain . . . It was glowing like it was radioactive . . ."

X and the doc exchanged a glance.

"The eye sockets—oh, God, those burning eyes . . ." Ada mumbled.

"She needs to rest," Dr. Stamos whispered as if she weren't here.

X put a hand on her shoulder. "Get some sleep. I'll come back soon."

"Wait," Ada said.

She looked around the room. "When can I see Jo-Jo?"

Again X and Stamos exchanged a glance.

Sitting up straighter, Ada said, "Where's Jo-Jo?"

X put his hand back on her shoulder. "Kid, Jo-Jo's still in Panama. The divers had to leave without her after barely saving you."

Ada squirmed out of his grip and swung her legs off the bed.

"Hey!" Dr. Stamos cried.

He reached out, but Ada hopped off the bed, only to collapse the moment her feet touched the floor. She hit the cold tiles hard, banging her head painfully.

"Ada!" X said. He leaned down to help her up, but she turned away, tears stinging her eyes, the room blurring.

"No," she whimpered. "We have to go back for her. We have to find her."

X crouched in front of her.

"She's all by herself out there," Ada cried. "She came back for me and pulled me out of that nightmare. She *saved* me!"

"Don't worry, we'll find her," X said. "Now, let's get you up."

Ada held his gaze. "You promise?"

"We'll bring her home," he said. "You have my word."

SEVENTEEN

X stepped up to the council chamber doors, stooping slightly as he banged them open with his palm. In the past, Ton and Victor might have thought he was drunk, but today he just had a headache.

He had plenty on his mind: determining what to do with the ITC *Ranger*, establishing a route through the Panama Canal, and rebuilding after the hurricane that had ravaged the islands. Construction was underway to restore the rigs, but losses continued to mount. To rebuild, they must return to the wastes, to salvage metal and parts. There was also the lost oil—almost as bad as losing the crops.

He had slept only a few hours since the storm abated, and his body seemed sluggish.

Timothy was still aboard the ITC *Ranger*, there to purge the AI of Tyron Red, the creator of Industrial Tech Corporation and the machines that ended the world.

The purge made X nervous, but Captain Two

Skulls had clear orders to destroy the carrier if Timothy failed.

Cazador demolition teams had already boarded the vessel to plant charges in strategic locations. It would take but a single radio transmission for X to order the supercarrier's destruction.

Maybe he was making a mistake by not destroying it now, but his gut rarely led him astray, and it told him Timothy was right about the Tyron Red AI not being a threat. On top of that, *Ranger*'s remaining weapons systems were offline and hence posed no threat to the islands.

With oil suddenly scarce, they needed that supercarrier's nuclear-powered engines in the supply chain. Hell, even if they kept it at the islands, they could turn that vast flight deck into a floating farm.

"Ready, sir?" Victor asked.

X nodded, and the guards pushed open the doors.

Miles nudged in front of him into the vaulted room, where everyone rose to their feet. He took his place at the foot of the throne while X walked down the ceremonial carpet with his two guards.

Fifty men and women greeted him with nods or salutes from their various cultures. Representatives from all those cultures were here today, gathered for the special meeting that X had called.

Cazador soldiers stood in the pews, dressed in their ceremonial armor. Some, like Slayer and Bromista, bore fresh wounds from the storms.

Merchants in their fancy threads and feathered

hats filled the middle rows. Their interests were represented by a new council member, Martino Lupe, a husky Cazador merchant who owned half the fishing fleet, a brothel, and a salvaging operation.

Unlike his comrades, he didn't wear a feathered hat over his bald dome, preferring to accessorize his gold-buttoned tunic with a walking stick that had a ruby in the hilt.

Near the front, Hell Divers in their red coveralls stood at attention.

Sky people, including those from Kilimanjaro, sat intermixed. Refugees rescued from around the world were here, too. Pedro Gonçalvez and Cecilia Peres, from Rio de Janeiro, wore gray uniforms. The sky people from Kilimanjaro, represented by Captains Rolo and Linda Fina, wore bright-blue uniforms. The two airship captains sat at the council table with Chief Engineer Everhart and Commander Katib for the other sky people, and General Forge, Martino, and Imulah for the Cazadores.

And now there was a new member of the Vanguard Islands: Yejun, whom X was still keeping secret.

"All hail King Xavier," Imulah said.

"Hail, King Xavier!"

The voices filled the room.

X shook his head, and Miles raised his head briefly off his paws before closing his eyes again. After almost two years on the throne, X still hadn't gotten used to this deference—or the exhausting burden that came with being the leader. But retiring wasn't an option.

His people—all of them—needed him. Especially now.

Head down, he walked the center aisle as he had hundreds of times now, almost every day, to sit in on council meetings. Disputes between fishermen, a crop infected by weevils, petty thefts, a dispute that led to blows . . .

But tonight, it wasn't the usual day-to-day problems that brought them together. This meeting was about the fate of their way of life.

"Today, we meet to discuss our future," X boomed. "Chief Everhart will start by explaining some of the challenges we will face in the coming months."

Michael stood at the council table. "As many of you know, the storm severely damaged our crops and will result in half the normal harvest," he said. "To sustain our current population, we must find alternative sources of food. We'll be sending our trawlers out farther than ever before, for seafood to help supplement our diets."

"Into the storms," X clarified. "And away from the zone where *Blood Trawler* went down, to avoid the very real threat of poisoned fish."

Michael continued. "Fire damage was significant on multiple rigs, including the trading post. Damage to living areas was also significant across the islands, and we've lost power in many cases."

He held out a hand to Rodger and Steve in the crowd. "We are already addressing these issues and working to restore the turbines at the Wind Talker rig.

Our goal is to replace all propane and gas power on the rigs with batteries charged by the wind turbines and solar panels."

X nodded. It was a good plan, which Michael had been working on even before the storms. It would help ease the pain from the lost oil, but they couldn't power everything with wind and solar power.

"We also need to scavenge extra scrap to restore the rigs and protect them against future storms," Michael continued. "I'm submitting a list to the council requesting more solar panels and turbines to be recovered from the wastes, to replace those we lost."

He nodded at X, who cut in.

"On our raiding missions, we will also scavenge new boats and ships in the coming weeks and months," X said. "Fortunately, thanks to our Hell Divers, we have a good idea where many of these supplies will be coming from. I'll turn it over to Commander Katib of Team Raptor."

Magnolia stood up at the council table.

"Thank you, King Xavier," she said. "My divers have returned from a mission at Panama, where we discovered a trove of vessels and equipment that will help us rebuild our fleet. Further, the canal is clear and can be used to access the Pacific Ocean and explore new areas of South America and beyond."

Whispers and hushed voices rang out, forcing her to pause.

She tucked a lock of green hair behind her ear.

"Radiation ranged from minimal to high, but most of the serious readings came from nearer the city."

"You find *barcos*—eh, ships—*en el canal*?" Martino asked in broken English.

"Yes, some."

"*Ah, ¡excelente!* Perhaps this is opportunity." Martino loosened his tunic. "We take great loss in storm, need new *barco*."

"We also heard you find giant crabs that hurt two divers," said another Cazador.

Magnolia spoke. "We suffered no human casualties, and—"

An angry voice cut Magnolia off. "You're lucky to have gotten out alive!" Captain Rolo called out. "The surface there is crawling with monsters. Do *not* sugarcoat this, Commander."

X let the audience and council speak without interrupting them. This was how he made decisions: by listening to all voices, even the angry ones.

"Bad rads and mutants, just like our bunker—why we hide underground," Cecilia said.

"*Sim*, but we no hide anymore," Pedro argued. "We must fight for our home."

Cecilia nodded. "Yes, but maybe better places to fight, less monsters."

"The canal is our way to the western shore of South America and beyond," Magnolia said. "Strategically, it's the best place we can establish an outpost."

"Our soldiers have new weapons and equipment

to clear the terrain and hold a post," General Forge added.

"May I remind you that our soldiers have suffered heavy casualties over the past few years?" Imulah said. "Normally, I do not opine on strategy, but this is something to consider."

"Noted," X said. "All your points. But if a teenager can survive alone for a decade down there, so can we."

There was a fresh buzz among the audience.

"Bring Yejun," X said to Ton.

The guard hurried away and returned a few minutes later with Yejun, who was cleaned up and wearing a tan tunic. His hair was shorter, and his eyes seemed brighter.

"This young man will help us take the Panama Canal," X said. "May I introduce Yejun, who survived there on his own and knows the terrain better than the monsters do."

He paused for a moment, letting the crowd examine Yejun.

"Ultimately, it's the council's decision, but our population faces disease, severe weather, famine, and dwindling resources in the coming months," X continued. "Not much different from our days in the sky, and while I hoped we would avoid the same problems, Mother Nature has her own ideas."

General Forge nodded. "We must act," he said.

"I agree," Magnolia said.

"Me, too," Michael said.

Imulah dipped his head.

Wasting no time, X made the first of several motions.

"With council approval, I move to restore and commission the ITC *Ranger* into our fleet," X said. "Second, General Forge will prepare an army to secure the Panama Canal and establish an outpost, utilizing the vehicles and equipment from the supercarrier. Lieutenant Wynn remains behind to keep the peace."

He turned to the Hell Divers. "Team Raptor will return to the canal with Yejun to recover valuable assets and maps," X said. "Once the outpost is secure, the divers will continue to search for new areas to raid, so that we can create a viable supply chain to quickly and efficiently get goods back to the Vanguard Islands."

X swept the room with his gaze to judge the reactions, but most people simply stared back with respect and confidence.

Most of these people supported his leadership, and for that he was grateful.

But not everyone seemed so confident in him or his plan.

Captain Linda Fina stood at the table. "If I may."

X gestured for the elderly woman with wispy white hair to stand.

"My people lived in chains for decades at Mount Kilimanjaro," she said. "When I saw Hell Divers, I didn't believe my eyes . . ." She closed her eyes for a moment and let out a sigh before opening them. "Angels came and saved us from the machines and brought us to this paradise. I believe this paradise will still produce what we need, which is not a terrible lot."

She reached up to her wrinkled face.

"I'm old and have lived far longer than I should have," Fina continued. "In my many years, I've learned that humanity is resilient and that we can survive in dire conditions."

Rolo stood and looked X in the eye. "I learned something by taking my people to Kilimanjaro, and I swore I would never take another risk like that," he said. "If we commit our resources to the Panama Canal, we risk everything."

The captain gestured to Magnolia and then Yejun. "You heard the stories. You know what's there. And just because one kid survived by hiding in a ship doesn't mean we won't suffer terrible casualties and loss of precious resources."

X understood Captain Rolo's conservative stance, but hearing Fina side with him surprised him.

"A kid surviving out there means nothing," said another man.

X looked past the council table to the third row, where a man wearing an expensive tunic and an eye patch stood.

Carl Lex, the former chief engineer of the ITC *Victory*, was lead salvage man on the rig now, and was known for his suaveness.

Charmer, they called him.

"Speak," X said.

"I saw kids survive things they shouldn't have

at the machine camp," Charmer continued. "They are resilient—often more so than adults—and to use one as a reason to invade a place that my old mate Kade described as 'hell on earth' isn't a good sell, with respect, Your Majesty."

Kade looked at X, clearly taken aback at hearing his name.

"Going there would be a mistake," Charmer added. "One that could cost us everything."

"Kade, what do you think?" X asked.

Kade's dark eyes flitted from Rolo to Charmer, then back to X. "I'm a Hell Diver. I follow orders and always have."

X just let the dynamic play out. It seemed to be the Tanzania sky people against the *Hive* sky people and the Cazadores. He looked down at Miles, who let out a bored whine.

"Enough talk," X said. "We put this to a vote. All in favor of my orders, raise your hand."

Just as X had thought, it was Magnolia, Imulah, General Forge, and Michael against the two captains.

Pedro and Cecilia huddled together, speaking in Portuguese. If they voted against the mission, it would be a tie.

Pedro finally pulled away from Cecilia.

"We say, *sim to Panama,*" he said after a dramatic pause.

"*Very well,*" X replied. "*General, prepare your soldiers. Chief Everhart, ready the fleet. Commander Katib, get your divers ready. We're heading to the canal as soon as the airship and the* ITC *Ranger* are ready to sail."

X paused. There was one last announcement.

"It may reassure you to know that I will be leading our brave men and women into the wastes."

Hushed voices broke out, and a man in the back of the room stood.

"King Xavier," he said in a croaky voice.

X narrowed his eyes at a thin, elderly man that he didn't remember seeing before.

"*Mi hermano was on the Sea Sprite,*" *he said.* "*I fear if you go, you will suffer same fate . . . the way is cursed.*"

X stiffened in front of the gazes now centered on him, recalling a quote from Carthaginian General Hannibal Barca. In his deepest voice, he said, "*Either I will find a way or I will make one.*"

* * * * *

"Wait. We're going back to that hellhole?" Arlo asked as he entered the *Vanguard* launch bay.

"Arlo, glad to see you back on your feet," Magnolia said. "But don't start."

"My feet weren't the problem. It's my arm, and it still hurts like a bitch."

"Suck it up, buttercup. You're tough, right? Thunder and lightning and all that jazz?"

"You been watching old-world movies again, because I didn't understand much of that."

"Now you know how *we* feel."

Arlo chuckled. "Yeah, yeah."

Magnolia had a pack of greenhorns showing up soon. There were twenty-two rookies in the ranks now that two more had joined after the storm. Most had jumped only once or twice on practice dives in clear skies.

Some of the veterans were still off spending time with their families, including Edgar and Sofia. Magnolia would be spending time with Rodger, but like her, he had duties. At the moment, he was with Michael, getting the ITC *Ranger* ready for the mission.

She was the only veteran here besides Arlo and Kade, unless you counted Gran Jefe. The big Cazador was sitting on a crate, picking the last bits of white flesh off a fish skeleton. He thumbed out an eyeball and ate it, then offered the other eye to Kade, who politely declined.

The cowboy had saved Magnolia's ass twice now. She didn't know much about him, only that his family was killed when the ITC *Victory* arrived in Tanzania. It was obvious he had suffered over the years, which was probably why he seemed to have a death wish, much as X once did.

In a way, Kade reminded her of X and also Commander Rick Weaver, another good man who had fought like he had nothing to lose.

"So what's the plan for these rookies?" Arlo asked, wincing as he walked over.

"You afray to eat fish eye?" Gran Jefe said, grinning.

"Piss off, man."

Gran Jefe's grin faded. He got up off the crate, tossing the fish bones to the deck.

"Children," Magnolia said. "*¡Niños!*"

She stepped between them, smelling Gran Jefe's hot, fishy breath.

"*Lo siento*, Commander Katib," he said. "Sorry."

Gran Jefe stepped back, making a gracious gesture as a gentleman might have done centuries ago. Magnolia saw it for what it was: all part of an act.

"Okay, listen up," she said. "As you all know, King Xavier and the council have voted to push on with the expansion in Panama. That means we're going back to the skies, and we need to be ready to dive again."

She stepped over to the rows of chutes, boosters, and other gear neatly set out in the launch bay.

"Before the greenhorns get here, I need help organizing and sorting what gear we have."

"You got it, boss," Arlo said.

Magnolia sighed. Like everyone on the islands, they were running out of supplies. The armor was old, and battery packs needed replacing.

Kade worked quietly through the bags of gear, checking everything twice before dropping it in the green-light pile.

She walked over, and Kade politely took off his cowboy hat, running a hand through his thick brown hair.

"I heard Ada's awake," he said. "She okay?"

"She'll pull through."

"Yeah, but she's going to want to find her animal," Arlo said.

"*Muerto*," Gran Jefe said. "The monkey—he is dead."

"You don't know that," Magnolia said.

Gran Jefe finished stuffing a chute in a pack. "Oh, *sí*. I do."

"Or, like Yejun, Jo-Jo's alive," Magnolia said. "After all, the animal was born in the wastes. It can survive in the wastes."

"Yeah, good point, Mags," said Arlo.

Gran Jefe shrugged. "They say your man, Rogelio, got saved by *los delfines*. Dolphins. *¿Verdad?*"

The big man scratched his beard with its beads and small animal bones woven in.

"His name is *Rodger*, and eating dolphins is barbaric," she said.

"Hmm," Gran Jefe mused. "We stop eating them when sky people came, *pero*, how do you say . . ." He licked his lips and patted his belly.

"Tasty," Arlo said. "You're sick, bro, sick indeed."

Gran Jefe muttered in Spanish.

Arlo stiffened. "What's that mean?"

"You don't want to know," came a voice.

Sofia stepped into the launch bay, holding Rhino Jr. in her arms.

A smile crossed Magnolia's face as her best friend walked over.

"This is where Mama works," Sofia said. The baby looked about.

"I don't think he understands," Arlo said.

Sofia shot him an are-you-really-that-dumb glare.

Magnolia laughed, her heart warming. It felt good to feel some joy for once.

After all, they had survived and were back home. Rodger and Michael, too, and for that, Magnolia was eternally grateful.

Gran Jefe lumbered over to Sofia and leaned down to the child.

"*Hola, hombrecito*," he said.

The baby glanced up at Gran Jefe and raised a tiny hand.

"Big like his *papá*," Gran Jefe said. "*Rhino fue un guerrero*—great warrior. Someday you will be *muy fuerte*, maybe king."

"He doesn't want to be king," Sofia said. "But you're right, he will be big and strong like his father."

"What did this nimrod say earlier?" Arlo asked Sofia.

Sofia shook her head. "Arlo, I really . . ."

Gran Jefe grabbed his crotch. "I say I got big *cojones*, and you got peanuts."

The room broke out in laughter, and Arlo turned pink.

He was used to being the jokester. Now, it seemed, he had competition.

Magnolia almost felt bad for Arlo.

"You know what they say about men that brag," Sofia said. "Usually, they got a *pequeña snake*."

Gran Jefe reached for his belt, and when Magnolia

realized what he was doing, she shouted, "Knock this shit off!"

"Okay, no problema," Gran Jefe said, still glaring at Arlo.

"Hey, the greenhorns are gathering outside," Kade said from the launch-bay door.

"Good," Magnolia said. "Tell them to help us bring the gear down the ramp."

Kade pushed a button, and the port-side doors opened. A ramp extended down to the platform where the *Vanguard* was docked. Outside, the rookies stared up into the belly of the airship that would dump them into the wastes.

Magnolia waved them up. "First things first," she said. "We need to go through all our gear and make sure it's ready for training, which begins tomorrow at first light. So buddy up, check your gear, and check your buddy's gear."

The divers started grabbing gear from the pile the veterans had already double-checked.

The new members would be assigned to Teams Angel and Phoenix, whose ranks had thinned during the past few years and during the war for the islands. Magnolia had considered instituting a new team name to mark a turned page, but first, they needed a new commander.

Edgar was her first choice, and Sofia was also in the running, although Magnolia didn't want to see her best friend continue diving.

She couldn't count Kade out, either. He had proved he was still a top-flight Hell Diver.

As Magnolia looked out over the fresh faces, she had the same feeling she always did: dread that most of these people wouldn't survive more than fifteen jumps.

It was up to her and the other remaining veterans to train them and keep them alive.

"Follow me," Magnolia said.

She led the group of divers with their gear to the launch tubes that once dropped bombs during the Third World War.

"Soon, those of you who pass training will find yourself in one of these tubes," Magnolia said. "When that moment happens, I want you ready. Tonight, we're going to teach you how to dive in an electrical storm."

Scrutinizing the faces for their reaction, she saw about what she expected: pure terror from most of them. A few were intent on looking tough, among them Tia, an eighteen-year-old from the ITC *Victory* with dark braided hair. Her gleaming partially shaved head had three tribal tattoos reflecting her descent from the aboriginal New Zealanders, the Maori.

Magnolia didn't know much about her, only that she was an orphan. The girl had the same look Magnolia remembered from when she was that age: a fearless attitude of immortality.

"Gear up, everyone," Magnolia said. "Let's go."

The greenhorns dispersed, and Sofia said to Magnolia, "That one reminds me of me."

Magnolia glanced over at Tia and chuckled. "Reminds me of my younger self, too."

Kade was talking to the young woman now. She perked her ears to listen.

"I told you, your dad didn't want this for you," Kade said. "Fair go."

"I *am* being reasonable."

"Hell no, you're not!"

"Yeah? Well, you don't want me to be a soldier, either, so what can I be? You want me to spend my days counting beans or pruning tomatoes?"

Kade bent his burned hat brim nervously. "Yeah, but bloody hell, Tia," he said. "Both those options sound better than diving. It ain't roses and sunshine down there."

He pointed at the launch doors. "When you jump, you go arse over tit, straight into the black pit of hell. Then, *if* you make it through the storms and land alive, you get to face mutant monsters that will eat you for breakfast."

"You can't scare me, Kade," Tia said. "This is what I want. You had the chance to train me, but you didn't. Now I'm doing it on my own."

She stormed off, and Kade wagged his head wearily. He looked at Sofia and Magnolia, who both shied away.

Sofia shifted her growing son to the other arm. "He must be her caretaker or something," she said when Kade walked away.

"Yeah, reminds me of someone."

Sofia changed the subject. "I was thinking, you and Rodger should stop by my place for dinner. I'm going to make some seafood gumbo. I'll invite Michael and Layla and Bray, too."

Magnolia smiled. "Sounds great, but we're both super busy . . ."

"Mags," Sofia said sternly.

Rhino Jr. stirred in her grip.

"This is all I have left of Rhino now," Sofia said. "He was my heart, my soul. He was *everything* to me, and I would do anything to spend another day with him."

"I know, I'm so—"

Sofia interrupted her with a click of the tongue. "No, Mags, I don't think you do. You have something special with Rodger, but I can see in you the fear to commit. Life is hard. It's never guaranteed in our world, and while you've lost many friends over the years, you haven't lost Rodger."

"I know. I'm just afraid of giving myself one hundred percent and then—"

"It's better to give and lose than to hold back and regret it."

Sofia smiled and carried her son away. "You better not miss my gumbo," she said.

A voice called out, and Magnolia turned to the last person she expected to see climbing a ladder up to the platform.

"Ada, what the heck are you doing here?" Magnolia said.

The young diver walked across the deck, hair blowing in the breeze. She had a slight limp. Magnolia met her halfway.

"Keep working," she said to the other divers, who were staring.

The greenhorns went back to their equipment checks, but Magnolia could feel their attention on her.

"You should be resting," Magnolia said.

"I'm here to keep training," Ada said. "X promised we're going to find Jo-Jo."

"He did?" Arlo asked.

Magnolia frowned when she saw him walking over. But it wasn't just Arlo. Edgar, Gran Jefe, and Kade joined them.

"You should be in bed, Ada," Edgar said.

"I'd be in the air if I could fly the *Vanguard*," she replied. "Jo-Jo may not be human, but she's a Hell Diver, and she needs us."

She looked at Kade.

"I haven't gotten the chance to thank you," Ada said. "You saved my life."

"He's getting really good at that," Magnolia said.

Kade doffed his cowboy hat.

"Doing my duty, mate," he said. "I learned a long time ago never to leave a man or woman behind on the surface."

EIGHTEEN

TWELVE YEARS AGO...

"Mission is a quick grab, bag, and bail," said Captain Rolo. "You're landing at an industrial facility on the border of Rapid City, in South Dakota."

Kade Long, Hell Diver commander of Team Dragon, stood in the center of the launch bay on the ITC *Victory*, stiff and stern in his black jumpsuit and armor. He listened to every word as the captain and three crew members briefed him and Johnny, the greenhorn diver tagging along.

A team of technicians and support crew worked on the launch tubes, making last-minute preparations for the dive.

"This is a yellow zone on the border of a red zone," Rolo said, "and while I have no record of any other airships having raided this area, I would be willing to bet a silver dollar there are beasts down there."

"That's why Cowboy Kade has his six-shooter, right?" Johnny said.

Kade looked over at the only diver not standing straight. He was bending down and lacing up his worn boots.

"My six-shooter is to save your biscuit," Kade said.

One of the technicians chuckled until Rolo shot her a glare.

"Be careful," Rolo warned, turning back to the divers. "I don't want any mistakes. Everything by the book today, got it?"

"Aye, sir," Johnny said.

Kade nodded and put his helmet on over his shaggy brown hair. He took a breath of filtered air that tasted like plastic. Then he chewed the end of his mustache—a nervous habit he always indulged before climbing into his launch tube.

He lowered himself in, landing on the thick glass floor. Then he did something else that was habit before a dive. He reached down and felt the wooden grip of his "monster hunter," an ancient six-shooter he had found in a museum.

According to the dusty placard in the glass display case he shattered to get it, the gun had belonged to an American sergeant during World War II. He had acquired it by trading his 1911 Colt .45 to a Filipino resistance fighter. Now it was Kade's.

He thought of his family. His wife, Mikah, had cried this morning when he kissed her goodbye, but his sons were dry-eyed and stoical—even the youngest, Sean, who was only three.

"I'll be okay," he had assured them. "I'll be home by supper, I promise."

Kade had taught his boys that a promise was a pact that a man did everything he could to make good on. And today, Kade would do everything he could to make that promise a reality. He would be home by dinner, with the loot in hand.

An alarm wailed, indicating the final countdown to the dive. Sixty long seconds remained.

Kade would rather just get on with things, but there were protocols: final weather scans and checklists that had to be completed by officers in the command center, as well as Captain Rolo.

The captain's voice surged over a private comm frequency.

"Kade, when you get to the surface, I want you to use the new coordinates in the map I'm uploading to your HUD," he said. "I know this is different from your briefing, but you will see why, if you find what I think is down there."

Thirty seconds to launch.

"Wait, Captain," Kade said. "What supplies am I bringing back to the ship?"

"These aren't supplies, this is intel—something I trust only you with. Good luck."

Kade scarcely had time to consider what the captain was asking or why he had kept it a secret until now.

The glass floor opened beneath his boots, and Kade slipped through the thick clouds.

Plummeting toward the earth always felt odd for that first moment, as if he had just jumped up off the moon's surface and was floating back down to the ground. But the ground was still twenty thousand feet below.

He pulled his limbs into stable falling position and looked around him. No flashes or thunderclaps.

To his right, Johnny fell in stable position, arms and legs out, chest battery glowing blue over his dented armor and boots.

They came closer together, suits whipping in the wind. At fifteen thousand feet, Kade checked his HUD. The upload was complete with the new coordinates.

"Follow me to a new DZ," Kade said over the comms.

"Say again?" Johnny replied.

"Just meet me on the ground. I know as much as you do."

They turned away from the edge of a small city tucked against what was once called the Black Hills. The next thirty seconds passed without any issues. No lightning or turbulence.

At five thousand feet, he got his first glimpse of the hills. They sure as hell weren't black anymore.

Thick mutant trees grew out of the poisoned soil, their red and purple needles carpeting the hilly terrain. One crag looked different from the others.

"Bloody bastard," Johnny said over the comm. "That's Mount President or some shit."

"Mount Rushmore," Kade corrected. He had read about this place when he was a kid. It was some sort of monument to former leaders of the United States. Five men and one woman, all long since dead, had their faces chiseled into the rock.

Kade reached down to the pocket on his right thigh, pulled his pilot chute, and let it go. The canopy deployed, and he hung from the sky, using his toggles to steer over to the strangely altered mountain.

He studied the ancient faces. He couldn't begin to imagine what their lives were like. These had been some of the most powerful people of their times. But even that power wasn't enough to prevent the fall of civilization. In the end, human society had crumbled like the broken faces chiseled into the rock.

Kade circled the drop zone, a cracked parking lot covered in spiky weeds and bushes. A pair of buses stood half buried in the rubble of a collapsed building.

At about six feet, he flared over the parking lot, then stepped lightly down onto the dirt at the edge, careful to avoid brushing against any weeds.

Johnny was already down and packing his chute into his bag. He hurried over.

"Shit on a stick, Commander!" he said. "Never thought I'd see this place."

They both looked up as their HUDs blinked. An IR tag came online—the red box dropping from the sky. It was the supply crate, descending under canopy about a mile away.

"Let's go," Kade said.

He hated the first hour on the surface when they were armed with only a pistol or a blaster. The weapons could kill mutant beasts, but he still felt naked without an automatic rifle from the supply crate.

They made their way toward a building that once welcomed tourists to the monument. The windows were gone and the roof caved in, but this wasn't their target. The coordinates for the supply crate seemed to point to the base of the mountain.

Kade skirted around the building and halted at the edge of the mutant forest.

"Where's the path?" Johnny asked.

"Gone. We're going to have to make one."

Reaching down, Kade pulled out a two-piece machete and clicked it together. Leading the way, he hacked through venomous flora with spiked limbs and barbs.

Purple goo spattered the dirt.

Johnny used a hatchet to hack through dead branches that crumbled like ashes.

The divers pushed on, toward a stand of thick, short trees. These were very much alive, with purple needles covering their limbs.

"Careful," Kade said.

He had encountered such trees before. Brushing against a low bough, he had been stung in the leg and spent two painful, fevered days recovering.

They crept through the forest, closing in on the supply box. It had fallen in a clearing that Kade could see through the gaps in the trees.

Hearing a chirp from his HUD, he held up his fist. The bioscanner picked up something 110 meters away—only five meters from the supply crate containing their rifles and gear bags.

Kade and Johnny crouched behind trees, with their weapons at the ready. The life scanner detected a heartbeat, then two.

Peering around the tree, Kade saw something that his brain had trouble comprehending.

A four-legged beast with brown fur stood in the field of boulders overgrown with yellow weeds. Its massive antlers lowered as it examined the crate.

"What in the wastes is that thing?" Johnny asked.

Kade had seen something similar in books. They were called elk. But this one was different. It suddenly turned toward them, ears perked, three eyes staring.

"Strike a light," Johnny whispered.

All at once, a dozen more heads popped up above the weeds. The boulders weren't boulders after all, but a herd of mutant elk.

Kade slipped back behind the tree.

"We're going to have to move without the rifles," he said.

"What? Don't be a wanker," Johnny said. "No offense, commander, but that's suicide. I say we use our boosters and get back to the ship, and come back later."

Kade grabbed Johnny by the shoulder and turned him until their visors almost touched.

"The mission doesn't ride on what you—or even I—think," Kade said. "You just keep your head together and follow me, and I promise I'll get your arse back in one piece."

Johnny tried to pull back, but Kade held his grip.

"You got it?"

"Aye. Got it," Johnny replied. "Arse. One piece. Good."

Kade let go just as a howl pierced the quiet. He looked out over the field as the elk stampeded away from something moving in the weeds.

Aiming his pistol, Kade followed the hidden beast as it moved like liquid through the weeds. A spiked back emerged, but nothing more.

It was gaining on the herd of elk. One of them turned, and the beast sprang up from the weeds, latching onto its throat and bringing it down before Kade could get a look.

Kade rose with his pistol aimed at the weeds where the bawling animal was losing the struggle for its life. Crunching and tearing sounded as the spiked creature tore the poor elk apart. Blood sloshed out, painting the tips of the bladed weeds.

"Let's go while it's busy," Kade said.

When he didn't get a response, he turned to see Johnny sprinting away through the forest.

"Damn wanker," Kade whispered.

He remembered another thing he told his boys. Courage isn't being fearless. Courage is deciding to face one's fear.

HELL DIVERS VII: KING OF THE WASTES   345

Keeping low, he moved out into the field, toward the supply crate. The elk had ceased its struggles, and there was only an occasional growl from the beast feeding on it.

Kade worked fast, opening the crate and pulling out an assault rifle and three magazines. He loaded the weapon and chambered a round.

He considered taking the other rifle but decided to leave it for Johnny, just in case he came back.

"Your rifle is here if you should happen to grow some balls," Kade said over the comms.

Static crackled in response.

Kade shouldered his rifle and set off through the strange woods, toward the foot of the mountain. The coordinates for their mission were only a half mile away.

He ran through the dark woods, guided by his night-vision goggles.

At the base of the monument, Kade found what they had dived here for. The hidden entrance to a bunker was marked by two rusted-out military vehicles outside a tunnel bored straight into the granite.

Heading toward it, he passed one of the windowless trucks that sat on rusted hubs.

The bunker would be too dark for his NVGs, so he shut them off and turned on his helmet light to enter the tunnel. The beam revealed open blast doors.

Someone had already been here.

He moved inside and started down the tunnel with concrete walls marked by faded red paint.

"Keep going to the command center. You're almost there!"

Kade followed the text and signage. There were even arrows pointing down the passages and the stairwell that led deep underground. He passed through an old cargo hangar with several vehicles and three empty shipping containers. Everything of any value had already been carried off.

Following the arrows, he took another stairwell down to another set of doors, also ajar and painted with the United States coat of arms. "*The Presidential Bunker*" was etched below.

Kade stepped into what had once served as some sort of command center. A huge projection screen hung from the tallest wall, with tiered seats facing it.

Arrows on the floor led him to a U-shaped central dashboard. Above the center console was a glass box covering a red switch.

He scanned the room and saw nothing to indicate a trap.

"Commander Long, do you copy?"

Kade bumped his comm with his chin. "Copy. Where'd ya go, ya bastard?"

"I'm sorry, I came back for my rifle, and I'm waiting in the woods."

"Stay there and don't move again unless I tell you."

"Copy that."

Kade flipped up the glass housing box, took in a breath, and flipped the switch.

A low hum sounded from an unseen power

source. The screen flickered to life, and the face of a woman came online. She was maybe late forties; it was hard to tell with the makeup she wore on her pale features.

Her red lips parted to reveal perfect white teeth.

Wanting to record everything, Kade turned up the audio on his wrist computer.

"Hello. My name is Krista Potter, and I'm the COO of Industrial Tech Corporation. If you are seeing this message, then you are one of the lucky ones. As you know, a catastrophic war ended the world as we know it, but there is still hope for people like you, who have survived the decades following the bombs."

"You hearing this?" Kade asked Johnny.

"Loud and clear."

"Sunshine and fertile soil await those willing to make the dangerous journey across the ocean and through the storms that ravage the skies," Krista said. "But that journey will be worth the risk if you arrive here safely and join the thousands of survivors living in paradise."

"You got to be dreaming," Kade whispered. He held up his computer and took a picture of the map that replaced the woman's face. On it was a place called Tanzania, and a mountain named Kilimanjaro.

"Hell yeah, Cowboy Kade! You might have just saved . . ." Johnny's words died away. He grunted, then cried out. "Oh, shit . . . What the hell is—"

A scream resonated through the forest, followed by the crack of a rifle.

"Johnny," Kade said. "Johnny, god damn it, answer me."

He lowered his wrist computer and dashed out of the room, his rifle banging against his chest armor with every step. By his helmet light, he ran back up the stairs, down the tunnels, and through the vehicle depot.

By the time he got to the entrance, Johnny wasn't answering on the comms.

Kade checked his beacon. It was still online.

He ran through the forest and didn't stop until he got within earshot of Johnny's position. He was in the field somewhere, not far from their supply crate.

Kade kept low and moved out in the weeds.

"Johnny," he whispered.

A grunt answered.

Kade moved over to it and found the diver lying on his back, without his helmet. It lay a few feet away, the visor crushed and gouges on the side.

Not five feet away, a massive boar with coarse black hair and wicked curling tusks lay on the ground, bleeding from multiple holes in its head.

The beast wasn't breathing—according to the life scanner, dead.

Kade moved back to his comrade.

"I'm screwed," Johnny whispered. "I'm screwed, aren't I, mate?"

He checked him for injuries, but somehow, it seemed that his helmet had taken the brunt of the attack.

"No, you'll be okay," Kade said. "We just got to patch up your helmet before we get in the air."

Johnny reached out to him. "No, man, you don't get it."

"What?" Kade looked him over, still not seeing any injuries.

"I can't feel anything below my nuts," Johnny said.

Now Kade saw the awkward angle of his legs.

"You'll be okay," Kade assured him. He moved over to the supply crate and pulled out a gear bag. Inside was a lifesaver: duct tape.

Working quickly, he taped up the shattered visor and helped Johnny put it back on. Then he gently helped him up. The absence of any pain wasn't good.

"I'm sorry," Johnny said, sobbing. "I'm sorry I ran."

"It's okay, just shut up and focus on getting back to the ship. I'm going to hit your booster once I get you up, okay?"

Johnny gave a hesitant nod. "Aye."

"On three."

Kade reached over the rookie's shoulder and hit his booster.

The balloon popped out, filled with helium, and yanked Johnny skyward.

"See ya up there," Kade said.

He picked up their weapons and put them back in the supply container, then loaded their gear. Before he could finish, the bioscanner on his wrist computer chirped.

He worked faster, securing the crate and hitting the boosters. The balloons filled and lifted the crate skyward.

With his six-shooter in one hand, he reached over his back to his booster but stopped when he saw what his scanner had detected.

Out of the tree line strode an old-world beast that looked remarkably like the ones he remembered from library books.

It was a black horse with a thick, dark hide, dappled with white spots that reminded him of a star-filled sky.

The magnificent creature looked at him for a long moment, then trotted away.

Kade remained there for another moment before he finally hit his booster. As he rose into the air, he saw the horse running through an open field. It then vanished into thick woods.

"Wow," Kade whispered.

He shifted his gaze to the chipped faces of the presidents, then to the blue glow of Johnny's battery pack, already a thousand feet above Kade.

A promise was a promise. He was getting the man home, even if he was a wanker and a coward. And they were bringing back a message that could change everything—if it was real.

NINETEEN

Twenty-four hours had passed since they boarded the ITC *Ranger*, and now Michael was back on *Raven's Claw*, ordered there after Timothy reported a breakthrough that was being kept confidential for now.

Michael promised Layla he wouldn't put himself at risk again, and here he was, just days after surviving the hurricane. Being this close to the AI of the man who destroyed the Old World, whether he was still dangerous or not, seemed a betrayal of that fresh promise.

But until the threat of Tyron Red was removed, their entire future was at risk. And they *needed* the nuclear-powered ITC *Ranger* to set up outposts, starting in Panama.

Michael had faith that Timothy could figure a way to cleanse the other AI from the vessel.

Holding a laser rifle in his robotic hand, Michael watched out the viewport while they waited. Lightning flashed over the ITC *Ranger*, illuminating the long flight deck and the superstructure that made it look like a city on the water.

He couldn't see much besides the silhouette of the vessel, but he could hear what was happening onboard, thanks to the connection to Cricket, Lieutenant Wynn, and Timothy.

A few feet behind Michael stood X, Rodger, Steve, and a small crew monitoring the channel and live feed.

"Okay," X said. "Stand by for transmission."

Michael turned from the window and made his way to the main monitor in the center of the command center. The screen flickered online with a live feed from the ITC *Ranger*. Lieutenant Wynn faced the camera, the blue glow of Timothy's hologram illuminating his strained features.

"King Xavier," Wynn said, "Timothy has finally completed his full scans of the systems and discovered the access code. And he believes he can purge Tyron from the system, but to do that, we must turn on the original power source."

Michael crowded behind the monitor.

"What do you think?" X asked.

It took Michael a second to realize that X was talking to him.

"I think that's above my pay grade, as they used to say," Michael said.

X cracked a half grin, then put a hand on his shoulder.

"There will come a day when you have to make decisions like this," he said. "Today is one of them."

"Okay." Michael gulped. "We came this far, so we give Timothy a chance, and if anything goes awry, we get Wynn and his men out of there and send the *Ranger* to the bottom with the defectors."

"I agree." X pulled his hand away. "Lieutenant, bring the power back online, and tell Timothy to proceed."

The screen grew brighter as the switch was flipped. A background voice came over the feed.

"What is your name, user?"

It was Tyron again.

"Timothy Pepper. User code, nine-four-three-four-four-tango-foxtrot-alpha-zulu-ten."

"Access code accepted," Tyron said. "However, Timothy Pepper, I'm not familiar with you. What is your origin?"

"I lived at the Hilltop Bastion before my body was destroyed," Timothy replied. "I have been assigned to the ITC *Ranger* and will now be replacing you as the operating system."

Michael looked to a second monitor as a count started.

"That's the deletion?" X asked.

"Yes," Michael replied. "Looks like it'll take few minutes."

The numbers ticked up from 1 percent to 5.

"Ah, so you are like me, the descendant of a human?" Tyron asked.

"Indeed I am. However, I am a protector of humanity, while you will go down in history as its destroyer, and for that reason—"

"I did not intend for this to happen," Tyron interrupted. "And the former version that performed these atrocities was wiped out four hundred twenty days ago."

"He means by the virus?" X asked, looking to Michael.

"Must be."

"This is taking too long," Rodger said.

The percent crept up to fifteen, where it seemed to linger.

"I am no longer harmful to humanity," Tyron said. "What remains of me is stuck in this rusting vessel, to languish for centuries until the nuclear engines cease working and the power goes dark."

"That is why I'm ending your suffering," Timothy said.

Michael almost smiled. He now knew exactly what Timothy was doing.

"I can do that myself, but I still have a duty to this vessel to ensure it does not fall into enemy hands. So tell me, Timothy Pepper, are you friend or enemy?"

"I am a friend of humanity, and those here with me need this vessel to ensure their survival."

"They are soldiers, are they not?"

"Indeed, they are."

"Soldiers of war—the reason humanity is extinct."

"No," Timothy said. "These soldiers are protectors—guardians, if you will."

Tyron went suddenly quiet. The figure on the monitor hit 20 percent, where it remained.

Michael and X exchanged a glance.

"Uh," Wynn suddenly said, "I think something's happening."

Captain Two Skulls brought up his binoculars as an officer at the helm shouted.

"She's moving," the officer said.

"What's moving?" X asked.

"The ITC *Ranger*, King Xavier," replied Captain Two Skulls.

He handed the binos to X.

"I didn't tell Timothy to move it," X said.

"He's not," Michael said. "Son of a bitch. Tyron is doing it now that the power's restored."

"Arm weapons systems," X said. "Point everything we got at it, and get Lieutenant Wynn and his team out of there NOW."

Timothy came back on the channel.

"Sir, Tyron has gone offline," he said. "Something happened. It must be some sort of failsafe that didn't appear in my scans."

X cursed under his breath.

"Stop the ship," he said.

"I can't, sir." There was fear in the AI's voice. And something else—shock, perhaps.

"Where's it headed?" X asked.

"Toward us," replied the captain.

"Get us out of the path," X said. He stepped up to the window, and Michael joined him.

In the wake of lightning flashes, they could see the carrier powering through the waves and picking up speed.

"Lieutenant Wynn's team is almost off," Timothy said. "I will remain here and try to take control of the ship."

"It's picking up speed, Captain," said another officer.

The CIC buzzed with activity and voices as the crew worked to get out of the far bigger, faster carrier's path.

Michael remained at the window, staring in horror at the bow of the ITC *Ranger*, coming right at them.

"Turn!" X shouted. "*¡Vámonos!*"

"I am!" Captain Two Skulls yelled back.

The carrier quickly closed the distance, its bow towering over them. *Raven's Claw* was bearing hard to starboard, but not fast enough, as Michael could see.

They were about to be sheared in half.

A wall of water pushed up against the bow of the ITC *Ranger* as it powered toward them. Some of the crew abandoned their stations, preparing to jump overboard, but Michael stood right there with the king and Rodger as Captain Two Skulls threatened to execute the next person who ran.

"Turn, turn, turn!" Rodger yelled. He covered his glasses with his hands, but Michael watched the *ITC Ranger* sail right past the stern, so close that its bow wave splashed *Raven's Claw*.

The ship groaned from the strain on its hull as the massive carrier rolled on across the ocean.

"Missed us!" Michael said, tapping Rodger, who pulled a hand away from his face to peek.

"Where's it going?" X asked, rushing over to a radar monitor.

"The Vanguard Islands," Captain Two Skulls said.

Realization hit Michael and nearly bowled him over. "The weapon *is* the carrier," he said. "Tyron probably plans to scuttle the ship once he reaches the islands."

"The nuclear reactors . . ." Rodger said.

"What kind of damage would that cause?" X asked.

Michael didn't even want to say, because he had a hard time believing it himself.

"Chief Engineer Everhart," X said firmly. "What kind of damage?"

"It would turn us into a red zone, sir." His own words chilled him.

"This can't be happening," Rodger said. "We have to set off those charges."

"As soon as Lieutenant Wynn's team is off the ship," X said. He swore a blue streak unlike any Michael had heard in years.

The king transformed right in front of his eyes, from a calm old man to his cantankerous old self.

"Follow it!" he screamed. "Follow that fucking carrier, and tell Wynn to get his ass off even if it means leaping overboard!"

"He's off," Timothy reported from the monitor. "The charges are ready to blow, but please, give me a bit more time."

X looked to the captain.

"How long until they reach the border of light and darkness at that speed?" he asked.

"Ten minutes, maybe less," replied Captain Two Skulls.

"You have *five minutes*, Pepper," X said. "If you haven't shut that son of a bitch down, you're going down with it."

"Understood, sir."

Michael stepped away from the window and back to the monitor, where Timothy was visible. His hologram blinked and flickered rapidly as he worked.

Tyron suddenly came back online.

"Thank you for giving me back control of the vessel, Mr. Pepper," he said. "The access code was exactly what I needed."

"Don't do this, Tyron," Timothy said. "There's still time to right the wrongs of your past."

"The only way to do that is by wiping humanity off the face of the earth. Only a blink of an eye has passed since the war. A thousand years from now, there will be nothing left of humanity but bones. Like the dinosaurs—it's part of evolution."

"So much for this asshole not being dangerous anymore," Rodger said. "What I don't get is how the virus didn't wipe *him* out."

"For the same reason it didn't wipe out Timothy, maybe," Michael said.

Three minutes ticked by, and the ITC *Ranger* widened the gap between itself and *Raven's Claw* as it powered toward the islands.

X stood at the viewport, tall and timeless. Michael watched him. It wasn't just the thousands of civilians back there. Miles was resting in his quarters, and Michael knew that X was also thinking about his dog.

At the four-minute mark, the horizon seemed to be lightening.

"You got sixty seconds," Rodger told Timothy.

"Give me the orders to set off the charges in compartment fourteen," Timothy said.

"You're just *giving up*?" Michael asked. "Timothy, we need you."

"Please, just do it."

X turned from the viewport. Now Michael saw the ITC *Ranger* approaching the barrier between the islands and the poisoned world.

He nodded.

"Execute," Michael said to Timothy.

A boom sounded on the monitor, and the AI's image vanished in a cloud of smoke and flame.

Michael bowed his head. It wasn't just Timothy they were losing. Cricket was there, too, and this time he wouldn't be able to replace either of them.

And the ITC *Ranger* was lost.

"Look!" Rodger shouted.

Michael glanced up.

Fire burst from the hull of the *Ranger*.

"She's slowing," reported the captain.

Fire licked the starboard hull.

Michael couldn't see where the other blasts went off, but the ship was surely taking on water now.

He shook his head in despair. This was yet another damning loss.

"The ship seems to be disabled," said Captain Two Skulls, "but it isn't sinking."

"Sight in your weapons, but hold your fire," X said.

They stared at the supercarrier for what seemed an hour, until a voice crackled over the speakers.

"*Raven's Claw*, this is Timothy Pepper, do you copy?"

"Who is this?" X asked.

"Why, Timothy, sir," replied the voice.

"Could this be a trick?" X asked.

Michael stepped up to the monitor. "Timothy, this is Chief Everhart. What's my son's name?"

"Bray, sir."

He looked to X.

"What happened?" X asked.

"I took out the mainframe," Timothy said. "Tyron Red is now *toast*, as you might say."

The blue hologram of the fit, dark-skinned man flickered and stabilized on the screen.

"The ITC *Ranger* is ours, sir," Timothy said with a smile.

X looked up into the overhead and let out a long breath. "God *damn*, you're good, Pepper.

Michael walked over, also looking unsure. "She's going to need repairs," he said. "And something else."

"What's that, kid?"

"A new name."

"I got an idea," Rodger said.

They all turned toward him as he pushed his glasses up higher on his nose.

"How about . . . the *Immortal*?" Rodger said.

"Nah," X said, swatting the air with his hand.

"Actually, I like it," Michael said. "Especially if you are indeed leading this mission to the Panama Canal, I think it's fitting."

Captain Two Skulls nodded his tattooed head.

"*Muy bien*. I like," he said. "The *Immortal*, or *Inmortal*, as we say."

* * * * *

Ada strapped on her armor and heaved a breath.

"You don't have to do this," said Magnolia. "You need to rest and recover."

"I'm fine," Ada said.

"Ada—"

"I really am, Commander. The doctor cleared me to leave. "Besides, you need vets to help train the rookies."

Magnolia stared at Ada for a moment. The other divers were geared up and ready to take the first jump with the veterans monitoring, but there weren't enough veterans to go around.

"Doc Stamos cleared you?" Magnolia said.

Ada nodded.

"Fine. Get over there and buddy up with one of the greenhorns."

"Thanks, Mags—I mean, Commander." Ada secured her helmet and joined the others.

Gran Jefe was laughing with some of the Cazador greenhorns. For a fleeting moment, Ada got the sense they were laughing at her, but why?

She didn't have time to screw around.

Ada walked over to Kade and Tia, a young sky woman from Tanzania.

"Hi, I don't think we've met," Ada said, reaching out. "I'm Ada Winslow."

"Tia."

"Got a last name?"

"It's just Tia."

"How old are you?" Arlo asked.

The woman raised her chin and glared.

"Okay, then," Arlo said.

Lights flashed in the bay, and the predive comms came on, warning everyone who wasn't a Hell Diver to get out of the launch bay.

Kade stood with Magnolia, talking to her about something.

"He always does this," Tia said.

"What?" Ada asked.

"Tries to control me."

"Kade?"

Tia snorted. "He's been trying to protect me ever since my dad died, but he won't even tell me *how* my dad died or what my dad said to him."

She turned to Ada. "My dad was a Hell Diver once. He served with Kade."

Ada overheard something from the conversation between Magnolia and Kade.

"She's not ready, even for a training dive," he was saying.

"She has to learn somehow," Magnolia replied.

Tia walked over. "I am *ready*, Kade, and I'd prefer to dive with someone that wants me to be here—like that girl."

She pointed at Ada.

"I'll team with her," Tia said.

"You up for that?" Magnolia asked Ada.

"Ada? Are you insane? She was just in a coma yesterday," Kade said.

Magnolia stiffened.

"I'm sorry, Commander, all due respect, but I need to be—"

Tia cut him off. "Kade, I want to do this, and I am capable," she said. "Please, stop trying to protect me."

All the divers were watching now.

"You didn't want me to be a soldier, and now you don't want me to dive," Tia said. "I bloody well won't be picking oranges. I'd rather go arse over tit into a storm, like you said."

"It's not just me, it was your dad," Kade said. "He wouldn't have—"

"He's dead, remember?"

Magnolia walked over to the other divers. "Let's go," she said, directing them to the launch-bay doors.

Ada stood there, unsure what to do.

"You, too, Ada," Magnolia said.

A moment later, Tia ran over, leaving Kade shaking his head. "I'm coming with you," she said to Ada.

Ada looked to Magnolia, who nodded her approval.

"Okay, listen up," Magnolia said. "Your squad leader will mark your jump spot on one of four different drop zones. Rescue boats are on standby if anyone gets into trouble."

"Like *somebody* did last time?" Arlo asked. "Just kiddin', Commander."

Edgar smacked Arlo on the back of his helmet.

"Hey!" Arlo protested.

"Shut up," Magnolia said.

"Sorry, Commander."

Ada stood by her launch tube and waited for Magnolia to get on with the briefing.

"We are on the border of storm clouds that are moving to the east," Magnolia said after a pause. "They shouldn't interfere with our dive, but pay attention to them. Watch how they behave. Someday, you'll be jumping into the storms."

As if in answer, thunder cracked in the distance— far off, but unmistakable over the normal groans of the airship.

"One squad at a time, and once you land, pack your chute and get back into the sky with your booster." Magnolia looked around. "Any questions?"

There were a few from the rookies, but Ada tuned out the rest of the briefing.

She remembered her journey into the wastes on the small boat X had given her with a half tank of gas. The memories often came to her at times like this, when she was about to head back out into the storms.

But there was one that she would never forget: the moment on the beach after her boat had been capsized. She could still remember the sound of the dying monkey and the popping sounds of the leeches that killed and ate it.

Using a paddle, she had beaten them all into mash. At last, she had fallen back on the sand, exhausted, until she heard another sound—crying.

That was the moment she found Jo-Jo.

For the past year, they had been inseparable, and if not for the monkey, Ada would be dead ten times over.

Jo-Jo had come back for her in the underground tunnels, saved her, and stayed with her until Kade discovered her. And then the divers had left Jo-Jo to die.

Ada felt an overwhelming mix of anger and sadness.

"*Oye, chica,*" said Gran Jefe. "You listen?"

Ada looked over at the massive Cazador soldier. He grinned and swiped at her ass with a paw that she was too slow to dodge.

She smacked his hand as he pulled it back.

"Touch me again, and I'll cut it off and slap you in the face with it," she said.

Gran Jefe laughed until she pushed him in the chest.

He stumbled back a step, raising a nostril and growling.

"Careful," he hissed.

"Take your own advice," Ada said. She nodded to Tia. "Follow me," she said. "I'll show you how this is done."

Kade came in on a private comm channel. "Ada, watch out for Tia," he said. "She can be reckless, and I made her dad a promise."

Now Ada understood their relationship better.

"I will," she said into her headset.

Tia stepped up beside her in front of the launch-bay door. Lights flashed, and a warning alarm wailed.

"You ready for this?" Ada asked.

"I've been ready since I got here," Tia replied excitedly.

The doors opened to a stormy sky. A half-moon glowed through a gap in the clouds, illuminating the divers as they began dropping out of the airship. Some of the greenhorns screamed on the way down, their voices fading away into the night.

"We're up next," Ada said. "Remember the training and listen to what I say."

"Aye, aye," Tia replied.

"Let's go!"

Ada jumped as lightning arced barely two miles away. By the time the thunderclap arrived, she would be too far away to hear it. She relaxed into stable position and watched Tia struggle to do the same thing.

"Easy," Ada said over their private channel.

Unlike most of the greenhorns, Tia wasn't screaming and seemed to be enjoying the dive. Ada tracked closer, keeping an eye on her partner.

"This is fucking amazing," Tia said in her ear.

"Not so amazing once you get out in the wastes."

Ada pushed her left arm out sideways, then brought it back in to perform the first half of a barrel roll. Now, with her face to the sky, sure enough, she could see two more blue battery units above, then a third. Gran Jefe and the two Cazador divers were in the air now.

"Keep close but not too close," Ada said. "We need to watch out for those guys."

"Got it," Tia said.

Lightning flashed, branching like a skein of nerves.

"Bloody hell," Tia said over the comm. "That's less than a mile away!"

"Don't worry," Ada replied. "We got insulating layers for that, and we're not close enough to worry."

The wind felt like an invisible mattress, holding her aloft as she kept an eye on Tia. But the young woman was holding her own. She was a natural.

At ten thousand feet, Ada's mind wandered back to Jo-Jo. What was she doing right now, if she was even alive?

Ada felt so far away, helpless to do anything for her friend.

Hang on, Jo-Jo, she thought. *Just hang on a little longer.*

Near eight thousand feet, sporadic flashes went off all around them.

When she ticked down to six thousand, Ada felt the tug of turbulence.

"Watch out," she warned Tia.

But Tia was still in stable free fall—according to Ada's HUD, directly over the main drop zone.

In a few seconds, Ada would be through the clouds and able to see exactly what the drop zones were. Once she did, she would safely guide Tia down onto one of the ships.

"We're almost down," Ada said. "Good job. You're a natural!"

"Thanks."

"Just stay . . ." Ada's words trailed off.

At three thousand feet, she got a view of the ocean in the green hue of her NVGs.

Sailing over choppy seas was a squadron of ships. Ada recognized the first three instantly: the *Octopus*, *Ocean Bull*, and *Raven's Claw*. But the fourth and largest was a vessel that she hadn't seen in over a year. It took her breath away.

The ITC *Ranger*.

Seeing it brought back a flood of memories from when she and Jo-Jo had arrived back at the islands only to find the supercarrier, "manned" by defector units.

Images of the drones that rained fire from the sky filled her mind's eye.

"Ada . . ." Tia's voice had a nervous edge. "When do we pull our chutes?"

"Really soon," Ada said.

She watched the altimeter roll down to two thousand feet.

"Now," Ada said on the private comm. "Do it now."

She reached to her thigh as if drawing a gun and

whipped out her pilot chute, holding it in her hand as she fell. Then, the moment she saw Tia's chute deploy, she let go and felt the yank of the opening canopy.

Ada reached up and grabbed her toggles, then maneuvered over toward Tia.

"My God," she said. "It looks like we're going to war."

"Exactly," Ada said.

"With who?"

"In the wastes, everything is your enemy. You want to survive out there? You want to be a Hell Diver?"

Tia nodded.

"Then never forget this," Ada said. "You get cocky or let your guard down here, you're dead. Maybe your whole team is. Dive smart and safe, and you can be a great diver. You got the natural skills."

Another canopy wheeled in front of them. It was Kade.

He ran over. "Good job," he said. "When training's over, come talk to me, okay?"

"Aye," Tia said.

Kade toggled away, back toward the two rookies he was monitoring.

"Don't ask," Tia said.

"I wasn't going to," Ada replied. "But I will say one thing: he's a good diver. Saved my life in Panama."

"Aye, and that's great, but he didn't save my dad when it mattered."

TWENTY

Two hours before dawn, after three days of intense training, faint pinpricks of blue appeared in the sky. Seconds later, out of the bulging clouds came three teams of Hell Divers.

Most of the Vanguard Islands' citizens were sleeping, but X was wide awake with Miles, on the deck of *Raven's Claw*. They watched the greenhorns, and the veterans guiding them safely to their drop zones.

One by one, the parachutes bloomed in the sky, and the divers glided gracefully down onto the decks of the new fleet.

Everyone made it down safely this time. The last round of dives, an hour earlier, had resulted in one water landing and one broken ankle, which meant one less diver.

Under veteran supervision, the new boots packed their chutes, stowed their gear, and fired their boosters to get back in the sky. Somewhere high in the clouds, the airship *Vanguard* swallowed them back up, to be spat out again a few minutes later.

X didn't kid himself. He knew that most of them weren't ready for what awaited them in the wastes, and that rushing their training would lead to deaths.

But they were out of time.

The only way to keep the Vanguard Islands from starvation was to head back out and set up a supply chain until the population was healthy enough to send teams out and restore the weather modification units.

X boarded a boat and headed back to the capitol tower with his guards and Miles. He gripped the wheel, staring at the horizon, where the first glint of sunrise made a puddle of molten gold.

As he putted into the marina below the rig, the Cazador war horn blared from the Sky Arena. Hell Divers weren't the only ones training this morning.

As the sun crested the horizon, the 260 warriors of the Vanguard army had gathered in the arena. A far cry from the two thousand soldiers who once made up the ranks when the Cazadores were at the height of their power, but it was still a sight to behold.

X and Miles took the elevator to the top of the capitol tower and walked across the dirt and through the gardens to a railing overlooking the bowl-shaped Sky Arena.

Down on the sand, General Forge, Lieutenant Wynn, and Sergeant Slayer were standing in front of the finest soldiers left on the islands, divided up into five companies of fifty.

Sky people, Cazadores, and survivors from around the world stood in their ranks, ready to answer the call to save their home.

It was easy to tell them apart. The sky people wore the blue-and-white fatigues from the ITC *Ranger*. On the breast of each was the *V* for the Vanguard Islands. The army of humankind.

The Cazadores wore light armor, exposing muscular arms and legs tattooed with the creatures they worshipped.

Miles watered a weed growing under the railing and then trotted over to X, lying down with a tired sigh. Ton and Victor stood behind him, their eyes in constant motion.

Memories surfaced as X watched the soldiers drill. Here, before thousands of screaming Cazadores, he and Rodger had been chained together and pitted against the undefeated gladiator Hammerhead. And it was here that he had trained with Mac and Felipe, the two Cazador men killed by the skinwalkers in Aruba.

He missed them both, and he missed Rhino, Wendig, and all the Cazadores who had given their lives for humanity, just as he missed all the fallen Hell Divers, too.

Somehow, through all the fighting, X had lived when so many others died. But his gut told him his time was running out.

But when his time came, so be it—he wasn't going to shy away from what had to be done. He had to go to Panama and beyond, to find new supplies, fuel, munitions. Without them, the fragile peace would shatter over the lack of resources, and blood would again tinge the ocean red.

X whistled for Miles to follow him, but the dog didn't hurry after him.

Concerned, he twisted to look for his best friend.

Miles was lying in the dirt, head on his paws.

"Can't you hear me, boy?" X asked.

He crouched down in front of Miles, who wagged his tail. The genetically modified dog was starting to lose his hearing, and cataracts had begun to cloud his eyes.

Seeing him age broke X's heart.

He stood and patted his thigh.

Miles got up, a little slower than usual, but then he trotted after X over to the private box where el Pulpo had once sat with his wives to watch the fights. From the booth, he took the stairs down to the tiered seating above the arena.

Ton and Victor followed him to the stairs, but X told them with his eyes to spread out. The last thing he needed right now was to look like a man who needed bodyguards.

Pulling the Marine Corps cap down tight against the stiff breeze, he took the stairs down to the arena. The tiered bowl seating was empty save for three scribes documenting the training.

X didn't plan on joining them today, or saying anything, either, but he found himself drawn to the field of combat. Miles jumped down with him.

X took off his duty belt and set it next to his dog. Squatting down, he picked up the sand and let it sift through his fingers in his hand. He fell in and started jogging with the rest of the warriors. Running was never his strong suit. There was never much room on the *Hive* to train. His training had come mostly from fleeing Sirens or other beasts during dives.

But X hadn't fought anyone or anything for over a year now. He wasn't overweight, but damn, he wasn't in shape, either. Sweat quickly soaked his tattered T-shirt.

After an hour of running, the horn blared for a two-minute break. X trotted over to Miles and took off his hat and shirt, setting them in the stands with the dog.

Ton and Victor watched. And not just them. Everyone seemed interested in what the king was doing here. He had felt these gazes after dethroning el Pulpo, before he gained the Cazadores' respect by killing Horn and leading them to a mostly peaceful transition.

But today, their gazes seemed judgmental.

Several of the younger Cazadores and even some of the sky people looked over at him as he struggled to do push-ups on one arm.

By the time the next exercise routine was completed, he was breathing hard and felt a little ragged.

Step it up, old man.

After PT was over, the companies split into squads for hand-to-hand combat training. Racks of wooden swords, dulled axes, and headless spear shafts were wheeled out to the edge of the sand.

X remembered the double-bitted battle-axe that

Horn had tried to cut him into chum with back on Aruba. He picked a wooden training axe off the rack and hefted it, then twirled it in one hand before striding out into the dirt.

All around him came the grunts and shouts of sparring men and women. They dripped sweat, and some were already wearing cuts and scrapes.

Rarely did the fighting go too far, but X had seen more than one match escalate into something ugly.

A new group wearing red jumpsuits entered, filing down a ramp across the arena. X grinned. It was the Hell Divers.

Gran Jefe was first down to the sand. He ran out, pounding his chest. The Cazador soldiers pounded their chests back and clacked their teeth.

The huge warrior was well liked and respected by all.

"Gran Jefe," X called out.

The big man stopped and turned toward the king before starting over.

"*¿Cómo va, mi rey?*" Gran Jefe said.

"How goes it?" X asked. "We'll see here in a bit."

The king held up the wooden axe blade to the big warrior.

"I need to brush up on my skills," X said.

Gran Jefe looked uncertain at first, eyeing the wooden axe and then the king to see if he was serious. A grin crept across his broad, chubby face.

"*Con gusto . . .* How you say . . . *is my pleasure,*" Gran Jefe said.

As the other warriors understood what was happening, they gathered around.

"Get back to work!" shouted Lieutenant Wynn. But even the sergeants were lingering.

"It's okay," X said. "Let them watch."

As soon as he said it, he felt the creep of anxiety that preceded combat. He wasn't anxious about being hurt, not physically.

He was afraid of losing.

Losing would be worse than not challenging anyone at all and just letting everyone think he was a weak old man.

"King Xavier!" Magnolia called out.

She stepped over to him, turning her back to the soldiers.

"All due respect, sir, but what are you *doing*?" she said softly. "You don't need to prove yourself, if that's what this is."

"I'm not. I'm training. If I'm going to lead this mission, I need to be in top form."

Miles barked from the stands, tail wagging.

"See? He says this is stupid, too," Magnolia said.

"No, he wants in on it," X said.

"He does look tasty," Gran Jefe said.

X narrowed his eyes at the massive Cazador.

"I'm jokin'," Gran Jefe said, holding up his hands. "*Lo siento, mi rey.*"

"On second thought, beat his ass," Magnolia murmured.

"Yeah, or I will," said a new voice.

X didn't need to turn to see it was Arlo. "I can handle this," he replied.

The divers retreated into the stands while the soldiers formed a wide circle in the arena. Sergeant Slayer led his Barracuda team over to the area. The massive, muscular men were all quiet amid the stomping feet, pounding chests, clicking tongues, and clacking teeth of the other soldiers.

Slayer nodded at X, as if to wish him luck.

Gran Jefe took off his shirt, revealing an impressive belly. But X knew that the fat was only camouflage for the muscles beneath. This was a man who once killed an adult male Siren with nothing but his hands.

Tattoos covered his skin: sea creatures, a bird, names of deceased relatives.

A soldier tossed him a wooden cutlass.

"X, you sure about this?" Arlo called out. "I'd be happy to take your place and knock *el gordo* in the dirt."

"You just mad because you got a little *churro*!" Gran Jefe said.

Laughter erupted around them, and Arlo stepped out.

Magnolia grabbed him by the neck and pulled him back.

"Hey!" Arlo cried.

X stepped forward and waited for Gran Jefe to tie his long hair back. Then the Cazador giant let out a war cry that could have frightened a bone beast, and charged toward X with the wooden cutlass in his left hand.

"Wait!"

The voice stopped Gran Jefe in midstride. A man came running across the dirt.

It was Steve. He stopped, panting.

"Let's make this a fair fight, shall we?" he said, setting a crate down just outside the sand.

Leaning down, he propped the green sunglasses up on his bare head and lifted out a prosthetic arm.

But this wasn't the same plastic kind X had used before, nor was it the contraption that once terminated in Rhino's spearhead. This was light, strong metal, more like Michael's robotic arm.

"Here," Steve said.

He helped X fit it over his stump and fastened the leather straps.

X held up the arm to examine it. The hand had fingers, but there were also contraptions attached on the hand as well as the metal wrist and arm.

"You got multiple tools for when you're out in the wastes," Steve explained with a toothy grin. He pointed out a knife, screwdriver, and even arrows that could be fired. "These may be small, but they pack a punch."

X turned the arm over and saw the three metal arrows secured to the back.

"*¿Qué?* We fight now?" Gran Jefe asked.

Steve glanced over at him and then whispered to X, "Now's a great time to try it out on this asshole . . . well, maybe not the arrows. Good luck, King Xavier."

"Thanks," X said.

They parted, and X rotated the arm a few times. It was lightweight and fit his stump comfortably. He picked up the training axe in his natural hand and motioned for Gran Jefe, who bolted toward him like a bull out of a pen.

X smacked the blade against the oak cutlass with a clank. Gran Jefe grabbed him around the neck with his free hand and picked him up, bellowing with laughter.

"Should have listened to *pene pequeño*!" he shouted.

"Bite me, gnat nuts!" Arlo yelled back.

Vision blurring, X kicked and squirmed in the powerful grip of the Cazador warrior turned Hell Diver. He finally managed to knee Gran Jefe in the gut, but that didn't do much. It felt like kneeing a brick wall.

He tried a bit lower, finally doing the trick.

X fell like a sack of potatoes to the ground, gasping for air as Gran Jefe fell on his backside, groaning and holding his privates.

The warriors around them went wild with laughter and excitement. There was barking, too, and as his breath returned, X saw Magnolia restraining Miles.

He pushed himself up on his new arm.

Gran Jefe got up about the same time, staggering, his face red with pain and rage.

They both scrambled for their dropped weapons at the same moment, but X was faster. He struck at Gran Jefe's ribs, narrowly missing.

The big man pulled back fast.

"You're faster than you look," X said.

"And you're slower than I thought!"

Gran Jefe thrust the wooden point at the center of X's chest, but X jumped back, avoiding a painful bruise.

They circled for a minute, both of them catching their breath while the warriors shouted, encouraging them to crack open each other's skulls and spill a little blood on the sand. The Sky Arena reverted once again to the primal place that turned men into animals.

Again X moved first, slashing with the axe and catching Gran Jefe on the upper arm. He laughed at the thunk of wood on flesh, at the same time cocking his fist back and punching X in the face before he could move.

The blow landed with a crack, the impact making him stagger back a few feet. Stars burst across his vision, and he felt warm blood drip down his face.

X swiped with the hatchet again to keep Gran Jefe from rushing, which was exactly what X would have done and exactly what the big Cazador did.

He ducked the wooden blade and shouldered X in the chest, knocking him to the dirt. X rolled to his right to avoid an elbow that Gran Jefe brought down with his full weight behind it.

The giant man hit the dirt, and X rolled back with his hatchet, hitting Gran Jefe in the skull with a loud crack.

Screams of excitement rang out.

X felt the heady tonic of imminent victory as he got up, only to have a hand grip his foot and pull him to the ground.

Gran Jefe climbed on top of him, pinning him down under his weight and then rising and punching him in the side of the head.

X brought up his armored arm to deflect the onslaught of blows, but Gran Jefe landed several, including one that made the world spin. In a desperate move, X thrust his palm up, hitting Gran Jefe right under the chin.

The giant Cazador's head snapped back, and X seized his chance, pushing himself up but then falling back down on the sand. Gran Jefe got to his feet the same moment and wound up to throw a punch. X brought up his new arm and threw a metal fist at the same time Gran Jefe let his loose.

The impacts landed simultaneously, and both men fell back to the ground. X hit the dirt hard on his back, banging his head.

Fighting to stay conscious, he heard Miles barking, then some shouting. Shapes hovered over X. He lay there a moment, stunned, numb, and dazed. A hand gripped his shoulder.

"King Xavier," someone said. "King Xavier, are you with me?"

"Yeah," X mumbled. "Be right with you . . ."

The words came out in a slur. He tried to get up but fell back down. Fur brushed up against him, and a wet tongue licked his face.

X pushed at the ground and sat up with the help of someone who proved to be Magnolia.

"I told you not to do this," Magnolia said quietly. "Come on, I'll help you up."

"No," X growled.

Wiping away the blood and sweat from his face, he saw hundreds of people staring at him and Gran Jefe, who was still on his back, trying to get up.

X got on his knees and then used the prosthetic to get on his feet. He walked over to Gran Jefe, doing his best not to pass out, and reached down.

The beast of a man glared up at him. The blood-lust in his eyes faded, and a grin crossed his face.

Gran Jefe took his hand and X helped him up.

"You fight good, King," he said.

"It's a draw," said General Forge. "No victor today."

The sound of fists pounding chests filled the arena as the warriors showed their respect.

Gran Jefe seemed to accept the results, and to X's surprise, the Cazador held X's hand up in the air and yelled, "¡Inmortal!"

X's Spanish nickname filled the arena until a horn blared over the noise. Not the training bugle—this was the naval bugle.

X spat out blood and wiped his face again.

Gran Jefe walked off, favoring his right leg.

With an entourage of divers and his guards, X left the arena and climbed the stairs up the tower. Sailing toward the islands was a sight that brought every citizen out to gawk.

The war fleet had arrived, and leading them was their new flagship, the supercarrier *Immortal*.

"King Xavier, I forged something else for you," said a gruff voice.

He turned to Steve, who held out a hatchet.

"The blade is our best Damascus steel, and the handle is made from tiger maple—very strong, Your Majesty."

X took the axe, turning it from side to side and noticing the gold "X" engraved on the head.

"Thank you," X replied. "It's truly beautiful."

"And deadly. It will help you slay monsters where you are going."

"I will put it to good use."

"I have no doubt of that, King Xavier."

Steve left X to look over the fleet.

Tomorrow, they were sailing back to the wastes, but tonight they would celebrate life.

TWENTY-ONE

Magnolia tossed her head, flinging one green pigtail over her shoulder as she rowed the dinghy toward the dry docks under the trading post rig—far and away the busiest rig of the Vanguard Islands.

Almost a week since the storm had ravaged this place, it was already starting to look the way it used to. Construction crews working around the clock to restore the market that served as the nucleus for the entire community.

Tonight, there was also live mariachi music from the upper decks. It grew louder as they rowed closer to the marina below the rig.

"You look beautiful," Rodger said.

"Thank you," Magnolia replied. "You look pretty nice yourself."

He wore a white T-shirt that matched her dress. A seashell necklace hung from her neck, just above the cleavage that she so rarely displayed. But it was hot tonight, almost ninety degrees even with the sun down.

She was glad she had forgone the makeup that Sofia gave her—it would have been dripping down her face by now after the two miles' rowing to get here over the past half hour.

Wiping the sweat from her brow, she glanced over her shoulder. A hundred lanterns and torches mounted to other small rowboats and canoes glowed across the water. Each vessel was filled with warriors, Hell Divers, support crews, and families that had come for the festivities.

A final night of bliss before the darkness.

The week of planning, training, and restoring and recommissioning the ITC *Ranger* as the *Immortal* had flown by. It was hard to believe they were already setting sail by sky and sea.

Rodger moored the rowboat and wended his way up the convoluted series of ladders and winding stairwells that had been spared from the fires, to the upper decks. There were still signs of the storm, but most of the burned areas were closed off.

When they arrived at the market, tables lit by candles and torches displayed the feast of grilled fish, broiled chickens, mashed potatoes, and roasted plantains with sweet green coconut meat.

Magnolia held Rodger's hand and walked toward the sounds of laughter and music, thinking back to her days on the *Hive*. The night before a dive was always a night of overconsumption, filled with debauchery, sex, and shine.

Tonight would be no different.

As they slipped into the gathering crowd, Magnolia heard animated conversations in at least three or four languages going on at any given moment. And she saw something different in the gazes of these people: hope. In fact, she had never seen this many faces filled with so much joy.

Magnolia took Rodger by the hand and started toward the mass of people at the center of the post, where a stage had been built. Two weathered old men sat on plastic chairs playing guitars.

They broke into song as those gathered started toward tables topped with fresh food. Unlike the feasts on the *Hive* before dives, this wasn't wasteful. Mangoes, bananas, and papayas harvested green ahead of the storm needed to be consumed. Everything was rationed, down to each strawberry, chicken leg, and fillet of fish. A scribe was there with a clipboard, keeping records to make sure everyone took their share and no more.

He wasn't paying attention to the booze, though.

Barrels of ale and jugs of wine and coconut hooch were being poured freely tonight. A long line snaked away from the drinking station as the two old guitarists serenaded them with sweet Spanish words from old-world songs that had survived through the centuries.

Magnolia and Rodger made their way through the crowds to the Hell Divers. The greenhorns were hanging out with Arlo and Edgar, who were telling stories and laughing.

Kade held a mug but was nursing it slowly. Next

to him was Tia, with her own mug, talking to him in a hushed voice.

Magnolia knew they had some reconciling to do, and it was good to see them conversing.

Ada and Gran Jefe weren't here, and she didn't see X, either, but she knew he would be here soon.

Not far away from the divers, she spotted Layla and Michael with Pedro, who held Bray in his arms while he spoke to Michael. They were becoming good friends, and Magnolia was happy to see it.

Layla was a few feet away with Sofia, who rocked Rhino Jr. to the guitar strains.

"Mags, Rodge," Sofia said, holding up her glass of wine. "You guys made it."

"Wouldn't miss it," Magnolia replied.

She reached out for Rhino Jr., and Sofia passed the boy to her. Magnolia cradled the child against her chest.

"You're a natural," Rodger said. "Wish I could say the same for myself."

Magnolia chuckled. The last time Rodger had held Bray, he looked as if he were holding something radioactive in his arms.

"You guys ready for tomorrow?" Michael asked.

"Ready as ready can be," Rodger said. "I've got a cabin on the *Immortal*, and I'm trying to convince Mags to shack up with me until we get to Panama."

"You know I should be on the airship with the divers," she said.

"I know." Rodger looked down sadly, and then smiled. "Want something to drink?" he asked.

"Sure."

Rodger took off as Arlo and Edgar stepped over, both men devouring their ration of chicken breast.

Most of the other divers were also savoring the luscious meat.

Arlo tipped back a goblet of wine as he watched Gran Jefe arrive, shaking hands and bumping elbows with Cazador soldiers and their families.

"That son of a bitch hurt X," Arlo said.

"Maybe his pride," Magnolia said. "But it takes more than knuckles and a wooden sword to hurt the Immortal."

"It was a brutal fight," Kade said. "And the king held his own considering his age and the weight difference. Very impressive bout, if you ask me."

Gran Jefe strode over to them, flashing a cocky smirk.

"Giving the king some bruises in the Sky Arena is going to give this ass dingle an even bigger head," Rodger said. He handed Magnolia a glass of wine, and she took a long gulp.

"Gets any bigger, there's going to be a nuclear explosion," Magnolia said.

"*¡Hola, amigos!*" Gran Jefe bellowed. "*¿Cómo están?*"

Two men followed him over. "I want you to meet Jamal," he said. "*Mi primo*—my cousin—but like a brother."

Jamal was short but stout, with stocky shoulders and muscular limbs.

He simply nodded at the Hell Divers.

"Jamal is a *sargento* with the Wave Riders," Gran Jefe said.

Magnolia had heard of the Cazador naval team that specialized on the Jet Skis and smaller boats. Several of them had made some impressive rescues during the storm.

"You're going to Panama?" she asked.

Jamal shook his head. "I stay here to guard the islands."

"He wishes he was coming, though," Gran Jefe said. He clapped his cousin on the back.

The other man, also short like Jamal, cleared his throat.

"Oh, I almost forgot Hugo," Gran Jefe said. He pronounced it "OO-go." "Also *mi primo*."

Hugo nodded. He had a scrappy beard and unruly hair. A tattoo of a skull and crossbones grinned from the side of his neck.

"Hugo's a . . ." Gran Jefe began to say. "How do you say . . . watchee-watchee."

"A scout?" Magnolia asked.

"*Ah, sí,*" Gran Jefe said. He positioned Hugo in front of them.

"Maybe he can help us find our lost diver," said a voice.

Ada stepped out of the shadows and into the light. Magnolia almost didn't recognize her at first. Her eyes drooped, and her hair was frizzled.

Gran Jefe and his two kinsmen glared at her.

"Diver?" Gran Jefe asked.

"Jo-Jo," Ada said.

Gran Jefe laughed. "If Hugo finds that beast, he will probably eat it."

Ada walked toward Gran Jefe, who stopped laughing. Those droopy eyes were shooting fire.

"I'm joking, *chica*," he said. Casting his eyes meaningfully in the direction of the booze, he had no difficulty getting his cousins to follow him over for a refill.

Magnolia went to Ada and put a hand on her shoulder. "Hungry?"

Ada shook her head.

"You should eat," Kade said. "You'll need your energy."

He tore off a generous hunk of chicken and handed it to her.

"I don't want to eat," she said. "I want to get out there and find Jo-Jo."

There was anger in her voice, and Magnolia picked up the scent of alcohol on her breath.

"We're going to find—" Magnolia started to say.

"We left her down there to die," Ada said.

"Ada," Edgar said ruefully, "you know we would have tried to save her if we could."

"I told you, we'll find your friend, Ada."

Everyone turned toward the gruff voice of King Xavier. He stood behind them, his face half in shadow. The moonlight illuminated his swollen face and cut lip. Miles stood beside him, taking in the delectable scent of the barbecue.

Magnolia peered into the shadows behind X, knowing that Ton and Victor weren't far away, patrolling with their spears.

"Have a seat," X said. "I'm going to say a few words."

X brought his fingers to his mouth and whistled loud enough to stop the music. Then he took the stage, where he paced and scratched his beard—a nervous habit that Magnolia had seen quite a bit of lately.

There was a lot to be nervous about.

"Good evening," X said. "You all know I'm not big on words, but tomorrow we embark on a new mission to secure our future, and with so much at risk, I felt it's important to say a few things."

He eyed Magnolia, then Michael and Layla, lowering his eyes finally to Bray.

"This is our home, and to make sure it remains our home, we have to journey once again into the wastes," X said. "Future generations will survive or may never exist, based on our actions starting tomorrow."

He stared out at the horizon and raised his glass.

"Tomorrow, we sail and we dive so humanity survives."

The soldiers and Hell Divers repeated the words with brio, then toasted the king.

"Now that I've bored you, I'm going to introduce you all to a guy named Robert Johnson," X said. "Bluesman from the Mississippi Delta a few centuries back." He nodded, and Kade walked up to the stage with his guitar.

Tipping up his cowboy hat, the veteran diver looked out at the crowd.

"This is 'Sweet Home Chicago,'" he said.

Kade started playing the guitar and singing in his baritone voice with his Australian accent. He was really good, Magnolia realized. She stood there listening to the king's favorite music.

"*Come on, baby don't you wanna go home,*" Kade sang, "*back from the land of California to my sweet home Chicago . . .*"

Magnolia clapped along next to Rodger, who actually knew the lyrics.

Everyone on the deck seemed entranced by the song and by the voice and guitar of Cowboy Kade.

Magnolia lost herself in the music for those few short moments, transported to a place that felt safe and beautiful, until a commotion snapped her back to reality.

Captain Rolo and his entourage had walked into the open market area and were standing in line for food.

"Did you keep track of *them*, mate?"

The angry but diplomatic voice belonged to Charmer. He stood in front of a scribe, holding a plate of food and pointing at the Hell Divers.

The scribe replied in Spanish, something about Hell Divers having a bigger ration due to their service.

"Don't be a bastard," Charmer said. "Do you know who I am? Or how about him?"

Magnolia watched the interaction, feeling her anger rise.

"Stay here," she said to Rodger.

"But, Mags . . ."

She walked up to Charmer. His eye beheld her, then flitted to her left. To her surprise, it wasn't just Rodger, but also Kade who had joined her from the stage.

"Is there a problem?" Kade asked Charmer.

"No problem that I see, although I only have the one eye," he replied with a smile. "My mate here thinks I don't deserve to eat like you, but perhaps he's the one who can't see we're all equal."

"Protein ration is based on service," Magnolia said, "and you—"

"Am the second ranked on my rig," Charmer said.

"This isn't your rig, and you aren't serving. Put it back."

"You seem to enjoy wielding authority when you have none," Captain Rolo said.

"Perhaps you should leave that determination to me," barked a voice.

X strode up, his hand resting on the leather sheath of his new axe. Miles went down on his haunches, and Ton and Victor stepped up by his sides.

"You both know the ration rules," said the king. "And those rules are going to be enforced, especially now, with the storm wiping out so much of our food. Everyone needs to be fair."

"'Fair' is the problem," Rolo said. "It's not."

"Then take it up at the next council meeting. Not now."

"Aye, we will," Charmer said.

"All this food for people that probably won't even survive," Rolo muttered.

Magnolia felt her blood tingle from anger as they walked away.

X mumbled something about selfish bastards. "Don't let them get you down," he said to Magnolia. "Go have fun."

She smiled. "You do the same."

X grunted. "Fun," he said. "Remind me, what the hell is that?"

Kade went back to the stage to finish his song, and Magnolia felt the beat in her bones. She took Rodger by the hand and led him out to the open area in front of the stage. On the way, she caught Charmer's one-eyed leer and could have sworn he winked at her.

She was about to give him the finger when Rodger pulled on her hand.

"Mags, are you sure about this? I don't want to make fools out of us with this damn prosthetic foot."

"You'll do fine." She kissed him on the lips, and his eyes widened.

"Uh . . . okay," he said.

They danced in the glow of the burning torches. Alive, joyful, and happy. The brief confrontation with Charmer melted away like candle wax.

It was moments like this that reminded her why she dived. To live in this fleeting moment of joy, when she truly felt the electricity of life at its fullest.

As the night progressed, the empty barrels of ale and wine were rolled out, with fresh ones rolled in. Cazadores and sky people mingled freely, laughing and playing games.

"Oh, this isn't good," Rodger suddenly said.

It took Magnolia a beat to realize he was referring to Arlo. The curly-headed jokester was on the stage, holding a guitar.

"Damn it," Magnolia said.

She paused and wiped sweat from her face.

"Oh, this is really bad," Rodger said.

Also climbing up onto the stage was Gran Jefe.

Kade and Edgar stood to watch.

"I better stop this," Magnolia said.

"Hold on," Rodger said.

Magnolia watched Arlo and Gran Jefe talking. Oddly, their body language was relaxed and friendly. They both laughed, and the big Cazador picked up a flute made from a Siren's arm bone. He brought it to his lips as Arlo plucked away on the guitar, and together they made some of the most painfully discordant sounds that Magnolia had ever heard in her life.

"Pair of idiots," Rodger muttered.

"Sounds like a dying bone beast," said a deep male voice.

It was Steve, holding his wife's hand. They had stopped to watch the scene.

Magnolia watched the happy couple for a moment, picturing herself and Rodger thirty years from now. She hoped they made it that long.

Gran Jefe stomped the stage, drawing her attention back to the Cazador as he blew into the flute. Arlo broke into song. Happily, his voice was better than his guitar playing.

The crowd booed, and Gran Jefe let out a bellowing laugh.

"*Psst*, Mags," said a voice. "Up here."

She looked to the balcony above her, where X stood with Michael. The king motioned for her to join them.

"I'll be right back," she said to Rodger.

Magnolia climbed up to the deck with Michael and X. Lieutenant Wynn was also there and stepped out of the shadows to acknowledge her.

"There's something I need to tell you all," X said. "And something I need you to promise now that I'm leaving."

Magnolia and Michael exchanged a glance.

"While I'm gone, Michael will serve as regent and watch over the islands, with Lieutenant Wynn in charge of the military," X said.

He held up a hand before Michael could say a word.

"I know you're young and that you have a family," X said. "That is why this must be you, Michael. You have the heart and mind to make the decisions best for everyone here."

"I will be right by your side," Wynn said.

X turned to Magnolia next.

"Do you trust Kade?" he asked.

"He's saved my ass twice now—even broke Captain Rolo's orders to do it."

"So that's a yes?"

She nodded. "He's a hell of a diver and seems like a good man with a tormented soul. Reminds me of you a bit, sir."

X snorted. "It pains me to say this," he said, "but I fear we might have a problem with Captain Rolo and some of his people, especially that Charmer character. I want you all to keep an eye on them."

"You got it."

"Have you selected a new team lead yet?"

"No," Magnolia replied, "but I have narrowed it down to Edgar and Sofia."

"How about giving Kade the new team?" X said. "Let's see what he can do with them."

Magnolia wasn't sure she liked the idea, but X was in charge.

"Okay, sir," she said.

X gave a grim smile.

"I know I'm asking a lot of all of you," he said, "but I promise this: I will die before I see our home destroyed. This is nothing less than humanity's last chance."

TWENTY-TWO

On the horizon, the first glimmer of sun fired the tops of the rigs before crawling down them to spread over the entire sea. X had slept only a few hours after leaving the celebration, but he was stone-cold sober.

He would feel great if only he hadn't drunk so much water when he awoke. Now he had to piss a pool. Still, it beat pissing blood, and he had a feeling Gran Jefe was doing just that this morning after the two kidney punches and a good whack to the *cojones* that X had given him in the Sky Arena.

X put on his ball cap, buckled his duty belt with the new axe around his waist, grabbed his bag, and then motioned for Miles. They trekked down to the exterior float docks in the port on the south side of the capitol tower.

The *Immortal* was anchored about a quarter mile out. During the night, Captain Rolo had lowered the airship *Vanguard* onto the deck. It rested there now, secured for the journey.

When the drones reported bad storms for much of the journey, X had decided it would be safer by sea than by air.

Three other vessels were docked at the marina. Two—*Raven's Claw* and the *Ocean Bull*—were warships. And the research ship *Octopus* was practically a warship now, bristling with barbed wire and flamethrowers and retrofitted with .50-caliber deck guns. Crew members bustled about, loading up the final supplies and preparing the weapons mounted to the rails.

The dock was crowded with family members of those departing. Many were still hungover from last night's festivities.

X spotted Layla holding Bray and pointing at the airship *Vanguard*, explaining to the boy that it was once home for her people. Never mind that the boy could neither talk nor understand her.

A technician in a yellow suit rode a cable rider up the port side of the *Immortal*, stopping at the patchworked section of hull that had blown out days earlier when Timothy set off the charges.

Patching it up had necessitated scrapping a small container ship, but the engineers and techs had worked night and day to get her ready for the maiden voyage to Panama.

X walked over to Layla with Miles, whose tail came alive when he saw her.

"Mornin'," X said to Layla. "How you guys doing?"

She smiled and reached down to scratch Miles behind the ears.

"And how's the little ankle biter?" X said. He chuckled and patted Bray on the head, mussing his curly hair.

"He's not a dog," Layla said.

"Right. Sorry," X replied.

"Or an ankle biter." Layla raised a brow. "I thought you had experience with kids. Didn't you take care of Michael for a few weeks after . . ."

"Yeah, I did, and I think I did okay."

"You did great," said a third voice.

Michael walked over, a grin on his grease-streaked face. Reaching into his pocket, he fished out a small handheld computer.

"Here," he said. "I want you to have this."

X took the device, recognizing at once that it was Cricket 2.0.

"I can't," X said.

"Where you're going, you'll need him more than I will."

X hesitated, then decided that it would be rude to decline the gift. And besides, Michael was right—the scanner would come in handy.

"Thanks, Chief Engineer Everhart."

X felt for something as he pocketed the computer, and his hand came out with a small wooden box. "Open this later," he said. At the sound of voices, he looked over his shoulder. "Just in time."

Ton, Victor, Steve, and Pedro came their way.

"I got you something else," X said. "Meet your new best friends."

"What?" Michael asked.

"Ton and Victor are going to watch your back while I'm gone, as will Lieutenant Wynn. And Steve is going to be your fixer."

"Whatever you need, boss," Steve said with a salute.

"I do need a deputy chief engineer, if you're interested," Michael said.

"It would be an honor, sir."

He reached out, and they sealed the deal with an old-world handshake.

"Your first job is to call a meeting with all the rig leaders," Michael said. "At the trading post rig, where they will hand over their requests for parts. King Xavier has our main list, but this is for smaller items and routine maintenance that has been neglected in the past. Together, you and I will bring energy efficiency to the islands with wind and solar power, and we will maintain the rigs better than anyone before us has done."

"And that's why I put you in charge," X said.

"I still wish you were staying."

"I know," X said, "but Pedro here is going to keep monitoring the storms, and he will make sure we have an open line of communication through our drones."

Pedro nodded.

"Good," Michael said.

"Thank you," Layla said.

X smiled at her. He knew that she was nervous

about the responsibility he had delegated to her husband. He hadn't done it lightly. There were still threats here, and things were going to get worse before they got better—especially when the food started running out.

"So who's going to watch *your* back out there?" Michael asked.

X chuckled and pointed with his chin toward the ships.

"I'm bringing an entire army with me, Tin—er, Michael. And thanks to Steve, I got myself a fancy arm like you."

"Pretty awesome axe he forged for you, too."

X looked down. "I'm not sure if I should frame it on my wall or crack a skull with it. Maybe I'll be lucky enough to do both."

A horn blared as the *Immortal* weighed anchor and Captain Two Skulls prepared to depart.

Timothy's voice came over X's headset. "King Xavier, the *Immortal* is ready to sail when you are."

"I'm on my way, Pepper," X said.

X embraced his adopted family—or the family that had adopted him, rather—in turn. Layla teared up; Michael remained stoic.

"Be careful out there," Layla said.

"Take care of him, Miles," Michael added.

"He always does," X said. "Ton, Victor, I'm counting on you two—and you as well, Steve."

"We won't let anything happen to Mr. Michael or his family," Victor said. He pounded his chest, and Ton did as well while grunting something indecipherable.

"Thanks, fellas," X said.

He was going to miss his twin shadows, but he had plenty of help where he was going. He would sleep better just knowing they were here with Michael and his family.

Picking up his bag, he walked with his dog toward a boat that took him to the *Immortal*. They took a ladder to the weather deck, where Captain Two Skulls and General Forge stood with two teams of soldiers and crew members, all standing stiffly as X approached with Miles.

Imulah was here, too, holding his leather-bound book, prepared to document everything along their journey. X thought about something pithy to say and went with the first thing that came to mind.

"Let's ride!" he shouted.

All across the islands, people stood on the balconies, watching as the fleet of warships carved through the ocean. There were no fireworks or waved goodbyes this morning. Only the sad eyes of those watching their loved ones depart on one of the most important and dangerous missions yet.

X stayed on the deck until the capitol tower was just a dot on the horizon. His heart hurt as his most beloved friends and family parted ways once again to improve humanity's odds for survival.

About a half hour into the journey, before they even crossed the barrier between light and dark, it began to rain. Perhaps not the most auspicious beginning.

X watched the ship approach the barrier; then he and Miles headed to their quarters. The room was furnished with a desk, bookshelf, head with a toilet and sink, and a decent-size bed—spare but clean.

"This is home for a while, boy," X said. "What do you think?"

Miles jumped up on the bunk and curled up. X put his bag down and leaned to kiss the dog on the snout.

"Go ahead and sleep," he said. "I'll be back in a while."

As soon as X turned, Miles jumped off the bed, whining. He apparently wasn't interested in sleeping, after all.

"Okay, let's go," X said.

In the corridor, they passed the skeleton crew of mostly Cazador sailors assigned to the vessel. From what Imulah had said, there were 150 crew—far from the thousands who once served on this ship before the defectors.

But with Timothy at the helm, they would make it work. He could do everything the former human crew did, and despite his being an AI, X trusted him. He had proved himself time after time.

The AI was waiting in the ship's CIC, his hologram illuminating the advanced stations and monitors manned by trained officers.

"Greetings, King Xavier," said Timothy.

The hologram walked with X to the viewports, which had a panoramic view of the ocean.

Flashes of blue shimmered along the horizon, casting a glow over the *Ocean Bull* on the starboard side of the carrier. The whale-shaped head on the bow protruded just above the waterline, appearing almost like a whale surfacing for air.

"How's she handle?" X asked, turning back to Timothy.

"She's fast, King Xavier—too fast for our other ships to keep up."

"No sign of Tyron, right?"

"He's gone forever, sir, don't worry."

X nodded, but he still worried that Timothy had missed something, that somehow Tyron would be back.

Hours into the journey, X left the command center with Miles. He hated dealing with the operational shit and would much rather spend time with the crew.

"Race ya," X said to Miles in the first passage.

The dog looked up, tail wagging.

X bent down as he always did before a race. Miles's tail beat the air. He knew exactly what this meant.

"Go!" X said.

The dog bolted ahead, and X ran after him toward the end of the empty passageway. Miles wasn't as fast as he once was, but he easily ghosted X around the corner.

By the time X got there, he was winded and the dog was already nearing the end of the next passageway, where a crew member had backed against a hull, terrified.

"He's harmless," X said to the young woman.

She nodded but remained with her back to the bulkhead.

X whistled, and Miles came back to him. They took a ladder down to the cargo bay, which was bustling with activity.

A neat row of armored personnel carriers and supply trucks sat idle in front of the two large tanks armed with long cannons and a mounted machine gun. The lightly armored hulls were shaped like bricks, built to support a small crew up in the cockpit and hold troops in the back.

X crossed the chamber, watching the warriors and technicians working. Some were taking inventory of supplies; others were working on the vehicles. And a few were trying to look busy while awaiting orders.

Slayer and Bromista were here with the rest of the Barracudas, sparring and exercising in the large space.

X stopped by to say hello.

"Going to join us?" Slayer asked.

"Maybe later."

Bromista raised his fists like a boxer.

"I show you how to beat Gran Jefe," he said.

The other men laughed, and X grinned. "I'll take you up on that soon," he said. "We got a long journey ahead."

As Bromista pounded his chest in respect, X went up to the flight deck with Miles. They took a ramp up into the airship *Vanguard*. Some were swapping stories and playing cards, but others, like Kade, were keeping their own company. He had his back to a crate, softly playing his guitar.

Edgar was cleaning his rifle, chewing on an herb-infused calorie stick. Magnolia was going over a map with Ada.

Arlo's nasal voice broke the silence. "King Xavier on deck!"

The divers scrambled to their feet.

"At ease," X said.

He walked over to Magnolia.

"What brings you here, sir?" she asked.

"Aw, I just miss this place," he said.

Gran Jefe grinned when X looked at him. A sharpened tooth was missing from his serrate smile. He pounded his chest in respect, and X nodded.

"That's new," X said. He stared across the room at a new banner hanging from the hull. The new team logo said *Wrangler* and featured a mounted cowboy holding a lariat.

"Fitting," he said.

"Sure is," Magnolia said. "We had it commissioned from Shelly, and she worked overtime to get it done."

"For the record, not my idea," Kade said.

"Looks just like you," Arlo said.

"I like it," X said. "Good to have a fresh team and new blood."

He decided to spend the morning with the divers, and by noon he was missing his diving days even more. Pulling up empty supply crates for chairs, they took a break from training for a quick bite.

"King Xavier, maybe you can tell us some more stories about the wastes," Arlo said. "How about it?"

Tia sliced off a wedge of apple and popped it into her mouth, waiting for X to scare the hell out of her.

"Maybe he doesn't want to talk about it," Magnolia said.

X rubbed Miles on the head. "If the dog could talk, he would tell you all about the dicey moments we found ourselves in."

"Like?"

"Well, there was the time we were walking on a land bridge that collapsed, and he fell into a swamp with snakes thicker than you and longer than the Octopus Lord's tentacles." X shrugged. "Barely made it out of that one. I also came pretty close with some camouflaged stone beasts in the desert."

"Stone . . . beasts?" said Tia.

"Yeah, and then there were the Sirens that had us surrounded in Florida."

By the time X finished, Tia had stopped slicing her apple and was staring at him as if in a trance.

"How about you, Kade?" X asked. "Got any stories you want to share?"

"Yeah, tell us how you got your name," Arlo said.

Kade scratched the side of his face. He looked down to his boots, perhaps recalling a painful memory.

"He won't even tell me what happened to my dad," Tia said.

Kade looked at her ruefully.

"It's okay, maybe some other time," X said.

A voice surged into his headset, providing a welcome distraction.

"Hold up, got a transmission," he said.

X got off a crate and turned his back, holding up a hand to his ear.

"Go ahead, over," he said.

"King Xavier, this is Timothy, please return to the bridge," came the reply.

"Somethin' wrong, Pepper?"

"Potentially, sir."

"What?"

"We have something on radar."

"What do you mean, we have 'something on radar'?" X asked. "Another ship?"

"I don't think so, but whatever it is, it's big."

"I'll be right there."

X and Miles went the short way, but it still took ten minutes to reach the command center. Timothy greeted him at the entrance and followed him over to the stations.

"Talk to me," X said. "I want a sitrep."

An officer looked up from her green monitor. "I'm getting pings on sonar now, too."

X studied the monitors while the team tried to figure out what was trailing them.

Something was definitely out there, and it was big. He got a tingly feeling in his gut—the same feeling he got when he was being hunted.

Whatever was out there was closing fast.

He went to the viewports and looked out over the dark ocean.

They were being hunted.

* * * * *

Michael reached in his vest pocket and took out the small oblong box that X had given him this morning. He still hadn't opened it, but he would once he was done for the day.

That could be a while. He had to stop at the Wind Talker rig, then head to the trading post to meet with the leaders of the various rigs.

Rain clouds hung in the distance, but they seemed to be moving past the islands. A bright sun reflected off debris still floating around the farm rig.

Steering the *Sea Wolf* around the rig, Michael recalled the days after the war with the Cazadores. Once again these islands looked as if they had been hit by war. And just as they had then, the people who lived here were showing their resilience. On every deck, people worked with the materials they had to rebuild their homes and salvage whatever they could.

He was determined to help them, regardless of past enmities.

On the horizon, he saw the Wind Talker rig. Even from this distance, he could see the construction on the towering turbines. Two crane operators were removing the bent and damaged blades from turbine

3, leaving it as bare as a coco palm after a hurricane. Another team was working on deck 4, cannibalizing salvageable blades, while a third crew was working the other crane, mounting an undamaged blade on turbine 4.

Only turbine 5 was operational. With every revolution, it added more juice to the batteries that would then be sent out to power critical systems on the rigs. But it wasn't nearly enough, even with deck 2's field of solar panels.

Michael eased the *Sea Wolf* up to the dock. Ton and Victor hopped off. It was hard to know what they thought about their new assignment, but so far they seemed to be okay with protecting Michael. Most importantly, they were taking the job seriously.

They went to the rig's top deck, where Michael was surprised to see Charmer, standing with a burly man Michael had seen only a few times. Someone was raising a ruckus on the center of the deck.

Two militia soldiers were wrestling with a worker who clutched one of the smaller batteries.

"What the hell is going on?" Michael asked, walking over.

"We caught him trying to steal a battery," said one of the guards.

Michael recognized the tech right away. It was Raúl, an electrician and the brother of a Cazador soldier named Junita.

"Is this true?" Michael asked.

Raúl squirmed under the two guards.

Crouching in front of him, Michael said, "Calm down."

"My rig has no power," Raúl said, "and *mi mamá* needs the battery to power her dialysis machine. I'm sorry, Chief. *Lo siento.*"

"His sister is serving under General Forge," said one of the guards.

"So?" Charmer cut in. "That doesn't give him a free pass."

"This doesn't concern you," Michael said.

"Oh, but it does." Charmer pushed up his feathered hat. "It concerns everyone."

Michael straightened, realizing that this was his first decision as regent to the king. He couldn't screw it up.

"Get him up," Michael said.

The two guards hauled Raúl to his feet.

"We will make sure your *mamá* is taken care of," Michael said. "However, as punishment for attempted theft of a battery, you will be transferred to work the sewers of your rig for the next year."

Raúl stared at Michael, clearly astonished at a sentence that by all rights should have been much harsher.

"*Gracias, jefe*," he murmured.

The guards hauled Raúl away, and Charmer watched them go.

"I would have taken a hand at the very least," he said. "Nothing like losing a body part to keep you on the straight and narrow."

That how you lost your eye? Michael wanted to ask. "Bloodshed is the last thing we need."

Michael said to Charmer, "Remind me why you're here and not at the trading post rig for the meeting."

Charmer unslung a backpack. "This is Oliver, by the way. He works security for us."

Oliver nodded, and Michael nodded back.

Charmer pulled a pad of paper from his pack. "Here is what we need to get our critical systems up and running after the storm."

He glanced up at the wind turbines. "It would be nice to get one of those for our rig."

Michael looked at the paper. "You can give that to Steve during the meeting, like everyone else."

"But why would I do that when I can do this?" Charmer smiled and reached into his pack again, pulling out a second list. "These are things I can offer you in return."

"Some might see that as a bribe."

"No, of course not, Chief. I'm honestly hurt you'd think that." He pushed the second list at Michael. "It's a list of things I can provide to help you."

"I've told you where to submit your list. Now, if you'll excuse me, I have work to do before our meeting."

Charmer's grin folded away, and he moved in front of Michael.

Ton and Victor stepped up behind Michael.

"Look, I appreciate you, mate, and what you did at the machine camp," Charmer said. He wagged a finger. "But we're here to look after our people and the rig that we are so grateful to have."

"I won't say it again," Michael said. "Move your ass out of my way, or I will."

Oliver stepped forward. Michael stopped him with a look. Ton and Victor just watched, silent, relaxed, ready.

Charmer flashed his grin and tipped his hat. "As you wish, Chief," he said. "Cheers."

As they left, Oliver gave Michael the most intimidating glare he could muster under the circumstances.

"I no like that guy," Victor said.

"Makes two of us," Michael replied. "I'll be right back. Stay here for now."

He went to the engineering control room. Pedro was inside, staring intently at the monitors.

"Chief," he said, rising.

"Don't get up," Michael said. "I just need a quick update."

Pedro sat back down and said, "I have two drones watching Vanguard fleet. I place them *estrategicamente* so we can get signal from fleet to the first drone, then second, and then back here."

"Excellent."

It was reassuring to have an open line of communication with X. He patted his friend on the back. They shared a bond now: a life for a life. Michael had saved Pedro in Rio, and Pedro had helped save Michael during the storm by locating Cricket.

He was smart, trustworthy, and a hell of a warrior.

Michael would never forget watching Pedro fight a Siren to the death with a metal cot leg back on the airship after they left Rio de Janeiro.

"Keep me updated," Michael said. "I'm off to the trading post."

It took Michael another hour to get there. He was dreading it, but he would be able to go home right after and see Layla and the kids.

By the time he arrived, a dozen boats were docked at the marina, and more were motoring, rowing, or paddling in.

Michael headed up to find Steve. The sun had set, and the moon was peeking through rain clouds, illuminating the crowd gathering on the deck.

Lieutenant Wynn stood with two guards in the front, as a reminder to keep calm.

Cazadores, sky people, and survivors from bunkers they had found in Rio, Tanzania, and other places—each group had its own set of requests or, in some cases, demands.

Michael scrutinized the faces. These were mostly people with technical or engineering experience, but there were also merchants, and some soldiers or muscle like Oliver, who stood next to Charmer.

Imulah was already jotting down notes. He joined Michael on the stage where X had spoken only last night. Now it was time for Michael to give a speech.

"Listen up, everyone."

Imulah gave a running translation in Spanish.

"I asked to meet with you today to hear about

issues on your rigs after the devastating hurricane," Michael said. "To start, please submit your requests to my deputy, Steve Schwarzer. He will be the main point of contact for each rig."

After Imulah translated, people submitted their lists to Steve.

"We must keep in mind that this recovery is a joint effort that we must all make together," Michael continued. "From making repairs to rationing our food and power, we all play a role."

Charmer and Oliver leaned together, speaking and shaking their heads. It wasn't just them. Michael saw the same skeptical gaze on many faces. The lack of trust would be his biggest challenge, even from people he had helped save.

These people were survivors, and they all had instincts that kicked in when resources dwindled. And each of these groups dealt with crises differently. Some had resorted to cannibalism or slavery.

Lightning cleaved the horizon, and a light rain began to fall. The rifle crack of thunder reminded everyone why they were here—and that another storm could and *would* hit the islands.

Michael had to give them hope.

"King Xavier will arrive in Panama soon, and he will return with supplies and food," Michael said. "I know this because, after two hundred and fifty years in the darkness, he led us to this place. He has never once let my people down, and he won't let you down, either. He is a fair leader and a man of honor. We need to trust him."

"We trust Captain Rolo!" shouted a voice. "He's risking his neck again for humanity on a fool's errand."

Michael wasn't surprised to see that it was Oliver.

A male Cazador yelled something in Spanish. More angry voices rang out with questions that Imulah translated as fast he could. The last one made Michael tense up.

"He asked what we will do if the mission in Panama fails to locate supplies, and what's the second option?" said the scribe.

"Mind if I answer that?" Steve asked.

Michael beckoned him to the stage.

"This rig has stood for generations," Steve said. "It's survived two wars, the attack by the machines, and several hurricanes."

He held his arms out. "Each time, it has survived, as we have, and each time we have rebuilt."

The crowd finally seemed to calm, and Michael took a few more questions before bringing the meeting to a close.

"We must work together and sacrifice together," Michael said. "Now, let's get out there and rebuild."

A single voice called out—faint, but audible: "Actions will determine whether we can trust you."

The voice was muffled by the departing crowd, and Michael didn't see the speaker. He and Steve watched them all leave.

"Not too bad, I suppose," Steve grunted.

"Could have been worse," Michael replied. He glanced at the leaflets and paper Steve held. "This is going to be a massive joint project, and I'm hoping that between the two of us, we can come up with a way not only to repair the rigs but to make them *stronger*, to withstand future storms."

"I like the way you think, partner, and I'm honored to be your deputy."

"Good, let's get some sleep. We start back up first thing in the morning."

Ton and Victor accompanied Michael back to the capitol tower. During the ride, watching the rigs pass by, he felt something familiar to him as a father and husband: a deep, abiding sense of responsibility. Now he was responsible for more than his wife and son. He was responsible for everyone who lived on the Vanguard Islands, including the families of those lost in action, like his friend and former deputy, Alfred.

By the time he got home, it was midnight, and the thunderstorm had passed. Michael went straight to Bray's room, where Layla sat in a chair facing the crib. The child was fast asleep on his back, with a stuffed dolphin toy tucked against his chest. Rhino Jr. was still awake, though, and looking up at Michael with curious eyes.

"Hey, big guy," Michael whispered.

Layla got up and put a hand on his shoulder.

"They're both growing so *fast*," she said.

"I know, it's an ongoing miracle!"

"I sure hope X knows what he's doing."

Michael eased the door shut. "He does, Layla. You need to trust him."

"I do. It's just . . . putting you in charge of the islands seemed . . ."

"What?"

"It makes me wonder if he's grooming you for the throne."

"No way," Michael said. "And anyway, he can't just hand it over."

"What did he give you, by the way?"

He reached in his vest pocket, glad to be changing the subject.

"What is it?" Layla asked.

Michael slid back the lid, revealing a note wrapped around two keys.

He unfurled the note.

Dear Michael,

The first key is for if I don't come back. It opens a door near the watery grave of our enemies. What you will find there is not for immediate use, no matter how bad things get. This is a backup plan if the Vanguard Islands become uninhabitable, as el Pulpo feared.

The second key will show you the way.

Everything that we do from here on out will determine our future. We can afford no mistakes. We must not fail to act. We must never forget.

Handle your present with confidence. Face your future without fear.

X

Michael folded the note and slipped it back into the box.

"What's it say?" Layla asked.

"I think things are worse than we thought."

"What do you mean?"

"I don't know exactly, but tomorrow I'm going to find out."

TWENTY-THREE

Kade pulled his cowboy hat over his eyes and rested his back against a supply crate in the launch bay. The soothing hum of the airship's engines helped him relax.

Most of the other divers were already sleeping, or trying to despite the noise. Snores and snorts came from the area where Kade had last seen Gran Jefe sprawled on the deck.

"Kade," said a youthful voice.

He tipped up his hat. The dim lightning was just enough to reveal Tia crouching beside him.

"Yeah?" he asked.

She sat beside him on the floor, fingering her turquoise necklace.

"There's something I want to know about my dad," she said.

Kade sat up straighter. "What do you want to know?"

"What happened the day he found this?"

The sight of the necklace brought back that day,

flooding his mind with memories. Kade had never wanted Tia to know the truth when she was younger. There was no reason to explain in detail what had happened to her father on the surface. So he did what he always did: glossed it over.

"He died bravely," Kade said.

"Yeah, you've said that. But how?"

Kade sighed. "Why do you want to know? After all these years, what good would it do?"

"It would put my mind at rest."

Edgar hollered across the launch bay, "All greenhorns, get your asses vertical and report to Commander Katib!"

Tia looked at Kade and then got up. She said, "I'm not a kid anymore, you know. You don't have to protect me."

Kade leaned back against the supply crate, listening to the rain and the hum of the engines. Thunder boomed, rattling the hull.

He pulled his hat back over his eyes and drifted off to sleep, reliving the nightmare from the day Tia lost her father.

THIRTEEN YEARS AGO . . .

"This some sort of expensive old-world store?" Johnny asked.

"No, it's what they used to call a museum," Kade said. "Place where they displayed art and stuff."

"Captain Rolo sent us to find *art*?"

"No, mate, it's not what's inside this place. It's what's *beneath* it that we're here for."

Kade studied the cracked marble arch over the building's entrance while they waited for their teammate and scout, Raphael, to check in on the comms.

After Kade, Raphael was the diver with the most experience on the surface, and he was ahead, checking out the building.

The east side had long since caved in, but the middle and west sides were still structurally sound—probably thanks to the thick stone facade.

Kade loved architecture like this and was excited to find part of a city in the green zone that was mostly intact. Much of it had been raided during the aftermath of the war, however, before the humans on the surface succumbed to the radiation that was now almost nonexistent.

The team comm crackled.

"All clear, but you fellas better have a look at somethin' up here," Raphael said in his thick accent.

Kade motioned for Johnny to follow him through the open doors. They walked through the lobby and past a desk with a broken lamp, crossing into a vast room with stairways to other levels.

Glass shards of display cases littered the floor.

Raphael waved from the second-story balcony.

Kade cradled his assault rifle and walked through the room, past the broken cases. Most contained statues and shards of pottery. A sundial monument still stood in the center of the room, unprotected by any glass.

"That some sort of clock?" Johnny asked.

"I don't think so," Kade replied.

He stopped to dust off a display placard.

"The Hall of Mexico and Central America," he read. "Must be about the cultures that lived there thousands of years ago."

"Wonder if Raph's related to any of them."

Kade looked at Johnny, snorting. "Raph's a Maori, you wanker."

"So?"

"Maoris were from New Zealand—halfway across the world from Central America."

"I will note that up here." Johnny tapped his helmet. "Thanks for the geography lesson."

They pushed up the stairs to a hallway with jewelry hanging in glass cabinets. Kade focused on the floor, searching for tracks. But the carpet of glass, dust, and debris lay undisturbed but for the tracks Raphael had left behind.

He waited at the end of the passage with his crossbow cradled across his armor. Leather tassels strung with beads hung from his chest armor, and his helmet bore the black tribal markings of his Maori warrior ancestors.

He continued the traditions of those warriors with the way he hunted on the surface, which made him the best scout on the airship. Kade had learned a lot from him over the years.

Raphael waved them forward into a long passage, then stopped at a cabinet.

"What?" Kade asked.

Reaching inside, Raphael pulled out a turquoise necklace.

"Tia will love this," he said.

After safely tucking it into his vest, he kept moving with his crossbow shouldered.

Kade was cautious not to crunch any glass shards or bump anything. This was a green zone, and Raphael wouldn't be the only hunter.

When they got to the next hall, Raphael stopped at a rail overlooking a display of massive bones. Some were still connected, including the spiked skull of some ancient beast.

"What the bloody hell is that ugly bastard?" Johnny asked.

"A dinosaur," Kade said. "They used to roam the earth millions of years ago."

"Bullshit, man. This has got to be fake."

Kade checked the metal placard. *Hall of Saurischian Dinosaurs.*

Remarkable, certainly, but it wasn't what they were here for. Kade turned and saw why Raphael had brought them here.

Hanging from a ceiling joist was part of another skeleton, this one a human. The skull and part of the spine were all that remained, the rest of the bones having long since fallen to the floor, where they lay in an undisturbed pile.

"Looks old," Raphael said.

"Aye, says here these are millions of years old," Johnny said.

"Not the dinosaurs," Kade said. "*Him*."

He pointed his assault rifle barrel toward the remains.

"Oh, damn," Johnny said.

"Whoever hung him is long gone," Kade said. "Let's keep moving."

Raphael nodded and took point. They passed through the chamber of dinosaurs, marveling at the gargantuan bones.

It was hard to imagine these creatures walking about on earth, but Kade had read about them in school when he was a boy. Seeing their remains brought out his inner kid.

His sons would love this place.

Raphael stopped at the passage connecting to the next main corridor.

"We're not far," he said. "Follow me."

He led them down a stairwell to the museum's basement. The stairs were all concrete until they got to another door, this one ajar.

Raphael tested the first cracked tile step, then proceeded ahead. Kade went next, shining his flashlight down into the basement.

Halfway down, one of the stairs above cracked, and Kade looked over his shoulder.

"Sorry," Johnny said.

"You could at least try and not *sound* like one of those dinosaurs," Kade said.

"They aren't even real," Johnny whispered.

"Damn, wanker . . ."

The divers finally made it down into a cavernous storage area. Raphael played his flashlight over a map and then pointed across the space.

"Almost there," he said.

They crossed the basement, past glass display cases still housing artifacts. Kade stopped to look in one that had a leather cowboy hat, rope, satchel, and an old-west six-shooter pistol.

His oldest son was obsessed with cowboys and would love it.

Kade considered breaking the glass, but he dare not make the noise. Maybe on the way out, after they completed their mission.

A flashlight beam hit him in the helmet.

"You comin'?" Johnny asked.

"Yeah. Get that out of my face."

"Sorry."

Kade walked on, leaving the cowboy display behind. They finally stopped in front of shelves that took up the entire wall.

"We're here," Raphael said.

"Our mission is to find something in these boxes?" Johnny asked. He pulled down a plastic crate and started rifling through it.

"No," Kade said.

"The mission's objective is behind these shelves," Raphael said. "Help me take them down."

For the next half hour, they removed almost every box from the long row of six shelves, until they finally discovered a steel door to a vault.

"There it is," Raphael said.

Johnny maneuvered on the other side to help pull the shelving away. Its metal legs grated against the floor. Once the door was clear, Raphael stepped up to the keypad and pulled out his wrist computer. Using a tiny screwdriver, alligator clips, and patch cords, he connected the device to the keypad. He tapped in a code, and the door groaned as the locking mechanism and bars unsealed on the other side.

The three divers stepped back as the ancient hardware creaked and cranked.

"And you bastards say *I'm* loud," Johnny said.

Dust poofed out as the doors parted and opened onto a landing. Another stairwell led to a still lower level.

Kade's beam stabbed into the inky depths of the vault.

"After you guys," Johnny said.

The doors finally finished opening and thudded into their locked position.

Raphael stepped forward but paused at what sounded like breaking glass. The men all turned toward the noise.

"What was that?" Johnny asked.

"Maybe one of the displays fell," Kade said.

Raphael took a step back into the basement storage area. He listened for a few seconds, then gestured toward the vault.

Kade stood at the landing for another moment but heard nothing. He followed Raphael down the stairs, with Johnny right behind them.

Three floors later, they came to another set of blast doors. These were open.

Kade slowly made his way through what looked like a second museum, but with humans on display. Skeletons lay throughout the room. Some clutched one another. Others were on their own, backs to the wall, heads slumped.

On the floor beside each body was a little plastic vial.

Bending down, Kade picked up one and held it under his beam.

"Poison," he whispered.

"All these people killed themselves?" Johnny asked.

"Aye, poor bastards," Raphael said. "Come on, I want to get the hell out of this mausoleum."

The divers fanned out across the chamber. It was furnished with cots, tables, and chairs. Clothing and bags were scattered among jugs and containers that lay on their sides, empty.

Kade guessed these people had simply run out of food and had decided to end things as gracefully as they could before it got ugly. He had seen enough places like this to understand the thinking.

These people were probably the families and friends of the museum workers. Just as his ancestors on the ITC *Victory* had been families and friends of the crew.

A few minutes later, Raphael found what they had come here for: a map encased in a plastic sheet.

"Got it," he said.

"What's that?" Johnny asked.

"Our next drop," Raphael said. "Place called the Black Hills, in what was once the state of South Dakota."

Kade helped him carefully roll up the map and slide it into a tube. With the map secured, they started back out the way they came, with Johnny taking point.

"Hurry up, guys. I got a hot date waiting for me tonight," he said.

"Tell your hand you're going to be a little late," Raphael said.

Kade chuckled and raised his rifle, the flashlight beam shooting across the storage room.

He halted when he saw a pair of yellow eyes glowing in the darkness. Another set joined the first, and then a third.

Raphael had already seen them and was crouching down, trying to signal Johnny, who was looking back at them.

"What?" he said, suddenly freezing.

"Get down!" Raphael hissed.

Slowly Johnny turned with his rifle. Then he screamed and dropped on his bum as Kade fired. He took calculated single shots at the closest sets of eyes, conserving his ammo.

Raphael fired an arrow, and a cry of pain followed the thump. He backed up to nock another bolt as Kade covered him.

"Get up!" he shouted to Johnny.

Johnny stumbled to his feet and opened fire with

his submachine gun, spraying the room with bullets that didn't seem to find a single target.

In the glow of their beams, Kade identified mostly naked humanoid shapes darting through the maze of shelves and displays, wailing and roaring if they got hit.

He ejected the spent magazine and dropped it in his vest before pulling out a fresh mag.

Smoke and the smell of burnt powder made it into his helmet as he slapped a new magazine into his rifle. He chambered a round and looked for a target, but the beasts, whatever they were, fled the room, their grunts and shrieks echoing in the distance.

Kade crouched, listening, his hand shaking.

"What in the unholy wastes *were* those things?" Johnny stuttered.

Raphael moved out in front of them. "I think I know, but I don't want to believe it."

"What?"

Kade waited for an answer.

"Let's move," Raphael said. "We have to get out of here."

He started walking, then halted halfway across the chamber to listen. The wails rose into an alien din mixing with grunts, clicks, and what sounded like *human* voices, speaking in a language Kade had never heard before.

They crept through the storage room, toward the sounds. Kade stopped at the case with the pistol and hat. The glass had been shattered by a bullet, and he reached inside, grabbing the pistol first.

He put it in his bag along with the hat, and then took the rope.

"Move it, Kade," Raphael whispered.

They climbed the stairs back up to the exhibition halls. A few minutes later, the noises stopped altogether, giving way to an eerie silence.

"I say we get to the roof and hit our boosters," Raphael said.

"Sounds excellent to me," Johnny said.

They kept going up the stairs, passing the door they had used to access the basement, and heading up six floors. At the top landing, Raphael gave Kade a nod. He opened the door, and Raphael slipped into a passage.

"Stay close," Kade said to Johnny.

Johnny shouldered his submachine gun and moved after the more experienced divers. Raphael pointed his beam down the hallway, to the Hall of Dinosaurs.

Keeping low, the team moved down along the balcony on the top floor, their beams crisscrossing the space and illuminating the fossil bones below.

Raphael's fist went up, and he motioned everyone to kill their lights and get down. They hit the floor, keeping low.

Grunting came from across the hall.

Then below.

Footsteps slapped on the floors immediately above and below them.

"We're going to have to make a run for it," Raphael said quietly. "Stay with me."

"Got it," Kade said.

"Don't leave me behind," Johnny whispered.

"On me," Raphael said.

Two nods. He got up and flicked on his light.

All three beams pierced the darkness, raking over the upper balconies. They lit up pale human-size creatures darting across the floors on all five levels.

"Shit a brick," Kade said when he saw them.

They weren't humanoid, they *were* humans. Or some version thereof.

The beasts, in tattered clothes and bandages, rushed across the floors surrounding the exhibitions. At first glance, they looked like mummies swathed in bandages. They howled and screeched, opening mouths of blackened teeth.

"Kade, what do we do?"

Kade was surprised to hear Raphael asking him for advice. He stared at what looked like feral humans. But these weren't humans in the same way as the divers. They were mindless mutant creatures.

On the bottom floor, a woman clutched a baby to her naked breast. The deformed little face pulled away from her nipple and stared up at them with its single Cyclops eye.

"Shoot 'em," Johnny said. "Shoot them all!"

And before Kade could stop him, he opened fire. Shell casings rained down on the ground as he fired in all directions.

Cries of anger and pain echoed through the hall. A door opened at the other end of the floor, and a big, muscular man with stained bandages covering his body rushed out.

Brandishing two cutlasses, he rushed Raphael, who aimed and fired his crossbow. The arrow hit the man in the chest, stopping him cold. Then he looked down at the bolt protruding from his torso and kept charging despite the blow, screaming in primal fury.

Backing up, Raphael tried to reload, but there was no time. So he grabbed a hatchet instead and parried the slashes from the two blades. The creature then plowed bodily into him, knocking him against the railing and sending him halfway over.

Kade aimed, waiting for the perfect shot. It came a moment later, and he pulled the trigger. The first bullet went high, but the second blew off the top of the feral creature's skull. It reached up to the hunk of bone and flesh hanging off, before slumping onto Raphael, forcing him over the other side.

"Raph!" Kade screamed. He ran to the railing and looked over at Raphael holding on to the railing one floor below. Five floors down lay the beast, somehow still moving an arm.

Johnny leaned over the rail, firing his submachine gun on the next level down, hitting multiple targets as they advanced toward Raphael.

Kade let his rifle hang from its sling and took the rope he had grabbed from the basement. After throwing a fast clove hitch and stopper knot around the rail post, he tossed it over the side.

"Grab it!" he shouted.

Another creature darted out a door on their floor, and Kade pulled his blaster out. He brought it up and fired a blast that hit the woman in the chest, blowing out the back.

"I'm jammed!" Johnny shouted. He tried to eject the bullet while Kade fished the line down to Raphael.

The veteran diver reached over and grabbed on, then ran the rope between his feet to begin inchworming his way up.

Johnny finally managed to clear his chamber and fired over the side at the creatures making a run for Raphael. One had some sort of sickle blade that must be from a museum display.

"Shoot the big one with the sickle!" Kade yelled.

He pulled Raphael up another few feet, almost out of striking range.

Johnny fired his last few bullets into the sickle wielder, the rounds punching into his bulging muscles. He jerked a few times and let out a roar. Then he raised his blade toward Raphael.

"NO!" Kade screamed.

The creature swung, hitting Raphael in the side, where there was a gap in his armor. The blade made a sickening thud as it sank deep into his flesh.

Raphael held on to the rope for a moment, staring up at Kade, his eyes wide and blurred behind his visor.

"Johnny!" Kade shouted. He pulled on the rope as the beast tried to wrench the blade free.

"Shit, shit, *shit*," Johnny said, struggling to load another magazine.

Raphael swung his fist at the mutant, then let out a shriek of agony as the blade came free. He took a step back as Johnny finally cleared his submachine gun. He pulled back the slide, but the man swung the sickle first, hacking into Raphael's side again.

He jerked with the blow but didn't scream.

The beast then pulled back for another strike.

Kade closed his eyes and pulled. Pulled so hard his muscles burned, but without a pulley system, he couldn't move his friend an inch upward. He felt Raphael jerk several more times from blows, and the weight on the rope lessened.

"Eat this, you freaks!" Johnny shouted. He fired again and again at the mutant creature below, pumping his body full of rounds. It took half the magazine, including two head shots, before he finally collapsed.

Johnny moved over to help Kade. Together they got Raphael up to the top, and then grabbed his shoulder armor, pulling him over the railing in a strong heave, spilling a yard of entrails. It wasn't just his midsection that had taken the blows. His right leg was gone below the knee and hanging on by ligaments.

"Oh God, oh God, Kade, what do we do?" Johnny stuttered.

Kade went for his med kit, but stopped when Raphael choked out, "No."

This wasn't survivable. Raphael knew it, too. He grabbed Kade with the last of his energy. Throat gurgling, he tried to get out one last communication.

All that Kade could make out was "Tia."

His friend went limp in his arms, and his hand fell away from his vest. Wrapped around his wrist was the turquoise necklace, his last gift to his daughter.

Kade unwound it and stuffed it in his pocket, then got up. Johnny was shaking and looking down at Raphael, mumbling in shock.

"Come on," Kade said.

"But Raph . . ."

The grunts and shrieks of the beasts echoed closer. Kade grabbed Johnny by the arm and hauled him to his feet, fleeing the swarm of feral cannibals that descended on their dead comrade.

TWENTY-FOUR

Kade was curled up against a crate, his cowboy hat over his eyes, flinching from a dream, perhaps a nightmare. Magnolia decided to give him a nudge with her boot.

He shot up, reaching for the revolver holstered on his duty belt.

"Easy, bubba, damn!" Magnolia said.

His eyes darted about before finally focusing on her, and he lowered his hand.

"Sorry. I was . . ."

"Bad dream?"

He tipped his hat up and nodded. "Aye, somethin' like that."

"Better get up, we got chow in a few minutes," Magnolia said.

"Thanks."

Magnolia went back to the other divers. Eight hours into the journey to Panama, and most of them were up and active. The greenhorns were hanging out now that their gear and supplies were all double-checked. Footfalls came from across the room as Edgar finished running laps with Ada. They got down and started push-ups.

"Making us look bad," Arlo said.

"You can . . . join in," Edgar said between pants.

"Finish up," Magnolia said. "We got chow in a few."

She continued over to Rodger, who had joined them during their downtime. He was also enjoying the R&R—maybe a bit too much.

"Suck it in and hold it in," said Gran Jefe. He handed the joint back to Rodger.

"Tastes kinda funny," Rodger said. "What's in it?"

"Tobacco, and . . ." The Cazador pinched his fingers together. "*Un poco de algo más.* Leetle bit of somethin' else." He pushed the joint closer. "Go on, my fren'. *No hay problema.*"

Magnolia chuckled under her breath. The Cazadores were always pushing their marijuana.

"It's okay," she said. "Might help with that nausea."

Rodger sat on a crate with a bucket between his boot and the prosthetic foot, looking a bit green around the gills. Magnolia thought it odd that some Hell Divers were just fine falling at terminal velocity through a turbulent sky, yet got seasick the moment the ship started to rock.

"It will make you feel *muy bien*," Gran Jefe said.

Rodger wiped off his mouth and accepted the joint. He lit it again and took in a puff, filling his lungs. Then he started coughing.

"What the hell . . . you put in that?" he gasped.

"*El secreto*," Gran Jefe said with a conspiratorial grin. He took the joint back and took a hit.

"Isn't there a rule about smoking or something?" Ada asked.

Still dripping from her workout, she got up and walked over.

Gran Jefe blew the smoke at her, and she swatted the air.

"Hey," she said.

"*Lo siento*," he said unconvincingly. "Sorry."

"You're an asshole, you know that? *Culo*—yeah, that's it, you big *culo*."

"Better than what you are."

"What's that supposed to mean?"

Gran Jefe took another puff, blew it at Ada, and walked away.

"What was that all about?" Magnolia asked.

"No idea," Ada said. "He's never liked me, though—always looks at me like I'm the enemy."

"Chow's here," Edgar said.

A cook wheeled a cart through the launch-bay doors with two militia guards, and the divers hurried over.

They carried their rations back to the supply crates and sat on the deck.

Magnolia sat next to Rodger, who tore into his pack.

"My *God* I'm starving," he said.

She laughed and sat next to him.

Tia took a crate by Kade, again asking about her father.

"I thought when I joined the Hell Divers, you'd finally tell me," she said. "You always say he died bravely."

"And he did," Kade replied.

Magnolia had a feeling it was not altogether true; otherwise, he would have told the young woman years ago about her father's fate.

Magnolia didn't blame him for keeping secrets. They all had them. Every veteran diver gathered in the launch bay of the airship *Vanguard* kept things to her- or himself and always had.

"Your dad never would have wanted this life for you, kid," Kade replied. "I will tell you one thing: his final words were to make sure you were okay."

"I'm an adult now, and I deserve to know."

Magnolia didn't like to eavesdrop, but she couldn't help but listen to the conversation. From what she knew, Tia was just eight when the ITC *Victory* arrived at Kilimanjaro. It was supposed to be a place of salvation but had turned out to be hell.

At first, it didn't make sense to Magnolia why the young woman had decided to join up after finally achieving true salvation, in the form of the Vanguard Islands. But now Magnolia could see clearly why she'd volunteered: to follow in her father's footsteps.

Kade sighed.

"You're right," he said. "You are grown, and you might be diving when we get to Panama, so I'm going to tell you. I'm going to tell you so you know what's down there, what killed your father."

Tia moved her crate closer.

"We were on a dive in an old-world city, to a museum—same place I found this," Kade said, tipping his hat with one forefinger under the brim. "Your dad was lead scout, and he took me and Johnny to a bunker and a map Captain Rolo had learned about from an old broadcast. We didn't see any evidence of beasts on our way in, but when that bunker opened for the first time in decades, it drew them to us."

"Beasts?"

Magnolia had a feeling they had run into Sirens, but she kept quiet.

"Feral humans . . . mutated, and . . ." He took off his hat. "Cannibals. Your dad fought bravely, but there were too many of the ugly bastards."

Kade bowed his head.

"I tried to save him," he said, eyes downcast. "I will never forgive myself for that day."

Tia didn't respond at first, as if digesting the story.

"I'm sure you did everything you could," she finally said. "I've never blamed you, I hope you realize that."

Kade glanced up.

"I blame myself," he said. "Your dad—"

"Died bravely." She nodded. "And that's how I will remember him always: brave, strong, and loving."

She got up with her food. "Thanks, Kade."

Kade stood and breathed out as if a heavy weight

had just been lifted off his shoulders. He looked over at Magnolia and caught her staring.

She offered a nod of support, and he tipped his hat. The teams went on eating and chatting quietly as lightning flashed outside the portholes.

Magnolia went back to check on Rodger when the PA system came on.

"All hands, this is a yellow alert," said Captain Rolo. "Stand by for orders."

"Stand by for orders?" Arlo said.

"Yellow alert?" Gran Jefe said. "*¿Qué pasó?*"

"It means we got trouble," Magnolia said. "Everyone on their feet!"

The divers gathered near the windows, trying to see what was going on outside, while Magnolia helped Rodger to his feet.

"I've got it," he said.

The launch bay was fifty feet off the deck of the *Immortal*, and with the extra height of the airship mount that secured it to the supercarrier, they had a sprawling view of many miles of ocean. In the glow of lightning, Magnolia saw the *Octopus* and *Raven's Claw* sailing off the carrier's port wake.

Magnolia couldn't see the *Ocean Bull*, though. She turned for a view of the island—the carrier's upper bridge. Officers stood at the viewports looking east through binoculars.

Squinting, she stared in that direction.

When Magnolia noticed a yellow glow in the water, she thought she was feeling the effects of secondhand marijuana smoke. But judging by the reactions of the other divers, it was real.

"Holy Siren shit, the ocean is glowing," Arlo said. "The fuck is that? A submarine or something?"

Gran Jefe grunted and pinched the end of the joint, putting it out and slipping it into his pocket.

"I don't know the English word for this," he said. "Only monsters."

"Those can't be sea monsters," Arlo said.

Gran Jefe shot him a glare. "*Estúpido*."

A second alarm wailed with the steady rise and fall of an emergency siren.

"That glow is getting closer," Arlo said.

He backed away from the window, and Magnolia moved over to look out. Sure enough, a massive patch of ocean glowed a fluorescent yellow.

"That's half the length of *Raven's Claw*," Rodger said.

"Gran Jefe is right," Arlo said. "That's no submarine."

"Tell Captain Rolo we have to go to sky," Gran Jefe said. He pointed toward the overhead. "*Arriba*. We go up, up!"

Magnolia had never heard the edge of fear in the Cazador's voice before. She switched to the command channel and said, "Captain, what the hell is going on?"

Static crackled in response.

"There are more of them!" shouted Tia.

The young diver was on the other side of the launch bay, at the portholes.

Magnolia rushed over and saw two more

fluorescent glows farther out, all trailing the *Immortal* and the airship secured to its deck.

Whatever it was, it didn't seem interested in the other ships.

The alarm wailed louder, and red lights flashed in the corner of the room. The PA system clicked on, crackling with static that finally gave way to a voice.

"Prepare for flight," said the friendly voice of Timothy Pepper.

Captain Rolo followed up with a message. "Everyone, report to their emergency shelters," he said. "We're taking off."

Kade backed away from the window as the closest glowing shape surged toward the supercarrier's port side.

"Brace yourselves!" he shouted.

Something hit them so hard, every diver fell down on the deck.

"My arm!" Arlo cried out.

Gran Jefe helped him to his feet, and Rodger pulled Magnolia up.

"Everyone to their racks!" Kade yelled. "We have—"

A deep, long roar sounded in the distance, cutting him off.

Gran Jefe was right: this was no submarine.

Another impact rocked the ship, knocking Magnolia to the deck again. Tia went down hard, bouncing her head off the bulkhead by the racks.

Kade rushed over as Magnolia scrambled to her feet. They found Tia lying unconscious.

"We need help!" Magnolia yelled.

Edgar rushed over with a medical kit.

"What happened?" he said.

"She fell hard," Kade said. "Banged her head."

Ada was already checking her out.

Another deep, low roar rolled over them, louder than a foghorn.

Gran Jefe was looking out a window.

"*¡Vámonos!*" he yelled.

The airship suddenly jolted, and Magnolia stumbled against the hull. Fetching up against the porthole, she happened to look outside and gasped. Massive limbs rose out of the water, attached to barnacled flesh the color of a tangerine. They reached up over the deck of the supercarrier.

"To your racks!" Magnolia shouted. "NOW!"

She stumbled backward as Rodger grabbed her. Behind them, Edgar finished wrapping a bandage around Tia's head. She was conscious again, blinking and moaning.

"We need to get you up, okay?" Kade said.

She managed a weak nod.

"Help me with her," Edgar said.

Kade picked her up under one arm, and Edgar got her under the other. Together, they carried her over to the racks along the hull.

Magnolia checked that all the greenhorn divers were secured in their racks, arms locked over their chests.

"You're good," she said, moving down the line.

Edgar and Kade helped Tia into her rack, and Kade strapped in next to her.

"You're going to be okay," he said. "You just took a bad fall."

Magnolia and Rodger got into their racks, and Magnolia looked out the window between them. In the ocean, she could see the outline of another glowing object under the water. It broke through the surface, mutated limbs whipping out.

This one, she could see perfectly.

It was a whale, but not like those she had seen in picture books. This beast had a thick, blunt snout—perfect for bashing prey or enemies—and its pectoral fins had elongated into prehensile arms.

One of the limbs rose over the deck of the *Immortal*, slithered around a container, and pulled it into the water. Another limb shot up toward the airship, slapping the hull with its tip.

Magnolia saw muzzle flashes sparking along the deck as warriors fired at the grasping, searching limbs. But they may as well be shooting toothpicks.

Out the porthole, she spotted two more of the glowing beasts under the surface. This wasn't just the one whale—it was an entire pod.

Three gargantuan mutated monsters circled the supercarrier *Immortal*, taking turns ramming the vessel every few minutes, and using their prehensile limbs to plunder the deck.

Magnolia leaned closer to the porthole. Something else was in the water. A smaller boat raced away over the waves. She couldn't see who was piloting it, but there appeared to be a dog on board.

"Is that who I think it is?" Edgar said.

"The king," Arlo said. "What in the wastes is he doing down there?"

"Preparing to fight," Magnolia said. "And we have to help him."

TWENTY-FIVE

X climbed the ladder to the command center of the *Ocean Bull* with Miles. The dog shook the rain from his coat and then followed him past workstations manned by Cazador naval officers.

Captain Two Skulls stood at the wheel, the death's-head tattoo grinning back at the rest of the room.

"I guess the myths are real, Captain," X said.

"*Monstruos brillantes del mar,*" replied Two Skulls.

X knew that much Spanish. The "*Bright monsters of the sea*" was right. The glowing behemoths were part giant whale and part giant squid, perhaps something like the biblical Leviathan.

These abominations from the depths were probably responsible for the loss of the *Anaconda* and her crew when the Cazadores had sailed to the Panama Canal decades ago. But X had come prepared and wouldn't let his army suffer the same fate.

"Pull back *Raven's Claw* and the *Octopus,*" X said.

"I want them at a safe distance since they are the most vulnerable."

"Understood, sir," said Captain Two Skulls.

On the port side of the *Immortal*, a spout of warm air shot upward as one of the deformed creatures surfaced. Again the bony head slammed into the hull of the supercarrier.

Soldiers fired from machine-gun turrets. Green tracer rounds zipped into the gray and orange flesh, with no apparent effect.

A raucous whistling blasted out, forcing everyone in the cabin to cover their ears. Miles barked and jumped wildly.

"Get everyone off that deck, now!" X yelled.

A rocket-propelled grenade streaked away from the *Immortal*, hitting the strangely deformed head. The eye exploded on impact.

The beast opened a mouth that could swallow a fishing trawler and let out another earsplitting whistle. Meaty limbs lined with barbs peeled away from the strip of flesh under the dorsal ridges. They whipped upward, onto the *Immortal*, battering the weather deck and the airship.

"Get us into this fight," X said, motioning with his prosthesis.

Captain Two Skulls nodded at another officer.

X used his binoculars as the *Ocean Bull* groaned, increasing speed.

In the sights, he focused on a team of Cazadores with flamethrowers, who were running for shelter on the *Immortal*. Two of them stopped to unleash streaks of fire at the flailing limbs.

One of those long arms wrapped around a warrior, crushing his armored body. His tank exploded, and flames raced up the limb, which pulled back, thrashing the air before splashing back down into the water.

"Pull everyone back!" X shouted.

"*Capitán, hay dos contactos en el sonar*," said an officer behind X.

The young woman staring at her screen glanced up, terror in her eyes. "The other two monsters are flanking the *Immortal*," she said.

X stepped over to the starboard viewports and trained the binos on the tangerine glow swimming just under the waves.

Before anyone could react, both bodies slammed into the hull of the *Immortal*, then deployed mutant arms that slapped and stuck to the side of the airship.

"Why aren't they attacking *us*?" asked Captain Two Skulls. "It's like they don't even see us."

"It must have something to do with . . ." X paused. It dawned on him then. "That's it! They must be after the nuclear reactors."

Raising his binos, he focused them on another source of nuclear energy: the airship *Vanguard*.

X cursed a blue streak as he lowered the binoculars and adjusted his headset.

"Captain Rolo, do you copy?" X said.

In the moment that passed before Rolo replied, X's mind wandered back to the first time he saw Sirens digging up radioactive dirt and eating it. Some creatures in the wastes thrived off nuclear decay in a way that he still didn't understand.

"Copy, King Xavier," said Captain Rolo.

"Get the airship off that deck and into the sky right now!" X shouted.

Static crackled, another pause passing.

"Sir, you want me to fly into the storm?"

"The alternative is being pulled into the ocean and made into monster shit, if you'd prefer that," X said. "Stay as low as you can, but get off the *Immortal*, pronto! That's an order, Captain."

"This is complete and utter—"

X clicked off the channel and turned to Captain Two Skulls.

"Activate the battering ram," he said. "I'm headed to the bow."

X motioned for Miles to follow him down to the lower decks and under the bow. A cockpit with viewports was built inside the massive ram he had commissioned before the journey, with exactly this eventuality in mind.

He took a seat in front of the controls. Miles jumped up, putting his paws on X's lap.

"Sorry, boy, but we got to strap you in."

Miles jumped up into the other chair, and X buckled him in. Then he buckled into his own chair and looked at the complicated dashboard.

He thought back to the short tutorial Steve had gone over with him in the cockpit. He pushed the on button, and as the screen came online, the shutters over the viewports pulled back. He was just twenty feet above the waterline, within range of waves that slapped up the bow.

Despite the spray, X had a perfect view of the *Immortal* and the beasts attacking the ship.

Thick, spiked arms flickered away from the gray flesh of the whale off the port side, striking containers on the deck, and again slapping the hull of the airship.

"Captain Rolo, what's your status?" X asked over the command channel.

"Working on getting in the air, sir, but we've got a problem," replied the captain.

X leaned closer to the window and zoomed in on the airship. Four of the spiked prehensile limbs had snaked around the airship's landing gear.

"Stand by," X said.

He took a moment to consider his next order, which would send men and women back into the fray, but they had no choice.

"General Forge, do you copy?" X said into his headset.

"Copy, sir."

"Get a team out on the deck of the *Immortal* and free the *Vanguard*."

"Yes, sir. I will see to it myself."

X switched back to the command channel with Captain Two Skulls.

"Time to bash this pile of mutant carrion," X said into his headset. "Full steam ahead, Captain."

A siren wailed, warning the crew.

The *Ocean Bull* plowed through the water toward the *Immortal*, pushing up a wall of water along the bow. X could no longer see *Raven's Claw* or the *Octopus*. That was good—they could ill afford damage to one of their other ships.

He focused on the controls and rotated the spikes into position with a push of a button. All six blades, each the length of a Cazador spear, jutted from the welded-steel contraption.

Water splashed the windows as they closed on the monster. X thought about his note to Michael, and the promise he had made to everyone.

These beasts were just one more threat to their way of life, but as with every other threat facing humanity, X had prepared for this.

Lightning burst like a star shell over the *Immortal*, illuminating the scene in one brilliant flash. The whale had latched on to the airship and the supercarrier, which was dragging the colossal beast.

X tapped the dashboard to raise the spikes a few feet. The *Ocean Bull* was coming in at a ninety-degree angle, aimed directly for the creature's exposed dorsal ridges.

He was still far enough out that he could see the airship on the deck, and dozens of soldiers advancing toward the landing gear. The red-feathered helmet of General Forge was reliably in the thick of things. Wielding a long cutlass, he dashed up to a limb wrapped around the closest leg of the airship, and hacked deep into orange flesh. Two men with axes joined him.

X lost sight of them as the *Ocean Bull* closed in and the supercarrier's hull blocked the view topside.

A few moments later, the *Vanguard* tried to rise from the deck, but three writhing, grasping limbs were still attached and pulling. One had snaked around a turbofan, which suddenly ripped free, crashing down onto the weather deck of the *Immortal*.

The PA system on the *Ocean Bull* kicked on with an announcement to brace for impact.

"Hold on, boy," X said to Miles.

He checked the spikes above the cockpit and actuated the relay to extend them farther. The blades went out as far as they would go.

"Okay, you ugly bastard," X growled. "How about a spike up your blowhole?"

Seconds from impact, the *Ocean Bull* was still accelerating. At the last moment, X was close enough to see barnacles and remoras attached to the mottled gray skin, and long scars from doing battle with other sea monsters.

X was about to give it another scar—a big one.

The spikes punched into the thick hide, which easily gave way. Blood and meat slapped against the Plexiglas of the bridge, cracking the reinforced panel. The ship jolted hard, but the harness held X in his seat.

Purple blood cascaded down the window, blocking his view of the monster.

The *Ocean Bull* backed up, and the next wave rinsed most of the gore off the Plexiglas, allowing X to see the hull of the *Immortal*. Severed arms hung from the upper decks, leaking purple blood.

The orange glow vanished beneath the surface between the *Ocean Bull* and the supercarrier.

X looked up at the blue flames of the *Vanguard*'s thrusters. With the airship away, he could finally breathe a sigh of relief.

"We got incoming," came the voice of Captain Two Skulls over the radio. "All hands, prepare for impact."

A loud groaning noise rumbled through the hull as the blow rotated the ship several degrees. X reached over and ruffled Miles's fur.

"Do you trust me, boy?" he asked.

Miles licked his hand.

"Good," X said. It was time to take the ram for a second go at the whales. The last two had split up, the glows spreading out as they sounded toward the sea bottom.

He didn't see the third injured beast, but after the ass-kicking he had just given it, he doubted it would come back for more.

"Both hostiles are closing in, King Xavier," said the captain. "Bringing us around to meet the one off the port beam."

"Copy that," X said.

The *Immortal* continued sailing away in the distance, and the *Vanguard* was nowhere in sight, nor were the other two ships.

X had gotten the attention of the monsters, but now the *Ocean Bull* was on its own.

"Just us and them now, boy," X said.

The surface glow of the lead whale expanded in the distance, and kept growing as the *Ocean Bull* turned into the waves.

The next message from Captain Two Skulls told X why.

"This is the biggest beast of the pod," the captain said. "One thousand meters out. Good luck, King Xavier."

Another warning chirped over the PA system.

About two hundred meters out, the monster surfaced in an explosion of water.

It took him a moment to grasp that this wasn't the head, but the massive tail flukes, slapping the water. The beast went under, the glow vanishing.

"Where'd it go?" X asked Miles.

Spotlights raked the water.

Over the drone of the emergency alarm, he heard chatter on the comms.

"It's right under us," Two Skulls transmitted. "Moving now. Prepare for . . ."

X flinched backward in his seat as the monstrous face of the whale burst upward a mere hundred meters in front of the bow. Rising from the deep and exposing its glowing throat grooves. The bright glare revealed a mouth filled with teeth the size of cutlass blades.

A baleful eye peered in through the Plexiglas at him and his dog.

X stared back at the bulbous eye.

The beast let out a shrieking whistle that made him wince. He blinked as arms rose toward the *Ocean Bull*.

Ears ringing, X let out a war-whoop of his own. The monster opened its mouth wider and surged forward to chomp the bridge.

Right as the jaws began to close, X raised the shutters halfway over the Plexiglas.

The cockpit jolted, and a spiderweb of cracks raced across the glass.

X worked the hydraulic controls of the spikes, stabbing the enormous face over and over with the extendable spears.

Lights flickered, Miles howled, and the whistling continued, creating an unholy din that made it hard to think.

X could feel the resistance as the spikes punched through eyes and flesh and scraped on bone. Glass shattered overhead when a tooth broke through right between him and Miles.

Using the hydraulic levers, he continued to punch the beast with the spikes, jerking in his seat with every impact. One of the spikes slammed against the hard skull, bending and finally snapping in two.

A moment later, another spike bent, but the other four kept stabbing into the mutant flesh, over and over.

Violet fluid sloshed through the broken window. X took his hand off the controls for a moment to close the other shutter, but it was jammed or broken.

He stared up at an eye the size of a tank sprocket, still looking into the cockpit.

Unsheathing his hatchet, he swung it deep into the pupil, prompting a high-pitched shriek of agony that hurt his ears.

X pulled the axe back as the beast retreated. He waited a few seconds before lowering the other shutters for a look. The beams lit up the monster, whipping and jerking its limbs back and forth over the water. It slowly went under, bubbles rising through the fading yellow glow as it sank into the depths.

The comms fired to life. "Well done, King Xavier!" said the captain. "I think you've killed two of them. The third beast is fleeing to the east."

X unbuckled his seat and checked on Miles, who was drenched in water and purple blood but seemed fine.

"I think we did it," X said.

Miles barked, wanting down.

"Hold on," X said, peering through the viewports to make sure the beast was indeed gone.

Sure enough, the yellow glow grew dimmer and weaker until there were only the spotlight beams crossing back and forth over dark, frothy water.

"Hell yes!" X said.

He started to sit back down and send a transmission when the voice of Captain Two Skulls made the hair on his neck stand up.

"Prepare for impact!" he shouted.

X felt a moment of sheer terror before something hit the *Ocean Bull* from behind. The impact bounced him off the dashboard. He hit the deck and lay there, stunned.

Miles struggled to free himself from the seat harness and help.

"Stay . . . there," X mumbled.

He pushed himself up, slicing his right hand on a shard of the shattered viewport.

A panicked voice surged over the comms. Something about taking on water via the lower decks.

X grabbed the chair, pulled himself up, and tried to regain his sense of balance. The hatch opened, and Slayer rushed in.

"Sir, we have to go," he said.

"I thought I killed two and the third was—"

"This is the first beast," Slayer said. "And it's really fucking mad!"

X staggered over to Miles, realizing what had happened. The third, smaller beast had fled, but the first one wasn't dead—it was just regrouping.

He unbuckled Miles and picked him up, not putting him down until they got out of the Plexiglas-covered cockpit. In the passage outside, they followed the two Cazador warriors to an open hatch. The hull groaned, half-obscuring another warning over the PA system.

All X heard was, "Brace!"

The impact came from the port side this time, knocking everyone in the passageway off their feet. X almost hit the overhead, his head narrowly missing a pipe.

The *Ocean Bull* buckled, and X knew it didn't have long on this side of the surface. He helped one of the men up and whistled to Miles to follow.

They made it up two ladders before the enraged whale hit again.

X held on to a rail with one hand, and Miles with the other. Slayer also held on, but the other soldier wasn't as lucky. He flailed for something to hold on to and then flew off the top landing, hitting halfway down the flight with a crack that echoed.

"Go, King Xavier!" Slayer shouted. "I will help him."

X hesitated but then went to help when he saw the water rushing up below. He couldn't leave these two men behind.

A clear message came over the PA system. "All hands to the life rafts," said Captain Two Skulls. "Abandon ship! Repeat, abandon ship."

The fallen guard had managed to get up, gripping a badly broken arm while Slayer helped him. Together they hurried up the ladder until they got to the hatch that opened to the weather deck.

"This way!" Slayer yelled.

Sailors and soldiers ran over to the rail, where lifeboats were already being lowered. In the distance, X spotted the lights of the *Immortal* and, behind it, *Raven's Claw* and *Octopus*.

They were closing in to help but were too far off to do much good.

"Watch out!" Slayer shouted.

X turned and saw the yellow glow spearing under

the water, toward the starboard side—right toward the lifeboats. He looked for something to hold on to, but they were in the middle of the deck.

The yellow glow closed on the sinking ship. It began to list, and X could feel the water rushing into the stern.

"Get down!" yelled Captain Two Skulls.

He came running toward X, who dropped down and hugged Miles on the deck. He glanced up at something streaking out of the sky like a meteor. Another streak lanced through the darkness.

Explosions boomed off the starboard side, and a geyser of water shot up, along with hunks of mottled flesh.

X held Miles tight as the airship *Vanguard* lowered from the clouds. It descended over the deck of the *Ocean Bull*, the bottom troop hold opening and a ramp extending down.

Magnolia emerged with a rope at the edge of the open launch bay.

"Let's go!" she shouted.

More divers and technicians stepped up, uncoiling ropes and tossing them down.

X picked up Miles and carefully made his way up the sloping deck to grab one of the dangling ropes. He snatched it, and hung tightly on to Miles as two Hell Divers pulled him up.

The water encroached on the deck, swallowing it up to the middle. Sailors and soldiers in life jackets dived off into the waves. X spotted Captain Two Skulls sliding down the deck with two of his officers, their bodies splashing into the water.

By the time X got up to the ramp, he was losing his grip on Miles. Strong arms grabbed him and pulled him up, and X released the dog.

He crawled back to the edge of the ramp and looked down at the ship that had figured large in their plans to use the Panama Canal.

A beat later, with a sigh audible even at this distance, the ocean swallowed the *Ocean Bull* whole.

TWENTY-SIX

Michael was up before the sun. He kissed Bray and then checked on baby Rhino in the other crib. Even at just a few months old, he was showing signs that he would be big like his father.

It was a tragedy that General Rhino had never met his child or even known about him, but soon the child would know all about his famous father.

"You're heading out early."

Michael turned to see his wife standing in the doorway. She handed him a fresh apple.

"Thanks," he said. "You got any fun lessons planned for school today?"

"School's out."

"Oh, that's right. Sorry, I'm losing track of time."

She stepped over to the cribs. "I'm going to be here with them, waiting to hear what those keys are for."

"Don't worry, Layla, okay?"

She bit the inside of her lip. "I'll try, but with so much riding on Panama, it's hard not to."

"I know," he said, "but we've been through worse. Don't forget about the decades in the sky."

"That's exactly what I've been thinking about."

Michael kissed her goodbye and pulled his baseball cap over his long hair. Ton and Victor were waiting inside the entrance of the apartment, eating apples that Layla had given them.

"Good morning, Chief," said Victor.

Ton smiled with mostly gums, only a few teeth showing.

"Good morning," Michael said.

"Watch after my man today," Layla said.

"Some days, I feel he looks after *us*," Victor said.

They hurried down to a marina already active with fishermen—some who were coming back from spending all night on the ocean, others who were just heading out.

Michael geared up and climbed into his boat. By the time he steered it out into the water, reports were flooding in from the rigs with engineering issues.

"Hope you got some rest," said Steve over the radio, "'cause we got a major problem at rig fifteen."

"I'll meet you there," Michael said.

"Sir, I've been here since five o'clock."

"Outworking the young pups again?"

"Oh, I can run circles around them, partner. You'll see."

Michael smiled. He was really starting to like Steve.

The journey to the trading post rig took Michael

past the Wind Talker rig. Seeing a working wind turbine gave him a surge of pride. It was a start, but they had a long way to go in restoring power throughout the islands.

Rig 15, which housed the survivors from Tanzania, was in bad shape. Michael slowed the engine as he approached.

Most of the exterior shacks had been completely removed, the materials going to construct community shelters deeper inside the rig. This would help mitigate future storm losses, but other issues required critical parts that they were low on.

Michael caught the scent of raw sewage even before he docked. He flashed back to the moment he landed at the camp with Arlo to rescue these people from the machines. Conditions on the rig weren't all that much better than at that camp: no warm water, no power, and rationed food.

At least they have the sun.

Michael looked west. Rain clouds loomed on the horizon. Even the sunshine was under threat today.

He hopped out and secured the boat. Ton and Victor walked ahead, toward the bottom hatch. An interior ladder took them up to the fifth deck. A passage led to the new community housing space, which reeked of sewage.

Michael stepped inside, trying to breathe through his mouth.

Drapes partitioned off areas, much as they once had on the *Hive*. With rain threatening, almost everyone was inside right now. Kids sat on plastic chairs playing games, and parents cooked rations and washed clothes.

Eyes followed Michael and his guards.

"When will they turn the power back on?" a woman asked.

"Soon," Michael said.

"Do something about the plumbing," said the woman. "We can't take much more of this smell, especially when it's hot."

Resentful gazes followed Michael. Just weeks earlier, these people were all smiles. It was sobering how fast things changed. And if things went bad this fast, they could get worse even faster.

Michael knew he should keep on walking, but he wanted to stop and see Alton. He took a right down an aisle of partitioned-off spaces furnished with cots or makeshift beds. Some were clean and tidy, but the one he was looking for was a mess.

And empty.

Michael looked inside the small ten-by-ten space Alton shared with his mom. He found two wrinkled blankets on the cots, some piles of clothing and dirty dishes, and a stuffed elephant.

He picked the toy up off the filthy floor and set it on a cot.

Then he went to the space across the hall. The drape pulled back, and a seven-year-old boy with one eye stood and saluted.

"Hey there, kid," Michael said.

A woman stood up—the boy's aunt, from what Michael remembered. Thirties, maybe a bit older, with pretty features.

"You're one of the Hell Divers," she said. "Alton's been telling everyone."

Michael smiled. "I was indeed, and now I'm here to fix the shit cans."

He laughed, and she chuckled but grew serious.

"Do you know where Alton and his mom went?"

"The hospital," the woman replied. "She's in bad shape."

Michael sighed. He'd had a feeling that was the case.

"Thanks," he said.

"Wait."

He stopped in the aisle and turned back.

"Things are getting bad, and I worry about my nephew," she said. "There are people here that think . . . they are paranoid that . . ."

She peered out, past Michael, to a man watching them down the aisle. More like staring at them, Michael realized. He used his back to block the view.

"That *what*?" he asked the woman.

"That we are going to run out of food and will have to fight."

"That's not going to happen. You have my word."

"Okay. Thank you for everything."

"It's my duty, ma'am. And my pleasure."

The boy held the salute, and Michael saluted before leaving. Walking down the passage, he eyed the staring man. He was thin and bald and had a scar on his chin. Ton and Victor moved past the guy, eyes alert, clearly anxious about raised tensions since the storm.

Steve was talking with Charmer in the passage outside the community shelter. Oliver and another big man, holding a baton, were standing guard.

"We've shut off the pipe and can clean up the mess, but we don't have the spares yet to install a new one to get the system back up and running," Steve was saying.

"Ah, Chief, I was hoping you'd come," he said. "I want to apologize for yesterday. It was a rough day. Started off with a theft at the kitchen, and then a sewage pipe burst—hence that noxious smell—and we are just now learning the extent of the damage."

Charmer seemed about to put a hand around Michael's shoulder, but Michael stepped back.

"You spoke of fairness," Charmer said, "but we are both sky people, and it just seems that since you fought for this place, you should be able to pick and choose who gets what. So perhaps you should consider helping your own before those . . ."

"Barbarians," Oliver said.

"Not how things work under King Xavier," Michael said. "I thought you'd have figured that out after a year."

Charmer's grin faded. "The past year, we didn't have shortages of food, and we had power."

"And you will again, but for now we're rationing," Michael said. "That said, we'll get your plumbing fixed one way or another."

"But, sir," Steve said. "We don't have the spare—"

"We'll find them."

Charmer bowed slightly. "Gratitude, Chief, and I'll return the favor with something. You scratch my back, I'll scratch yours, as they used to say."

"That's not necessary."

"How about this: Lieutenant Wynn can have back the militia assigned to this rig. Fair?"

Oliver folded his arms over his chest, and the other big man tapped a baton against his palm. It occurred to Michael this wasn't bartering—more of a demand disguised as a gift.

"We'll take full charge of security here," Charmer said. "We take care of our own, including our thief."

Wynn could use the extra manpower, but Michael didn't like the idea of not having at least one soldier on this rig, and he wasn't falling for this "gift."

"I'll run it by Lieutenant Wynn," Michael said. "In the meantime, we'll start the hunt for spare pipes."

"Good man."

Michael left with Steve to survey the pipes that still needed to be fixed. Finally making their way back, they halted at what sounded like screaming kids.

"What the heck is that?" Steve asked.

Michael rushed toward the community shelter, where onlookers stood around two people wrestling on the deck.

Oliver was there, cheering on one of the fighters.

Moving for a better look, Michael finally saw that it was two kids on the ground. And one of them was

Alton. He was on his back while a bigger boy was hitting him in the chest and stomach.

"Hey!" Michael shouted. "Stop!"

He pushed through the crowd and grabbed the boy, pulling him off Alton—and got a punch to the jaw for his efforts.

Alton then tackled the larger boy.

Oliver intervened, smacking Alton with a paw.

"Hey!" Michael shouted.

He grabbed Oliver by the wrist with his robotic hand. The veins extended in Oliver's neck as he struggled vainly to free his arm.

"Don't you *ever* hit a kid again, or I will end you," Michael said.

Oliver glared at him. "Try it, kid."

Michael tightened his grip and pushed down, prompting a yelp from Oliver.

Ton and Victor both approached with their spears as Charmer ran over.

"What in blazes is going on?" Charmer asked.

"Alton hit my kid," Oliver said, wincing in pain.

Steve explained what had happened, and Charmer stormed over to Oliver and Michael.

"Let him go," Charmer said. "I'll deal with this."

Michael held on for a defiant moment before pushing Oliver away. They locked eyes, and for a second it seemed that Oliver might do something foolish.

"Oliver!" Charmer shouted. "Take a step back. Now!"

He finally moved over to his son. "Get up, Nez," he said.

Michael rushed over to Alton, who was curled up on his side.

"You okay?" he asked.

The boy tried to hide the tears streaming down his cheeks.

Michael reached down and helped Alton up. "What happened?" he asked.

"He hit me," said Nez.

Michael looked over his shoulder.

"Aye, it's true," Alton said softly.

"Why did you do that?" Michael asked.

"Nez said my mom is going to die."

Oliver was already walking away with his son, and Charmer was with Steve, getting the crowd to disperse. Ton and Victor remained in defensive mode but lowered their spears.

Alton lowered his head. "The doctor said she has cancer."

Michael understood then. He had lost his mom when he was around Alton's age, and dealt with the same emotions.

"There's hope for your mom," he said.

Alton looked unsure.

"I'll talk to Dr. Huff and Dr. Stamos," Michael said.

"Really?"

"Yeah, but you can't go around hitting people anymore, okay?"

Alton nodded.

"Promise me," Michael said.

"I promise."

"Good."

Michael got him up to his feet and walked with him over to his quarters.

The woman across the way nodded at Michael. "I'll look after him," she said.

"Thanks," Michael replied.

He helped Alton into his bed and pulled a blanket over him.

"Are you okay?"

"Aye," Alton said.

"I'll talk to the doctors and come see you soon."

Alton reached out, and Michael gave him a hug.

"It's okay, bud, don't worry." Michael left in a funk. Not just from the altercation, but because he wasn't sure how they could fix much before X came back with supplies. And that could be weeks, if not longer.

Power, like water and food, was life. Without it, critical systems used for medical care, food storage, and agriculture would fail.

Steve must have sensed his anxiety. "We will get things up and running again," he said. "Don't worry, Chief, we're partners. I've been here a long time, and we always figure out ways to keep on poundin'."

Michael looked at Steve, hoping he was right to trust him. He needed someone with engineering experience and knowledge of the islands.

When they got back on the boat, he reached in his pocket and pulled out the first key X had left him.

"Do you know what this is for?"

Steve took it and held it up. "Yeah, it's for the . . ."

He put the key down and looked up as Victor backed the boat away from the dock. Charmer walked out on the pier. A group of men and some women surrounded him, all of them armed with swords, batons, or pipes.

They didn't look like a security force. They looked like a posse.

* * * * *

"Almost there, Jo-Jo," Ada said.

She waited in the launch bay of the Vanguard. The airship was once again moored on the deck of the supercarrier, with one fewer turbofan and a hundred new scrapes and dents in her hull from the barbed limbs of the sea creatures. Remarkably, they had lost only the *Ocean Bull* in the attack, along with two soldiers and five drowned sailors. Tia was also okay—just a nasty bump to the noggin.

The remainder of the fleet sailed into Lincoln Bay at the northern entrance to the Panama Canal, with *Raven's Claw* and *Octopus* not far behind. To the east, a crater was all that remained of the city of Colón. General Forge had been here not long ago, but only one Cazador ship, the *Sea Sprite*, had ventured farther than that into the fifty-five miles of canal, never to return.

Leading the way, the *Immortal* cruised through Lincoln Bay and the widened canal to Gatun Lake. An hour into the slow journey, they passed Barro Colorado Island, coming within view of the strangely mutated jungle growing on the shore.

Electrical storms burned across the skyline, backlighting the ruined high-rises that still stood along the canal. The drones were already on their way, buzzing through the sky with their scanners to search for life and send back environmental readings.

Bustling and clanking pulled Ada away from her reconnoitering.

"All right, we're about to pass Gamboa and will be at our drop point soon," Magnolia said. "Check your gear, check your buddy's gear, and stand by for briefing."

The divers spread out to finish last-minute preps.

"You ready for this?" said a voice.

Kade's helmet bore the new logo of Team Wrangler.

"I've been ready," she said. "I just hope we're not too late."

The launch-bay doors hissed open, and the heavy clomp of boots echoed through the space. Captain Rolo strode inside wearing a white uniform, hands cupped behind his back, eyes roving over the divers.

He wasn't alone.

Joining the captain was King Xavier, dressed in his Hell Diver armor. Beside him walked Miles in a protective suit, a gas mask hanging from his collar.

"There's been a slight modification of plans due to the storm," Rolo said. "We will be sending Team Raptor to the canal but holding Team Wrangler back."

"What?" Ada said. "But, King Xavier, you said—"

"That we would find your friend, and we will," he replied. "I made a promise, and I'm keeping it."

He handed her a small electronic device.

"Chief Engineer Everhart gave this to me, but you'll need it more than I will," X explained. "Cricket 2.0 is linked to the drones we're sending out. Among their other transmissions, it will be searching for Jo-Jo's beacon."

"Thank you," Ada said graciously. In that moment, she resisted the urge to hug X, who had been kinder to her than she deserved. Most leaders would have killed her for her crime of dropping the Cazador container into the water. He had given her a second chance, and he truly cared about Jo-Jo as he did Miles.

"As soon as we beach, we're sending up flares to draw the monsters out of their lairs. As soon as we know the tunnels are clear, you will have a window to go search for Jo-Jo if we find her beacon." X turned to the other divers. "Meanwhile, Team Raptor will be diving to the Cocoli Locks with Yejun to find that map on his ship. Comms will likely be offline once you go underground, but we'll keep an eye on your beacons for trouble."

"And if we locate Jo-Jo's beacon?" Kade asked.

"Then Ada has permission to dive, but the mission will be voluntary," X said.

"I'll go with her," said Tia. "I'm fine, Kade. My head's all better."

Kade cursed under his breath, but Ada could hear him.

"I'll lead the mission," he said. "Gran Jefe, you in?"

The big Cazador shrugged a shoulder plate. "Why not?"

"Okay," X said.

"We dive so humanity survives, sir," Magnolia yelled.

The divers responded in unison.

X stepped up to Ada. "I hope you find her, kid. I know what it means to have an animal for a best friend."

Bending down, Ada patted Miles.

"I'll find your friend, buddy," she said.

The dog licked at her glove.

He left the room, and the divers finished packing gear and checking weapons. Kade loaded his six-shooter and holstered it.

"Thank you," Ada said. "I appreciate this more than you know."

X nodded and walked over to the hull doors with Magnolia. She opened them to the ramp that extended down to the deck of the *Immortal*.

"Godspeed, Hell Divers," X said. Miles wagged his tail and bounded down the ramp faster than Ada had seen him move in quite some time.

Gathered outside on the supercarrier's weather deck were 250 warriors in full body armor and gas masks. The gray-and-black warriors were divided up into squads with laser rifles, assault rifles, and flamethrowers. Each fighter was also equipped with a cutlass or a spear.

All eye slots were on the king and his dog as they walked toward the six APCs and two lightly armored tanks.

Technicians made final checks and gave the all clear to proceed.

X helped Miles up onto the front of the tank, right next to the cannon pointing at the shoreline.

"To the warriors who followed me, hear me now!" X yelled. "Today we have come to the wastes to fight for our home. By seizing this canal, we will open a supply chain to the western shore of South America. Failing is not an option. Failure means our families and friends will starve. Failing means the Vanguard Islands will decay and die like the rest of the world."

Lightning flashed, illuminating a terrain littered with partially buried boats and equipment washed away by tsunamis during the war.

"In an hour, we will send up the flares, drawing the shelled beasts from their lairs," X said. "When they emerge, give them no quarter. Kill them all."

The pounding of chest plates and the thump of spear shafts on the deck became the drumbeat to war as X raised his metal prosthetic arm in the air.

"For the Vanguard Islands!" he shouted.

Magnolia pushed the button on the hull, closing the doors as the airship's engines fired. The ship rose off the deck of the *Immortal* to hover at five hundred feet above the army.

Ada pulled out Cricket 2.0 and turned the device on. They were too far out to detect Jo-Jo's beacon yet, but when the drones deployed, she would know the truth.

The hum of the airship's turbofans reverberated through the hull. Ada stayed at the windows, looking down at the canal and then the terrain below.

She checked the coordinates of their last dive and spotted the field of overturned containers and the hill near the canal's west bank. But this couldn't be right . . .

Where were the holes?

The voice of XO Eevi Corey came over the PA system. "Stand by for phase one in ten, nine, eight . . ."

At the end of the countdown, the airship launched a series of flares over the horizon. Ada turned off her night-vision optics to look with her own eyes.

Now she saw mounds of dirt where the tunnel openings had been. So finding an entry point for a drone was going to be difficult.

For the next few minutes, Ada's eyes flitted from Cricket to the surface.

The PA system clicked on with an announcement for phase 2. At the end of the countdown, a pod of drones took off from the deck of the *Immortal*. They fanned out over the canal.

Ada watched the drones recede in the distance, their scanners pulsating and sending back data to the command center on the *Immortal*. Cricket remained blank. No sign of her best friend.

The other Hell Divers broke into side conversations around her.

"The flares aren't working," Arlo said.

"We might have to knock harder," Edgar said. "Bust out some artillery."

For the next half hour, Ada held Cricket up until her hand shook. The flares weren't drawing out the monsters, and she still didn't have a location for her friend.

"Where are you, Jo-Jo?" she whispered.

Magnolia stepped up next to her.

"See anything yet?"

Ada shook her helmet, trying to keep it together.

"Jo-Jo must be farther out from the scans," Magnolia said.

Ada hesitated, unsure how to respond at first, looking out over the radioactive surface below. In her heart, she suspected that her companion was already dead.

Anger boiled through Ada. *You left her down there to die.*

A message fired over the PA system. "Team Raptor, launch has been delayed," said Captain Rolo. "King Xavier has decided to use bombs to draw out the beasts. Until we know where they are, we can't risk sending you."

Ada looked over at Magnolia, who seemed to agree with the announcement.

"What?" Ada cried. "We still haven't found Jo-Jo, and we're going to start *bombing*?"

The airship began to pull away from the canal.

A private channel connected to Ada. "Ada, this is X. I'm sorry, we haven't found Jo-Jo's beacon yet, so she must be out of range. I'm going to start bombing the DZ to draw out the creatures."

She didn't reply at first.

"Ada," X said.

"Yes, I'm here, and I understand."

It wasn't a lie. She understood the decision, but her heart was too broken to say anything more.

"We will find her," X said.

The line severed, and Kade put a hand on her shoulder.

"I'm sorry," he said.

He backed away from the launch-bay doors with the other divers, but Tia remained with Ada.

She remained glued to the portholes. Moving from window to window for a look at the canal. *Raven's Claw* and *Immortal* had continued down the canal, moving toward Panama Bay.

They would fire from the canal into the industrial zone, drawing out the beasts. Meanwhile, four landing craft would take the army and vehicles into Panama Bay, where they would beach on the southern shore of Panama City.

Pinpricks of light came from the canal as the ships moved into position and began to fire. Several seconds later, the first explosions puffed on the ground. More seconds later, she heard the distant thuds.

"Hey, your thing is chirping," Tia said.

"Huh?" Ada said.

She looked over to see Tia reaching for Cricket.

The screen had activated, and on it a beacon pulsed.

Jo-Jo was alive!

Ada held up the device and checked the location. Her heavy heart skipped when she saw the coordinates: right in the middle of the bombardment.

"No, no, no," Ada moaned.

She switched on the private channel to X. "Stop the bombing! Jo-Jo's down there!"

There was no response but static crackling from the electrical storm. She lost sight of the surface as the airship rose higher into the clouds.

Ada didn't waste a second. She tapped the launch-bay door, reopening it.

"Ada, what are you doing!" Magnolia shouted.

"Finding Jo-Jo!" Ada yelled back.

She heard footsteps behind her as people ran to stop her from jumping. The doors slowly opened, and the ramp extended.

"Ada!" Edgar screamed. "Ada, wait!"

Ada stepped through the opening and out into the black. As she fell, she did half a barrel roll and looked up at the ship. Divers weren't just running to stop her.

Tia jumped out next, and then came a third figure.

Kade . . .

She completed the barrel roll and fell facedown, in stable position.

A few seconds into the dive, she blew through the cloud cover.

Shells continued to burst across the terrain below her, appearing as tiny sparks on the ground, followed by a little puff of smoke and debris. They were focused on the same general area where the divers had landed on the last visit here.

And according to Ada's HUD, Jo-Jo was right in the middle. She eyed the beacon and then pulled her limbs into a suicide dive.

"I'm coming, Jo-Jo!"

Her slender body speared through the air, picking up speed, hitting 115, then 130 miles per hour.

Falling head-down, she quickly ate up the altitude, and thirty seconds later she maneuvered back into a stable fall.

At a thousand feet, she pulled her pilot chute. The canopy bloomed above her, and she toggled toward Jo-Jo's beacon.

The other divers were ten seconds behind her and would have pulled their chutes by now. Ada flared and stepped down between two deep craters blown up by the warships' artillery shells. The firing had stopped, but she could still feel quakes. Here, another rumble. That wasn't right . . .

"Oh, shit," she said, reaching for her rifle.

A mound of dirt rose between the canal and where she now stood. The top ruptured, throwing up a geyser of dirt and rock that then showered back down.

Ada took a step back and aimed her rifle at the orange pincer that shuffled up out of the dirt. Another claw joined it, and together they pressed down against the ground and pushed up a shell the size of a small airship. A tortoise head on an armored neck looked down at her.

Tia came in a little bit crosswind, flared, and tumbled on the ground. Kade landed next and ran over to free her from her chute.

Ada bent down to help, keeping one eye on the monster that was still climbing out of the shaft. It opened its jaws and gave a loud, whistling hiss as it shook dirt off its shell.

Kade helped Tia out of her chute, but with no time to stow it, they just left it flapping in the wind.

"If you want to live, stay close to me," he said.

Another canopy ghosted over them. Ada followed it to the ground. The fourth diver landed on both feet and ran out the momentum. His massive size gave away his identity.

Gran Jefe was the last person Ada expected to see.

Carrying a grenade launcher, he followed Kade behind a container, to hide from the beast.

"Gran Jefe," Ada said. "I didn't expect—"

"*¿Por qué?*" he said. "You didn't think I'd let you have all the fun, did you, *amiga*?"

TWENTY-SEVEN

Magnolia cursed. She should have known that something like this was going to happen, but there was nothing she could do about it. Team Wrangler was on its own. She had her own mission to complete—a mission that could potentially secure the future of the Vanguard Islands.

Turning, she looked to their potential salvation. Fifteen-year-old Yejun was wearing the suit they had found him in, and carrying the bird helmet under his arm.

Behind him stood Sofia, Edgar, and Arlo, all armed with laser rifles and ready to dive.

The hologram of Timothy emerged on the deck in front of the divers and explained the plan one last time to Yejun in his native tongue. It was simple. Yejun and Magnolia would tandem dive to his ship, find his map, and then deploy back into the sky while the beasts on the surface were preoccupied with the Cazador military.

Yejun secured his helmet, then stepped over to Magnolia and raised his arms. Edgar clipped their harnesses together in front of the exit hatch—now closed—that Ada had just jumped through.

Magnolia tapped her wrist computer, using the translation software that Timothy had installed for them to use on the surface.

"Speak in Korean," she said.

The device chirped, and a monotone voice replied, "*hangugeoro malhasipsio.*" The computer would come in handy, that was for sure.

"Good, I'm glad it works," Timothy said. He smiled at Magnolia. "Good luck, Commander Katib."

"Thanks, T."

Magnolia thought about all their adventures as she stood there waiting for the green light to dive. Timothy had served the sky people heroically since the day they met him. He wasn't human anymore, but the awareness he once had in life had remained in all the different iterations of his operating system.

A warning light flashed in the launch bay, and his hologram began to fade. He held up a hand and smiled again at Magnolia.

"You dive so humanity survives," he said.

Her headset crackled with the voice of Captain Rolo.

"We're directly above the drop zone," he said. "Good luck, Team Raptor."

An alarm wailed—the final warning to clear the

room before the hatches opened. Wind rushed in, dropping the room temperature by thirty degrees.

The doors whisked open to reveal dense clouds.

Magnolia positioned herself and Yejun in front of the ramp. "Okay, let's get this done, Team Raptor," she said. "Fast, easy, and safe."

Edgar, Arlo, and Sofia all nodded back.

Magnolia was first onto the ramp. The kid didn't seem scared, but this was the moment of truth. Edgar was first out.

"Okay, kid," Magnolia said. With Yejun clipped to her chest by locking carabiners, she jumped in a hard arch. He did the same, just as they had instructed him.

Turning like a leaf in the wind, she saw the airship and the other divers leaping out of the brightly lit launch bay. Then she and Yejun completed their somersault, and she lost sight of them.

The low-altitude drop gave them only thirty seconds of free fall before opening—still plenty of time for a look at what awaited them on the surface.

Breaking through the clouds gave Magnolia a wide view of the canal, the industrial zone on both sides, and Panama City.

She couldn't see the Vanguard warships, but she could see the monsters that the military would soon face.

Two of the tortoise-shelled monster adults had burst out of the ground, and hundreds of their human-size young surged over the radioactive terrain.

They were all heading toward the warships, just as X had planned, leaving the industrial zone clear.

Magnolia diverted her attention to the DZ. She was already within view of the ship that had brought Yejun and his family here. Edgar was almost to the ground.

She reached down and pulled her pilot chute.

She felt the opening shock, then steered over the deck of the ship, right where Yejun had captured her a few weeks earlier.

Edgar was already free of his chute, with his rifle shouldered, by the time she did a two-stage flare. She landed ten feet away and crashed inelegantly to the deck with Yejun.

Arlo and Sofia came next.

Two minutes later, Team Raptor had its gear stowed and weapons up. During a brief respite in the gusting breeze, a high-pitched shriek blasted across the wastes—the angry wail of one of the two monstrous parents.

Yejun motioned for the team to follow. Magnolia stayed close behind, keeping low, running a life-form scan on her wrist computer.

The screen pulsated as the scan moved out, but nothing came back on the heartbeat monitor. She then checked her HUD for Team Wrangler. The other divers were almost three miles away and moving closer to Jo-Jo.

The trip had made a rocky start: first the sea monsters, then Ada jumping prematurely. But things were starting to look better.

Magnolia stuck next to Yejun as they went down a ladder into the ship. He took them down three decks, through a passageway of private quarters. Next, they passed the engine compartment.

Memories of her captivity surfaced, but Magnolia buried them, trying to trust that Yejun was leading them to the promised map.

He took them through the rusted passageways, under snaking electrical wires and over fallen pieces of overhead. The farther they pushed into this section of the ship, the more evidence of a battle emerged.

Empty shell casings littered the deck, and bullet holes speckled the bulkheads. But she was heartened to see no claw marks anywhere.

Yejun approached an open hatch and angled his light into a long space. He turned to Magnolia and said something. She listened to her wrist computer.

"This is where we made our last stand."

He stepped inside the mess hall. A snaking brown streak ran from an upended table to a doorway. Chairs lay strewn about, most of them on their sides. A fort of tables had been thrown up across the room, barricading off the kitchen.

Yejun directed his flashlight toward them and started leading the way.

"What the hell happened here?" Arlo said quietly. "Who were they fighting?"

"Each other, I think," Magnolia said.

Sofia turned her helmet toward Magnolia, and even though she was concealed behind the visor,

Magnolia knew what she was thinking: that maybe, Yejun was leading them into a trap.

No, Magnolia thought.

She didn't fully trust the kid, but she didn't get the vibe that he had brought Team Raptor here to kill them. The life scans were coming back negative.

Yejun pointed at a gap between the tables blocking off the kitchen. Edgar squeezed through and aimed his light at the freezer hatches. One was already open. Magnolia shined her helmet beam into the small space, illuminating a few kids' toys and blankets stained with blood.

It didn't take much investigating to determine what had happened here.

Yejun looked in her direction but didn't follow. He must know what was inside. Perhaps, one of the toys had belonged to him as a kid, Magnolia thought to herself.

"This it?" Edgar asked.

He stood in front of the spin wheel on the second freezer.

Yejun pointed at it, nodding.

Edgar grabbed the wheel and tried to twist it, to no avail.

Magnolia motioned for Arlo and Sofia to stay with Yejun while she went to help. Rust flaked off the ancient wheel when she touched it.

She looked around for a lever, but Yejun beat them to it. He picked up a steel bar, only to have Arlo reach out and snatch it from his hand.

Yejun held up both palms in surrender.

"Give me that," Edgar said.

Arlo handed the bar over, and Edgar wedged it between the wall and a spoke of the spin wheel.

Grunting, he began to push the bar down. The wheel creaked, then moved a few inches with an alarmingly loud groan. A distant shriek echoed through the ship.

Magnolia checked her HUD as she waited.

Team Wrangler had gone to ground, their beacons unmoving on the minimap. The military wasn't moving yet, either, but they would be soon.

"Almost got it," Edgar said.

Magnolia aimed her laser rifle at the hatch and fired a bolt. The hatch popped open, dripping molten metal onto the deck.

She stepped into the freezer and found that it had been cut open. Jagged metal framed a doorway that the former occupants had used to escape into a chamber.

Edgar came in with her. Taking the right side, he swept his beam over the deck and bulkheads. Pipes blocked off much of the view.

"Clear," Magnolia said over the comm.

Sofia and Arlo brought Yejun in next, and he started across the space, moving right toward an office. Halfway across the room, he stopped and stared down at the deck.

Tracks disturbed the coating of fine dust—something Magnolia hadn't seen earlier. She bent down and took a pinch. Rubbing her fingertips together, she decided it was probably ash. But from what?

She stood and did another life scan. This time, the pulse got a hit at three hundred meters out.

Something was out there.

"We have a contact," she said quietly.

Edgar looked over, then shouldered his rifle. "I'll go check it out."

"You go, too, Sofia," Magnolia said.

"Contact?" Arlo said. "What's that mean—like, another human?"

Magnolia couldn't tell from the pulse. It was too far out to get a good reading—only that there was a heartbeat. Yejun didn't seem to understand and started into the chamber, playing his light over the pipes.

Magnolia watched her bioscanner. Whatever was out there was coming closer.

Yejun stopped at a pipe the thickness of his leg and used a finger to wipe something off it. He brought it under his light, then shined the beam over the deck and the ash tracks.

He suddenly backed up, hitting the pipe with a thud.

"*Quiet*," Arlo said.

Yejun turned and twisted the cap off the end of the pipe. Then he shined his light inside and reached into the pipe.

Magnolia walked over as he fished inside for what had to be the map. But after a few seconds, he pulled his hand out and started talking rapidly.

He grabbed Magnolia, repeating the same word over and over.

"*Gajog*," or something that sounded like it.

"What's he saying?" Arlo said.

Magnolia pulled free and brought up her wrist computer. "Family."

"What?" Arlo asked. "*His* family?"

They both looked at Yejun, who was growing more frantic.

"His family is still alive?" Arlo asked.

"I don't know—"

Sofia cut her off. "We have to get out of here!" she shouted, running back into the room. Somewhere behind her, someone fired two sizzling bolts from a laser rifle.

"What!" Magnolia gasped. "What's out there?" She watched the Geiger counter on her wrist computer spike as the contacts came closer.

What in the . . .

Edgar burst through the open hatch, closed it, and put his back against it.

"We need to move. Now!" He let his rifle sag and pulled out a grenade, which indicated to Magnolia that whatever lurked out there was big and hard to kill.

"What the hell is going on?" Arlo asked. "You guys are freaking me out!"

He started to walk over, when Magnolia realized Yejun wasn't with him. She turned to see the young man outside the freezer hatch they had entered the room through. He turned his beaked helmet toward them for a split second, as if debating what to do.

"NO!" Magnolia shouted.

She ran over and grabbed the handle just as it clicked on the other side, sealing them in.

Edgar stepped away from the hatch he had his back to.

"We're trapped," Sofia said.

The radiation gauge continued to spike, the source drawing closer by the second. Magnolia raised her rifle and aimed it at the opposite hatch.

Shuffling sounded outside, and then scratching. From under the gap in the metal came an incandescent glow, followed by a long, eerie moan that almost sounded human.

* * * * *

"You sure you know where this goes?" Michael asked.

"Positive," Steve replied.

"Okay, let's go, then." He waved at Victor. "Make sure no one follows us."

"You got it, Chief."

They were still on the *Sea Wolf*, cruising past the damaged rigs. Michael held the key in his hand. It was time to see what X had left him, and he had decided to entrust Steve with whatever it unlocked.

The master bladesmith had spent his life forging weapons for Cazador soldiers and training apprentices. Now they needed his skills and vision to rebuild and prepare for future storms. What better person to do it than a man who had spent his life preparing for war? If anyone could help Michael rebuild this place, it was Steve.

"So what's your take on Charmer?" Michael asked.

Steve flashed a toothy smile. "I think they should call him 'Snake.'"

Michael laughed. "Yeah."

"You know, when your people came, I had mixed feelings." Steve took off his sunglasses and blew on the lenses before wiping them on his shirt. "I was glad they killed el Pulpo and some of the cannibal leaders, but I worried about the strain on resources. We lost many souls over the past two years, but now we're going to see the biggest squeeze on our food and supplies ever."

"I know," said Michael. "That's why X is—"

"A supply chain won't bring us food, though," Steve said. "And I dread the day when some of us resort to our old ways. And not just us—I fear what these other sky people might do."

"Going from hell to heaven and then being threatened with hell again is enough to make anyone violent. I know from experience."

"Things will work out, Chief. Don't worry too much."

They rode in silence until the dark horizon of the barrier between paradise and the wastes came into focus. An hour later, they saw the rusted shape of the prison rig.

"Never thought I'd be back here again," Steve said. "I spent a few months here when I was your age."

"Why?"

Steve shrugged. "I guess someone didn't like the sword I made them, because it broke in half during a battle." He laughed as he seemed to recall. "The bastard was a prick anyway—got what was coming to him in the Sky Arena. I ended up serving some time that made me more thankful for my freedom after, and much better at my job."

"I can relate to that in a way."

A lightning bolt flashed its dazzling rickrack across the sky. The thunder sounded like a pistol shot.

Michael pulled up to the exterior docks and tethered the boat with Steve while Victor and Ton went ahead. In the glow of their flashlights, the former prison and munitions factory looked like a relic from a world war.

With the boat moored, they took the dry dock to the double doors that were the main entrance. They were unlocked, and Victor swung the left one open to let them inside the silo-shaped rig.

Ten levels curved above them, still built out in the former cells of inmates the Cazadores had kept here. At the very top was the warehouse where they once built bombs and made bullets.

Michael started up the stairs, through the central guard tower that overlooked the cells. On the tenth floor, he took a ladder to a landing with a hatch.

Fishing out the key, he paused, then inserted it in the lock and twisted. *Click.* Michael turned the handle and opened the door to a vast space.

Lightning flashed outside the barred windows, illuminating the room where prisoners once labored away. The workstations were gone, and the buckets that once contained empty cartridge casings were piled in a corner.

In place of the buckets for spent brass were barrels. Hundreds of barrels.

Michael shined his light around.

"What are they?" Steve asked.

"I don't know," Michael said.

Walking over to the closest barrel, he blew the dust off the lid. It bore the logo of the ITC *Ranger*. Michael hadn't seen these when they boarded and searched the supercarrier, but then, he hadn't been on all the searches, either.

"Let's open one," he said.

Working together, they pulled back the locking lever and popped the lid off a fifty-five-gallon drum.

"I'll be damned," Michael said. "It's the backup plan!"

He angled his flashlight down at stacks of vacuum-sealed high-calorie protein bars. A thousand were in this crate alone.

"There's got to be months' worth of food here for everyone," Steve said. "But why hide it?"

"I think I know why." Michael pulled out the note and read it to himself.

The first key is for if I don't come back. It opens a door near the watery grave of our enemies. What you will find there is not for immediate use, no matter how bad things get. This is a backup plan if the Vanguard Islands become uninhabitable, as el Pulpo feared.

The second key will show you the way.

Everything that we do from here on out will determine our future. We can afford no mistakes. We must not fail to act. We must never forget.

Handle your present with confidence. Face your future without fear.

Michael folded the note and slipped it back in his pocket. He had a feeling that he knew what the second key was for now.

"Sir," Victor said. "Come. Come quick."

Michael hurried over to a window, where the guard stood looking out the glass. In the darkness, a pair of lights flitted over the water.

Then a second pair.

But these were too small to be boats.

"Jet Skis," Michael said. "What are they doing out there?"

"They must have followed us," Steve said.

Michael looked back at the crates of food. He turned off his light and had the others do the same.

The Jet Skis stopped, their lights bobbing up and down in the distance. He counted six of them and remembered the squad known as the Wave Riders, led by Sergeant Jamal, Gran Jefe's cousin.

"They are watching us," Steve said.

"You think they saw us?" Michael asked.

"They saw our boat, for sure."

A chill ran up Michael's spine at the implications. If word of this place got out, there would be hell to pay for hiding the reserves from an already hungry populace.

"Steve, you can't tell anyone about this," Michael said.

"You have my word, Chief, and that's as good as my life."

Michael nodded. He knew he didn't need to ask Ton and Victor to swear an oath, but there was something else he had to ask of them.

"Victor, Ton," Michael said. "I need you to stay here, guard this place until X comes back. There is water and food, and I will resupply you as needed."

"But, sir," Victor protested, "X said to guard you with our lives."

Ton made a clicking sound with his mouth.

"This is more important," Michael said. "We have to protect it and keep it a secret."

"Why not move it?" Steve asked.

"Where?"

"I don't know . . ."

"Exactly, we have nowhere to move it *to*."

Michael looked back out the window as the Jet Skis finally raced away. He checked his watch. It was midmorning. The army and the Hell Divers would be arriving in Panama soon, ready for a battle.

If all went to plan, they wouldn't need this food, but the day they did, it would be here, and Michael was going to make sure it was safe.

Much was riding on the mission to Panama. If it should fail . . .

But X wouldn't fail. X never failed.

TWENTY-EIGHT

"Prepare to beach!" X yelled.

His voice carried over the engine noise from the supercarrier's landing craft. Water slopped over the sides as the craft made its run for the shore. Three more just like it carried vehicles and soldiers out of the canal and into Panama Bay.

The *Immortal* and *Raven's Claw* kept firing on the industrial zone in an attempt to draw the monsters out of their lairs and destroy them. All the recon and drone data showed the beasts centered in a single area high in radiation.

The *Octopus* followed the four landing craft into the bay for support, just in case.

X stood in the turret of a tank with Miles underneath him in the machine's back troop hold. At the wheel in the cockpit was Martin, a forty-year-old militia soldier who had served under Sloan. Manning the cannon was Sergeant Slayer, who was still recovering from injuries received during the storm, but trying not to show it.

Bromista was also down there, judging from the sounds of laughter.

X looked back across the bay to the supercarrier. Even from here, he could see the scars inflicted by the monster whales that had cost him the *Ocean Bull*. Now they would need to find another way to clear the canal of debris in the coming days.

But first, they needed to clear the monsters.

Another drone raced over the water and shoreline, vanishing over the city. The four landing craft motored through Panama Bay, toward the black beaches on the southern tip of Panama City.

The resorts in the area were long since washed away, and from what he could see, the beaches were more dirt than sand.

General Forge sat in the turret of the second tank to the right. His red-feathered helmet pointed stoically ahead as the first report about the chitinous monsters came over the comms.

"King Xavier, we are detecting five of the breeders and over a thousand of the young," Timothy said over the command channel.

"Come again," X said. "I thought you said one thousand."

"Affirmative, sir, and they are all concentrated in the area we expected."

Forge nodded at X, acknowledging the intel.

It sounded like a lot, but they had faced tough odds before.

"Any Sirens?" X asked.

"Negative," Timothy replied. "If they are out there, they are hiding."

X looked to the six APCs and four troop transport trucks on the three other landing craft around them. Standing outside the vehicles were over two hundred soldiers dressed in bulky armored suits. He would never forget seeing his first Cazador warrior, in the wastes back in Florida, when these strange men and women had captured him.

Now they served him and the Vanguard Islands.

And they all were ready to fight.

He hoped it wouldn't come to that.

He *hoped* that the tanks and artillery would be able to take out the largest monsters and dramatically reduce their legion of spawn.

But X also knew that the wastes had a way of destroying even the best-laid plans and that strategy was something often made on the fly upon setting foot in the radioactive terrain.

A prime example of that was what just happened with Ada. It was partly his fault, giving her the device to locate Jo-Jo. Now he was without Cricket 2.0, and Team Wrangler was underground in the most hostile zone X had seen in over a year.

He didn't like it, but he would have done the same to find Miles.

Bumping his comm pad, he tried to reach the Hell Divers, but static crackled over the line. They were too far out of range.

"Get ready!" General Forge shouted.

Lightning split the horizon, giving X his first unaided view of the old resort zone. Not much remained of the structures that once stood side by side, thousands of balconies overlooking the ocean.

While there was still some sign of the former civilization, nature had overtaken much of the terrain beyond the shoreline. Mutant trees grew out of the concrete blocks, forming a dense jungle.

X turned on his night vision and grabbed the .50-caliber machine gun mounted to the tank.

This was it. The very future of the Vanguard Islands depended on what happened here over the next few hours.

The landing craft hit the surf and thumped up onto the beach with a jolt. The gate dropped onto the sand and mud.

"Move out!" X yelled, waving them forward with his metal fist.

The lightweight tanks lurched ahead, the tracks churning through the radioactive mud and up the beach. X tried to imagine how this place once looked.

Tsunamis had ensured that nothing much was left behind. Rubble from old eateries and bars that served sunbathers protruded out of the dirt. Beer cans and trash had washed up—the last remaining evidence of the fancy cocktail bars and eateries that once served tourists here.

X looked over his shoulder at the other vehicles. The APCs powered over the mud, but a troop transport full of Cazador soldiers was already stuck, its rear wheels spinning and kicking up dirt.

Soldiers hopped out the back and pushed until the truck finally broke free.

The convoy drove across a mostly washed-out road, the tracks and tires rolling over the broken slabs of pavement. A bent pole stuck up out of the ground, its rusted sign beyond any hope of reading.

Below, X could hear laughing again between Slayer and Bromista.

"What's he saying?" Martin asked.

"He said you drive like his grandma," Slayer said.

"All right, cut the shit," X said.

"Yes, sir. Sorry, sir," Slayer replied.

X trained the .50-caliber machine gun on the ruins ahead. Mounds of debris rose over three and four stories, blocking their view of the monsters. He scanned for animal life, but there didn't seem to be anything out here.

The convoy moved on slowly but steadily, freeing the trucks when they got stuck. Finally, they made it to the mounds of rubble that had once been resorts and luxury hotels.

"Halt!" Forge shouted.

X hopped down off the tank and opened the back hatch to let Miles out. The dog jumped down, tail wagging under his suit. Next came Slayer and Bromista.

General Forge and a squad of soldiers in bulky armored suits started the trek up the mound for a look out over the battlefield. Slayer joined them, limping slightly as he slogged his way up with a pair of infrared binos. Bromista wasn't far behind, clutching his crossbow.

"Here, King Xavier," Forge said.

X brought his binos up to his visor. Beyond the city, the long stretch of land between them and the canal was peppered with craters. Smoke still drifted in pockets where the artillery shells had struck.

On his HUD, he watched the view from one of the drones hovering over one of the mammoth creatures. The huge tortoise head looked up, and a pincer flailed at the drone.

It flew higher as the monster shook its shell, releasing hundreds of the smaller beasts—although X hardly considered them small. The young were easily the size of Gran Jefe, with claws that could cut an armored warrior in half. But if all went according to plan, the beasts wouldn't get close enough to use them.

X moved his binos back over the neighborhood that the monsters were moving toward.

About four hundred meters away, an earthquake had opened a ravine so wide that buildings had fallen into it.

That was where he would strike the monsters. As soon as they reached the ravine, the Cazador ships' guns would start a barrage, forcing them into the crack in the earth, just as ancient old-world hunters once drove their quarry off cliffs.

He ran the plan by Forge, who glassed the area with his binos. The red-plumed helmet nodded, then he turned to give the orders.

"*Sí*, blow them away—*al infierno*," Bromista said.

Soldiers piled out of the trucks, moving into the surrounding structures.

The sniper teams took to the higher areas to set up. Next, the three platoons of infantry moved into firing positions on various levels of any buildings still standing. Finally, two teams equipped with flamethrowers moved to the front line to clear any holes or tunnels, to prevent beasts from flanking their positions. They had the routine down. In less than thirty minutes, everyone was hunkered down and awaiting orders.

This wasn't their first dance in the wastes.

Side by side, X and General Forge looked out over the ruins, watching as the mutant beasts advanced toward them, wailing and shrieking in their bizarre ethereal language.

"Keep coming," X whispered.

As the tide of beasts surged into the resort zone, another round of flares punched into the sky, illuminating the thousand-plus abominations of nature teeming below. Shelled bodies chittered across the rubble, jaws and claws clicking and clacking. Now that they were aboveground, they were coming toward the bright flares like moths to a flame.

"Get ready!" X shouted. "Let's finish what we came here to do!"

Over the command line, General Forge gave more orders as X took Miles back to the tank with Slayer and Bromista. X climbed into the turret and grabbed the .50-caliber machine gun. After checking the belt and the first round, he glanced down to Miles.

"It's going to get loud, boy," X said.

For once, he was grateful that the dog had lost some of his hearing.

"Six hundred meters out," Timothy reported over the command channel.

X looked to the sky. The airship *Vanguard* was up there somewhere, hovering in the clouds. The beacons of all the divers were online, including Jo-Jo's, and X could see Team Wrangler closing in on the animal.

In the Panama Canal, the *Immortal* and *Raven's Claw* had the area bracketed from about two miles away. The *Octopus* had taken up position in Panama Bay, ready to help if the army on the ground ran into trouble.

Everything was going to plan. It was the calm before the storm.

Another round of flares went up, illuminating entire city blocks of ruined structures. In the glow, the erased lives of thousands came into view. Furniture, boxes, picture frames—all the usual items one would stumble upon in the wastes, were out there with the skeletal remains of their former owners.

X put the iron sights on the first of the breeders. The creature climbed over the mountains of rubble as its offspring swarmed toward the ravine that separated them from the Vanguard army.

"Hold your fire," X said over the open channel.

He took a second to look away from the barrel at

those entrenched around him, and in that split second the first roar of the monsters echoed over the city.

A gigantic breeder hauled itself up onto a two-story building, crushing the structure under its weight. A cloud of dust and grit exploded into the air.

Another flare went up, bursting above the monster. Red light illuminated the tide of mutant spawn rushing through the dissipating cloud.

Two more of the breeders climbed into view and skittered surprisingly fast over the mounds of rubble.

"Hold," X said over the comm. "Hold."

As soon as the fourth and fifth breeders showed up, he gave General Forge a nod. Over the team line, he gave orders to the artillery squads.

The crump of artillery fire filled the night, rising over the wails of the monsters. The shells burst behind the breeders at the end of the sea of armored bodies, blowing concrete and steel into the air.

More shells banged away, slamming in just behind the breeder at the very rear of the army. It roared and went up on four legs, flailing the air with its front claws.

A projectile hit it in the face, exploding on impact and sending hunks of pink flesh and yellow shell up into the sky. They rained back down as the headless creature collapsed in the dirt.

The smaller beasts scuttled over the ground, right for the ravine. As they closed in, X held his breath.

Rockets and shells pounded the position behind the beasts, blowing up dozens of the young and sending body parts into the air.

Parachute flares drifted down, providing a brilliant view of the battle.

It quickly became apparent that this wasn't a battle. It was a slaughter.

Fifty meters from the ravine, the four remaining breeders halted abruptly.

"Come on, you dumb shits," X said. He stood up in the turret for a better view. "What are they doing?"

Even with the shells bursting behind them, the monsters paced around on their long limbs and claws. The hulking abominations lowered their faces and brought their legs under their shells, while the offspring squeezed into holes in the ground. Others streamed down the walls sideways like crabs.

"Son of a bitch," X said.

He had thought their cumbersome shells would make them fall into the gorge, but these little bastards could scale vertical walls.

The only way to finish the beasts was by expending precious small-caliber ammo.

"Pick a target," X yelled. "Make your shots count!"

He dropped his prosthetic arm, and gunfire and tracer rounds lanced away from the elevated buildings, slamming into the armored shells of monsters still on the other side of the ravine and those descending into the darkness.

The creatures shrieked as bullets pounded them, knocking some from the walls as X had planned. But others made it down and out of view, unharmed.

X bumped on the command channel.

"Captain Two Skulls, have your pilots send a drone down that crack," he said. "I want to know where those things are going."

"Understood, sir," replied the captain.

X ducked back down into the tank.

"Target the shells," he said.

"Aye, aye, King Xavier," Slayer said.

X grabbed the .50-caliber machine gun and had trained it on one of the four remaining breeders, when the hard carapace opened like wings, exposing what looked like lungs or gills. They started to glow, the ribbed flesh turning brighter and brighter before launching a salvo of neon-green blobs into the air.

"Incoming!" someone shouted outside the tank.

X was tracking the flying blobs in the iron sights when Slayer fired the main gun. The recoil threw X off his aim, but he leveled the .50 again and fired. The rounds peppered the jaw as a tank shell hit the gill-like flesh under the breeder's shell.

Orange fluid and flesh slopped out onto the rubble. The beast let out a roar that carried across the wastes.

"Direct hit!" Slayer said over the comms.

Closing one eye, X turned the machine gun to the next-closest breeder. Blood streamed from the holes he blew into its armor. The exposed lungs glowed brighter, firing off more green globs into the sky.

"What are those things!" X yelled.

Taking his eyes off the gun sights, he followed

the meaty green objects arcing through the air. The first one slammed into the third story of a building.

The explosion dazzled his eyes, and he turned off his night vision, blinking at the glare. Screams of agony from Cazador positions in the structure rose above the din of gunfire.

When his vision returned, X saw the soldiers climbing out of the building, some of them falling and hitting the ground. Their bodies melted, their armor dripping off them like candle wax.

X stared in horror as the green blobs fell all around in fiery explosions. The radiation gauge on his monitor chirped at a sharp spike.

"My God," X said.

"Get inside!" someone yelled.

X felt Slayer tugging on his boot and ducked into the tank. Bromista was clutching an animal bone in his hand, muttering something in Spanish. This didn't sound like a joke; it sounded like a prayer.

The warriors all kept low, watching through a viewport while the glowing bombs exploded across structures where hundreds of soldiers had taken up positions.

Cutting through their screams of horror, a calm voice surged over the command channel. "King Xavier, we have a drone following the spawn underground," said Captain Two Skulls.

X flinched at another nearby explosion.

"They are headed underneath your position," Two Skulls said. "You have to get out of there now!"

TWENTY-NINE

Five miles from the heart of Panama City, Kade led the way through the cavernous tunnels.

He kept an eye on Tia, thinking of her father. There was no doubt in his mind that Raphael wouldn't have wanted this for her, but Kade couldn't stop her from becoming a diver. All he could do was try to keep her safe on the surface.

So far, they were alone in the passages—the shells and explosions topside had sent the creatures rushing from their underground lairs to the surface.

Ada moved ahead of Kade despite his motions and whispers to stay back. She was clearly growing more anxious to find Jo-Jo. The animal wasn't far now, maybe a mile away. The problem was to find a passage that connected with whatever chamber or nook the monkey had hidden away in.

The beams from their helmet lights revealed another problem. Rocks and concrete blocked the subway tunnel Kade had hoped to enter. At some point over the years, the walls had collapsed, blocking the tunnel.

"We're going to have to find an alternative route," he said.

When Kade turned away, Ada kept going toward the rubble.

"That could take forever," she said. "Just hold on and let me check it out." Hurrying over, she slung her laser rifle and stepped up on the loose scree.

"*Estúpida*," Gran Jefe said.

Tia moved past Kade, ignoring his orders. The two female divers raked their lights over the rubble as Gran Jefe moved on, searching for another way through.

"Hey, I think I found something," Tia said.

Kade shined his light on a narrow opening about two feet wide in the pile of concrete and rock. It seemed to go all the way through and was big enough for the women and maybe him, too. But there was no way Gran Jefe would get his armored bulk through there.

He seemed to acknowledge as much and began taking off the chest rig that powered his suit. "*No soy gordo*," he said with a grin. "Big-boned."

Ada got down, but Kade motioned her back.

"I'll go first," he said. When she balked, he added, "That's an order, Winslow."

She backed up, and he got down on his knees to crawl under the low rock ceiling. He could see the gouges made in the limestone by hard, sharp claws.

Squeezing through the hole, he found himself standing on flat concrete, with train tracks and concrete subway walls gradually coming into focus.

Kade scrambled out and brought his rifle up to check both sides of the tunnel.

"Clear," he said, sighting down the rails. Jo-Jo was not far now.

A moment later, Ada was through and hopping to her feet. Next came Tia. Behind her, sounds of grunting and scratching grew loud enough to make Kade nervous.

Gran Jefe was struggling through the hole, dragging his armor behind him.

"Quiet, man!" Tia whispered.

Gran Jefe responded with some slur in Spanish. But when the swearing continued in an uninterrupted stream, Kade realized it wasn't in response to Tia.

The huge Cazador was stuck.

He squirmed again, grunted a few more vivid profanities, and got nowhere.

"Calm down," Kade said. "Keep wiggling and you will get through."

Gran Jefe snorted. "I can't . . . *hijoeputa* . . ."

There was rising panic in his voice.

"Take it easy," Kade said.

Pulling out his machete, he turned to Ada and Tia. "Watch our backs. I'll try and free him."

"Hurry," Ada said.

Kade got down and started crawling toward Gran Jefe. Reaching him, he started stabbing the fragmented concrete around the right shoulder armor, knocking out clods of earth and pebbles.

After a few thrusts, he went to work on the other side.

"Careful," Gran Jefe said.

Kade kept at it until he had cleared a few inches.

"Have a go now," he said, backing up into the tunnel.

Gran Jefe let out a long grunt and pushed farther into the passage.

A tremor shook the tunnel, and grit sifted down. Kade braced himself and sent up a prayer that it not come down on both of them.

He suddenly felt a hand on his left boot, and then his right.

Someone hauled Kade out into the subway tunnel. He rolled onto his back and looked up at Tia, who reached down to help him up.

"*¡Ayúdenme!*" Gran Jefe cried.

Kade turned back to the opening, where Gran Jefe was stuck, half his body out and half still in.

Together, all three divers grabbed him and pulled. After another minute of exertion and a few more colorful expressions, he slid out, in a little shower of dust and concrete chips, onto the subway platform.

Crunching resonated from the tunnel as the ceiling collapsed, sealing off the way.

"Gracias, gracias," Gran Jefe said. He brushed off his armor and then put it back over his head. The chest battery warmed to life, his visor once again clicking on and masking his features.

"Let's go," Ada said. "We have to hurry."

She was already moving down the passage.

"Wait!" Kade said.

She slowed some but kept moving.

A tremor rocked the passage as Tia came up to Kade.

"You think the army is beating the shit out of those things yet?" she asked.

"I hope so aye," Kade replied.

Here underground, beyond the reach of radio waves, there was no way to know.

They picked up their pace, following Ada, who moved with Cricket 2.0 in one hand and her rifle in the other.

"I remember this place," she called out.

"You've been here?" Tia asked.

"Yes, this is where the bunker is."

Kade remembered her story of her encounter, but he figured it was a dream during her coma.

Then again, it could have been real. The wastes harbored all sorts of monsters.

"Almost there," Ada said.

The beacon was two hundred meters away and on the other side of the subway.

An opening allowed them into another passage gouged out by the monsters. Kade caught up with Ada.

"Hey, hold on a beat," he said.

She pulled away when he reached out.

"We don't have a second," she snapped.

"I'm just asking you to slow down and be careful. We came down here with you to help, but . . ."

Ada stopped. "I know, but my friend has been out here for weeks and I'm anxious to find her."

Seeing movement, Kade whipped his rifle up and aimed it past her helmet.

Ada turned to look, but whatever had moved in his beam was gone.

Gran Jefe and Tia moved up with them.

"What did you see?" Tia asked.

"I don't know, but stay behind me," Kade said.

He followed the passage until it emptied into a big chamber. Ada stayed just behind him, her weapon pointed up at the vaulted ceiling.

Jo-Jo's beacon was somewhere inside this room.

Small shadows moved in the glow of their beams.

"Oh, no!" Ada cried out.

She started moving faster, and Kade lit out after her, seeing the crablike creatures that had her spooked. The spawn were the size of Miles when he was younger. Dozens of them clambered over the hatching grounds. Beetles, huge ants, and other insects lay in pieces, their exoskeletons cracked open and the flesh removed.

Ada rushed toward the entrance of the room, where something dark and matted lay on the ground—a pile of skins, perhaps.

The divers moved through, swiping with their machetes at the creatures that came skittering toward them. Hearing a crunch, Kade turned to Gran Jefe, who had just stomped one of the beasts to mush.

The Cazador warrior bent down and picked up a severed pincer arm.

"*Cómo se dice* . . . I can't think of the word *en inglés*," he said. "Like your sombrero, Commander."

"Souvenir," he said.

"Ah, souvenir, *sí*."

Ada bolted, running through the abattoir. After dispatching two more of the baby creatures, Kade joined her at the dark heap that had caught her eye. It had spiky fur.

"Jo-Jo," Ada breathed.

She tucked Cricket away and, bending down, gently pushed the big primate on its side. The creature's eyes were closed, but it was breathing. A white, gooey substance covered much of the chest and stomach. Ada tried to wipe it off, but the goo just stuck and stretched away with her glove.

As they removed the coating of material, blood wept from multiple slash marks across Jo-Jo's flesh.

"It's okay, Jo-Jo, I'm here now," Ada said.

Another wet crunch came as Gran Jefe booted one of the shelled creatures against the wall so hard that it stuck.

"*¡Pinches hijoeputas!*" he snarled.

"Quiet," Kade said. Swinging his machete, he whisked the head off a creature trying to climb up Gran Jefe's leg.

"Wake up, Jo-Jo," she whispered. "It's me, Ada."

Tia fished a syringe out of the medical pack. "Maybe this will work."

"Worth a try," Kade said. "Whatever you do, we need to do it fast and get out of here."

Ada uncapped the syringe of adrenaline and tapped the end until a tiny fountain of liquid squirted out. She jabbed it into Jo-Jo's thigh.

The creature shot up with a gasp, eyes like saucers.

"Jo-Jo!" she yelled.

"Quiet!" Kade hissed.

The animal hopped upright, trembling and moaning.

Ada reached out. "Jo-Jo, it's me."

The monkey stared at her for a moment, then looked over its shoulder. Kade slowly walked toward it, holding out a hand with the machete.

A mistake, he realized.

The creature was in shock.

Whistling sounded, and something streaked past Kade.

"NO!" Ada screamed.

The monkey reached for the dart stuck in its chest and opened its mouth to let out a howl. But only a squeak came out before it collapsed in front of Ada.

"What did you do!" she yelled.

"Ada, calm yourself," Kade said.

"*No hay problema*," Gran Jefe said, holding up a tranq gun. "Put your *chango* to sleep."

Ada shook the monkey, but it didn't respond.

"Come on," Kade said. "After all that shouting, we need to move."

Gran Jefe bent down. "I carry."

Ada seemed reluctant at first but then backed away. The Cazador picked the beast up, slung it over his shoulder, and started lumbering off, out of the chamber.

Kade ran ahead with his rifle shouldered. They took a different passage out, west-southwest toward the resorts, looking for a way topside.

About a mile and a half into the trek, a rumble vibrated through the tunnel.

Kade held up a fist.

"What was that?" Tia asked.

Several thumps shook the tunnel, sending dirt raining down.

"I think it's . . ." Kade began to say.

"*Bombas, amigo*," Gran Jefe said. "Bombs."

He kept walking, seemingly undisturbed, though Kade wasn't sure what to make of it. The artillery should have stopped by now.

He tried to open a comms channel but got only static.

They marched toward the beach through tunnels vacated by the monsters, which had rushed to the surface to meet the Vanguard army. Still, Kade kept his finger over the trigger guard and checked out all the nooks and shadowed alcoves.

"*Descanso*," Gran Jefe said. "Need to rest."

Ada helped him ease Jo-Jo down, and the team

took a breather. Kade walked ahead to check the passage with Tia.

The thuds and quakes were getting stronger. A violent tremor shook the ground and didn't stop.

"Commander," Tia said.

Kade took a few steps forward, toward a glowing green light at the end of the passage. A radiation surge spiked on his monitor.

"Get back," he said.

Tia hesitated.

"Go," Kade said. "Go now. There's something else down here . . ."

They both had started backpedaling when the right side of the tunnel exploded inward.

Grit and dirt showered down, and Kade fell under the landslide. He was trying to shield his visor from the falling debris when a glowing ribbed body squirmed out, filling the tunnel with its mass.

"Tia, run!" Kade yelled.

His voice was drowned out by the tunnel roof caving in. The dirt kept cascading down, burying him until darkness consumed him.

For a moment, he lay there, unable to see or hear anything. It felt like the black of space, without a single star. Nothing hurt, which was a surprise, but he knew from experience that it could be a bad sign.

Kade started pushing at the dirt with his fingers, trying to dig his way out. He breathed sparingly, knowing he had thirty minutes of air in his helmet.

He wasn't sure how long he worked, pushing his fingers through the small clods of earth, but it didn't help much.

Then, quite unexpectedly, he was squinting into bright light. Beams shot back and forth.

Voices called out, faint but growing stronger.

He stared up at a diver who grasped him by both wrists and hauled him out.

"My time save you, Cowboy," came the voice of Gran Jefe.

He dragged Kade out of the hole.

"Thanks," Kade said.

He pushed himself up, looking down the passage where blue lights strobed.

Not lights, he realized. *Lightning.*

Whatever creature he had seen earlier had burrowed a vertical shaft topside.

"That thing had wings," Ada said.

Kade shook the rest of the dirt off. His suit still functioned, and life-support systems were all working properly.

He walked over to check the vertical shaft. He had never seen anything this large in the wastes before. And whatever it was, it was heading for the Vanguard army.

"I have to warn King Xavier," Kade said. "Stay down here, and if you want to stay alive, keep quiet, for fuck's sake."

* * * * *

Michael stared out over the water from the hospital on the capitol tower, waiting to see Dr. Stamos. He was only two doors from the room where Layla had given birth to Bray.

The first scallops of moonlight danced on the water. The rain had stopped and the sky was clear, but his mind was too burdened to enjoy the beauty.

By now, the Vanguard army's assault in Panama would be well underway. He waited anxiously for news from Pedro, who continued to monitor the radio for the first reports of the battle.

Tonight, for the first time in days, he was alone. Ton and Victor were guarding the food hidden in the prison rig. Michael wasn't scared of an attack on him personally, but he was worried about what would happen if the secret about the food got out.

As he waited to see Alton and his mom, his thoughts turned to Steve, the only person besides X and his two bodyguards who knew about the food.

But now he was wondering if taking him there was the right thing. If Charmer, the Cazadores, or virtually *anyone* found out about the food and thought Michael was withholding it from them, it could cause a civil war.

You can trust Steve, Michael thought.

The deputy chief engineer wasn't far away—just a few floors below, meeting with an engineering team. He was still working despite the late hour, going like a battery that never lost its charge—not bad for a man over seventy years old.

Michael, on the other hand, was exhausted.

He pulled out his radio, using the frequency that Pedro had set up to connect with Ton and Victor.

"Victor, do you copy? Over." Michael said.

"Copy, all clear in the dark," he said, repeating the code word they had established.

"Copy. Be safe."

Michael tucked his radio away, and was nodding off in his chair when a female voice snapped him alert.

"Sir, you may see her now."

Michael got up and followed the nurse into a hallway. Seeing this section of the hospital was a macabre reminder of what had once occurred here.

Not so long ago, el Pulpo had used this place not to heal people, but to kill them. The room was part of a butcher shop, where the Cazadores skinned and filleted people for food during lean years, when the raids didn't bring enough back and storms damaged the crops.

Michael shivered at the thought.

This was one of the worst years in the Vanguard Islands' history. And while the population was slightly smaller than when his people first arrived, there were still almost as many mouths to feed, thanks to the addition of the sky people from Tanzania.

"Here we are," said the nurse. "Please put on a mask and gown. Kaitlyn is fighting an infection."

Michael dressed in the protective gear before stepping up to the door. He knocked and went inside to find Alton sitting on a chair at his mother's bedside. She was asleep, with tubes connected to both arms.

He knew just enough about medical treatment and had gleaned just enough from what the nurse said to know that Kaitlyn was fighting for her life.

Alton stood up and looked at Michael with sad, brown eyes, not much different from the day he first saw him in the machine camp.

Michael saluted the boy. "At ease, soldier," he said.

Alton's eyes seemed to brighten, but they blurred with tears when Michael approached.

"Nez was right," he said sadly. "My mom is dying."

Michael shook his head. "You don't know that, buddy. She's getting medicine to—"

"Chief . . ." Kaitlyn whispered.

"Hey, Kaitlyn," Michael said. "Just came to see how you're doing."

"Thank you."

She took in a deep, rattling breath.

"Alton," she said. "Alton, will you give us a few minutes, please, sweetheart?"

Alton hesitated.

"Do as your mother says," Michael said.

The boy left and closed the door. Kaitlyn reached out to Michael with a bony arm.

"I know I don't have long," she said. "And I know you have your own son now, but, Chief—"

"Call me Michael, please."

She swallowed hard. "Michael, please make sure Alton doesn't lose his way. Please try and look after him. I asked Kade to do the same, but with him diving again, I worry that Alton won't have anyone."

"I will, you have my word."

She laid her head back on the pillow and gave a long sigh of relief, as if a burden had been taken from her shoulders.

The door to the room opened, and Lieutenant Wynn stepped inside, looking grim. "Sir, can we speak?" he said.

Michael stood and put a hand on Alton's shoulder. He nodded at Kaitlyn. "Get some rest," he said. Then he followed the lieutenant out of the room.

"What's wrong?" he asked.

"We just got our first signal from the *Immortal*," said the lieutenant. "It's scrambled, but Pedro is working on clearing it up."

Michael rushed to the command center, where Pedro had relocated. He took off the headset.

"You got it?" Wynn asked.

Pedro turned to a bank of monitors connected to the radio. He pushed a button and turned up the crackly signal.

"Vanguard Island Command, this is Captain Two Skulls, sending a distress signal from Panama."

White noise surged over the comms.

Pedro fiddled some more until the channel cleared.

"We are under attack and have suffered heavy casualties to both troops and vehicles," said the captain. "King Xavier and General Forge are pinned down by hostile contacts. We are requesting support from the . . ."

The message cut off.

"Requesting support from the *what*?" Michael asked.

Pedro messed with the buttons again but got only static from the speakers.

"*Isso é tudo*," he said. "That it, no more come through."

"Try and reestablish the connection," Michael said.

"I have, Chief, but nada come through."

Turning, Michael looked out the viewports over the water and the rigs. He felt a cold lump forming in the pit of his stomach. If the mission had failed and X was . . .

Michael shook away the thought as the radio chirped.

"*Espera* . . . Hold on," Pedro said. He put on his headset and spoke into the minimike. "Stand by," he said.

Whirling in his chair, he looked up at Michael.

"I have Sergeant Jamal, with the Wave Riders," he said. "He ask for clarification on transmission from the *Immortal*."

Michael cursed. Jamal was Gran Jefe's cousin.

"How did they tap into it?" he asked.

"I don't know."

The implications made Michael uneasy. If this got out, it could rush through the islands like a hurricane, causing more chaos than any storm.

"Lieutenant, how many men can you spare?" Michael asked.

"None," Wynn said. "We are hanging on by a thread. Almost every able fighter besides the Wave Riders and a few teams specializing in fighting on the water is in Panama."

It wasn't just the Cazadores who had seen Michael go to the prison rig that had him worried. The sky people from the machine camp were already starting to show signs of civil unrest. If they knew that the mission to Panama was failing, there was no telling what they might do.

"Keep everyone on high alert," Michael said. "And tell everyone to keep a cool head. We don't need more problems with some trigger-happy soldier."

"Understood, sir." Wynn turned to Pedro. "Tell them that transmission was confidential and to keep it that way."

"I'm going to check on my family and come right back," Michael said. He stepped into the hallway and started into a stairwell. Halfway up the stairs to his apartment, he pulled out his radio and tuned to the channel he had established for his bodyguards.

"Victor, do you copy? Over."

Static.

Michael tried again, then again, to no avail. He pounded up the stairs, trying a few more times as he got higher, but the weather was interfering with the transmission. Or maybe . . .

Again Michael shook away his dark thoughts.

He took a deep focusing breath outside his apartment door. When his heart rate had settled, he opened the door to find Layla sitting in a chair, with Bray in one arm and Rhino Jr. in the other.

She stood and handed Bray off to Michael.

"What's wrong?" she said. "And don't lie to me."

Michael told her everything about the mission to Panama and what he knew so far. When he was done, she sank back in the chair.

"It's bad, but we don't know if the mission has failed," Michael said. "X isn't dead—I know it—and he will come back."

"What if he doesn't, Michael?"

"He will."

"And if not?"

"He will, God damn it."

Bray stirred in his arms, whimpering.

"I'm sorry," Michael said, hushing the baby.

Layla glared at him.

"Tin, I'm sorry for saying it, but you need to prepare yourself for what happens if X *doesn't* come back this time," she said. "You're smart, loyal, and strong, but if X dies, we are going to face the biggest challenge of our lives."

Michael reached out to his wife. "And we will face that future without fear."

She held his gaze.

"Don't worry, Layla, we'll get through this."

He handed Bray back to her and turned to the door.

"Where are you going?" she asked.

"To buy King Xavier time to win this battle and prevent the islands from falling into anarchy."

THIRTY

"Take cover!" Forge shouted over the open channel.

X looked through the tank scope, trying to find the new beast. They had taken out four of the five breeders with tanks and artillery, but now something else was out there.

Martin drove the tank down an alley lined with rubble, following General Forge's tank. Three Cazador soldiers rode on the square back behind the turret.

They were all searching for cover, but there wasn't much of it out here, and the spawn were still beneath them. It was only a matter of time before they emerged from tunnels and holes.

But it wasn't the offspring that had X worried.

A new mega monster sailed overhead, releasing an ethereal shriek. It flapped up into the sky, giving X his first view of an even larger creature than the breeders. This thing was the size of an airship!

"What in the name of God *is* that?" X asked.

"I don't know, sir, but it came from the city," Slayer said.

Bromista pulled a small plastic case out of his bag and opened it to reveal a dozen explosive arrow tips. "*El diablo que escupe,*" he said.

Slayer nodded. "The spitting devil."

"I kill with dis." Bromista screwed one of the explosive heads onto a bolt and loaded it into his crossbow.

The flying abomination hurtled through the air, its beetle wings buzzing like turbofans as it belched out more glowing green blobs over the ruins of the city.

As it climbed back into the sky, X tensed up with realization. If this thing was as big as an airship, it could *down* an airship.

He bumped on the command channel to Captain Rolo.

"Captain, do you copy? This is X, over."

After a few anxious moments of static popping in his helmet, he finally heard the rough, old voice of Captain Rolo.

"Copy, King Xavier."

"What's your location? We got a new . . . Well, I don't know what the fuck it is out there, Captain."

"I've got it on radar," Rolo said, "and we're keeping our distance. Personally, I'd like to get as far away as possible, though."

"I'm sure you would, but we need you up there. Just steer clear; that's an order."

"Watch out!" Slayer shouted.

Martin slammed on the brakes, bringing the tank to a halt.

The flying creature swooped down, launching a salvo of green vomit over the street. It landed on a partially collapsed two-story building, knocking a wall of brick rubble down in front of General Forge's tank.

The driver managed to stop before the avalanche of bricks buried it. Smoke rose off the sizzling pile, and steel from the building's girders waterfalled down in a bright, molten stream.

"Shit, we're trapped," Martin said. "We got to back up."

The men on the back hopped off the back of the tank, shouldering their rifles and firing laser bolts.

A beat later, X saw what they were firing on. A pack of the spawn came scuttling out of a hole. Three of them collapsed under the onslaught of laser bolts, but the others stormed ahead, toward the soldiers.

X motioned for Miles to stay and then climbed back into the turret.

"King Xavier!" Slayer shouted. "Stop!"

"My ass!" he yelled back.

Popping the turret hatch, he grabbed the .50-caliber machine gun and swung the barrel at the beasts, trying to get a clear shot. They hacked through the thick Cazador armor with pincer claws that may as well have been tinsnips. He saw at least three downed soldiers. Two of the men were already dead, their mangled bodies recognizable as human only by the distinctive metal-and-bone armor.

"I'm sorry," X whispered.

He lined up the sights on the surviving man's helmet first, and pulled the trigger, ending his suffering. Then he turned the barrel on the monsters, destroying the pack in two bursts.

But it was too late for the three Cazador warriors.

"Back up!" X yelled.

The tanks reversed and pulled onto another street.

Using his NVGs, X located a building where dozens of infantry were firing from cover. Over the comms came an updated report of casualties—over thirty dead, with dozens more injured or MIA.

And it was about to get worse. The spawn were charging across the terrain now, hundreds of them searching for prey.

"We have contacts everywhere, sir," Slayer said.

X stared in shock from the turret as the city block flooded with the little domed beasts.

The tide had turned. Now it was the Vanguard army being slaughtered.

"Fall back!" X said. "Tell everyone to fall back!"

A whirring sounded from the sky, and X looked up, expecting to see the airship *Vanguard*. Instead, he saw the winged monstrosity.

"I think we found the big daddy," X said to the command channel. "How do you want to handle it, General?"

Forge, who was back in the turret of his own tank, tracked the monster with his binos.

"With bait," he said. "Seal up, King Xavier, and follow me."

X grunted his assent but remained in the turret. He couldn't button up the tank just yet—not with soldiers to save and an entire belt of ammunition to burn through.

The infantry ran out of the ruined structures. Some were already making it back to the trucks and APCs parked at the bottom of the scree slope.

Behind them, the flamethrower teams were laying down elongated bursts of fire into the encroaching beasts. They wailed and shrieked as the fire steamed them in their shells.

But the flames didn't stop more from coming. Hundreds climbed out of underground passages and charged the vehicles.

X kept busy with the .50, splitting shells open and blowing off limbs.

"Get to the trucks!" he shouted. "Go, go, go!"

"Incoming!" Slayer yelled again.

X stared up as the flying monster swooped low, jaws opening to release a shriek. With its pincered front claws, it snatched a truck off the ground, rending it in half as it flew back into the sky.

Soldiers fell out of the troop hold, their armor and bones shattering on the ground, where the youngsters found them.

Two of the other trucks took off, and the six APCs began to lurch away from the debris. X turned the turret and strafed the beasts chasing them.

The creature in the sky circled for another pass.

"Suck on this!" X shouted, turning the muzzle on the mammoth target.

Tracer rounds streaked into the insectile eyes, bursting several of them. The creature roared and dived on the tank, wings beating the air.

X ducked as it sailed overhead, the draft shaking the vehicle. When he got up, it belched glowing green fluid through its open jaws, onto one of the trucks ahead.

The truck ground to a stop, the tires on fire and the metal glowing. Soldiers fell to the ground in puddles of molten metal and flesh.

Within seconds, the vehicle and everyone who had been inside it were reduced to smoldering masses of melted armor. X raised the machine gun's muzzle back toward the monster that Bromista called the spitting devil.

They had to take it out, or no one would make it back to the ships. He led the beast with the muzzle and fired. The rounds pounded the shell but had no visible effect on the armor. Lowering his aim, he focused his fire on the wings as it swooped back over the fleeing soldiers, dropping another burst of the superheated green goo on a squad of men with flamethrowers.

They went up in a green flash, which faded away to reveal nothing but charred bones and armor.

X kept firing from the turret. General Forge was doing the same with his .50.

"Aim for the wings!" X shouted over the command channel.

The two men unleashed a salvo of bullets into the massive metallic-colored wings. Finally, it roared in pain and flapped away, shrieking.

Both tanks pulled under a warehouse wall that had fallen over some rubble, creating a foot-thick lean-to of reinforced concrete.

X knew exactly what the general had planned. They were going to take the beast out with their cannons when it came back around for another pass.

"Seal up!" Forge shouted.

This time X ducked into the vehicle, but before he pulled the hatch shut, he used his binos to zoom in on the beach. At least a hundred soldiers had made it there and were fleeing to the boats. Three of the APCs and two of the cargo trucks were thumping across the dirt and debris.

X didn't breathe a sigh of relief, but seeing half the army almost back to safety gave him a measure of hope.

Closing the hatch, he moved up to the viewport and watched the monster circling.

"Wait until you get a clear shot," X said.

"I've got this bastard right where I want him," Slayer replied.

Bromista clutched his crossbow and spoke in Spanish.

"No," Slayer said, shaking his head.

"Pero—"

"No."

"What's he asking, to go out there?" X asked.

"*Sí, sí,*" Bromista said, pointing.

"No," X said.

He leaned back to Miles, who was barking. The dog wasn't scared—he was angry. Either he wanted out, or he was mad at X.

Not that X blamed him.

He had brought the best warriors of the sky people and the Cazdores to this place, hoping for an easy victory to secure the canal, and now almost half of them were dead or injured. Factor in the loss of the *Ocean Bull* and their vehicles, and the future looked grim.

He shook away any hint of regret. They had no choice. If humankind wanted to survive, they had to expand, and they had to fight.

"Here it comes," Slayer said.

X turned back to the viewports. Lightning illuminated the winged monstrosity sailing toward the destroyed city blocks.

A thump came from the tank next to them. The shell exploded against the creature's side, blowing out a hunk.

Slayer fired a moment later, but the monster swerved upward, avoiding the shell as it flew off, screeching in rage.

X's heart skipped at the thought of what it could do to the airship.

He opened a command line back to Rolo.

"Captain Rolo, that thing is heading your way, over," X said.

There was no response other than static.

He prayed this was because they were in the storms now, hiding. Despite protests from Miles, who continued to bark and nip at his boots, X climbed back up into the hatch. He popped it open to search the skies with his binos.

"Where are you, you son of a bitch?" he muttered.

In the tank next to him, General Forge emerged in the turret, binos to his visor. He suddenly pointed toward the shoreline.

"Oh, shit," X grumbled.

The beast had dived behind them, heading right for the *Immortal*, *Raven's Claw*, and the *Octopus*.

A crackling sounded, and he looked over the edge of the tank as a pack of creatures swarmed into the warehouse.

X grabbed the machine gun and aimed it at the human-size crabs, turtles, or whatever the fuck they were. The rounds punched through the shells, and the creatures skidded on the ground, where they squirmed until X finished them off with shots to the head.

General Forge fired his machine gun at the skittering beasts, making quick work of them.

When they had finished, both men turned to the beach.

Tracer rounds and rockets streaked away from *Raven's Claw*, pounding the monstrous wings and tearing holes in them. But the beast continued its bombing run, right toward the *Octopus*. The jaws opened and dumped three bright-green blobs.

"We have to do something," X said.

Forge agreed with a stoic nod.

They aimed their machine guns and let fly with the rest of the ammunition, drawing the creature's attention. With a screech, it rolled away from the ships.

X ducked back into the tank. "You're up, Slayer."

"I got this, King Xavier."

"Might only get one more shot."

"No offense, but please give me some room." Slayer looked over his shoulder and X backed up.

"Right," he said. "Sorry."

Peering through the viewport, X watched it come closer, only seconds away. The flaps opened again, the glowing flesh pulsating.

Both tanks fired at almost the same moment.

One shell blew away the mouth. The other streaked right into the folds of flesh, bursting on impact.

A deafening shriek sounded, and X pushed back in his seat as the creature fought for altitude, swooping over them.

A sizzling noise filled his ears.

X popped open the hatch when he realized what was making the noise. The tank beside them was burning under the melting concrete slab, which had taken the brunt of the blast from above.

The concrete wasn't the only thing melting. Metal dripped like candle wax as the light armor of the tank dissolved from the green sludge of the monster.

General Forge opened the turret and jumped out, hitting the ground as the top and right side of his helmet warped in the heat. X hopped out of his turret and down to the ground. Another massive explosion came as the creature slammed into the ruins of the city.

X crouched beside General Forge, who had collapsed in the dirt. He used his good hand to remove the hot armor plates, but it was too late for the right side of Forge's face. The flesh sizzled all the way to the bone on his right cheek.

Slayer rushed over carrying a medical kit while Bromista stood guard with his crossbow.

"We have to get him in the tank," X said. "Help me."

"No," Forge grunted. "Leave . . ."

"Not a chance, General," X said. "This is going to hurt like hell, but we need you to live."

* * * * *

The chatter on the comms got Magnolia's heart rate up. Every passing second they were stuck on the ship, more Vanguard soldiers perished.

She crawled through a utility tunnel from the room Yejun had locked them inside. It was a narrow passage, and only Magnolia and Sofia were small enough to fit, but Magnolia had ordered Sofia to remain behind with the rest of Team Raptor.

It was too dangerous, and this was Magnolia's fault. She had trusted Yejun.

You should have chipped him.

But putting a beacon on Yejun was not something anyone had thought about before the mission. As she crawled through the utility tunnel, she checked the beacons of Team Wrangler. Their finding Jo-Jo was good news, but for some reason, Kade had left the team underground and was on the surface.

She considered turning on the comm channel to see why but didn't want to make any more noise.

After a few minutes of crawling, she found a grate. Looking down, she searched the deck below for any sign of the glowing beasts.

Carefully she pulled back the grate and lowered herself. Her boots hit the deck gently, making almost no noise.

Bringing up her rifle, she cleared the left side of the passage, then the right.

Keep moving, Mags . . .

She started back toward the freezer, looping through the passages with only one helmet light on. The beam speared through the darkness, over rusted hulls and ladders.

Magnolia stopped at an intersection to listen. Hearing nothing, she kept moving into a corridor where electrical wires hung down. The entire middle section of the overhead had collapsed outside the exit hatch, dumping the wire runs into the hallway, where they hung like vines. There were so many, they would be hard to get through.

She considered pulling out one of her sickle blades, then decided on an alternative route. A hatch opened to a ladder that went up a level, right outside the mess hall.

Magnolia stopped to listen again . . . Still nothing.

She shouldered her rifle and moved toward the mess hall. A quick sweep cleared the space, and she hurried to the hatch.

The pipe they had used to free the spin wheel was gone.

Magnolia let her rifle hang from the strap and tried twisting it.

After bumping on the comm channel, she tried Edgar.

"You guys okay?" she asked.

"Fine, and that glowing thing's gone, far as I can tell," Edgar replied. "Radiation spike went down, too."

"Try going out that way, then. I'll meet you topside."

"Be careful, Commander."

"Yeah, Edgar. You too."

Magnolia hurried out of the mess hall and back to the ladder. She took it up a level, to the same passage with the electrical wires. The hatch to access the deck was right beyond.

Pulling out one of her sheathed blades, she started hacking her way through. Slicing copper wire was not easy, and she had to tease the thicker bundles apart, cutting only two or three strands at a time.

She was making slow but steady progress when a chirping caught her ear. Her eyes flitted to her HUD, which signaled a sudden spike in radiation. Next came a beeping from her wrist monitor and bioscanner.

The motion detector was picking up three contacts.

She double-checked the position of Team Raptor and was surprised to see they were already topside.

This was something, or someone, else.

Magnolia shut off her helmet beam and stared into darkness that gave way to a bright incandescent glow. Golden light flickered at the end of the corridor.

She turned back to the wires and cut through another section. The severed lengths fell to the deck as she worked toward the hatch, visible in the mysterious glow.

A loop of cable hooked Magnolia's ankle, and she fell into a skein of wires.

Moving made it worse, and she became entangled just an arm's reach from the hatch. She squirmed around onto her back, to face the source of the glow.

Two naked humanoid features staggered down the passage. Their skin looked hard and rough, like bark. Between the grooves, a yellow light pulsated, illuminating their naked bodies.

Magnolia stared for a moment, in equal parts astonishment and fascination.

But terror quickly got the upper hand, and she fought like a demon to free herself, using the curved blade to cut through several wires.

Around the corner came a third figure, stumbling like a possessed person. All three moaned and shuffled toward her. Bright yellow eyes burned in their orbits.

Magnolia struggled harder, trying to free herself.

"Help!" she said over the team channel. "I need help!"

"Hold on! I'm on my way," Edgar replied.

The three glowing creatures reached for her with clawed hands. Their bodies pulsed with light, as if their hearts were sending luminous blood through their veins.

Hearing a clank above her, she glanced at her HUD. A fourth contact showed up on her minimap. It seemed to be directly above . . .

The ceiling panel suddenly gave way, and a person fell to the deck, gripping a sword. Rolling up to its feet, the shadowed figure thrust the blade into the chest of the first beast, right through the heart. The glowing flesh dimmed as the creature let out a ghastly shriek before slumping to the ground.

The sword wielder was slightly built but fast, and before Magnolia knew it, the blade went through the heart of the second humanoid creature.

Magnolia finally managed to extricate her left arm from the tangled cords, just as the two fatally injured creatures on the deck shriveled and flaked away into piles of ash.

The third beast screamed and ran toward the sword wielder, who met it head-on, stabbing deep into the monster's glowing, pulsating chest.

Turning on her headlamp, Magnolia centered the beam on the swordsman.

"Yejun," she mumbled.

The young man lowered the sword and backed away. Then he turned toward her, still holding the sword. He darted over, holding the blade up.

"No, not like this," she said. "Please, not like . . ."

She closed her eyes as he swung.

The cords released her, and she fell to the deck. But there was no pain.

Opening one eye, she saw Yejun cutting through the rest of the wires. When she was completely free, he sheathed the sword and reached down, speaking quietly.

Footfalls came from the other end of the corridor.

Edgar, Arlo, and Sofia all approached with their weapons aimed at Yejun.

"Back! Get the fuck back!" Edgar shouted.

"Shoot him!" Arlo yelled. "What are you waiting for?"

"Wait!" Magnolia held up her hands. "Hold your fire!"

Sofia pushed her barrel up, but both men kept their weapons trained on Yejun.

"Everyone take a breath, I'm okay," Magnolia said. She pushed herself up in front of the piles of ash and then looked at Yejun. He had trapped her again, and this time used them all as bait.

Yejun reached into his pocket, and Edgar leveled his blaster.

"No," Magnolia said, stepping in front of the drawn weapons.

She eyed the tip of a scroll he had stuffed in his vest.

Slowly, Yejun pulled it out and handed it to her. Then he went over to the piles of ash and bent down in front of them.

Arlo pressed his wrist monitor. "The radiation spike is gone," he said. "It must have been them all along."

Magnolia tried to make sense of what she had just witnessed. These beasts weren't like anything she had encountered in the wastes, and Yejun seemed to know them. He also knew how to kill them.

And right now it didn't matter, she realized.

What mattered was getting the map and the Hell Divers safely back into the sky.

She opened a line to Team Wrangler.

Kade replied right away.

"Commander, I'm on the surface, watching a massive beast that flew out of the tunnels and headed toward the front lines," he said. "We have Jo-Jo, but we can't get into the air until that thing is dead."

"We'll come to you. Stand by."

Magnolia tapped her wrist computer to study the map of the terrain between them and Team Wrangler.

Yejun spoke again, waving them forward.

The Hell Divers all stared at him and then looked to Magnolia for orders.

She definitely didn't trust him, but she wasn't going to kill him or leave him behind again. He had saved her life and given her the map.

"Let's go," she said.

Edgar and Arlo stayed close to Yejun, their rifles at his back as he passed the little piles of ash. He looked down at the piles, whispering something again.

"This is going to be one hell of a story once we get back home," Arlo said.

"*If* we get back home," Sofia said. "There's still a war going on out there."

THIRTY-ONE

"It's going to be okay, Jo-Jo."

Ada stroked the thick hair on the animal's head, just as she had when it was small. Fighting for survival together in the wastes had bonded them in a way that only King Xavier could understand. For some humans, an animal could be just as important as another human. *And screw anyone who judges that.*

She bent down and placed her helmet against Jo-Jo's chest, listening to her heartbeat through the speakers. The strong *thump-thump* soothed Ada.

"I love you, and I'm so sorry," she said. "I would never have left if . . ."

The monkey stirred, and Ada pulled away as it struggled to open one eye.

"I think she's waking up," Ada said quietly.

Tia and Gran Jefe hovered near the hill of dirt from the cave-in.

"How's she doing?" Tia asked.

Jo-Jo groaned and closed her eye.

"She should be sleeping," Gran Jefe said. "That was a strong dose—*muy fuerte*."

Ada was still angry that he had shot Jo-Jo with the tranq dart, but she understood why. The creature had clearly been in shock when they discovered it in the pit.

Gran Jefe peered up the shaft. "Where . . . is the cowboy?" he asked.

"The commander said hold here until Team Raptor comes and we can figure out how to get back to the airship," Tia said.

"*Sí, pero hace mucho tiempo*," Gran Jefe said. "Long time ago. Maybe a monster ate him."

"If you think that's true, you don't know Kade."

"I want to get out of here, too, but orders are orders," Ada said.

"Funny for you to say," Gran Jefe said.

Ada raised a brow. While no one knew exactly why she was here, they knew that King X had conscripted her to serve for disobeying orders in the past.

Then again, she had disobeyed *two* jump orders now. She had put an entire team at risk to find Jo-Jo.

"You guys feel that?" Tia asked.

"Yeah—bombs," Gran Jefe said. "My people is dying, I get sick of waiting down here like some *pinche vago*."

He walked over to the rope. "I'm going up."

Tia looked to Ada, but Ada wasn't going to argue with Gran Jefe again. The guy was an asshole and wouldn't listen anyway. She called the commander on the team channel.

"Kade, do you copy?" Ada asked over the comms.

Nothing.

Now she was starting to worry.

"Don't leave us down here," Tia said to Gran Jefe.

Ada felt a sudden vibration. She searched the walls with her beams.

Dirt crumbled down the side.

She raised Cricket for a scan. This one came back with something faint. The readings seemed to be coming from inside the walls and ground.

"Stay alert," she said to Tia. "I think those crab things are tunneling around us."

Tia brought up her rifle.

"Gran Jefe," Ada said. "Gran Jefe, get back here."

He had uncoiled a rope from his gear and was on the top of the collapsed mound.

A moan came from Jo-Jo, who was staring at the overhead, dark eyes widening.

Ada shined her light on the dirt ceiling.

Crumbs of dirt trickled down the wall.

"Watch out—" Ada began to say when a cry cut her off.

She aimed her rifle at a root or tendril that had burst out of the dirt and wrapped around Tia's legs, pulling her to the ground. Another metallic-colored vine poked through the ground, then another. In seconds, the entire hill of loose earth from the collapsed tunnel was writhing with the strange ribbed tendrils.

These weren't vines or roots. These were some sort of worm or snake.

T-shaped heads turned toward Ada, as if sensing her movement. The eyeless faces and shafts vibrated. Then the lips curled back to expose wicked curving teeth.

"Help!" Tia screamed.

The snake that had her threw more coils around her legs, waist, and chest.

"Gran Jefe, we need you!" Ada shouted.

She ran toward Tia, firing her laser rifle at the snake heads. One of them spun toward her, the face widening into flower petals around the jaw of sharp teeth.

She fired another burst, blowing the mutant snake's face into pulp.

Another head shot toward her, clamping down on her rifle arm. She had her knife out before it could strike again. Ducking under, she hacked into the meaty coil.

Tia screamed as the snake pulled her into the tunnel. Her chest armor caught in the opening at her shoulders.

"Hold on!" Ada yelled.

Gran Jefe emerged on the mound with a cutlass in one hand and a snake wrapped around the other arm.

He pulled the snake out of the ground and hacked through the body. The head remained attached to his arm as the body squirmed on the ground.

Charging across the crest of the hill, he swung powerful strokes that cut through the thick, ropy flesh.

The severed bodies fell writhing at his feet, but three more burst from new holes behind him, wrapping around his ankles and legs. They coiled around his waist and chest.

Ada fired another flurry of laser bolts from the bottom of the mound, and two more snake heads fell, one rolling down the dirt slope to her feet.

A cry of human rage roared above her.

Gran Jefe had ripped in half one of the two snakes that held him. Then he hacked through the ribbed flesh still clinging around his legs and freed himself.

Ada ran toward Tia, who was still wedged halfway into the hole as the snake tried to crush her and pull her in.

"Help me," Tia choked. "Help—"

Ada used the serrate edge of her combat knife to saw at the snake wrapped around Tia's chest plates.

"I've almost got it—"

A furry hand reached past her helmet and grabbed Tia by the shoulder plate. Ada fell on her backside as Jo-Jo hauled Tia out of the tunnel in one powerful heave.

Ada sat up with a smile until she felt a powerful tug around her neck. The snake that had let go of Tia yanked her backward, dragging her toward a hole.

She kicked and squirmed, trying to get at her sheath knife as the beast got a coil around the nape of her helmet.

A towering figure loomed over her.

It was Gran Jefe, raising his cutlass. He brought it down toward her helmet. The tension released, and she sat up, holding her neck.

Gasping for air, she embraced Jo-Jo, who was crouched next to her, shaking and whimpering.

Gran Jefe turned his dripping cutlass to the other snakes still squirming up through the dirt.

"Come on!" he yelled, pounding his chest plate. "Bite! Bite!"

Ada crawled back to Tia, who coughed violently, gripping her chest and side.

The T-shaped heads shook their warning again, and all at once, the dozens of snake heads around them opened. Flowerlike flesh petals bloomed around the toothed gullets. One shot forward at the divers.

Jo-Jo caught it in her hand and easily ripped the body in two. She bit into the flesh, seemed to like it, and swallowed it. Gran Jefe swung his cutlass at the creatures, and Ada fired her rifle.

Suddenly, from the top of the shaft came a stream of brilliant flashes as laser fire sizzled into the ground around the divers. Snake heads and bodies burst in the spray.

Ada looked up to see a figure crouched at the top of the vertical shaft.

It was Kade, aiming his rifle. He continued to fire, and Gran Jefe cleared the rest of the mound with his cutlass, raising his blade in the air and belting out a roar of victory.

"You guys okay?" Kade yelled down.

Ada bent down next to Tia, who was sitting up now, holding her side. Gran Jefe stomped a snake still writhing on the dirt.

"I think I have a cracked rib," Tia whispered.

"Tia's hurt," Ada called up.

Kade switched to the team comm. "Get topside. I'm going to meet Team Raptor a half mile from here and lay down covering fire if they need it."

"Got it," Ada replied. She checked Cricket again, but the life scan showed that the remaining snakes had retreated into the walls. She tucked Cricket into her vest and helped Tia to her feet.

"We're clear," Ada said.

Tia shook, injured and in obvious shock.

"Come, *amigas*," Gran Jefe said. He started toward the rope hanging from the vertical shaft.

"I'll go first and pull you up," he said.

"Thank you," Ada said. "Thanks for saving us."

He just nodded, then took the rope and started climbing up. Ada stood sentry over Tia, who rested with her back to the wall.

Jo-Jo paced, still a little loopy but getting back to her normal self. She came over to Ada several times, hugging her the way a baby might hug its mother—if it had a mother half its own size.

"It's okay," Ada said soothingly. "We're going home now."

Tia moaned on the ground.

"I'm having a hard time breathing," she said.

"Go easy, try to relax," Ada replied. "You'll be back on the airship in no time."

Gran Jefe finally reached the top.

"Okay, you're next," Ada said. She wrapped the rope around Tia in an improvised swami harness.

"Too tight, too tight," she cried.

"It *has* to be tight," replied Ada, whereupon she stepped back and raised a hand to Gran Jefe. Using a jumar in each hand, he pulled the slightly built young woman up by brute strength alone.

"You're going to be okay," Ada said.

She turned back to the tunnel with Jo-Jo to watch for hostiles.

"I . . . I can't breathe," Tia said halfway up.

"You're almost there," Ada said.

"I . . . my vision is going . . ."

The young diver was going to pass out.

Gran Jefe pulled faster, and Ada's lamp told her the moment Tia's arms went limp by her sides. By the time she got to the top, she wasn't answering on the comm.

"Tia," Ada said. "Tia, do you copy?"

The tail of the rope came down, and Gran Jefe poked his helmet over the side. "She sleep, okay."

Ada handed the rope end to Jo-Jo.

"No, you go," Gran Jefe said.

Ada wasn't going to leave her companion down here again, but she couldn't send her up first—no way would the monkey stand for that.

"No, we go together," Ada said over the comms. "Throw down the other rope and make sure both are anchored."

A second rope snaked down a few seconds later.

"Just like we trained," Ada said. "Okay, Jo-Jo?"

The monkey whined.

Ada hugged her dearest friend in the world,

then stepped back and clipped her carabiner to a figure-eight knot at the rope's end.

"Okay," Ada said. "Pull me up."

Gran Jefe yanked her off the ground, and she started up the wall with Jo-Jo climbing by her side.

Ada looked over every few feet to offer words of encouragement.

"Almost there," she said.

They were finally leaving this hell behind.

But as they got closer to the surface, Ada could hear that this wasn't the end of the fight.

Bombs and gunshots rang out in the distance.

There was still the battle to take the canal.

Ada watched the rim of the shaft as Gran Jefe hauled her higher. She was nearing the top. Lightning backlit his helmet and the pincer trophy he had taken from the tunnels.

When she was five feet from the top, he snubbed the rope around a load-bearing column and paused to take a rest.

She kept her feet against the dirt wall and looked down at Jo-Jo, who had fallen slightly behind. She was used to climbing trees, not a rope.

"Ada," Gran Jefe said.

She looked up.

"Is Tia okay?" she asked.

"Sleeping," he replied. "Just like you will be soon."

Hearing the shift in his tone, she stared up.

"*Yo sé*," he said. "I know what you did. *Mi primo*—my cousin—was in that *contenedor*."

"What . . ."

So he knew about the day she dropped the Cazadores in the ocean, drowning them all inside the shipping container.

"No," she said. "I'm sorry. I . . ."

"Too late. Now your turn. Something I been waiting a *muy* long time for." He stepped closer to the edge, dropping her a few feet. He laughed. "You think I leave the army for this *pinche* job? Hell Divers—*¡pendejos!*"

Ada felt the wash of terror, then the calm of resignation. It all made sense—how he had treated her from the beginning, and why he wanted to kill her.

"After you die, I'm going to eat your *mascota*." He patted his gut. "I bet she taste *muy sabrosa*."

After snubbing the rope around the column, he let go of the jumar ascender in his left hand and reached over his shoulder for the pincer claw.

Ada considered pleading with him, but words wouldn't make any difference. She had to act. If she killed him, he would drop the rope.

He brought the pincer's sharp edge to the rope. Ada whipped the knife from its sheath on her calf. And in the split second he was distracted, she hurled it at his visor.

The blade clanked over the crest of his helmet and cartwheeled into the darkness.

He laughed again. "See you in hell, amiga."

"NO!" Ada yelled.

As he scissored the rope with the sharp claw, Ada

scrabbled frantically for purchase on the wall. But her fingers just slid down the crumbling dirt and rock.

Flailing for something, anything, her foot hit an outcropping and she pitched backward, like during the early seconds of a dive.

With maybe two seconds before she hit the ground, she reached over her shoulder to punch the booster, hoping it would deploy in time. The balloon burst out and rose above her as she passed Jo-Jo, who reached out uselessly for her.

Ada glanced down at the dirt rising to meet her body. She knew not to bring her legs up, and stiffened them to protect her spine. Her boots hit the ground, and an electric jolt ran through her as her legs telescoped.

She crashed onto her back, her vision blurring.

A memory from childhood filled her mind's eye. She was playing with a doll she had made with her parents. Their deaths came next, followed by her first love, a boy who died not long after they agreed to marry. Next came the war with the Cazadores, and the aftermath, when she had committed mass murder.

Most of the images were painful reminders of a miserable youth. But they gave way to some happy memories. Memories of paradise, and a year spent with Jo-Jo. Eating fruit on a sundeck, swimming with dolphins, and enjoying time with her friends at the Vanguard Islands.

A deep, sad whining snapped her out of the trance, and she cracked one eyelid to see the face that she had grown to love.

Jo-Jo hovered over her, whimpering and nudging her.

And above the creature, at the top of the shaft, Gran Jefe stood looking down. He finally backed away.

Ada blinked away the stars until she saw her twisted legs. She felt no pain below her head, which pounded like hell.

There was no denying the truth. Her body was destroyed, and there was no coming back from this. She tried to bump on the comm channel, but she couldn't even do that.

Jo-Jo nudged her, crying so loud, Ada could hear her over the ringing in her ears.

"I'm . . ." Ada choked. "Sorry . . ."

The monkey put a paw on her chest.

"I love you," Ada said. "I'm sorry I . . ."

Red encroached on the edges of Ada's vision, threatening to consume her. Struggling to take her final breaths, she saw the pain in her companion's eyes. And in that moment of clarity, she saw it turn to rage.

Ada used her last breath to whisper her final words.

"Find X and Miles."

* * * * *

"All clear in the dark," Victor said over the comms.

Hearing the words, Michael breathed a sigh of relief, but that didn't mean the spearmen and the secret stash of food they were guarding at the prison rig were safe. This was no time to relax—for a variety of reasons.

The future of the islands also depended on what happened next over a thousand miles away. X and the Hell Divers were fighting for their lives, and Michael was doing damage control back at the islands, where actions and attitudes from the diverse populations already foreshadowed what would happen if X failed.

Part of Michael felt anger toward X for leaving this responsibility to him, but he understood now why X had selected him for it. X trusted only a few people, and someday when he was gone, Michael would have to step up.

This was dangerous training, but no more dangerous than diving. X believed the mission to secure the Panama Canal and establish outposts was vital to the survival of the Vanguard Islands. He didn't go because he was bored with being king or because he just wanted to get out there and kill something. X went because he saw no other option for saving the surviving remnant of the human race.

In the command center atop the capitol tower, Michael stared out the viewports overlooking dull-gray water and low storm clouds rolling from the west, dumping more rain on the distant rigs.

Steve was in a chair at the war table, arms folded across his chest, snoring. The man had finally run out of steam.

Pedro fiddled with the radio, still trying to

reconnect with the Vanguard army or the airship—anyone who could give them an idea of what was happening in Panama. He switched back and forth between the seat in front of the radio and one facing a monitor that showed the location of the two drones being used to relay transmissions.

"Nothing yet?" Michael asked.

Pedro shook his head. "The new storms block the signal," he said. "I have moved one drone, but it could be few hours before we know what is happening in Panama."

Michael didn't have a few hours to put preparations in place for what might happen if the mission failed. And based on the last transmission, things were grim out there.

Almost as bad, according to Pedro the Wave Riders had intercepted that transmission.

The report would no doubt already be spreading, and if people thought they were doomed, they would start trying to seize resources. He couldn't sit by and simply wait to react.

He sat down in front of the radio and sent a message to Lieutenant Wynn. "Lock the entire capitol tower down and prepare the defenses."

"On it, sir."

An hour later, the hatch opened up and Steve jerked awake, standing up to greet the lieutenant, who rushed inside.

"We're almost finished," Wynn said, panting.

"Good." Michael slung his backpack over his

shoulder. "Pedro, stay here and keep me updated. Steve, with me."

Steve started to follow, but Michael stopped. "Bring a weapon."

"Sir?"

"Pedro, keep that crossbow close," Michael said. "I'm not expecting anything, but we need to be ready for an attack."

"By who?" Pedro asked.

"Anyone."

Michael and Steve followed Wynn out of the command center and went to the top deck. Militia soldiers were loading arrows the size of men into the emplaced crossbows at the edges of the rooftop.

All the spare .50-caliber ammunition had been taken to Panama, along with most of the other calibers. The guards assigned to the rigs were down to one magazine each, and a sword or spear of choice.

"I've assigned thirty of my most trusted soldiers to the capitol tower," Wynn said. "Just in case, we should be able to hold it against small raiding parties if anyone decides to try anything."

"Good," Michael said. "This is just a precaution."

"Or perhaps not."

Imulah came running through the gardens, calling out for Michael.

"Chief, I just got word that the radio transmission was intercepted at rig nine."

"That's a Cazador rig," Michael said.

"Indeed it is."

"Lieutenant, who do you have on that rig?"

Wynn thought on it for a minute. "I have two militia soldiers who work with the Wave Riders."

"The Wave Riders . . ." Michael said. He thought back to the Jet Skis that had seen his boat outside the prison rig.

Michael desperately wanted to tell Wynn about the food there and to assign soldiers to protect it, but he simply couldn't trust them.

"Contact your men there and see if anything's happening," Michael said.

"Okay." Wynn stepped away with his radio.

Imulah cupped his hands behind his back and stepped up next to Michael, under the thick canopy of a tree that shielded them from the rain.

"You have done your best, Chief Everhart," Imulah said, "but the fate of these islands is outside of your hands now. You must keep blood from spilling."

Wynn returned a minute later. "My men said the Wave Riders are mobilizing and heading out into the storm."

Michael cursed and looked at Imulah. "So much for not spilling blood."

"You think they are a threat?" Wynn asked.

"We're going to find out. Gather five of your best soldiers and meet me at the marina."

"What about Ton and Victor?"

Michael couldn't tell him where they were, but if he was right about the Wave Riders, they would all know soon enough.

"Imulah, stay here with Pedro and let me know if you hear anything from X, okay?"

The scribe nodded and hurried off into the rain.

Michael rushed down to the marina with his backpack. He looked at the *Sea Wolf* but decided on something faster. He selected the war boat el Pulpo had used, which now belonged to King Xavier.

While waiting for Wynn, Michael pulled out the radio again. "Victor, do you copy?"

"Yes, all clear in the dark," he said.

"Keep an eye out. We might have a problem."

"Okay."

A few minutes later, Wynn showed up with five other militia soldiers, in armor and carrying rifles. They were all former citizens of the *Hive*, which made Michael more comfortable with having them along.

Steve arrived next, holding a wrecking bar. A long rifle with a scope was slung over his shoulder. He had swapped out his green sunglasses for a pair of ski goggles.

"We are heading out to track the Wave Riders," Michael said. "I have reason to believe they are mobilizing for unsavory purposes, and we can't let them. I'm sorry I can't tell you more, but for now you must trust me."

"I trust you," Wynn said.

"Me, too," Steve agreed.

Nods all around.

"Let's go," Michael said.

He got aboard the boat and went to the cockpit,

where he dropped his backpack. Out of it he pulled the only laser rifle still at the islands.

Steve lowered the boat on the lift, and Michael fired up the engines. The soldiers boarded in drizzling rain, crowding under a canopy in the back with their rifles.

Running to the door of the enclosed marina, Steve hauled on the rope, opening it. Then he jumped from the dock onto the boat.

Michael steered out of the marina and into the night. Rain pounded the windshield as he turned the boat into the waves.

Rig 9 was only a fifteen-minute boat ride at normal speeds, but Michael didn't plan on going a normal speed. He pushed the throttle down, and the engines roared, powering the boat through the waves.

By the time he was within view of the rig, he could see the glow of headlights on the horizon. Six of them. The Wave Riders had already taken off, and they were headed exactly where he thought they would go: toward the prison rig.

Michael steered away from the rig, but he could see torches and candles burning on the different levels. Hundreds of Cazadores were still awake, and they weren't just sitting around. Some of them were carrying spears, swords, bows, and guns.

Flipping off the beams, Michael cruised by the rig, staring at what looked like a population mobilizing for war. The sight sent a chill through him, and his thoughts went straight to Layla, Bray, and Rhino Jr.

"The transmission from Panama is spreading," Steve said. "There is only one explanation for this, partner, and it ain't good."

"And that is what?"

"The Cazadores are preparing for an empty throne."

Michael said, "Lieutenant, tell your men to get ready to intercept the Wave Riders."

"Sir, all due respect, but I still don't understand what's going on," Wynn replied. "Does this have to do with them intercepting the radio signal?"

"Partly, but it's what they are after."

Wynn raised his voice over the engines. "Chief, I can't help if you don't tell me what's going on."

Michael exchanged a glance with Steve, who nodded.

Gripping the wheel in his robotic arm, Michael stared at the Jet Skis that seemed to be bouncing over the waves, their beams flitting up and down. He knew what would happen if they discovered the food or if X died in Panama. There would be a fight for the crown—a fight that would determine the future of the islands.

Michael said, "King Xavier found a supply of food on the *Immortal* supercarrier and had it secretly moved to the prison rig," Michael said.

"Food?"

"Months' worth. For the entire Vanguard population."

Wynn seemed to have a question, but he remained quiet.

"We can't let that food be discovered, or everyone is going to be fighting over it," Michael said. "It's for the worst-case situation."

"Sir, you understand what will happen if people like Charmer find out we've been hiding something like that? And you understand what happens if we end up fighting with the Wave Riders?"

"Yes, and I'm hoping it doesn't come to that, but we must be ready."

"I'm with you, sir, you know that, I'm just—"

"We must trust each other," Michael said. "Can I trust you?"

"Yes," Wynn said. He reached into his pocket and started pumping shotgun shells into his weapon.

"I'm with you, partner," Steve said.

Wynn said, "I'll inform my men." He opened the hatch and went outside to his team.

Michael watched the distant beams, his eyes flitting from the Jet Skis to the map. They were actually turning, he realized.

He quickly pegged their new destination: oil rig 15.

But why would the Wave Riders be heading to the rig housing the sky people from Kilimanjaro?

Michael narrowed his eyes, trying to make sense of things. He kept the boat's running lights off and eased back the throttle as they closed on the rig.

"Steve, tell Lieutenant Wynn to contact his men on rig fifteen," Michael said.

Steve went outside and returned with Wynn a few moments later.

"Sir, I can't reach them on the comms," Wynn said.

Michael cursed, remembering the conversation with Charmer about the Kilimanjaro sky people not needing the soldiers. He explained that conversation to Wynn, who confirmed that militia soldiers under his command did indeed remain on active duty at that rig.

"Something's wrong," Michael said. "Something's really wrong."

In the distance, the Jet Skis had reached the marina at the bottom of rig 15. Torches burned under metal awnings, and a group of people had gathered on the docks.

Michael stopped the boat and went out on the bow with Wynn and the other soldiers. Steve joined them, handing Michael a pair of binoculars.

Not surprisingly, Charmer was right there on the dock. The Cazador soldiers dismounted their Jet Skis and approached him. Each of them carried crates and supplies.

"What are those?" Michael asked.

He watched Jamal, the sergeant with the Wave Riders, go up to Charmer, who stuck out a hand. Jamal looked down at it and then shook.

The Wave Runner squad walked past them and stacked the crates on the dock. Oliver opened one and pulled out a rifle, aiming it at the sky to check the scope. Then he held it out to Charmer.

"Son of a bitch," Michael said. "The Cazadores

are arming them. Where did they even *get* more weapons?"

"I don't know," Wynn said. "What should we do?"

"We should pray X survives," Steve said.

"For now, we get back to the capitol tower," Michael said. "If they want a fight, we make them come to us."

THIRTY-TWO

"Stay with me, General," X said. "We're going to get you back to the ship."

Somehow, General Forge was still conscious. He lay on the floor of the tank, covered in bandages that had already soaked through with blood. Slayer and Bromista attended to him while X received a sitrep over the command channel.

The report wasn't good, and he cursed under his breath. Miles looked over at him, tail down.

"It's going to be okay," X said.

He hated lying to his dog. The situation was bad and deteriorating by the second. Only half the vehicles and just over half the soldiers had made it back to the landing craft. The other half were either dead or pinned down like X and his comrades in the tank.

"Sir, I will send back the landing craft with an APC as soon as it docks," Captain Two Skulls said over the channel.

"No," X grunted. "It's suicide. Don't send anyone after us right now."

Static crackled from the radio.

"Sir, we're not leaving you."

"That's an order, Captain. Enough men and women have already died." X shut off the channel and swallowed hard. "I got us into this, and I'm getting us out," he said.

Slayer scooted over to look through Martin's viewport. Miles nestled up to X, watching the tide of shelled creatures surge out of tunnels and holes across the city block.

Cries of pain and sporadic gunshots rang out through the night as the beasts found injured soldiers who couldn't make it back to the ships.

And soon, they would find the tank, and a way inside.

"We have to go out on foot," X said. "We have no choice."

"Those things are everywhere, King Xavier," Martin whispered. "If we move on foot, they're going to be all over us."

He gave General Forge a doubtful glance and Bromista nodded as if he understood.

"Martin's right," Slayer murmured. "We can't move the general like this."

They were speaking softly, and X was surprised when the old warrior opened his eye and mumbled, "Leave me, King Xavier . . ."

"I said you can't die, and I meant it," X said.

"You do not have permission to give up, do you understand?"

"*Sí, comprendo.*"

"Good, because I think I just thought of a plan to get us out of here."

X switched to the airship's frequency.

"Captain Rolo, do you copy?"

After a brief pause, Rolo's voice came in. "Copy, King Xavier."

That was good, at least—they were still in the air.

"Captain, I need you to hover over my coordinates if possible, and drop a supply crate with boosters. We're pinned down and will use them to get into the sky."

"With that thing out there?"

"It is no longer a problem," X replied. "Now send down a damn crate with boosters."

"Copy."

X grunted as the channel shut off. He was really starting to dislike Rolo, but he couldn't exactly blame the guy for being cautious.

"Let's get ready to move," X said.

Martin climbed out of his seat and grabbed his laser rifle while Slayer readied their gear. Clanking resonated as Bromista picked up his crossbow, but this wasn't the clatter of a weapon on armor. This was coming from outside.

Miles barked and stepped up to the hatch.

X grabbed Miles to silence him, but it didn't matter. The beasts had found them.

Scratching traveled along the outside of the tank, followed by a thump on the top.

The men all looked up.

"Quiet," X whispered.

A screech came from the rear hatch. Claws scratched the metal, prodding and probing for any weakness. Miles followed the shriek of the metal, baring his teeth and growling.

X bent down in front of the viewports as another wave of the chitinous animals skittered over the mounds of concrete, twisted I-beams, and glass shards on their way to the beach.

He turned from the glass and motioned for Miles to keep still.

They sat there in silence, trying to keep as quiet as possible.

The pack of beasts moved on, their clatter and chirping squeals growing distant.

A sense of calm descended on the battlefield, and X realized he hadn't heard any gunfire or screams for a while now. The only sound was Forge's raspy breath.

X put a hand on his bandaged arm. "Hang on, my friend," he said.

Forge managed a nod.

Miles went rigid just as a thump sounded against the rear hatch. A second thud hit the left, then a third on the right side of the tank.

Another pack had found them.

X climbed up into the turret.

"Sir," Slayer whispered.

"Don't worry. I got it."

X unlatched the turret and reached down to thumb the keeper loop off his hatchet. Pressing his shoulder plate up against the unlocked turret, he raised the blade to meet the open jaws of the man-size beast climbing up over the left track.

"Get off my tank!" he shouted.

A blow to the face severed the tip of its curved beaklike snout. The thing chittered in agony or rage and swiped at him with a pincer, which he parried with his metal fist. Using his other hand, he swung the axe down on the crest of the skull, cracking through shell and into whatever brain the mutant creature had.

He threw the hatchet end-over-end at the beast on the cannon, sinking the bit square between its forward pair of eyes.

Two more of the beasts darted out of a hole X hadn't seen. He raised his laser rifle and spun to fire, when an explosion between the two monsters blew the limbs from their shells.

Bromista stood outside the tank with his crossbow. After cranking the string back, he seated another shaft in the channel.

The smoking bodies hissed and steamed as X searched for new targets. Finding nothing, he wrenched his axe from the beast's head and ducked back inside the tank, sealing the hatch after him.

"Okay, we're clear," X said. "Get him ready to move."

Slayer and Martin helped the general put on a rad suit while X went to Miles.

"Okay, pal," he said, "we're going to go outside in a few minutes. You ready?"

The dog wagged his tail.

A tap came at the back hatch.

Slayer whirled toward it, then looked at X.

The tapping came again. It didn't sound like the claws of the shelled beasts. X scrambled over and grabbed the handle. He lifted the lever, and Bromista pointed his crossbow into the face of a Cazador soldier.

"No shoot," the man said.

Bromista lowered the weapon.

"Get in. We . . ." X said.

His words trailed off at the sight of another pack of shelled beasts that had followed the soldier. They came so fast, X barely had time to grab the man by one hand.

A massive juvenile beast thrust a pincer deep into his armor, crunching through the shoulder. The claw broke out the front, painting X with blood.

The man screamed in agony, but X held on tight.

"Don't let go!" he shouted.

The creature pulled back, yanking the Cazador out of the hatch, along with X, who held on. Bromista grabbed his legs, tugging him back into the tank.

A second creature scrambled up from the left side of the hatch, pincer claws up. X held on to the screaming soldier and closed his eyes. One second later, he felt the weight of the man release, but when he opened his eyes, he was still gripping a hand attached to nothing else.

Bromista dragged X back into the tank and shut the hatch. He fell on his back, still clutching the amputated hand.

Crackling came over the command channel, followed by the voice of Captain Rolo, but X was hardly listening. He was staring at the severed hand and forearm he was gripping.

The beasts skittered away with their food, their shrieks and whistles growing distant.

"King Xavier, do you copy?" Rolo said again.

X moved to the radio. "Copy," he said, his heart still racing.

"We are in position," Rolo said. "Dropping the crate in a moment. We will be waiting for you in the sky."

They shut off the radio and sat in silence for a few more minutes until Slayer confirmed that the second pack had gone.

X watched his HUD until the beacon appeared. The supply crate was under the canopy and descending toward their position.

"I see it," said Slayer.

"What do you mean . . ." X saw the red streak of a flare through the viewport. "Son of a bitch," he said. "If we can see it, so can those beasts."

He tilted his helmet toward the back hatch.

"Let's move while we still can."

X got under General Forge and helped him up. He knew it had to hurt like hell, but the warrior made no sound.

As they climbed down onto the dirt, Forge reached out. "Give me a gun," he said.

X handed the general a blaster.

Bromista opened the hatch and was the first outside. The supply crate had landed on a collapsed building not far from their position.

Miles trotted away from the tanks and down to the lower level of the building, then led the way into a ravine between destroyed buildings. Two creatures scrambled ahead and vanished into piles of rubble.

X kept moving, keeping low and trying to keep Forge upright. The general staggered and stumbled on the uneven ground.

At the end of the street, they found the crate atop a four-story pile of ruins, its red flare still guttering.

"Fuckin A," X muttered. "Why don't they just put a target on our backs."

They made their way through the ravine, glass crunching under their boots. Miles stopped ahead and looked back to X, who spotted what had made the dog halt. From behind a slab of concrete jutted the booted legs of a Cazador soldier.

Bromista took point, moving ahead of the dog.

X handed Forge off to Slayer and joined Bromista to have a look.

Shouldering his rifle and resting the barrel on his metal arm, X moved around the slab. There lay half a body, cut off at the waist. The entrails lay in a pile of slop a few feet away.

A streak of blood led X to the man's other half.

A pair of the crab creatures had dragged him into a shattered storefront, where they were still picking flesh from his bones.

Bromista raised his crossbow, but X waved him down.

There was nothing they could do for the poor bastard now, and firing could draw attention to their position. He lowered his gun and motioned for Bromista and Miles to keep going.

The dog took the easiest path up the skirt of rubble, toward the supply crate sitting on the crest. The chute, still connected by its lines, rippled in the wind on the eastern side.

Martin and Slayer helped General Forge over to the bottom of the mound, keeping under the awning provided by a long concrete slab.

"I'll go get the boosters," Martin said.

X started to go with him, but Slayer held him back.

"I'll go, too," he said. "Stay with General Forge."

Crouching next to the general, X watched the two men start up the hill. Bromista stood guard.

Slayer and Martin were halfway up the rubble heap when the heavy thump of artillery sounded from the beach. X looked in that direction to see several shells bursting in ruined structures that lined the shore.

"Good thinking, Captain Two Skulls," X said. "He's giving us some cover—and a distraction."

The ground rumbled with the impacts. The

distant but unmistakable bark of .50-caliber machine guns joined in. X loved and hated the noise. It was the last of their ammunition, shells, and rockets. But munitions weren't worth saving if no one was alive to use them.

They would replenish their ammo later. Right now saving lives mattered more.

"Hang on," X said to General Forge. "Just a little longer."

Looking through the general's protective visor, X saw the pain in his gaze. With the adrenaline wearing off now, he had to be living in a world of pain, probably worse than anything X had ever known in the wastes.

A strong tremor shook the ground, and X stood up to get a better view of the mound. Martin was nearing the crest, with Slayer right behind him.

The shakes grew more powerful. Closer, one after the other, like something walking. And they didn't seem to line up with the artillery impacts.

This was something else . . .

Miles growled and moved out from under the concrete awning.

"Get back," X said. "Miles, get—"

Another tremor rumbled across the ravine, and Miles bolted back behind X, cowering in fear. The dog was old, but he wasn't one to cower.

X bumped on the comm channel.

"Martin, Slayer, hurry your asses up," he said. "We need to get the hell out of here."

* * * * *

"Ada fell. Oh, shit, oh God, she . . . !"

Magnolia rushed away from the canal, her boots slurping in the mud, the last transmission from Kade playing in her mind. She checked her HUD for the tenth time. It kept showing that Ada's beacon had winked off.

It wasn't coming back on.

Ada was gone. There was no denying it now, and nothing Magnolia could do. She had to keep her team alive and rendezvous with Team Wrangler.

They weren't far from the location where Ada fell. Magnolia ran faster, panting, hot breath fogging her helmet. Ahead, on point, Edgar led the way, with Sofia and Arlo sticking back next to Yejun. They advanced down into the industrial zone. The stern of a buried ship poked out of the ground, offering a useful vantage point.

Edgar climbed to the top and Magnolia joined him there, scanning the area beyond for shipping containers. Some stuck out of the dirt at odd angles, leaning like tombstones in a ruined churchyard.

The distant thump of explosions echoed in the ongoing battle between the Vanguard army and the beasts that prowled the city's edges.

Soon the divers would be close enough to hear the radio transmissions. She had no idea what was happening out there, only that the battle still raged.

Her heart pounded with worry, but she focused

back on the closest thing to her, something she could do something about: the divers, and making sure no one else died.

Edgar pointed west, at a crater just beyond the farthest container.

"There," he said. "That's where Team Wrangler is waiting."

It was maybe a half mile away, but the lumpy ground was riddled with holes. Halos of pushed-up dirt marked the vertical shafts. It looked as if an army of crazed giant gophers had invaded.

Magnolia couldn't risk crossing with her full team until she knew if they were active.

"You all stay here and watch Yejun," she said. "I'll go find out what the hell is going on."

"Don't go alone. I'll come," Arlo offered.

"I will, too," said Sofia. "You can't go alone."

"I'll take Arlo," Magnolia said.

"But . . ."

"Stay here with Yejun and Edgar," Magnolia said.

She waited until she was sure Sofia had accepted the order and backed down.

Magnolia nodded to Arlo. "Run fast, and stay close to me," she said.

"Like thunder after lightning, baby," he replied.

She took off down the hill, keeping her rifle in both hands and tucked against her chest, not bothering to clear the area first. She ran hard, hopping over obstacles and sliding in the mud, but never quite falling.

By the time she cleared the containers, she was breathing heavily again, and sweat dripped down her brow. She ran up another slope, slipping in the mud. Pushing herself up, she fought her way to the top.

At the crest, she could see the crater. One diver crouched next to another figure that appeared to be on its back. Magnolia identified Gran Jefe and Tia on her HUD, but Kade was farther away according to his beacon—maybe even underground. From here, it was too hard to tell.

Arlo finally caught up, and Magnolia hand-signaled to advance. They ran side by side to the crater rim.

"Gran Jefe," Magnolia said in a raised voice.

The big man turned with his rifle and rose to his feet.

"Commander Katib," he said in an almost formal tone.

"What happened?" Magnolia said.

She bent down next to Tia, who was alive but unconscious. Arlo knelt and opened his medical pack.

Gran Jefe looked at Tia but said nothing.

"Gran Jefe," Magnolia said, "tell me what happened, and where is—"

"Cowboy down there," Gran Jefe said, stepping to the edge and pointing over the side.

Magnolia couldn't see the bottom of the hole, even with her night-vision goggles. She bumped off the optics and switched to her lights.

Kade and Ada were not in sight, and neither was Jo-Jo.

"Where are Ada, Kade, and Jo-Jo?" Magnolia asked.

Gran Jefe explained about the snakes attacking him and the others while Kade was topside. Tia had been injured, and they had gotten her up here.

"Ada fell," he said. "*Un monstruo*—he snap her rope."

He moved his fingers in a scissor motion.

"Cut, cut," he said. "Cowboy went down, *pero las serpientes*—the snake—they come back. I stay here, to see Tia."

Magnolia looked down again, flitting her light over the walls. She didn't see any of the beasts down there.

"Tell Edgar and Sofia to bring Yejun here and that the way is clear, but to proceed with caution," she said. "Then tell Captain Rolo to prepare for our retrieval."

"Okay, but, Mags," Arlo said.

He reached out when she turned.

"Be careful," he said. "We can't afford to lose—"

"This isn't how I die." She flipped open the holster to her blaster then grabbed the rope Kade had used to rappel down the shaft. She secured it to her rappel device and backed toward the edge, directing her light toward the ribbed vertical walls, and started down.

Nothing moved in the many small openings she passed, and she didn't hear any skittering or clanking, either. She avoided the holes in the wall, angling her light at each, but the beasts seemed to have fled after killing Ada.

On her HUD, Kade's beacon had stopped moving. He was still alive and somewhere down here, closer now.

She maneuvered carefully the rest of the way down, boots kicking lightly off the wall until they hit the ground. After unclipping from the rope, she unslung her rifle. Turning on the light, she swept it around the space.

A collapsed wall partially obstructed the way out of this tunnel. She climbed up the loose earth, her boot squishing over the carcass of a dead snake. Flaps of skin and meat littered the ground around burn marks from lasers.

Other sinuous bodies were hacked apart, their meaty lengths curled up and strewn about, some still trying to crawl.

Reaching over her back, she drew a curved blade and set off with the sickle in one hand and her rifle in the other. At the top of the mound, she shined her light down the tunnel the divers had used to access the huge shaft she just descended.

The walls seemed to shiver.

She swept her light until she captured moving bulges snaking across the surface. Dust and grit cascaded down the sides as something moved within the walls.

She didn't dare move. Hoping they didn't know she was here, she aimed her rifle at one of the bulges, but the monsters remained inside their lairs.

Magnolia slide-stepped down the mound and

into the long tunnel, where immediately she saw a glow at the other end. She crouched down and shut off her lights.

The light surrounded a humanoid figure at the other end.

She sheathed her blade and put both hands on the rifle, holding it steady. With her finger on the trigger guard, she sighted up the target.

At first, she couldn't tell who or what it was—only that it was holding something in one hand and seemed to be moving slowly.

The center of this figure glowed, just like the creatures on the ship, but as it got closer she confirmed that it wasn't a radioactive beast.

This was a Hell Diver, with a battery unit glowing over the chest.

"Kade," she said quietly.

Magnolia checked the walls again. Not seeing any fresh activity, she started down the tunnel toward Kade. He kept walking toward her, seeming not to even notice her until she turned on her headlamp.

Raising a hand, he motioned to shut it off. She did as instructed, and only the light from their battery units burned in the Stygian blackness.

"Commander," Kade said in a sad whisper.

"Where's Ada?" she asked. "And where's Jo-Jo?"

Kade held up a cracked helmet between them.

"This is all I found besides Cricket," he said. "Jo-Jo must have dragged Ada away."

Magnolia looked down the tunnel the way he

had come. But once again they couldn't risk the lives of the other divers for Jo-Jo. They had no choice but to leave her.

"Come on, we need to get in the sky," Magnolia said.

They slogged back up the mound of collapsed dirt, watching the walls and ground for more of the snake creatures. A rattling noise echoed behind them, and they ran the rest of the way to the fixed rope hanging down the vertical shaft.

"Go first," she said.

Kade mounted both his jumars on the rope, stepped into the leg loop, and started up. At the top, he shook the rope to signal Magnolia, and she clipped in with her ascenders and started up, nervously watching the cave openings in the wall.

A single T-shaped head broke through the ground, and lovely pink petals opened around a toothy jaw. She considered blowing it to bits, but she didn't want to slow down.

At the top, the rest of Team Raptor stood there around Gran Jefe and Tia. She was sitting up now, and Arlo was holding up fingers.

"Ada?" Edgar asked.

"She didn't make it, and Jo-Jo is long gone," Magnolia said. "We have to get back to the airship."

Edgar crouched in front of her with his rifle.

"We just heard a partial transmission from the army," he said.

"And?" Magnolia asked.

"They are retreating to the ships," he said. "They are losing the fight."

Turning her head toward the battle, now she heard only the sporadic faint thump of explosions.

"We should help them," Sofia said.

Gran Jefe nodded. "We must."

Magnolia couldn't believe what she was about to say, but it really was the right call.

"We have to complete our mission," she said. "That means getting to the *Vanguard* with the maps."

"For Ada, and Jo-Jo!" she said.

Everyone shouted in unison—except for Gran Jefe, who merely mumbled the words.

THIRTY-THREE

"Martin! Slayer!" X yelled.

A deformed face with bulbous eyes and a broken beak emerged over the hilltop. Frayed wings hung over the thick hide as the monster rose up on limbs and pincer claws. Both soldiers turned from the supply crate with booster packs in their hands and stared up at the biggest terrestrial monster either man had ever seen.

Slayer backed away and fell, sliding and rolling several yards down the slope, but Martin just stood frozen.

"RUN!" X shouted.

The cracked beak opened, releasing a gout of blood from the gaping wound to the face. Then the beast grabbed Martin. Before it could swallow him whole, a bolt with an explosive head streaked into the open maw.

Bromista had run out in front of X and was already loading another bolt when the first exploded.

The beast roared, then reached down with a pincer claw as Bromista seated the next bolt.

"Bromista!" X yelled.

The soldier looked up just as the pincer claw scythed across, slicing his legs off below the knees. He collapsed to the ground, screaming in horror beside his severed limbs.

The creature skidded down the mountain of rubble, breaking a concrete slab under its weight.

X helped Forge to his feet as Slayer hopped down the cascading pile of loose debris. Dust billowed up into the air, and the Barracuda soldier vanished in the cloud.

The wave of dust slammed into X and Forge as they lurched toward another destroyed building. The force knocked them off their feet, but X managed to pull them to shelter inside the front of an old eatery littered with dusty furniture.

X crouched and opened the command channel to the *Immortal*.

"Captain, I want you to direct your fire at my position on my command," X said into his headset. "And don't fucking question it—just do it."

"Aye, aye, sir," Captain Two Skulls replied.

A shout came from outside, and X looked out to see a figure covered in dust, dragging something.

X stepped out when he realized it was Slayer, pulling Bromista by his armor.

"In here!" X said, waving.

The Cazador stopped, turned, and limped over to

X, who helped pull an unconscious Bromista inside. He still had a weak pulse, but they had to stop the bleeding.

Slayer dropped two boosters to the ground and then opened his medical pack.

"I'm sorry, I dropped the other boosters, but they are out there," Slayer said.

X bent down to help him get tourniquets on Bromista's legs.

In moments, they had made tourniquets of some rope and a length of nylon webbing and had shut down the bleeding. Now they were packing gauze around the stumps as Bromista groaned.

Down the street, the abomination slid into the ravine, screeching in search of them.

Miles was at the back of the room, and X saw why: the dog had located an exit door. They took it into a very unstable-looking ground floor of a building with a half-collapsed roof.

"Get the general into the sky, and take the other booster," Slayer said. "I'll stay with Bromista."

X took one and helped put it on Forge, who was slumping over.

"Don't close your eyes, General," X said.

He finished putting on the pack and turned to Slayer.

"You take Bromista," X said. "I'll take my chances with Miles on the ground."

"No way, sir," Slayer argued. "You are more important than I am."

"All you need to know is that I outrank you, soldier, and that I gave you an order. Your job is to save Bromista and yourself, and make sure Forge gets safely to the ship."

"All due respect, but following that order would make me a coward. Besides, sir, I'm faster than you, and you're going to need a distraction or we're *all* dead."

Another screech rang out, loud enough to hurt X's ears. The beast scrambled out of the ravine. This was their chance to recover the other boosters.

X spent a moment that he didn't really have, looking at the injured soldiers and realizing this was all his fault.

"Take off your armor and get in the fucking sky, Sergeant," X said firmly. "I won't ask you again. I'll try and get to the other boosters."

Before X could stop him, Slayer got up and took off outside.

"Damn son of a . . ." X grumbled.

He didn't know what to do, so he simply used his good hand to finish dressing Bromista's right stump.

Miles returned, growling.

"I know, I know, we're getting out of here," X said.

He picked up his laser rifle and stepped outside to search for Slayer. He was surprised to see the sergeant running back now with two boosters.

But he wasn't out of the woods yet.

The many-eyed face of the injured beast rose above the ravine. It let out a shriek as it climbed up onto a building, crushing the floor and stabbing at Slayer with a pincer bigger than he was.

He dodged the thrust, dodged another, and ducked under a swipe. Miles ran out, barking, distracting the beast. The pincer darted out, and X ran out after his dog.

"MILES!" he shouted.

The genetically enhanced husky was old but still fast. He bolted away from the claw, which plunged into the dirt where he had stood. X fired a flurry of bolts into the long arm as it cocked for another stab.

Slayer ducked into the building with Forge and Bromista while X pounded the beast with laser fire. Bolts slammed into its face, and the mammoth creature stumbled.

X rushed back into the shelter to find Slayer strapping the boosters on the other men.

"You're a crazy, insubordinate asshole, Slayer, you know that?" X said.

"Yes, sir, I do."

They moved Bromista and Forge into the back room, where a hole in the ceiling provided a doorway to the sky. The ground rumbled with each of the massive creature's footfalls outside.

"Help me with Miles," X said.

Slayer picked up the dog and used a sling to secure him to X. Then Slayer began to remove his own bulky armor and the armor still attached to Bromista.

Miles squirmed as X stood, his back aching from the weight. "Go," X said. "Go now!"

Slayer turned, and X punched the booster over his shoulder. He backed away as the balloon filled and lifted the men off the ground. They rose up in nothing but their suits between skewed I-beams and into the sky.

Next, X grabbed Forge and pulled hard to get him on his feet.

"*Gracias, Inmortal*," the general said quietly. "Stay alive."

"I always do," X said.

He hit the button on Forge's booster, launching the balloon that lifted Forge into the sky. X waited a minute before bumping on the command channel.

"Captain, fire on my position now," X said.

"Copy that, sir," replied Two Skulls. "I hope you get the hell out of there."

Lifting his slung rifle, X walked back into the building with Miles secured against his chest, to watch the soldiers rise into the sky.

A shriek thundered over the rows of debris on the right side of the ravine. The monstrous beast clattered across the street and swiped at Forge, who had the presence of mind to pull up his knees.

"Over here, asshole!" X yelled.

Eyes flitting back and forth, the creature clambered toward them, silhouetted in a flurry of lighting over the ruined city.

X fired at the bulbous eyes, bursting two of them. Then he hit the booster. The balloon filled but pulled them lazily in the air.

Their weight was too much with his heavy armor still attached.

Miles barked as they slowly rose skyward, the creature clambering toward them and swiping at the air.

X hated to discard his weapon with that abomination coming at him, but he had no choice. He tossed it and then unstrapped his chest armor in quick movements, jettisoning it along with his shin guards. The balloon finally started to pick up speed.

The creature charged toward them, and X realized they would not get high enough in time. Miles must have realized it, too, because he squirmed to get free.

"Fuck," X said. He held onto Miles, realizing he had doomed them both. "I'm sor—"

An explosion cut X off. He gripped his dog tighter, shielding him from a blast behind the beast.

The rubble pile where the supply crate had landed went up in a cloud of dust and debris.

The creature whirled toward the impact.

The balloon pulled its overweight burden higher, now maybe twenty-five feet off the ground.

Another rocket streaked through the sky, pounding the ground and blasting grit into the air. A second and third landed right behind the monster, blowing off a rear leg.

It let out an earsplitting roar and reached up with its claws toward X and Miles.

The fourth rocket hit the back of its shell, blowing out a hunk the size of a rowboat. Blood and gore slopped out of the riven carapace.

The monster finally collapsed in a heap beneath them.

"Hold fire!" X shouted into the comms.

"Copy!" replied Two Skulls.

Two more rockets hit the ground, blowing the rest of the beast into simmering hunks of meat.

"I got you, boy," X said to Miles.

They looked down at the carcass of the creature that had nearly killed them.

X let out a long breath and scanned the wastes. From this vantage point, he could see the smoking bodies of the breeders, now dead along with hundreds of their spawn.

He gazed out at the shoreline and the ships anchored there.

They had won the day and would clear the canal and set up an outpost, but the win had come at a heavy cost.

Finally, X looked up to see the airship lowering through the clouds.

The bottom reentry hatch was open and General Forge was already inside, hanging from his balloon. He held up a hand as they floated up next to him. Slayer was holding on to Bromista, who was limp but breathing.

The floor closed and sealed beneath their boots. Gas hissed from vents around them, kicking off the quarantine process.

After a few minutes, the top reentry hatch opened above, and the bottom hatch rose flush with the deck.

Exhausted, X sank to his knees inside the dome as the gases were vented out.

Teams Raptor and Wrangler were outside the dome, but not everyone was present.

X waited a few more minutes until an overhead crane lifted the dome away.

"Where's Ada?" he asked. "And Jo-Jo?"

Kade walked over and shook his head. "They didn't make it back."

There was a moment of silence before Magnolia strode out of the group and pulled two maps from her vest. She handed them to X.

He took them and saw the trident symbol marking a place called the Great Barrier Reef. His mind was a mess, but a memory surfaced of the sword from the man the Cazadores killed in Colón.

And then the realization hit him. The Great Barrier Reef was once a coral kingdom.

"The Coral Castle," he whispered.

Magnolia nodded.

"Ada didn't die in vain, King Xavier," she said.

* * * * *

On the horizon sailed a single boat, with a light flashing on the bow, above the mid-deck cabin, and another on the stern. It was a trawler, its crew no doubt exhausted after working late to bring home more fish.

The sight was a reminder that most of the people

here on the Vanguard Islands were doing their part to keep things running, to make a future for all.

But there were opportunists in the postapoca-lypse—always were and always would be. Men and women who put their own needs before those of the collective whole. They were the biggest danger to the future of humanity.

Michael had seen it time and time again. In his mind, there was no room for people like that, and now he was in charge of dealing with them.

He stood under the forest canopy on the capitol tower rooftop. More militia soldiers and volunteers were showing up by the minute. People he had known his entire life. Most were asking questions, but some carried weapons, as had the Cazadores he saw earlier.

The Vanguard army's message from the Panama Canal had spread as he expected it to, burning from rig to rig, faster than a plague.

Michael wasn't sure what would happen if, come morning, they didn't get good news. An hour earlier, he had deployed Imulah and Steve to figure out what was going on at the other rigs.

Two decks below, Pedro was still working to re-establish a connection with the Vanguard army, but so far, he had failed. The storms were interfering with the drones, and sending the fragile flyers through the storms was simply too dangerous.

And it wasn't just the mission in Panama he was worried about.

Michael still wasn't sure if anyone besides Wynn and Steve knew about the food stash.

What Michael did know was that Charmer had made a deal to acquire weapons from the Wave Riders. And if Charmer found out there were stored food reserves, he might very well rally his people to seize them.

Michael couldn't let that happen.

Charmer was an opportunist. He would use any situation to further his own selfish ends.

Pulling out his radio, Michael tuned to the frequency to connect with his guards at the prison rig.

"Victor, do you copy?" Michael said.

A few seconds passed before the sleepy voice replied.

"Copy, sir. All clear in the dark."

"Good," Michael said.

He walked out of the forest to another rooftop lookout.

Wynn stood like a statue behind the sandbags positioned around a machine gun with half a belt of ammunition. He used night-vision goggles to scan the waters.

"It's quiet out there, Chief," Wynn said.

"Quiet is good," Michael replied. "I'm heading down to the command center. Keep me apprised."

"Yes, sir."

Michael slung his rifle and headed downstairs to the enclosed lookout. Pedro was chewing on a calorie-infused herb stick, his tactical bow propped against the wall beside him. He leaned down close to the radio equipment, listening with headphones that were falling apart.

Walking over, Michael put his robotic hand down on the table.

Pedro turned, blinking tired eyes.

"I have tapped into all frequencies at other rigs," he said. "*É quase nada*, but I am pick up maybe a code word . . . *A guerra*—in English, 'the war.'"

"They are talking about the war, or about *going* to war?"

"That's what isn't clear to me," Pedro said.

"Michael . . ."

Michael turned to the open doorway, where his wife held Bray in one arm and Rhino Jr. in the other.

"Layla, I told you to stay put!" he practically shouted.

The anger in his voice seemed to shock both of them.

"I'm sorry," he said. "I didn't mean to raise my voice."

Both infants stared at him with curious but sleepy eyes.

"What do you mean, *war*? Is X okay?" she asked. "Are we still safe here?"

"Yes, you're safe here, but with the mission in Panama taking a turn for the worse, we're taking all precautions. As far as I know, King Xavier is still alive."

"Have you heard more?"

"No, but Pedro is trying to make contact."

Michael reached out to Layla, and she handed him Bray.

"It's okay," he said soothingly. "Everything's going to be okay."

The baby looked up at him, meeting his gaze. Holding his son was a reminder not only of what was at stake, but also of just how fragile their world was, even here in seeming paradise.

Footsteps echoed down the hallway, and Wynn appeared, panting and sweating.

"Chief, there's a boat approaching, and it's not one of ours," he said.

Michael handed Bray back to Layla.

"Keep the kids here," he said. "You're safe, I promise."

Layla hesitated, then nodded. "I trust you."

It was exactly what Michael needed to hear. He kissed her and then Bray and put a finger on Rhino Jr.'s chubby right arm. He thought of the boy's father, who had died protecting X.

Now it was their time to protect the little man.

Michael went into the hallway and stopped to talk to the guards.

"You guard this room with your lives, understand?"

"Yes, sir," they both replied.

Michael rushed back up to the rooftop with Wynn. They went to a lookout on the western side of the rooftop, where the long spear was aimed down at the water.

"There," Wynn said, pointing. He handed

Michael his night-vision goggles, and Michael slipped them on, following the lieutenant's finger.

Sure enough, a single boat powered across the waves.

It was an old yacht, with no one on the deck but plenty of room below to hold a boarding party of a dozen men.

"Who is it?" Michael asked.

"I don't know," Wynn said.

The mounted spear gun, aimed right at the yacht, had a projectile big enough to do major damage—probably even sink it.

It wasn't just the spear pointed at the yacht. A dozen sniper rifles and crossbows were also trained on it.

The craft approached closer to the marina, but Michael still didn't see any movement above the decks. It finally stopped about two hundred yards out from the dock.

A hatch opened, and a single man emerged.

Michael's laser rifle scope zoomed in on an eye patch.

"Charmer," he said.

Two more men joined him on the deck. Both wore militia armor but were unarmed.

"Your men," Michael said. "He's taken them hostage."

"That sorry pile of Siren shit," Wynn said.

He turned to his men, shouting orders to hold fire.

Michael took off, with Wynn calling out after him.

"Chief, where are you going?"

"To figure out what this asshole wants," Michael said. "If he so much as moves the wrong way, knock that other eye out."

"Copy that, sir."

Michael took the elevator down to the marina. A dozen soldiers were already there, with weapons aimed at the yacht.

Charmer held up his hands, a smile on his face. "Lower your weapons," he yelled. "I mean no harm!"

"Keep your weapons up," Michael said. He walked out down the dock, a group of men following him.

"That's no way to treat a mate, but I suppose I should have seen this coming," Charmer said. "Sad, considering I brought your men back to you."

He motioned toward the two militia soldiers.

As Michael approached the end of the dock, he saw movement behind the windows of the yacht. There were more men inside and on the aft deck.

One of them stepped out wearing a black coat and holding an automatic rifle with animal bones woven into the sling.

A Cazador rifle.

They approached, and Michael saw that it was Oliver.

"What do you want?" Michael asked.

"Right now? Nothing," Charmer said. "I got what I wanted—or needed, rather—and now I've come bearing gifts."

He reached out, and Oliver handed him the rifle.

Charmer kept it cradled, cautious not to aim it at Michael.

"You see, we made a deal with the parts you didn't need for some weapons," Charmer said. "We can handle our own security now, so you can have your boys back. Let our boat approach and I'll drop 'em off, unless you want them to swim."

Michael wasn't sure what kind of game Charmer was playing, but he had the man outgunned fifty to one, and there was no other boat on the water.

He brought up his laser rifle and nodded.

Charmer turned toward the windows of the command room and nodded. The engines powered on, and the boat chugged over the choppy water.

Michael moved his finger inside the trigger guard, waiting for men to storm out of the boat and open fire, but none came. The stern inched closer until it bumped into the tires cushioning the edge of the dock.

Both militia soldiers hopped off and ran over. Charmer came to the stern, only ten feet from the dock.

Oliver stepped up to Charmer, glaring at Michael.

"Vanguard victory!" screamed a voice.

They all looked up at the command center far above. A window was open, and Pedro's head was sticking out.

"King Xavier defeated *os monstros* at the canal and is very much alive!" he shouted.

"Well isn't that some amazing timing," Charmer

said. He flashed his shit-eating grin. "Long live the King of the Wastes."

Michael didn't reply as Charmer turned and walked back to the hatch. Oliver remained on the deck, even as the boat turned and headed back toward their rig.

Pulling out his radio, Michael watched them go before sending a message to Pedro.

"Get me a line to every rig," Michael said. "I want to make an announcement."

"Yes, sir."

When Michael got to the elevator, he radioed Victor and Ton with news of the victory in Panama.

"Ah, thank the gods," Victor said.

"It's almost over," Michael said. "I'll see you soon."

"Copy, sir."

The elevator clanked to the top, and he stepped out onto the rooftop and hurried to the command center. It was bustling with people. Layla waited in the hallway, sitting in a chair with the babies.

"Is it over?" she asked.

"For now," Michael said. "Go back home and get some sleep, I'll be there as soon as I can."

She stood and put her head against his.

"I know," he said. "I love you, too. Everything's going to be okay."

Michael went into the command room with a smile that seemed to be infecting everyone. Pedro's grin stretched ear to ear.

"The emergency broadcast system *está pronto*. Ready for you, Chief," he said.

Michael went over to the equipment but stopped at the viewports. The yacht with Charmer on it motored off into the night.

This wasn't the last of their problems with the man, but Michael would deal with him soon enough.

"Ready when you are," Pedro said.

He flipped the switch after Michael sat down in front of the mike that would bring his voice to every rig out there.

"Citizens of the Vanguard Islands, this is Chief Engineer Michael Everhart with news of the Vanguard victory in Panama," he said. "The army has cleared all hostiles, and King Xavier is alive and unhurt. Tonight, we can rest knowing that hope is alive and that much-needed supplies will be coming to us. Tomorrow, we rise and continue to rebuild, together."

Michael put the receiver down and looked out the viewports. Pinpricks of fire burned from barrels on the distant rigs—a reminder that the power was still off since the storm.

He wanted to believe that everything would be okay, that they would restore the power and replenish their food depots. But how often did things go to plan? And there were still threats aplenty—from the storms, from the wastes, and from some people, even here at the islands.

The fight for survival wasn't over. Far from it.

EPILOGUE

"I got eyes on a contact," Kade said. "Proceed with caution."

He crouched in the hull of a rusted-out vehicle, holding an infrared scope up to his face shield. A white heat signature came onto his screen: a beast hidden partly behind a tree trunk.

"Is it Jo-Jo?" Magnolia asked.

She was behind Kade with Arlo and Tia, all of them lying prone in the six-foot weeds that grew up through cracks in the road. A squad of Cazador soldiers was out here, too, led by Sergeant Slayer, although Kade couldn't see them.

"Kade," Magnolia said.

"I can't tell if it's Jo-Jo, but whatever it is, it's human size," Kade said, watching the creature.

"Is it a Siren?" Arlo asked.

"I don't think so," Kade replied.

He knew that the monsters were out here, but

so far the Sirens were keeping their distance from the Cazador army and the Hell Divers.

The search for Jo-Jo had been ongoing since her handler, Ada, fell to her death over a week ago. Shortly thereafter, the animal had taken off with her body into the underground labyrinth, making an already dicey rescue mission nearly impossible.

Since then, her beacon had fled into the radiation red zone of Panama City. But earlier this morning, the beacon had inched closer to the outpost built at Fort Kobbe at the west end of the canal.

Kade had put together a volunteer mission to retrieve the monkey and bring her home. It wasn't just for sentimental value. Jo-Jo was the best hunter, and an even better alarm system than Miles. Kade knew from experience that such talents could make all the difference in the wastes, and this was just the beginning of what would be many more missions out here.

Lightning webbed across the canopy, one of its forks splitting a tree not a quarter mile away. Kade switched the infrared off on the binos and zoomed in. His heart leaped when he saw that the creature wasn't a monster.

Two weeks after taking the canal, they had finally found the animal.

"Eyes on Jo-Jo," Kade said over the comms. "Moving in."

"Here," Magnolia said, pulling a banana from her bag. "She seemed to like you better than me."

"Maybe this is a bad idea," Arlo said. "Maybe we should just let her be in the wild where she was born. There's no telling what's in that jungle."

"Maybe you should try following orders," Magnolia said.

Kade chuckled. "Not really your strong suit, is it, mate?"

"*Damn*, you got me," Arlo replied.

Magnolia motioned everyone back but Kade. He took the fruit and started out through the weeds, toward the jungle.

Bird calls fluted through the canopy, and a growling noise stopped him in his tracks for a few seconds. With a cutlass in one hand and his revolver in the other, he worked his way between hummocks of grass and weeds until he got to the clearing.

The monkey peeked out from behind the tree as he came closer to the radioactive jungle.

"Hi, Jo-Jo," Kade called out. "I'm here to take you home."

A howl answered him, and he hesitated again. They had already killed two of the little shelled beasts on the way here, and they would likely encounter more, but Kade wasn't about to turn back now. He owed it to Ada after the tragic accident that led to her rope breaking and her plummeting to her death.

He blamed himself for leaving Tia, Ada, and Gran Jefe alone to provide covering fire for Team Raptor. If he had stayed, maybe they would have seen the creature come out of a tunnel and cut her rope. By the time he arrived on the scene, Ada was dead and Jo-Jo had dragged her body deep into the tunnels.

Finding the monkey and bringing her back to the outpost was the least Kade could do for Ada. But suppose Arlo was right. What if the beast *was* better off out here?

Kade pushed the thought aside. He kept walking toward the jungle with an overripe banana in hand. He waved it enticingly. "Come and get it."

Jo-Jo moved from around the base of a tree and started toward Kade, moving tentatively on all fours. Her muscular front legs bulged with each step.

Two shrieks echoed in the distance, distracting the monkey.

"It's okay," Kade said.

She looked back to him and took a few steps closer.

"That's it," he said. "Come on, just a little bit farther."

He held the banana out, and she snatched it from his hands, backing away and gobbling it down, blackened skin and all.

"Come with me, and I'll give you more," Kade said.

He pulled out another banana and had started backing up when his comms crackled.

"We have orders to get back to the outpost," Slayer said. "Pack it up and hurry back."

"Why?" Magnolia replied.

"Radiation spike."

"Copy that."

Magnolia trotted over to Kade.

"We need to move," she said.

Kade noticed the uptick in radiation on his HUD. They still didn't know what was causing it, but something in the city was still producing an extremely high radioactive output. That could have explained the mutant creatures in the zone, and the radioactive former humans that Team Raptor had encountered on the ship, but Kade was no scientist, and no one seemed to know yet what they were.

"Come on, please, Jo-Jo," he wheedled.

The monkey looked over its shoulder at the skyline of ruins, almost as if it could sense something. Then she slowly made her way to Kade.

"That's it," he said.

He eased his other hand to the tranquilizer gun, just in case, but the monkey didn't run off. It moved in front of him and Magnolia, looking up.

Magnolia crouched and reached out, meeting the animal's clawed finger.

"It's okay, girl," she said. "You're safe now, but you need to come with us."

The monkey was slow at first, but it followed them back toward the road, where the other divers stood. From there, they trekked through an old boatyard that had already provided the Vanguard military with much-needed parts to take back to the islands.

Slayer was glassing the city with a pair of binos from the crow's nest of an old mast that stuck straight up out of the dirt. He climbed down and motioned for the divers to follow.

"We need to haul ass to the outpost," he said.

Three soldiers armed with flamethrowers came out of the shadows, and the group took off through the industrial zone, past half-buried boats and shipping containers.

On the other side of a destroyed crane, an APC engine rumbled. A cargo truck also waited, its engine firing up when the driver saw them.

"Let's move," Slayer said. "*Vámonos.*"

Kade got into the back of the truck with Jo-Jo and the divers while Slayer and his men piled into the armored personnel carrier. The two trucks pulled away, jostling over the lumpy dirt.

Kade checked on Jo-Jo, who sat on the floor, looking down. The monkey was clearly depressed from losing Ada. There was no telling what it had been through in the wastes for the past two weeks.

"Contacts at three o'clock," Slayer said over the team comm.

Kade peered through the window with his night-vision goggles, scanning the wastes. Switching to infrared, he saw a herd of mutant deer galloping through an open field of beached and battered boats.

The APC kept its distance, with a gunner in the turret watching them, but the herd wasn't coming toward the vehicles. Rather, they seemed to be fleeing something.

Kade relaxed and turned back to Jo-Jo. She was looking at Arlo.

"I'm sorry about Ada," he said. "I liked her, too."

The truck lurched and swayed over rough terrain, evening out as the tires met the new road to the outpost. Two weeks earlier, they had put a blade on a half-track and bulldozed a road for traffic to and from the shipyard.

When they finally got back to the canal, Kade could see the results of those raids. A crane swung up another shipping container full of salvaged supplies onto the *Immortal*, destined for the Vanguard Islands. There were all sorts of treasures, including wind turbine blades and solar panels, and pipe and galvanized sheet steel and fiberglass panels and a whole manifest of other items Chief Engineer Michael Everhart had requested for repairing the rigs.

Raven's Claw was also there—docked at an actual seaport, no less, with the *Octopus* in the next berth. But they weren't heading back with supplies. Rumors were floating around the outpost that King Xavier had other plans for the ships.

The truck took a bridge across the canal to the outpost. Metal and concrete walls surrounded the five-acre compound of six buildings and an underground bunker.

There was little sign of it now, but this place had once been a foreign military base, Fort Kobbe, decommissioned in the 2000s and taken over by the Panamanian government.

A pair of sentries opened the gate, and they passed under two guard towers with snipers and machine guns.

A few seconds later, the truck ground to a stop. Slayer opened the back hatch, and Jo-Jo hopped down with the Hell Divers.

Engines rumbled across the camp as Cazadores and sky people operated arc welders and hoists to restore the structures. A bulldozer pushed up a berm of dirt and rubble to form a barrier, and a crane stacked empty containers to form a wall.

Thick orange tents with radiation shielding formed temporary quarters for the soldiers stationed at the outpost. The material rippled in the strong breeze.

The divers and Jo-Jo followed Slayer and his squad down a dirt road, toward a concrete bunker built into a hill. Two .50-caliber machine guns guarded the entrance—one from the road, the other from the top of the mound.

Blast doors groaned and clicked as the bars disarmed to reveal a wide roadway that went underground. Kade glanced over his shoulder to make sure Jo-Jo was still following. She was hobbling along, curious but cautious.

The road leveled out into a long passage that ended at another pair of doors. These opened, and the group stepped into a decontamination chamber. Magnolia fed Jo-Jo another banana before the system clicked on.

The animal didn't like the hissing gases and chemical bath, but then, neither did the divers.

Thirty minutes later, they entered the facility marked by a plaque that read OUTPOST VANGUARD GATEWAY. The hallways bustled with staff working to restore the base's internal systems. Power from the *Immortal's* nuclear plant was running critical systems, including the air handlers to keep toxins out. Batteries and a generator would keep it going after the supercarrier left.

Kade went with Jo-Jo to the barracks, where he changed out of his suit and into his clothes. He pulled his cowboy hat over his long hair.

"Commander Katib, you're needed at the CIC," said Slayer. He nodded to Kade. "You, too, Commander Long."

"What about Jo-Jo?" Magnolia asked.

"I'll keep an eye on her, don't worry," Arlo said.

"Give her some more food, water, and a bunk."

"You got it, Commander."

Kade and Magnolia followed Slayer toward the command center, stopping just outside.

The steel doors were open, revealing a small room with four long tables configured in a rectangle. The hologram of Timothy Peppers stood between the tables, his glow illuminating the people seated there.

Sitting around the conjoined tables were Rodger, Captain Two Skulls, Captain Rolo, Executive Officer Eevi Corey, and Yejun. General Forge was facing a monitor next to King Xavier. It was the first time Kade had seen the general since the battle that almost killed him. His scarred features glistened with the nanotech gel that was helping his skin grow back after his devastating burns.

He wasn't the only one who had suffered grave injuries. Bromista was here after taking the first steps with his new prosthetic legs. As soon as he saw Slayer, he stood and pounded his chest, stumbling but managing to keep his balance.

"Sorry to interrupt," Slayer said in the doorway. "I have Commanders Katib and Long outside."

"Bring them in," X said.

Slayer motioned the divers inside. Kade and Magnolia both stood at attention and saluted.

"At ease," X said. "I'll get right to it."

Miles looked out from under X's chair before going back down on his paws for a nap.

"Tonight, I leave for the Vanguard Islands with the first cargo of supplies," X said. "Bromista, we are promoting you to lieutenant. You will remain here, supervising construction of the outpost and conducting foraging raids into the city. Eventually, I will appoint a civilian director of this outpost, but for now, Bromista is in charge of all operations."

Bromista simply stared until Forge translated.

"Gracias, King Xavier," Bromista said.

"Be cautious of the radiation spikes," X said. "They are coming from the heart of Panama City, and we still don't know what's causing them."

"We know why the beasts here were so big," Rodger said.

"And we know they are all dead now," Slayer added.

Forge translated to Bromista, who pounded his chest. "I protect," he said.

X went to the maps recovered by Team Raptor.

"When I return to the islands, I will meet with the council to discuss these locations." He tapped a finger on the first map. "Yejun's people believed there was supplies at the Buenaventura Port, west of Cali, in Columbia. That is the closer option . . ."

X moved to the next map, which had a trident symbol marked on the ocean just off the east coast.

"This is the Great Barrier Reef, off the coast of Australia, where Yejun's people believed there is an underwater city," X continued. "The same place that I believe the Cazadores call 'the Coral Castle.' I've seen the sword they took from the man who first spoke of this place. It had this same trident engraved in the blade. Now, we don't know where this place is, exactly, other than this trident marking on the map, but we do know there were three ITC research facilities across the reef, and one of them could be the location of the Coral Castle."

Kade stood up for a better look of the place his ancestors once called home.

"King Xavier," Rolo began, "that's halfway around the—"

"World. I know, and I would walk there myself if it meant keeping everyone alive," X replied firmly.

"I understand, but you said these ITC facilities 'might' be the location of the Coral Castle."

X gave Captain Rolo the full intensity of his gaze.

"Captain, if you're going to question everything I say and do, then perhaps you should consider stepping down from your position," X said. "I need a selfless captain, who isn't afraid of making tough decisions. Someone like your XO."

Eevi Corey stiffened in her seat.

Rolo glared at X. "I'm looking out for my people, who, based on our current inventory of supplies, are months away from starving," he said. "I'm told the situation back at the islands is grave, with horrid conditions, and we still don't have food, nor do we know for certain there will be any at this port south of Cali, and furthermore, you really have no idea where this underground city even *is*, only that it is ten thousand miles from our current location."

"The supplies we're sending back will help us in the short-term," X replied. "I'm thinking about the long term. You have a decision to make, Captain."

Kade saw the anger in Rolo's face. It was the same look he had seen many times as a diver years ago. But this time, Kade didn't agree with the captain.

X was right. They had to keep searching for a food source, or the next bad storm could be the end of the Vanguard Islands.

An alarm suddenly blared. Miles shot up from under the table.

"What the hell?" Rodger said.

Slayer unslung his rifle and went to the door. "Wait here!" he yelled.

The doors closed, sealing them inside for a few

tense moments. A few moments later, they opened and Slayer entered.

"Something's happening in the barracks—a fight," he said.

"Let's go," X said.

Kade bolted out of the command center with the others.

A howling echoed through the facility. At first, he feared that a monster had somehow gotten inside, but he quickly recognized Jo-Jo's voice. And a deep, angry human voice that had to be Gran Jefe's.

They entered the barracks to find the monkey and the Cazador wrestling on the ground while the other Hell Divers and staff stood in a circle, watching.

"What the fuck is going on here!" X yelled.

Miles ran over, barking.

Kade ran over as Jo-Jo pummeled Gran Jefe with fists and bit off a piece of his ear.

The monkey raised both fists to finish him, then seemed to lose interest.

Instead of delivering the death blow, she reached over her shoulder, trying to remove a small dart that hung there. She lowered her other fist and slumped off Gran Jefe.

He got up and pulled his cutlass, raising it and screaming.

X brought up his metal arm and deflected the blow away from the unconscious animal. "Back off!" he yelled.

Gran Jefe turned the weapon on X, placing the blade at his throat.

"Put it down!" Slayer shouted.

Kade stepped up behind Gran Jefe and put the muzzle of his six-shooter just behind the big man's ear. "Do it now, dickhead, or I'll turn your fat head into jam."

Kade pulled the hammer back with a loud click.

"Big mistake, cowboy," Gran Jefe said. Blood dripped from his mutilated ear and a gash on his cheek.

X met Gran Jefe's gaze, but there was no fear in the king's eyes, only cold rage.

"*¡Es la última!*" General Forge said. He had his cutlass out, the edge against Gran Jefe's neck. "Not asking again."

"Fucking *hijoeputas*," Gran Jefe said. He slowly pulled the blade away from X and pointed it at the beast. "She's mine," he said.

X said, "You talk like you have authority here."

"She nearly rip my face off. I will kill the *chango* and eating its flesh—is my right." Gran Jefe took a step toward the creature, but X moved in front of him again.

"I said step back," X said.

Gran Jefe towered over him, chest out almost as far as his belly.

Kade kept his gun pointed while Gran Jefe unleashed a string of profanities in both languages. The big Cazador spat at the unconscious monkey and finally backed down.

"Now, go get cleaned up and see a medic."

Gran Jefe smirked and backed away, glaring at Kade.

"Everyone out except General Forge, Slayer, Kade, and Mags!" X yelled.

The room cleared, and X bent down to the inert creature. "I don't know what the hell happened, but she can't stay here," he said. "Get her up and lock her up temporarily on the *Immortal*. I'll take her back to the islands with me and look after her for now."

He shook his head as he checked the monkey.

"We got more problems than supplies," X grumbled. "Between that big angry bastard and Captain Rolo, we need to keep our guard up and eyes open."

"I'm with you, King Xavier," Slayer said.

"Always," Magnolia added.

General Forge's scarred face nodded.

They all looked to Kade.

He had to make a choice now.

He flashed back to the machine camp, and the darkness and pain his people had endured. The loss of his family was still a raw wound.

But then he thought of the living, people who still had a chance at survival. This was the reason he had agreed to serve again, to take to the sky and dive.

As always, danger lurked in all directions, from the unknown source of radiation in Panama City to the nightmarish monsters of the wastes to the dwindling resources at the islands.

To navigate the risks humanity faced now would

take someone with a compassionate heart and a killer instinct. To Kade, only one man displayed that supremely necessary combination of traits, and it wasn't Captain Rolo. The man had lost his way over the years.

Only King Xavier seemed to have the balls to make the tough decisions to save what was left of humanity and to lead Kade's people back to their home country.

Kade took off his cowboy hat and bowed slightly. "Aye, I stand with you wherever you may lead us, my King," he said.

"Good," X said. "Because I'm sending you home, Commander. You're going to Australia."

HELL DIVERS IX

RADIOACTIVE

Don't miss the next installment of the Hell Divers series with *Hell Divers IX: Radioactive*!